THE IRISH-AMERICANS

THE IRISH-AMERICANS

OUR OWN KIND

EDWARD McSORLEY

ARNO PRESS

A New York Times Company

New York — 1976

Editorial Supervision: ANDREA HICKS

———◆———

Reprint Edition 1976 by Arno Press Inc.
Copyright © 1946 by Edward McSorley

Reprinted by permission of Lina McSorley

Reprinted from a copy in The Princeton
   University Library

THE IRISH-AMERICANS
ISBN for complete set: 0-405-09317-9
See last pages of this volume for titles.

Manufactured in the United States of America

———◆———

Library of Congress Cataloging in Publication Data

McSorley, Edward, 1902-1966.
   Our own kind.

   (The Irish-Americans)
   Reprint of the ed. published by Harper, New York.
   I. Title. II. Series.
PZ3.M24840u7 [PS3525.A2914]   813'.5'4   76-6357
ISBN 0-405-09350-0

OUR OWN KIND

OUR OWN
KIND

BY

EDWARD McSORLEY

HARPER & BROTHERS PUBLISHERS

NEW YORK AND LONDON

5-6   FIRST EDITION   D-V

TO MY WIFE
LINA ALLEGRINI

OUR OWN KIND

Chapter One

WILLIE McDERMOTT nestled warm and deep in the dark trough of the vast feather bed, squinting into an aluminum April morning. The lashing rain chased fretful little streams into the March dust which had spread itself thinly over the panes, and the rivulets, frantically twisting their way down to the sill, swelled to globes and quietly dropped away. His grandfather's croppy head, white as a gull's back, rode easily on the crest of the gray and brackish pillow slip. On the other side of him his grandmother's long braids, black and heavy as a tarred mooring line, but spun through with strands of silver, floated with the sour flowers on the comforter that eddied and swirled with their breathing. Above their heads, yellowing and crisp, withered fronds of last year's palm sagged in dying blades from the varnished fleur-de-lis of the filigreed bedtop. Scummed over like a stagnant pool in the mill lots, a mirror was braced on top of the broad-beamed dresser on his grandmother's side and near its edges drifted a host of seraphs, cherubs, angels and archangels. They mourned and wept for James John, May He Rest in Peace; Margaret Mary, *Requiescat in Pace*; and one brawny heavenly aide de camp to Gabriel heralded the ordination of Michael Francis Ryan at the Church of the Assumption of the Blessed Virgin, Providence, Rhode Island, June 10, 1912.

A wafery linen cover which his grandmother had washed thin as a Holy Communion wafer in years gone by, crusted the top of the dresser, now a melancholy gray that seemed not to end with its own frayed edges but to swoon forlornly into the powdery dust like the last March snow on the wood. The cloth was littered with a miscellany of shedding hairbrushes, pins, gas bills, a comb with its eyeteeth gone, a pair of black stained prayer beads with the crucifix missing, and a small thin figurine of St. Anthony, shaven headed, who held a little blond boy child in one hand and a blue ball, capped with a golden crucifix, in the other. The grandmother could take away any or all of the articles on the dresser in a day's time and put them all back again without leaving the bird's flight of a wake of where they had been moved.

Tethered in the dry wastes of the wallpaper was the Agnus Dei

Qui Tollit Peccata Mundi and a more robust angel, snow sparkling on the sweep of her wings of eagle feathers, who brought the season's greetings from F. X. QUINN, CHOICE MEATS AND GROCERIES, 132 Pine Street. The commode was on his grandfather's side, sturdy squatting oak, or the next thing to it, you might say, holding inside the delft blue scrolled porcelain washbasin and a cracked pitcher that looked forever like a little-necked duck. In the shelter of the bowl was his grandfather's black clay pipe, a plug of dark Mayo and a width of sulphur matches whose red tips, like the pears of the Precious Blood dropping from the Sacred Heart of Jesus in its pearl shell frame above, purpled in the damp morning light. Begrimed and scanty scrim curtains drooped from the window frame, lingering, it seemed, like Nora's foggy weekday drawers still listlessly hanging from the back yard clothesline on a Tuesday.

The boy's eyes sped from wall to window and window to wall while his brief yesterdays with their triumphs and defeats schooled in the green shoals of his thoughts. The Church of the Mediator bell thundered six times in the mist, shattering the quiet, and as its notes were still hurtling through the quivering house his grandfather stretched out his legs and groaned as he threw the covers off himself.

With his head propped on his elbow Willie watched his grandfather perch there on the spavined rocker's edge to light his pipe with quick gasping puffs before he pulled his socks over his feet and up over the legs of the heavy ribbed underwear. Peg, his grandfather's Boston bull bitch, fretted in the doorway to the dark dining room and longingly whined to be let in. She dared not enter, even with a papal dispensation, while his grandmother was still in the room, or the old woman would fling a shoe with Annie Oakley aim at the white crescent which cleft Peg's brindled head between the twirling eyes; or perhaps, as the dog retreated, the pimpled German silver hairbrush would fly end over end at her stern. Peg had one brown eye and one blue one, the blue ringed with narrow fringe of lighter blue. Peg spun her eyes at the heaving hulk of his grandmother and again appealed to his grandfather. The old man sadly shook his head and taking the pipe from his mouth jabbed in the air in the direction of his wife. He thumped the couple steps from the rocker to the bedside in his stocking feet and cuffed the boy gently on the head.

2

"Up," he commanded.

The grandfather smiled and trotted away to the kitchen, gaited in the same stride he used every afternoon in the foundry, carrying the iron ladle. It was his custom on days when the foundry was shut down to get up first with the booming of the Mediator's bell and make the breakfast. On working days the grandmother was first up to shake down the fire and make the breakfast. She would have liked to change the order because he worked more days than he loafed, and for more than thirty years had been suggesting the change, but he ignored her without ever once answering her.

The cairn on his back which grew there from his years of toil seemed to be getting larger and weighing his shoulders deeper and farther down. Peg nosed at his legs as he whipped by her and tossing a glance of contempt at the old woman in the bed, softly padded away after him. Long shreds of blue smoke cut over the room when they had gone and settled slowly to the floor. Soon the grate in the kitchen stove was rattling and the kettle clattering over the lids; the tiny shovel scraped in the hearth as he cleaned out the ashes and a wordless, toneless song rose and fell with each shovelful he dumped into the coal scuttle. The boy hated to hear the ashes dropping into the scuttle; he knew he would have to pick over every one of them to salvage what could be burned again. He could feel their raspy texture on his fingers now.

"Treasure," he could hear the old man grunting to Peg in the kitchen. "Snowy breasted Peg. My popeyed little Peg."

The boy plunged sleepily through a gritty cloud of powdery ashes which swept through the kitchen. His grandfather was hooped over the pantry sink sloughing cold water over his face, spitting and grunting while the tap poured an inch-thick wabbling stream into a dappled enamel washbasin. Peg was halfway under the stove, her forepaws stretched out in front where his grandmother would surely trip over them. Peg snorted the ashes out of her black wet snout. The teacups, bottom-up in their saucers, were on the table and the oatmeal steamed and thumped at its cover. His grandmother drummed her bare feet into the kitchen, taking a little slap with the one nearest Peg as she passed. Her hair was skewered into a tight bun on the top of her small head and her stained corsets, with a metal tip peeping out here and there, brimmed over. Her small bird's beak of a nose was sliced with a deep red

3

mark where her glasses should have rested and the eyes, without those smeared shields in front of them, were contracted and hard. She squalled into the pantry and bumped her husband out as he groped for a towel. The washbasin clattered in the sink as she dumped the water. Soon, her back to the kitchen, she was splashing cold water against her chest, the surest way of avoiding t.b.

"Call Chris," she chattered. "Get Nora out of the bed."

She meant anyone within the sound of her voice. Chris was her son, her pride and joy that never caused her a day's worry in her life, that never missed mass on a Sunday or a holy day of obligation, that never did so many things his father did it was a great puzzle and a mystery until the day he died how he spent his life when he was not keeping books in Ryan's ship chandlery, presiding at meetings of the Catholic Club or marching in the Holy Name parades.

"Nora is long out of it," cackled a wisp of a voice from the other room.

As the voice croaked a chain rattled briefly and a door clicked to. The muted roar of a boxed Niagara was still gurgling when Nora, the grandmother's older sister, minced into the kitchen, and a moment later they were jostling each other in the cramped alleyway of the pantry. Nora's glasses, their gold rims tarnished like the severed claws of an old hen, were caught up above her wrinkled forehead in scrambled puffs of steel-wool hair. Except that she was thinner and her face more tallowy, it might have been the grandmother's good and evil selves wrestling there with each other. They had spent their lives together, sniping and snarling with the venom that only sisters spew at each other. Uncle Gyp McGlinn, who once owned the blacksmith shop across the street but later drank himself out of it, said Nora had been forever pushing Nell, the grandmother, into trouble and out of a bed and that give her time and she'd push Nell the hell out of Ned McDermott's bed, too. Nora was a spinner in the Glendale mill, and it never happened that when the Ship Windlass Company foundry where Ned worked was shut down that Nora wouldn't have some reason or other to be at home, too. Nora was that damned lazy, Willie's grandfather always said, she wouldn't wipe the dirt from a dish unless she was to eat with it. She bickered like a guinea hen as she sprinkled a few drops of water over her face and Nell answered each sally. Neither the boy nor his grandfather in the kitchen could tell what they were saying.

4

The old man restlessly pitched and dove in a rocker by the window smoking his pipe. The boy, staring at a chromo of Robert Emmet on the wall next to one of Frank Quinn's calendars, wondered why his aunt Nora always called his grandfather a mickey thick of an ignorant man that didn't know his letters because time after time, as long as the boy could remember living with them, the old man had read to him word for word the imperishable damnation Emmet was hurling at the oppressors of his country there in the courtroom. Often, when they were reading it together, the boy would ask his grandfather what the judges said when Emmet told Norbury he was impatient for the sacrifice.

His grandfather was looking out the window into the furrows of muck in the street where big drays were plodding past to the warehouses and the coal piers a few streets away. The heavy low gears and hooded vans rolled along in the mud with hardly a sound from their heavy steel rims. On the piles of lumber in old man Tanner's carpenter shop yard on the other side of the high board fence the boy could see the rain splashing up in bright little spurts. Beyond Tanner's he could see the Armenian women, their hair braided in black halos on their heads, walking along the rickety balcony to the stairs that led down to the bakery. His grandfather would nudge him when a steaming chestnut mare, flinging the mud with her heels, would slide along with a grocer's wagon. They would both turn away when a scrawny nag hauling a bearded, blanketed ragman on a sad and tired wagon would plod along after such a fast-trotting little beast.

"Gyp's there," said the old man, pointing across the street to the blacksmith shop where the black smoke from the forge was just beginning to rise from the chimney. They could see the wide doors slowly swing open and from nowhere a couple horses appeared in the yard. The smoke from the forge hung low, clouding across the branches of the naked elm at the end of Tanner's yard as a gust of wind tried to lift it. The gilt face of the Mediator clock showed seven and the bell beat out the strokes. Nora ladled the oatmeal while Nell poured the tea. His grandfather, setting the pipe down on the table beside his bowl, took one more look out the window and said it was the hell of a cold rain for April, surely.

5

Chapter Two

THEY blessed themselves and started eating without talking. Chris appeared at last in his bathrobe with the silver figs splashed in and out of its blue folds. For him there was hot water and toast with his oatmeal. He ate as he lathered his face and shaved, moving back and forth from the big mirror to the table for a sip of tea and a hasty bite of the toast. The storm gusts, singing mournfully, beat against the clapboards of the house, the one or two on that side which were loose slapping like the ratlines of a schooner in the wind.

"Rain before seven will clear before eleven," said Nora, sipping her tea with the spoon slanting saucily up out of the cup. She spoke of the weather, religion and sins of the world with such unrestrained authority no one ever thought of disputing her except Nell.

"Wear your rubbers, pet," said Nell to her son. "And don't forget to bring your umbrella home with you when you come to your dinner."

He gave her no answer.

"He's off," said Ned, as Chris gathered the folds of his bathrobe around himself and cut away from the table, still chewing a piece of the toast. The boy was glad to see him leave the table, and Chris's mother trotted after him to be sure he found the clean socks and a clean collar. Soon he was pounding his feet into his rubbers in the musty carpeted hallway at the front door and umbrellas were rattling in the black tin stand that had the lovely red roses painted on it.

The day's work was now in full swing for the sisters. Nell, humming to herself, whipped cyclones of dust out of the dining room carpet while Nora, sedately contemptuous of the chore, cleared away the dishes and began to wash them in the sink.

Knowing the rain couldn't possibly stop before the Mediator was striking eleven, the boy watched across the street where Gyp McGlinn was letting his pigeons out of the tiny dovecote on the roof of the blacksmith shop. The birds soared up in widening circles and wheeled around the Mediator steeple. Then, as though

6

they were weighted with leaden wings, they coasted slowly down, avoiding the elm tree and lighting in the yard where their arrival scattered a flock of sparrows who were breakfasting there on the remnants of oats from the nosebags and whatever else they could pick up. The pigeons retired quickly from the rain to their house on the shop's roof and down the sparrows swooped again to their feast.

"D'ye see that?" his grandfather said disgustedly. "Them pigeons might be as hungry as could be but they'd never touch that manure. Now look at them sparrows cut into it. English birds. Be God, even the birds of the air is hogs in England."

The boy brought the funny papers from last Sunday's Boston *Globe* to his grandfather to read for him. The old man always read him the most wondrous accounts from them about great and gay and witty Irishmen who were always getting the best of it. The stories he read were always different from the ones the boy himself was beginning to read from the same papers and never at all like the ones Nora or his grandmother read from them.

"That's the great scholar for you," sneered Nora from the pantry as the old man began a story about a tinker, a great fighting tinker, right from the funny paper. "Why do you fill the boy's head with them lies when they ain't in the paper there at all? Should think you'd be ashamed to be telling him them things and you not able to read a word of truth if it slapped you in the face."

"You be damned," said the old man reading on about the tinker.

There it was again. She was always saying something like that. She was forever cruelly torturing them both with her hateful accusations that his grandfather couldn't read or write. The boy grew restless under her jibes and the tinker was lost. He can read and write, he can read and write, he repeated to himself.

"It says here," said the grandfather, "it says here that the tinker won the battle, all right, but that it'll be next Sunday before the outcome is generally known."

Bold Robert Emmet was their refuge, their well of courage. Dear Emmet standing there in the courtroom face to face with the British judges that condemned him to his death and ordered his noble head cut from his body and thrown to the dogs in the dirty Dublin streets to be devoured by them. They would stand beneath the picture and his grandfather would say, "Here, Will,

7

now, I'll read what Emmet said." Or perhaps the boy would seize the old man by the arm and beg him to read what Emmet said. Their arms would be around each other or the boy would stand in front of his grandfather while he read.

Sometimes they would read it together, the old man going slower so that the boy could keep pace with him. The old man's brown eyes would never waver an instant from the picture, although he might now and then shake a fist at the judges or perhaps, "when the grave opens to receive me," his voice would be lowered a trifle.

"When my country takes her place among the nations of the earth, then, and not until then, let my epitaph be written," they would always read together. Each passionate word eternally damning the bewigged judges and especially Nora for daring say he could not read.

That morning they read it again. This time together and in spite of the racket Nora set up with the pots and pans and clattering dishes in the pantry, the wind blowing a gale against the house and the kettle screeching on the stove. The boy watched every word of the printing, now that he was learning to read in school, and every word they read was printed there on the picture. Some of them, the boy knew, were never printed anywhere else and no one but Emmet himself ever used them. Every shining word was there. They marched in joy around the kitchen when they finished reading.

"Send that boy down cellar for a hod of coal," said his grandmother from the dining room.

"Fetch us the coal," said his grandfather.

Down he went into that fearful gut of blackness and gloom with the coal hod over the crook of one arm and the end of a candle in his hand. In the other he carried his peggy-stick, a short length of broom handle which he kept hidden away under the stairs below and which he used to swipe at the big rats that now and again would spurt out from dark recesses. He would slash at British judges or any other monsters who happened to be dwelling in his mind at the time. Yes, he would take a whack at Nora's thun or clip his uncle on the knuckles or the ankles where it hurt when you got hit there. Setting the candle on a little dusty shelf, he took up the shovel and laid down the peggy-stick. A couple of shovels and the hod was full. The boy shoveled on, flinging the coal around as Gyp McGlinn did in the forge or as his grandfather

8

told him Torpedo Casey used to fire those big navy vessels. He flung the shovel away, snatched the hod and candle and in a breathless moment was upstairs again in the kitchen.

"Was it the tinkers after you?" said Nora.

It was hopeless to think his grandmother would let him out with Peg to chase rats over Tanner's lumber piles with the rain pouring down. He wished he could go across the street to the Riordans' where Joseph and Eddie and Margaret were and where Rose, a little older than any of them, would be helping her mother. But his grandmother always told him there was bother enough for poor Mrs. Riordan with that brood of hers. He would gladly have stayed the rest of the morning watching Gyp across the street or have gone to the Bernsteins' house where there were Sammie and Mark and Esther. Their father was a tailor and their mother, his grandmother swore up and down, said that the Jews didn't kill Christ.

His grandfather went into the dining room to lie down on the couch for a nap, as he always did when he was home from the foundry. Desperately the boy began to explore the contents of the small drawer in the kitchen table where there was always a scramble of nothing at all and everything under the sun. He found unpaid bills from Frank Quinn, a lump of beeswax, an old slicker from the foundry, a bone-handled jackknife with both blades gone, some matches, the stub of a carpenter's pencil, a corkscrew, a small broken whetstone, a plug of dried-out tobacco. He soon tired of it. Ages would linger before it cleared before eleven. He thought it might be a good plan to bring his grandfather a pencil and have him write something on the back of one of the bills, but he remembered that whenever he did that the hand his grandfather had hurt in the foundry would always be bothering him. Peeking into the other room he could see that the old man had fallen asleep, anyhow. His pipe was hanging upside down from his mouth and Peg was curled up at his feet.

He went into the parlor where, under oval glasses, funeral flowers waxed and preserved kept green the memories of dear Aggie and Willie, Lord have mercy on him. There was a picture there of his uncle, with candy-striped stockings and long curls, and another picture of that lovely brown-haired girl with a lock of her curls hanging down over her shoulder. She stood with her arm on the shoulder of a young man seated in a fringed armchair. They

9

always told him that it was a picture of his grandfather and his grandmother on their wedding day. But there was nothing about his grandmother now to make him think so and he wondered that she could ever have looked so pretty.

In the corner were two huge volumes of Civil War drawings which Mick McDermott, Ned's oldest brother who had been sixth corpóral in a troop of the First New England Cavalry, bought from a salesman one day when he was sobering up from a drunk. Toothless and lonely now, his big frame sagging (he and their brother Pete were the big men of the family), Mick lived in the Soldiers' Home in Bristol. The only times the family saw him were on a payday when he would come to the house reeking and sodden with drink when his money was gone. He would slyly try to maneuver old Ned into a corner somewhere so that he could give him a touch without Nell's hearing him. She never quite dared put him out of her house, though many times she threatened it. She would tell him to come sober or not at all and, whichever it was, she didn't care. At night the boy would be awakened by her rancorous tirade against his grandfather for giving money to Mick.

Ned drank very little whisky, but when Mick came he knew the best thing to do was to slip out with him to Jimmy Deignan's around the corner. The boy had learned their strategy and, when he could manage it, would try to be with them on the pretext of taking care of Peg. These were great adventures because Deignan's was in the middle of a dingy alley where no one lived but Negroes, and one time when his grandfather came home from Deignan's he told them he had met Sam Langford there, the great fighter. The boy hoped that someday he would meet the Boston Tar Baby there with Mick and his grandfather and perhaps see him fight. There were many fights in the street.

In spite of all, the boy knew, Mick was a great man, because his uncle Pat McDermott, the family's authority in such matters, often said that if it were not for the Irish that shed their blood and sacrificed their lives the naygurs would never be free today, Lincoln or no Lincoln. In fact, his ruling was that the fetters of slavery England bound around the liberty of this glorious nation would never have been torn asunder had not so many Irish laid down their lives during the dark days of the Revolution.

The boy lugged the heavy volumes from the corner to one of the windows, which in this room were shrouded with lace curtains, and opened one to look at the drawings of battles; Antietam, Chancellorsville, Bull Run, the Wilderness, Sherman's march to the sea and the barefoot Negroes waving to the dusty troops, generals sitting stiffly outside field tents or pointing with their swords toward the enemy redoubts.

He was always searching for Mick's picture, because one day when he asked the old soldier if it were in the books Mick said: "Is it? That's me there on the horse. I rode all over on the finest piece of horseflesh in the Army, the finest horse ever you seen, smashing me way through the ranks of the Johnny Rebs. That's me there on the horse with me saber swinging."

Mick would have told him more that day, perhaps, but the grandmother shut him up with a burst of fury and in the excitement the page was lost forever. Mick was no help in finding it because when the boy asked him what battles he was in, he would say, every damn one of them.

He was with McClellan along the Potomac and with Grant in the Wilderness and riding with General Phil Sheridan or another time it might be Burnside he was with. The boy had to search for the finest damn horse he ever seen among all the thousands of cavalry horse, artillery horse, army mules and the piles of corpses.

Near the middle of the first volume that morning he found a large yellowing envelope and in it a folded and official looking document, stiff and printed, but with spaces where there was handwriting scrolled with long tendrils of E's and M's and D's which he made out to be his grandfather's name, and in other places the word William, his own father's name. The long words baffled him but he could read the words FINLEY STOVE COMPANY from having seen them so many many times. It was where his grandfather had worked once and where his own father was working when he got the iron burns he later died from. He thought it must be something like the report cards the teacher gave at school. A strange looking one, but a report card, and there over the pages his grandfather's handwriting. He flew to the kitchen.

"Nora, Nora," he cried.

"For the love of God what is it now?" she said.

He pushed the papers into her hands as his grandfather came bounding in from the couch and his grandmother hurried in after him.

"There's the writing," the boy screamed. "There's my grand-

11

father's writing. You always say he can't write but there it is. It's all over those pages. His own writing."

His grandfather dropped into the rocker at the window, staring at the boy in bewilderment.

"What is it, then?" asked his grandmother.

"God save us do you know what it is?" said Nora grimly without taking her eyes from the papers.

"What in the hell is it?" asked the old man.

"It's Willie's papers," Nora said. "Willie's 'prentice papers, Lord have mercy on him."

"Where did you filch that?" asked his grandmother.

"In Mick's books," the boy said. "It has my grandfather's writing all over it, hasn't it, Nora? Hasn't it, Nora?"

"Oh, yes," said his grandfather. "Yes indeed."

"Read it, Nora," the boy pleaded.

"Read it to the boy, Nora," the old man said.

"Why don't you, then?" Nora said. "You're the great scholar."

"Poor Will, Lord have mercy on him," moaned his grandmother.

Nora settled her thun against the stove and pinched at her glasses.

"I'll read it then with your lordship's name all over it."

This indenture [she read], made this first day of October, 1887, by and between Edw. McDermott of Providence, R.I. of the one part and the Finley Stove Co., a Corporation created and organized under the laws of the State of Rhode Island and having its principal office in the city of Providence in said State of Rhode Island, of the other part,

WITNESSETH

That the said Edw. McDermott hereby binds out his son William J. McDermott of the age of sixteen years as a servant and apprentice of said Finley Stove Co. to labor for the said company for the full term of two years of working days from the date hereof as a moulder and iron founder.

And the said McDermott doth covenant, agree and promise with and to the said Finley Stove Co. in consideration of its receiving said William McDermott as such servant and apprentice as aforesaid that the same William shall and will during said full term of two years of full working days well and faithfully serve and demean himself and be just and true to the said Finley Stove Co.

12

as his master and keep its secrets and everywhere promptly and willingly obey all its lawful commands made by its officers, agents or employees authorized by said Company to direct and command said William;

That the said William shall do no hurt or damage to his said master in its goods, or estate or otherwise and shall not willingly suffer any to be done by others; that he will not embezzle or waste the goods or property of his said master or lend them without its consent to any persons whomsoever, and will not during the hours required of him to labor by said company depart or absent himself from the service of said company without its leave duly obtained and that he shall and will in all respects during said term demean and behave himself as a good and faithful diligent and sober servant and apprentice.

And also that the said Edw. deposits the sum of $100 with the said Finley Stove Co., the said sum to be held by the said company during said term of two years to be and become forfeited and to become the property of and belong to, said Finley Stove Co. absolutely upon breach by said Edw. of any of the covenants, promises and agreements herein before made.

And the said Finley Stove Co. for and in consideration of the promises covenants and agreements hereinbefore made and of One Dollar to it paid by said Edw. doth on its part covenant, agree and promise to and with the said Edw. that if the promises covenants and agreements hereinbefore made by said Edw. shall be well, duly and truly performed and observed in all respects it will teach and instruct said William as its servant and apprentice and cause him to be taught and instructed in the trade of a moulder and iron founder for and during the said term and will also for and during said term except as hereinafter provided pay to said William the sum of 75 cents a day for each and every day of labor performed hereunder during the first year of service and the sum of 92 cents per day during the second year of service of said William and which said sum shall be payable weekly. Provided, however, that if said William shall not labor, when able to do so, as servant and apprentice as aforesaid and shall not well duly and faithfully perform all the said promises covenants and agreements by him to be performed hereinunder, then in that case the said Finley Stove Co. may without liability terminate this agreement and be forever discharged of all its obligations hereunder or otherwise and may also have and hold as its own said sum of One Hundred dollars deposited as forfeited.

IN WITNESS WHEREOF, the Finley Stove Co. has caused these presents to be signed and executed and its corporate seal affixed hereto by R. T. Finley Jr., its treasurer, for this purpose duly authorized and the said Edw. McDermott has hereunto set his hand and seal on the day and year first above written.

Finley Stove Co.
R. T. Finley, Treas.

Signed sealed and delivered   his
M. L. Saunders   Edward (X) McDermott
         Mark

Finley Stove Co.
Incorporated June 1859

"See, see," the boy cried happily, "you always say he can't write but there it is. Lots of his writing."

"There it is for all the world to see," said his grandfather.

He took the boy into his arms, rocking jubilantly so that the old chair creaked. His tired eyes were sweating tears, but his face was radiant.

"Poor Will," said the grandmother leaving them.

"Yes," sneered Nora, "for all the world to see. And what is this here, then, where it says 'his mark' with a cross between it. And a scraggly damn cross it is, too. Did your lordship write that by yourself, too?"

The chair fetched up as though it had crashed against a stone wall. The old man groaned. The boy was bewildered.

"You bitch," said the old man, his voice racked with rage.

From that day there were never any more Irish heroes in the funny papers getting the best of it, and they never again read Robert Emmet's bold words together. Many times, though, when disaster would threaten the boy's world he would think of those words and remember just how they had read them together so many many times. The old man and Emmet were forever his allies, sustaining him in many a lost battle, many bitter defeats, though the old man died soon afterward when the boy grew to need him more and more; and dear Emmet, he knew, was dead there in Dublin, three thousand miles across the sea.

Chapter Three

FOR years now, Ned knew, Nora had been letting her hatred of him, for having married Nell instead of herself, gather like maggots in the rancid tub of her heart. He knew she wouldn't hesitate a minute to ruin her sister's life and happiness, such as it was, if she were not afraid of making a shambles of her own. Indeed, as Gyp McGlinn said once when he had a drink too much, for he never would even have referred to it sober, Nora could no more help hoping that one night, if it took her a lifetime, Ned would climb into her bed instead of Nell's, than she could help letting that tongue of hers swing like an old gate in the wind. Once, he laughed to think of it now because his contempt for her had grown so strong and firm over the years, he had walked perilously close to the brink of her trap and if she hadn't sprung it wider open, instead of letting him go his own way, he might have tumbled into it. It was the night of the day Willie's father was born and before Nora had come to live with them. She was there, of course, helping Nell and waiting on her. When Nell sank at last into an exhausted sleep he had gone out with his brother Pat for a drink, and Nora promised to stay with Nell until he got back, or all night, if need be, she said, if need be. She was a pretty thing then, too, prettier than Nell even. What things a man will think, God forgive him, on a night like that when you'd think he'd get down on his knees and thank God for having brought his wife safe through the peril of bringing a child into the world. But no. It's out to the bar with the first one that comes along, though Pat meant no harm in asking him, and drink and drink until he wouldn't know whether it was his own pride or the whisky made him that drunk. Then Pat goes his way, but he don't remember Pat ever leaving for there was something on his mind that nothing would drive away and he felt—dear God, what a fool a man is at them times—he felt he could father a race; and there was Nora waiting cosy and willing in the warm kitchen when he got home and Nell still asleep. What he said or what he did skipped away from him now like a mouse in the dark, but the first thing he knew there was Nora in his arms, and he wanted her there, too, crying to him, "Why wasn't it me,

Ned? Why wasn't it me?" She was that greedy, though, that was it, greedy—she was that *goddam* greedy she was like a wild thing clawing him with all fours, a wild hungry thing. Whether the baby cried, or Nell moaned first—it was one of the two—he didn't know. He tore away from her and went into the bedroom where it was so quiet and the lamp, shining down on Nell's face made her look like a pale little angel lying there with the dark curl rolling down around her neck and rolling still on her white breast. Nora stood with the paisley shawl in her hand, waiting only for the kind of a look he would give her when he got back into the kitchen, to decide whether she would put it on her or rip off the rest of what she had on. The look he gave her told her, and the look she gave him back was her hating hateful answer. Let it be. He knew it was still there today melting at the ice of the glasses behind which she hid it.

When she came back again she came to stay, and many a time since then he wished he might have shown her the door again but Nell would never have that, he knew—not her sister. He could never tell Nell about that night; it would break her heart. Nora was always there in his house, wearing Nell's castoffs or what Kate Reagan might give her, like a sin repented but unforgiven on his conscience, like the sore on the back of his hand that he got from a splash of iron and that would never heal. His scorn for her never abated and he would let his contempt roll like a sea over her, hissing as it swamped her.

Now she was at the boy, because she knew how dear Willie was to him. It was a stab here and a cut there with the little knife of spite she carried in the sheath of—of a petticoat, maybe. When she could slash them both with the same stroke she would, and love it the more. Let her try to interfere with what he wanted to do for the boy, though, and he'd crush her again as he crushed her that night years ago. That boy would not walk his life through the mean alleys of his own days. No by God, he'd be there to help him on his way to the broad streets and find whatever there was good to find and nothing would stand in the way of it. No Noras, no nothing, while God gave him strength to sweep them away out of the path.

I'll always find work, he would say, and he always had, except during the panic when he would tramp home in the middle of the night with a sack of coal on his back, plundered from the barges in the river. He would say it to Nell when, as sure as the shop shut

16

down for a spell, Frank Quinn would come crying for his bill. His horizons held no day when the last ladle would be poured into the flask and he would pick up the tools to say the work was done for good and all now. If even his dreams held such a day, he never spoke of them to anyone and he was content to know that when the hour came that he could no longer ram the sand in around the pattern and no longer catch the first bright iron as it spouted from the cupola, Sergeant Death "with his cold arms" would soon embrace him. Time and again he had been licked, as he said, and his cherished hopes swept away from him, his darling boy and his girl taken from him by the hand of God before their time.

These were fresh new days coming and better days than when the signs, "No Irish Need Apply" hung, if you could read them, on the shop gates and the mills. Evil days when the bastards had threatened to burn down the convent on Claverick Street and the Irish gathered from all parts of the city, marching around it day and night for three days, while the sisters went on with the scholars inside and never missed a lesson. Yes, God bless them, today the spires of their churches reached higher into the skies than anything in the city, proud and enduring with their altars of Carrara and Connemara marble, their stained glass and their loud defiant bells. There was hardly a parish now without its own school. The days were gone when you came into the foundry and some son of a bitch said you were all so drunk at O'Toole's wake you buried the pig and left the corpse in the parlor. For now many a one had come to the top of the heap, like Nell's cousin Pete Carron; and no matter how he did it there he was. Ned remembered the day Pete arrived in Boston years ago, with no more than the shirt to his back and, managing somehow to get to Providence where the others had come, knocked on the door and asked Nell if he could sleep in the attic. And he did, too—the long cold winter in the attic, and happy to get his cup of tea in the morning, saving every penny he could get his hands on when he went to work for the railroad. Soon he was riding around in a buggy hauled by one of Malley's old nags on Sunday mornings. He got to every police station in the city, bailing out the drunks and the brawlers so they would get to last mass at least. He charged them a pretty penny, too, for the favor, and sold most of them insurance when it was paid back. That was his start, God knows, and today he sat in the bank, with the gold watch chain swinging across his Donegal home-spun and himself pulling at the gray beard that he started to raise,

17

they said, to save the price of a shave on Saturday. Visiting his rows of tenements and counting his mortgages by the dozen, there he sat, banking the bishop's money for him and doing a charitable deed when the fancy struck him. True, as Pat said, Pete Carron never did a dishonest thing in his life—without a profit. He wasn't one you'd be proud of among yourselves, but a damn good thing to let the Yankees know they weren't the only ones in the banks these days.

Some got into a store or a saloon and soon owned it, or one of their own across the street, and raised a priest or a doctor or maybe a smart lawyer; there was no telling what else they mightn't do. But most of them like himself, try as they would, never owned their own houses and never could put by enough in good times to tide them over the bad times. Nor was it from want of hard work, for there were few that he knew that you would say were drinkers, except they might get over the bay once in a while in company or at a wake or a wedding. As soon as one bill was paid along came another on its heels. Some had a trade and others never got the chance to learn one, though, all in all, counting the days the shop would be shut down for the moulders or the weather too wet for the building trades, they came out about even with the one that had a tidy little job without a trade but no time out. Some were smart and struck when the others did, eating crusts for a while to make sure of a full loaf later, and others scabbed on them, coming out as well in the end when all was forgotten; brought up their families well or had one here and there turn out no good like Pat's Eddie.

There was his own Will, a good moulder and a hard worker. Lost his wife when the baby was born in the little house on the other side of the Armenian bakery. Well, she was worn out, poor thing, nursing her family, the four of them dying of t.b. the year before Will married her. Let him come home again, he said then, so that Nell can nurse the baby, if it lives. So home he came, but not for long. He stumbled with the ladle one day in the foundry a short while later, and died of the burns. It couldn't have been that drunken Pig-eye Owens nor his lazy brother Tom that had to go; no, it had to be Will. Well, God's wisdom in all things.

The boy's world was bounded by his grandfather's; a world that began with early mass on Sunday, and Willie polishing the family's shoes by the kitchen fire while the rest of the house was still in bed; a world that included trips to Narragansett Park to watch the trotters and to the country towns outside, perhaps, where the old man would hold him up over the railing around the pit to watch the cockfights. Nights after supper there were trips around the corner to Deignan's where Ned drank the little he did drink, while Willie played outside with Peg and the colored boys that lived there, throwing sticks for Peg to chase. On a warm day, when there was no work, they might set out for a trip across the bridge, stopping at Owen Tegue's harbor master's shack on the way just to say hello, and then on to Tim Lee's little cottage. They might walk out to his Uncle Pat's house where he could play with his cousins, John and young Pat, pelting stones at the chickens in the big yard in back of the house. But they were not friends like Joseph and Eddie Riordan; just cousins. He didn't like to visit them or his cousin Fred Kane. He always had the feeling when he was at the Kanes' house that his cousin Fred was going to say something that would make a fool out of him. Fred Kane managed to know many things the boys knew but didn't talk about when their fathers and mothers were around. Fred would always talk about them.

But mostly the people his grandfather liked, he liked, and the people his grandfather didn't like, he didn't like. It was that way about Nora, who was always ordering him around the house and finding things for him to do. He did them sullenly because his grandmother would make him do them anyway, but it was against her, his aunt, old, sallow and toothless, that he first revolted. He could never define the reason his grandfather didn't like Nora, but he knew that the old man didn't. It was she who made sure that Willie went into the cellar, or out in the back yard if the weather were warm enough, to sift the ashes. "For if you don't," she'd say, "I'll have to do it myself and you're better able than I am." She would tell his grandfather, too, if he didn't do as she told him. He wanted to rebel, defy her, but if he did it would mean a sharp crack on the head with his grandmother's thick wedding band and a look from his grandfather when he was told, a look of pain.

"Willie," she said one afternoon when he came from school, "there's a pile of ashes in that cellar that'd reach the moon. Get down there and sift them. Bring them up in the yard a little at a time."

He had a sieveful of them done, carefully picked over, when Joe and Eddie Riordan came to the gate. They started over the fence to Tanner's when Nora, looking out the window, called him back.

"Do you have to do what she says?" Joe sneered.

Willie McDermott was straddling the fence. It was a great chance.

"Go to hell," he called up to Nora. "You can go to hell." His grandmother appeared at the window beside Nora.

"Willie, come back here," she called.

"You can go to hell," he shouted.

The boys leaped down between the piles of lumber, Willie trembling with the intoxication of his challenge to them.

"That boy," said Nora as soon as Ned got inside the door, "has gone the limit this time, swearing and cursing at Nell like a trooper."

Peg, as always, was leaping with joy at Ned's arrival, bounding up and down from a chair. Ned set his dinner pail on the kitchen table and hung his hat on the hook. He leaned over and patted the dog.

"Did you hear what she said?" Nell screamed out of a cloud of smoke from the frying pan.

"What did he say?" Ned asked, still patting the dog.

"Not to mention what he said to me," Nora said.

"You'll punish him this time, do you hear?" Nell threatened. "Yelling out there on the back fence and calling me every black name he could lay his tongue to."

"It's come to a pretty pass," Nora said, "with a boy that age swearing and cursing at his own grandmother."

"I want him punished, do you hear?" Nell cried above the hissing of the frying pan. "Punished!"

Ned sat in his rocker carving a plug of dark Mayo and slowly crumbling the chunks between the palms of his hands. He scraped out the bowl of the clay pipe with the knife, blew the stem clean and carefully packed the tobacco into the bowl.

How could the man sit there and do nothing about it? Nell and Nora were both infuriated, Nell springing away from the stove at him, slashing a large meat fork in the air in front of her. She thrust the fork menacingly in Ned's face.

"I want him whipped!" she shrieked. "I want him whipped! I want him whipped within an inch of his life!"

"My dear woman," said Ned, looking disinterestedly at the fork, striking a sulphur match on the sole of his shoe and watching it slowly grow from a tiny blue bud into a dancing yellow flower, "I will not fight with my own for a stranger."

Chapter Four

THE desperate little lilac in the back yard had long since been stripped of its last flowers, but its dusty leaves looked silvered and extravagant in the waning daylight. Patches of coarse, scraggly grass had begun to sprout around it and Peg, lying with her back against the slender trunk, bit casually at the narrow blades. Ned McDermott and his friend Tim Lee sat on the top step, watching the fire of the sun burn itself down behind the spires of the cathedral down the hill.

"Red sky at night sailor's delight," said Tim. "It'll be a grand day for the voyage, Ned."

"The boy has his heart set on it," Ned said. "It'll be his first journey over water, God knows."

The darkness dropped over them as they discussed the details of the trip they planned for the morning. They were bound for Block Island to see Kit Somerville and would spend at least a couple of days there at Kit's farm, with at least one cockfight in Kit's barn. It was a cosy place for a cockfight, because the farm, on the edge of a salt marsh, was far away from any other farms and Kit, besides, was a deputy sheriff, the only one on the island. He was Republican representative in the state legislature and held a license as pilot for the Providence River, Narragansett Bay and all contiguous waters. It was a full half day's sail from Providence to the island with a stop, usually, at Newport.

They had decided when the last snow began to thaw that, as soon as the weather broke, they would make the excursion. Every time they met they mulled it over, though in their minds everything had been settled but the day, and that depended only on when the Ship Windlass, the foundry where Ned worked, would be shut down. Two steamers made the run: the *Mount Hope* and the *Warwick.* This in itself had presented a problem because the *Warwick* cost half a dollar less than the *Mount Hope* and neither of them was against saving a penny where he could. Another consideration, which both of them had known for months but never mentioned, was the fact that the skipper of the *Warwick* was a nautical gentleman by the name of Olsen whereas the skipper of the *Mount Hope* was an intrepid navigator by the name of O'Flaherty, a Galway man.

"D'ye see, Ned," Tim said, "I happen to run into Will O'Flaherty in McGarraghan's the other night after he tied up, and he says 'Lee, begod, I met an old friend of yours in Newport the other day.' 'Who is that?' I says. 'Casey,' he says, 'Torpedo Casey . . .' "

"Torpedo Casey," Ned mused. "The son of a bitch. And how is he?"

"Wait now," Tim continued. "It seems Casey is working on some boat that's tied up at the other side of the wharf where O'Flaherty docks. He says you'd never know Torpedo for a machinist mate, first class except for the cap he wears. They have a chin for half an hour or so every time. . . ."

"Machinist mate, first class," Ned scoffed, "why the man couldn't wind an eight-day clock and have it keep the time of day."

"That I don't know," said Tim, "but he has the rating and draws the pay. That I *do* know."

"How long is Casey in now?" Ned asked.

"Due for a pension any time he wants it," Tim said. "And a fat one, too, besides what he has put by."

"Put by?" Ned snatched the clay pipe out of his mouth and spat. "Many's the time I gave him the fare back to Newport when he'd be on a toot. You did yourself, Tim."

"Not in late years, Ned. Torpedo's a changed man, they tell me."

"For his own sake I hope so," Ned said fervently. "Though he has neither kith nor kin."

"Not a soul," Tim admitted.

"Not a soul," Ned echoed.

They sat in silence for a long while. The skies darkened except for a spot over the Butt Company, where the heat was on for the moulders on the night shift. The flames there reached up and down from the stack.

"Well, it's dark, Tim, and we might step around to Deignan's for a drink. I never drink during the day myself unless I'm drinking."

"Yes."

"Come along, Peg," Ned said and the dog, stretching herself and yawning, followed them out the gate.

Tim Lee was about eighty years old at the time, he thought, but he wasn't sure and cared little as long as God gave him the strength to get around and take care of Annie in her last days. He was a carpenter by trade, but he had not worked at it for many years now. Annie was his sister and they lived together in a sway-backed little cottage on South Water Street on the other side of the river where there wasn't another Irish family but themselves now. Winter or summer he wore a greening derby hat, a stiff white collar and a green necktie with a huge horseshoe stickpin thrust into its wrinkles. The pin was rimmed with tiny emeralds and chip diamonds which, as he went on in years, were disappearing, diamond after emerald. He chewed ten-cent cigars. Near the cottage was a two-story frame house which he and his sister owned and rented to families of Bravas, giant Negroes from the Portuguese islands who worked on the river boats along the docks, and some of the young girls in the textile mills.

The only other white men in Deignan's were Mick Hanley, the bartender, and Deignan himself, standing down at the end of the bar in his shirt sleeves. All the others were Negroes and a Negro woman in neat rags was standing at the side door waiting for Mick Hanley to fill her pail.

"Good evening, Ned. Hello, Tim," said Deignan courteously.

They greeted him and, when Mick gave the woman her pail, had a beer and a whisky.

"These niggers all speak English, Ned," said Tim. "Them Bravas that rent the house can hardly speak a word of it, you know."

"So, I'm told," Ned said. "These is damn nice fellows. Never had an off word with one of them except the time Pat's Eddie come and smashed the glass after drinking from it. They were mad, but I says nephew or no nephew, that is no kin of mine. I disconnect him entirely."

"Never amounted to much, did he? Where is he now?"

"In the Army," Ned said.

"And Pat is still in the foundry?"

"Ah, sure."

"Good man, Pat," said Tim. "By God, Ned, do you know them Bravas is a strange breed of man? There's countless generations of them has passed through that house since Annie and me started renting to them. They breed like pigeons, anyhow. They come and go like birds in the fall and spring. They're up and off home, you know, to Portygal or wherever the hell it is they come from. Some comes in and some goes out. But, though I never know their names at all, only Joe and John or something like that, I never lost a penny with them yet.

"I mind the time I says to Annie, I think I'll put an inside toilet, lift-up seat and all, in No. 80, I says. You're a fool, says she, sure you have no inside toilet, seat or no seat, to your own house and you want to go putting one in there for the Bravas. Don't be stirring them up with your nonsense. They're happy and content as they are. Annie, I says, I'm going to try it out. I'm going to do it, I says, if I can drive a bargain with that crafty Mulvey. It's the coming thing, Ned, everywhere, the same as in your own house, now. What the hell, I put the gas in for them, I says to Annie, and I might as well go the whole hog and put the toilet into the cellar."

"They're fine comfortable things," Ned said. "A great comfort on a cold day."

"D'ye still own that shack on South Water Street, Tim," asked Deignan.

"Shack? It's a damn sight better built than many a coop on Christian Hill. Anyhow, it was a hell of a job to get that damn thing into the cellar. Mulvey let me have the bowl and the flush parts for a good price second hand, see, but no, Mulvey, says I, let the seat be brand new. The second hand bowl is good enough, I says, for anybody, but let the seat itself be new. Well, Mulvey is days and days getting the damn thing in the cellar. He had pipes to the sewer and pipes to the water main and pipes strewn all over me cellar. I thought to meself one day down there watching him and Gaffney at work how damn much hard work goes into providing the simplest comforts of man. Then I thought to myself he's been a hell of a long time at it. Well, me gossoon, I'm onto you with your cheap price for the secondhand bowl, I thought, and you making it up on the labor end.

"Mulvey, I says, is it a throne for the King of Ireland long dead you are contriving there or is it a simple inside lift-up seat toilet you are installing for me? That fetched him, and the work wasn't long after that being done with . . . Mick, give us another of the same. I must say it was a fine job, though, neat as you please and the seat itself a fine piece of woodwork. Oak, it was, white oak. Best o'health, Ned.

"One day, a week or so later I was passing No. 80 and I says to myself I'll just drop in and see how me new inside lift-up seat toilet is. Down I go by the cellar door without saying a word to the Bravas and struck a match to have a look at it and there, by God, Ned, is my new toilet, stripped naked as the day it was born. The seat that was brand new is gone and the mouth of the bowl gaping at you. I hunted high and low for it.

"By God, I says, I'll put an end to this and up I go to the Bravas on the first floor and into the kitchen. There's a ship's company of them sitting around the table with a bottle and jabbering away at each other. But they damn soon stopped when they see me. They don't know what to make of it for I never go there until the first of the month if it falls on a Sunday or a holiday and then the day before.

"Where the hell is my new lift-up seat to my toilet? says I. Who in the hell is plundering and stealing my property now? Who done it?

"Well, they start to tell me they have no money until the first of the month. No money, no money. One of them shows me the calendar and points to the twentieth. I'll never forget the day, Ned. To hell with your calendar, says I, where the hell is my plumbing?

"While they're staring at me I look around the walls and what do I see hanging there but my brand damn new lift-up seat toilet. And what in the name of God do you suppose they have inside it but the Blessed Virgin herself, Ned!

"Now what the hell breed of a man is it will put the Holy Mother of God's picture inside a lift-up seat toilet?"

"Well, by God," said Ned.

"Or any other kind of a toilet," said Mick Hanley.

"A sacrament," Ned said, aghast.

"Sacrilege," Deignan corrected.

"Hell of a damn thing whatever it is," said Ned.

"I thought it would kill Annie, poor soul, when I told her about it," Tim shook his head and finished his drink. "Well, you can't take it down and leave the Blessed Virgin with no frame at all around her, says Annie. And sure I couldn't. No, Annie, I says, that one thing I can't do! Ah, let them squat on the naked bowl as their fathers did before them, Annie says. Well, there she hangs to this day, Ned, at No. 80 South Water Street—the blessed Mother of God inside a lift-up seat toilet, though not brand new any longer, God forgive them."

Chapter Five

STANDING like an admiral of the fleet in the cockpit of his tiny bewhiskered launch, the great trunk of his arm casually resting on the tiller bar, Harbor Master Owen Tegue steered his craft through the foul-smelling night vapors the sun was beginning to burn off the river and headed for the float anchored just below his little shack on the bridge. He spied Ned McDermott crossing the bridge with his grandson and hailed them. They stood at the head of his gangway until he had made the boat fast to the float and joined them. He was a cousin, or something, of Nell's, a huge, rusty man who was crafty enough to have himself elected to his job as the candidate, unopposed, of both parties for many years. His face was weather-red and abundantly freckled and he wore large round gold-rimmed glasses with thick lenses in them. When Willie looked at him, peering up in front of him, the blue eyes behind the glasses looked very merry and large, but when the boy looked at him from the side, where there was no glass to cover them, the eyes were drawn and had a narrow squint to them, as hard and sharp as his grandmother's when she was angry.

Owen Tegue was the only one of Nell's family, excepting her brother Bill, long since dead, whom Ned liked. The rest of the Flynns? No.

They were a mousy family, scampering into so damn many other families Ned could never put his finger on which was which of them. They were married to Pryors, Doonans, Deignans, Carrons, Faheys, Ryans, Sweeneys, Cassidys, McGlinns, Monaghans, Caseys, Carrolls, or they were cousins to them, or they were something to them. There was one of the Caseys from Fall River, he must have been the first one of them ever came out here, and the ship he was on was wrecked in a storm on the shoals off Cape Cod. Hardly anyone was saved when she foundered, but, when the dawn came, some of them drifted ashore on pieces of the wreckage, Casey among them. They said he sat there in the lee of a sand dune, cold and shivering, huddled close to the one alongside him, and looked out at the vessel breaking up on the shoal, her sails torn

26

and dragging in the surf, her bows under. They said he looked at the poor stricken thing there and shook his fist at her crying, "Damn you, damn you, if I'd known you'd dump me where you did—if I'd known I'd have to swim half the way, I'd never have started! Never!" That was years and years ago and Ned had never seen the man, but it was the one thing and the only thing, he said, that any of them—Flynns, Caseys, Pryors, Faheys, Doonans, Deignans, Cassidys, Carrons, or Ryans, McGlinns, Monaghans—the one and only thing any of them ever said that anyone would ever remember. No, Owen Tegue was the only one of them he liked.

"Where are you bound so early in the morning?" Owen Tegue asked Ned.

"The island," Ned answered. "We're meeting Tim Lee in McGarraghan's. Come along with us and have a drink. You look chilled to death."

"I am. Chilled to the bone. I was up half the night with a fire on a coal barge. Had to see it was towed away from the pier before half of Fox Point was burned up. How is Nell and Nora? It's a little early for a drink, ain't it?"

"Nell's fine," Ned said. "Come along. What would start a fire on a barge? There's no boilers in them, is there?"

"That drunken squarehead of a captain—captain they call him, yes—fell asleep with his pipe in his mouth and set the whole thing ablaze."

"I done it many a time," Ned said. "And co'd sober, too. It's a dangerous thing."

McGarraghan opened early in the morning, as most of the waterfront saloons did, for the longshoremen and the teamsters. The coal teamsters had just won a strike under the leadership of Larry Ganley. One of the concessions they won was that they no longer had to harness up mornings; the helpers did it, giving the teamsters that much more time free in the morning to spend in McGarraghan's if they wanted to. McGarraghan, a teamster once himself, let them use the bar as a headquarters and swore in court that two of them, arrested for beating up a scab, were standing in the bar at the time of the attack.

Tim Lee was already there, leaning against the bar talking to McGarraghan. It would be more than an hour before the *Mount Hope* sailed, but they always made sure to be ahead of time when they were starting a trip as important as this one. All of them knew

Torpedo Casey, and McGarraghan said the man must be in the Navy all of twenty years. Owen Tegue said Casey was as good a seaman as there was around those waters, and because of his position he was not disputed. He wondered how Ned come to be so friendly with that Yankee, Somerville, whom he knew by sight because Somerville often brought a ship up the river. Ned said he had known him ever since they both had to run the hell out of a barn in Fall River together when the sheriff raided a cockfight that was going on. Neither one of them had an overcoat, Ned said, and it was a hell of a cold hike into Fall River from the barn. They didn't dare take the main road, he said, but had to go around by the shore with the wind blowing a mile a minute.

"There's good and bad in all kinds, you know," he said. "We've been friends ever since that day. Never mentions a word about the church or religion to me, nor I to him."

They were well fortified, indeed, by the time they had each bought one and McGarraghan himself treated. It was more than either Tim or Ned usually took at one time, but, what the hell, it was an occasion, you might say, that didn't happen every day in the week. Tegue left first, saying that he was going home to his breakfast, and he gave the boy a dime as he went out.

Since Tim lived on that side of the river, he was their guide down to the wharf. The sun was now well up over the city and it skimmed its reflection over the waves as Tim, Ned and the boy walked to the long wharf shed where the tickets for the boats were sold. Tim went to the window and bought two tickets and a half-rate one for the boy. Other boats left from the same wharf, the steamer for New York and the Fall River boat. They went astern on the main deck, sheltered from the wind by the boat deck above them and the housing of the cabins at their backs. The engines were already making steam and the vessel trembled like a mare that is ready for the first heat. It was a weekday and too early in the season for many passengers. The boy ran fore and aft, above and below, peered down the engine room and watched them bringing the freight aboard forward. Her whistle screamed, terrifying him, and in a few short minutes there was shouting fore and aft as the lines were let go. Like a tired old cow leaving the tie-up, she waddled slowly away from the wharf and out into the stream.

Ned and Tim smoked contentedly as she headed down river with her black smoke feathering out astern of her toward the white dome of the Statehouse on Smith Hill. They stretched out on deck chairs of flowered carpeting to watch the thriving hills of the city retreat from them, the shafts of the foundries, the coal bunkers, lumberyards and gashouses and desolate old wharves along the riverside, the creeping barges and tugs and above them, crowning the hills on which the city was built, the steeples of the churches, their own churches. The gray twin spires of the cathedral were off the starboard side; halfway up College Hill, it seemed from where they sat, was the yellow tip of St. Patrick's with its golden cross proudly stretching its arms into the sunlight. They spoke very little and the wind, slipping by the cabin-housings, snatched their words from them and carried them off in whispers. There was nothing to mar their view of the city except the flashes of swift spring lavenders, the tangerine organdies or greens and plaids of girls' dresses as they paraded the deck. Tim gave Ned a nudge with his elbow when Topside Mary—no one ever knew her by any other name—casually sauntered by in a matronly black chiffon with white polka dots. Mary usually rode the overnight boats to New York, but sometimes she'd take a stateroom for just the down-river trip during the spring and summer. She loved the water and lived a very pleasant life during the summer months, extremely selective of the company whom she entertained in her stateroom and a great favorite of the stewards, whom she tipped with a free hand.

The boat was gathering speed now, like a horse breaking into a slow and easy trot. The river was widening out and the sturdy tower of St. Malachi's caught the sun on its raspberry bricks off the starboard side. The boat left Starve Goat Island on her starboard and drew away from the dilapidated little shacks that lined the east side of the river. The boy, kneeling in the arc of the bench that curled around the stern, watched the frothing path of the wake and the boats putting out behind them in the city, their walking beams crawling spiderlike over their topsides like great dream creatures who walked and walked forever to nowhere, who grew larger and sharper and even faster, monsters who crowded his heels but never overtook him.

"It'll be a surprise to Casey when he sees the two of us walk down the gangway," said Tim, "if we happen to run into him."

"God, I hope we do," Ned answered. "I want the boy there to see him, too, dressed in his blues and all."

"Oh, there'll be nothing fancy about him, Ned," said Tim.

"He'll be in his work clothes there with only a cap or something on him showing his rank."

"Is that so?" Ned was disappointed. "Well, no matter, I want the boy to see him, anyhow."

A quartermaster, relieved from his turn at the wheel was making a round of inspection, flipping a careless eye at the rows of life preservers stacked neatly under the circular bench and fastened to the deck above with a thin narrow stripping of wood.

"How's Will O'Flaherty?" Tim asked him just to let him know there were passengers of some consequence aboard.

"Who?" the quartermaster asked, puzzled. He didn't mind talking with the passengers when they were in a free and easy mind down at the bar, but he disliked them really, and didn't want to be bothered with their dumb questions if there were no drink to accompany them.

"The captain," said Ned sharply. "The captain."

"How'n the hell do I know how he is?" said the quartermaster sullenly. "Ain't seen him this morning."

He moved around on the portside, still carelessly scanning the life preservers.

"T'hell with him, Ned," Tim said. "We'll wait a while until things is all snugged down for the voyage and we'll take a walk around the deck and go up on the bridge and see Will—I promised I'd say hello if we made the trip."

They were well below the city now where bright new homes with wide screened porches lined the shorefront with their green lawns stretching down to sea walls. Watching from the stern, Willie McDermott could see the other river boats slowly overhauling them. One side-wheeler, its white paint outlined by freshly gilded trimming, was coming along faster than the others and making ready to pass them on the starboard side. The boy watched her closely and as she came abreast about seventy-five yards away he could see the name, black letters in scrolls of gilt, on her bows, *Mount Hope.*

"That's the *Mount Hope* over there," he told the old men.

"Yes," said Tim Lee. "What's that you say?"

"This is the *Mount Hope*, Willie," his grandfather said quietly. "We're on the *Mount Hope* ourselves. Try to read it again, now, and see do you make it out any better this time."

"I can spell it for you," the boy answered firmly. "Want me to?"

"Spell it out, boy," Tim challenged him, smiling indulgently.
"Let's hear you spell it out for us. . . ."

"M-o-u-n-t-h-o-p-e, that says Mount Hope. . . ."

"Try again," his grandfather said, "practice makes perfect, as
they say. . . ."

Tim Lee went to the rail, his watery old eyes squinting at the
boat which was now almost directly abreast of them, walking
primly along and overtaking them. Tim threw the butt of his
cigar into the water and peered again at the name on the boat's
bow. It was repeated again in a semicircle over the rim of her side
wheel.

"Before God, Ned," he said, without turning his eyes from the
boat. "Before God, I believe the boy is right after all, Ned."

"What the hell kind of a dirty trick is this?" Ned roared springing over to the rail beside him. "Read it again, Tim. . . ."

The quartermaster, strolling aft for a smoke before reporting at
the pilothouse again, walked innocently into the squall of their
anger.

"Look here, you," Tim Lee blazed at him. "What the hell ship
is this we're sailing?"

"No guff, now," Ned snapped. "What ship is it?"

The quartermaster scrutinized them carefully, not wanting to get
into a snarl with a couple drunks. No, he decided, they weren't
drunk, either of them.

"When she left the wharf she was the *Edgemont*," he answered
disdainfully. "Prob'ly still is. . . ."

"Where's the *Mount Hope*, then?" Ned demanded. "What's
become of the *Mount Hope*?"

"That's her alongside us there," said the quartermaster.

"That's her all right," Tim agreed.

"Where's Will O'Flaherty, then?" Ned was fuming.

"Who's he?" asked the quartermaster.

"Who's he? He's the captain of this ship. That's who he is,"
said Tim mimicking the quartermaster's tone.

"The hell he is," the quartermaster sneered.

"Who is then?" Ned asked.

"Swanson," said the quartermaster.

"We're in a trap of some kind, Ned," Tim shook his head in
bewilderment.

"Where in the hell is *he*, then?" Ned snarled.

31

"Go look for him." The quartermaster was disgusted and turned his back on them.

The old friends glared at each other, half suspicious of their own thoughts.

"Come along, Ned," Tim said finally. "We'll find this Swanson and see what he's up to."

They scurried along the deck, up a passage and to the pilothouse, the boy skipping along behind them, dodging in and out among passengers and wondering what the trouble was. Tim Lee pounded on the white door of the pilothouse. A deck hand opened it and told them to go away; passengers were not allowed there, he said. They stalked in, however, and found a large friendly looking man in his shirt sleeves lolling on a bunk reading the sport page of the *Journal*. He looked up in surprise and told them passengers were not allowed there. If they had complaints about anything, he said, they should refer them to the purser's office off the main saloon.

"Where is the captain?" Tim cried.

"I am the captain," said the big man on the bunk.

"It's you we want," Ned said shortly.

"What kind of cutthroat shanghai ship is this," Tim said, "snatching passengers from the wharves."

"Gentlemen," said the captain. "I don't know what you're talking about, but if you have any complaints bring them to the purser."

"Look here," Tim said. "We bought tickets for the *Mount Hope* this morning. The *Mount Hope*, do you hear? And there she is off there."

The captain asked if he might see the tickets and Tim thrust the pasteboards at him. The captain glanced at them.

"You see what it says, don't you?" he asked quietly. "Steamer *Edgemont*, Providence to New London and return. Maybe you bought them at the wrong window on the wharf. . . ."

"Wrong window," Tim whacked his hands together. . . .

"Step aside, Tim. I'll handle this my own way," Ned ordered. "Now then, my man, your little game is up, whatever it is. We're going to Block Island, see, not New London nor anywheres else."

"Not on this boat," said the captain.

"You're in trouble enough as it is," Ned continued, ignoring him, "but we'll give you a chance to get yourself out of a bad scrape. Put us aboard the *Mount Hope* there and the rest'll be forgotten."

"That's fair enough," said Tim.

"That's impossible," the captain answered. "Impossible."

"Come now," Ned went on. "Don't make a fool of yourself into the bargain. Put us aboard the *Mount Hope* there while you have the chance. . . ."

"The last chance," Tim interrupted.

"Be quiet, Tim," Ned admonished.

"Gentlemen," the captain said. "There's some mistake here."

"There's no mistake," Tim began.

"Come, my patience is running thin with all this talk," Ned cut in. "Will you or won't you do as you're told? . . ."

"Gentlemen," the captain was threatening a little. "You can refer your mistake to the purser. Get out of the pilothouse now, or I'll have to call the deck hands to put you out. Passengers are not allowed in here."

The quartermaster, reporting, stepped into the pilothouse.

"Calling your cutthroats and your pirates, are you?" Ned doubled his fists.

"Come, Ned," Tim urged, taking his friend by the arm. "Let's get out of here. Owen Tegue'll hear of this, you goddam squarehead. . . ."

"Yes, by Jesus," Ned echoed, "and damn soon, too. Wait'll Owen Tegue hears of what goes on. . . ."

They tramped out and went below to the sloppy beer bar on the freight deck forward. There a sallow little man in last week's apron set a bottle of Hanley's Peerless in front of them in a frothy puddle on the oilcloth bar. Looking out the big cargo porthole on the starboard side they could see the steamer *Mount Hope*, Captain William O'Flaherty, bound for Newport and Block Island, rapidly pulling away from the steamer *Edgemont*, Captain Ivar Swanson, bound for New London.

Chapter Six

THERE was nothing more to be said. The old men stood for a long time at the bar while the boy explored the boat. He peered down into the overpowering heat of the engine room, hardly able to breathe as he looked over the tops of the shining cylinder heads and watched the Brava oilers at work. He went aft, down the reeking alleyway and looked down over the humps of the boilers into the blackness of the stokehold, the thunder of the engines, the pumps deafening him. Dripping Brava firemen, up for a blow, cautioned him against going below into the inferno and wiped their dark faces with their begrimed sweat rags, which looked to the boy like the dishcloths in his grandmother's pantry; they rolled cigarettes from long, curling tobacco out of paper packages that had George Washington's picture on its blue and starry sides. The fumes of the coal, the cooking oils and the smoke of their cigarettes seemed to be filling his stomach and he went on deck again, walking from stem to stern, leaning sometimes on the rail and trying to absorb this beautiful world ashore, a world of long stretches of yellow beach, houses with the red tiles of their broad roofs gleaming, islands of trees rimmed with necklaces of grim rock. In the stern, his arm hooked around the staff that reached out over the water where the flag flapped and swirled, he listened to the whispering music leap from the boiling cream of the wake. It terrified him to look down into it, and the wind, when he turned his head toward the bow, made him gasp. He found his grandfather and Tim still standing at· the bar and together they went to the stern where they had first sat, and ate the lunch his grandmother had packed for them in a shoe box. He ate ravenously at first but by the time he was peeling the bruised, warm bananas he could eat no more.

Newport Harbor lay to their portside with its torpedo station, its naval vessels and long rows of barracks and pancakes of parade ground where they could barely make out little white dots of men marching and running. There were shabby commercial wharves where boats of every kind were docked and the harbor was peopled with busy little boats coughing their ways in every direction. The white wings of sailboats scudded over the green waters around them and somewhere ashore there was the great Torpedo Casey. The Edgemont waddled along, her course veering over toward the starboard shore and Point Judith where the sea was; and its tumult began to juggle the Edgemont. It was somewhere along here, Tim was saying, that the Larchmont went down that winter night with nearly everybody aboard her when she was rammed or rammed the schooner. They were a long time talking about it, whether the captain of the Larchmont was to blame or the captain of the fishing schooner or whether it might have been the man at the wheel or the lookout that was at fault. Don't forget it was blowing a gale of wind that night, Tim said, and it was snowing harder than it ever snowed before of since probably. The boy wondered how so sturdy and beautiful a ship as this one, riding along so surely could ever sink, but he could see those people thrashing around in the water, cold and frantic like the kids down at the coal pier who sometimes waded out beyond their depths and had to be hauled in to the safety of the shore. But there was no shore and no helping hands for those poor souls, Tim told him, perishing there on the Larchmont. Ned added that many's the disaster at sea could have been avoided if those concerned paid attention to what the hell they were doing.

Riding into the Sound, the water grew calmer for a while, but then heavy, lumbering asphalt clouds rolled across the sun and a wind, carrying scattered splashes of heavy rain, rushed down over the steamer. Tim said it was no more than a shower at all and they sat for a while where they were, waiting for it to pass. But it didn't pass; it grew, moaning and howling in spurts until they had to retreat to the stifling plush prison of the saloon, where they found seats and sweltered for the remainder of the trip to New London, listening to a restless pigtailed girl beating out scales on a huge upright piano, babies crying and parents scolding, a group of young people chorusing, and Topside Mary, her green silk parasol twirling beside her knees, joking and laughing with a cigar-smoking sport wearing pin-striped white flannel pants and a wide-brimmed sailor straw. At last he wandered off in one direction, and Topside Mary, disdaining even a glance at anyone in the saloon, waited defiantly a few minutes and walked away in the other. Willie McDermott running out the athwart-ship alley to the deck saw them meet again on the lee side of the *Edgemont* and go into one of the outside cabins.

The rain beat ceaselessly down while they were tied to the wharf in New London and the passengers crowded on the decks for a breath of fresh air in the shelter of the buildings. The starched dresses were wilting and the people were sticky and irritable, chafing to go ashore for a few minutes anyhow, but held aboard by the downpour. The benches along the deck were wet and they couldn't sit. They milled and prodded one another along the decks and through the alleyways, littering the decks with orange skins, eggshells, stray banana skins and crusts of bread, while the deck hands rumbled up and down the gangway with their hand-truck loads of a desultory cargo of small crates, sacks and a few lengths of galvanized pipe. They were all relieved and happier when the lines were cast off again and the *Edgemont* inched her way from the wharf, like a fat lady edging her way backwards out of the pew into the aisle, stern first into the rain and the fairway.

The voyage home to Providence was even worse than the trip to New London. The pigtailed girl in the saloon was tired and hungry and irritable, smacking viciously at the keys of the piano; all the babies were crying, and even the young people abandoned their singing after a few off-key attempts at songs they couldn't remember. While the *Edgemont* was rounding Point Judith again, parents who had been scolding and wheedling their children forsook them and, their faces turning a horrid greenish-yellow, made wildly for the alleyways to the deck, groaning and vomiting. Not all of them reached the rails in time. They closed the windows of the saloon to keep the rain out and closed them again to sweat and stifle in the oppressive stinking air there.

Ned and Tim stood it as long as they could and then went below to the little bar near the cargo hold. They brought their bottles to the port on the lee side and drank, staring out into the rain which was steady and fine now, curtaining off the shore lines. They had passed Newport Harbor and were cutting into smoother water with the evening falling over it before they knew where they were. Sometimes the steamer would ride up on a bell buoy or channel marker so close they could see them tossing and pitching in the dappled, rolling water only a few yards away from them. When they reached a gap in their talk they couldn't bridge, one of them would get up from the burlap-covered bales on which they were sitting and go to the bar for more beer.

36

Willie curled up on the bales behind them, the burlap burning like a banked fire under him, wretched and tired. He was soon asleep.

His grandfather and Tim raced trotters and pacers; they fought cocks and bulldogs; built houses and poured castings. They talked about all the people they knew, and Ned told Tim that only that morning he had been thinking about the Flynns. And now, he said, he knew he was right all the time, for this was the kind of a thing, missing the boat and all, that would happen to a Flynn. He hoped none of them ever heard about it. Of course, they would never say anything to him about it but the news would fly among the Deignans and Doonans and Carrons all over the world. The whole clan would know it. Just a whisper was all they needed, a whisper like a ladies' maid would bring down to the kitchen. That was the thing about them, Tim, that was one of the things he didn't like about that clan, there were so damn many servants in it and the richer the man or woman they worked for, the more they were looked up to. Now who in hell would look up to a servant but another servant, Tim? All right, no, you don't have to look down on them, but, for the love of God, if that's the way they have to earn their bread and butter—not a goddam McDermott, Tim, was ever anybody's servant—let them have the common decency not to go around from house to house bragging about how much money or how many houses the people they worked for had. But they do, as though they owned it all themselves, and that's it, see, Tim, as soon as they get into one of them places they clap their eyes on a house or a mention in the will somehow if they behave themselves, and that finishes them.

When the *Edgemont* was passing Starve Goat Island again the bartender said they could have another bottle of beer each, if they wanted it, before he started to clean up and close for the night.

The world was still pitching and tossing under him when Willie, holding his grandfather's hand, went ashore between the old men. The rain was pelting down now on the tin roof of the wharf shed. Tim said it was lavish, fairly pissing, but he would walk them as far as the trolley car, anyhow, rain or no rain, finish the day off together as far as they could. He had only a few steps to go from the shed to his little cottage and Ned told him not to be a fool and run along home.

"Sure, it's only a drip now, Tim," Ned said. "We'll use shank's mare and be home almost as soon. Sure we're both wet to the skin as it is and a bit more won't hurt us. Make the boy grow, they say. . . ."

They said good night to Tim under the shed, and struck out across the mud of Water Street to the bridge where the lights across its span were shedding the rain like buds drip the dew in the morning. Ned wanted to walk, because while he was sitting on the boat with Tim he couldn't think and he wanted time to do a little of that before he got to the house and Nell would be asking him why they hadn't stayed the night in Block Island with Kit Somerville. His derby shed the rain and the boy's thin little cotton shirt was plastered to his body. Tired as he was, though, he felt secure and even happy trudging along with his hand in his grandfather's. He could feel the hard scales of the calluses on his grandfather's fingers. They waded over the inch-deep creek that had swelled on Eddy Street and were soon at the long brick wall of Finley's foundry. There were so many things Ned wanted to begin telling the boy he didn't know where he would begin, but this was as good a place as any. . . .

"Well, please God," he began as they passed the high picket gate that led to the foundry yard, "you'll never have to be tramping down here of a cold morning when you get to be a man and you'll never have to be pounding sand nor pouring a floor on a hot day either. That's what going to school will do, you see, Willie . . ."

They plodded along, finding a little shelter every few yards under the few dreary elms, the boy only half awake and Ned talking as though only himself could hear or was the only one listening.

Crushed by the disastrous events of the day, he had begun to be afraid for the first time that in spite of his determination his plans for the boy's future might slip out of his grasp, that he might not be able to achieve what he wanted to for him, and he wanted to reassure the youngster, who understood nothing of what he was thinking, that everything would be accomplished. If, he thought, even with Tim Lee along that could read and write with the best of them, the day—the one day—had turned out so badly, who could tell what would happen to such a great undertaking as the education of a boy? Yes, he was troubled, for there's many a slip. He grasped the little hand within his own tighter.

"Wait'll you see," he said confidently, "there you'll be one day with stacks and stacks of books piled around you and in'll come Tim Lee for advice. You'll be a lawyer or a doctor or something of the kind I don't doubt a bit, and Tim Lee'll come in to ask your advice on this question or that and you'll say, as like as not, 'Oh, yes, Mr. Lee, I remember you well. I remember the day you and me grandfather took me on the boat to Block Island that got us in the end to New London and we didn't know where the hell we were bound. But no matter,' you'll say, 'bygones is bygones and mistakes is bound to happen to the best of us. Think no more about it, Mr. Lee,' you'll say, 'and what is it I can do for you now?' "

"Why will he come to ask me something?" the boy asked.

"Why? Why, my God, boy, because you'll be a doctor or a lawyer or something with a grand education about things that Tim Lee never knew, and he'll come to you asking you for your advice on this matter or that that he wouldn't know a damn thing about himself. Of course there'll be thousands of others coming in to ask you for your advice on this or that and you'll have to tell them what they want to know, you having an education and all that they don't have, most of them working in a foundry or a shop or a mill or something or other. . . ."

"How will I know what to say to him if he comes to ask me something about a matter or this matter?" The boy was troubled because the older people were forever asking him questions that he was sure they knew beforehand and that he couldn't answer, anyhow.

"Why . . . why you'll know all about this or that from the books you'll be studying that has the answers to everything that he'll want to know," Ned said. "Why you'll read all them books at one time or another and you'll know just what to say."

"And besides, if they get too damn nosy up there when we get home, asking questions and all, we'll tell them that we changed our minds about the Island and decided to take a little trip to New London, anyhow, since none of us had ever been to New London before in our lives and we can go to see Kit Somerville at Block Island or Torpedo Casey at Newport any old time for that matter. . . ."

"Did you?" the boy asked.

"Well, in a way we did, you see," his grandfather answered. "If it had been O'Flaherty or any other decent man was captain of that boat, he might have put us aboard the other one, you see, with no trouble at all. But that goddam squarehead son of a bitch, you see, was so mean about it I says to meself to hell with him, I says, we can see Kit or Torpedo any old time at all and none of us ever seen New London in our lives, I says, so why the hell not stay right where we are now and see it this once since we're here? That's when I made up my mind we might as well go right along to New London on that goddam boat. Besides, I says, it looks to me as though there might be a storm coming up before we get halfway to the Island and that'll spoil the whole thing. Though there wasn't a cloud in the sky at all then, I just had the feeling there might a storm come up as we were going to the Island and that would spoil it all. D'you remember there wasn't a cloud in the sky then. . . ."

"It's raining hard now, though," the boy said, wiping his face.

"Not a cloud in the sky," Ned said pushing open the back gate.

Chapter Seven

KATIE Daly scattered cracked corn to the Plymouth Rocks in their piano-box henhouse at the far end of the grape arbor before she opened the wicket to let them out into the sun. "Surely, Catherine darling," she declared, "surely you, a schoolteacher and an only child and all, can do better for yourself than Chris McDermott. Not that I have anything against him, but there's a streak of something or other in the McDermotts that I don't like, a wild streak, and they're rough people and you're all we have, dear. Now you, Dolly Varden (snatching up a heavy bird and holding it head down while she probed its innards with her knuckled, stubby fingers), you will make a Sunday dinner this week for there hasn't been an egg out of you these two weeks past." She dumped the hen into an old strawberry crate where it would get no more to eat that day and when Joe came home at night he would chop its head off.

"Catherine, dear, you can pick and choose as you please," she mumbled, feeling in the warm straw of the nest for the eggs and putting them into a berry box stained with purple. "There's Walter McGuinness, the wholesale liquor dealer's son that's running after you like a dog and he'll have a fine business, too, when old man McGuinness dies. Or what's wrong with young Farrell, the lawyer, now, though his mother's a widow and they have nothing to speak of today. If it was me I'd say Farrell and be done with it. Your father thinks well of him, too. And young Pat O'Neill that's just set himself up in practice. A young doctor must have a wife in his house if he wants the respect of the people. Wouldn't you like to be a doctor's wife, dear?

"The McDermotts! Pooh! Look down the lane, Catherine, at Chris's own brother Pat, his own brother. Poor Tessie Butler has kept a roof over him and Mollie and their boys all their lives. You don't remember Mollie before she was married to a McDermott, Catherine, a pretty girl, strong as a man and look at her now with not a sound tooth in her head and her hair as gray as a gull. Or look at Ned himself, and I won't say he's not a good man, either, but what has he to show for working all his life? No, Catherine, you don't want *his* brothers, Pete or Mick, staggering drunk to your house to pay their respects. Or maybe one day an old tramp would knock on your door, bold as you please, and that would be the other brother, Joe. He drifted away years ago. They're ignorant people and quarrelsome. If it wasn't for Pete Carron bailing them out of jail they'd have spent half their lives in it.

"No one could say it about Chris, I know, he's bound to make something of himself sooner or later, I suppose, for he's refined and smart and honest, too, I suppose. But he has a long way to go, dear, before he'll have what your own father has and why do you want to grow old, as I did, waiting for something that you might have now for the asking? Why must you begin where I began when you could start where I waited all my life to get? But there's no talking to you, is there? Well, God knows, it's your bed that you're making and it's you (booting a hen out of her way as she opened the latch of the door), it's you, Catherine, that will lie in it."

Pouring down over her shoulders as she dried it in the May morning sun, Catherine Daly's long red hair wavered in the gasps of wind that trembled the pale green shoots of the vine near her. She opened her eyes and glanced down the arbor as her mother fumbled with the plug in the hasp of the henhouse door and closed them again as the old woman walked up to her. Saturdays were Catherine's own. No school, so she slept later and her mother wouldn't let her lift a finger around the house except to tidy up her own dainty little room upstairs in the cottage. In the afternoon she might go downtown to walk through the stores, play the piano a little before supper when she came home, and in the evening go to confession. There were dances Saturday nights, but Joe Daly, a fairly prosperous saloonkeeper, insisted no daughter of his was going traipsing around to a Saturday night dance and get home at midnight or after. She never thought of disputing her father although now that she had been teaching more than a year she resented his unrelenting dominance over her thoughts and actions, and it seemed to her that marrying Chris McDermott, whom she could twist around her little finger, would provide more than merely an escape for her. Her father had a "little money" and one day, if she ever needed it, the cottage would be her own. Her days were full and she wanted nothing she couldn't have. She sang in the choir at last mass and was always one of the soloists in St. Malachi's

Catholic Club Minstrels. The last time she sang "I'm Afraid to Go Home in the Dark," a ragtime tune, and made a hit with everybody. She sang "Mandy, Mandy, Sweet as 'Lasses Candy" for her encore and brought the house down. Maria Fahey the dressmaker made her costume, a Southern Belle with flounces galore. She carried a little parasol and wore a little bonnet that set off her hair wonderfully under the jets of light the spotlight flung over. Clara Louth, who taught in the same school with her and sang in St. Malachi's choir, said Catherine was simply born for the stage. Every St. Patrick's Day, which always fell in Lent, Catherine played the "Colleen Bawn" or the "Dark Rosaleen" in the Irish play given by the Catholic Club in St. Malachi's old church that had been made over into a hall since the basement of the new church was opened. It was after one of the Patrick's Day shows she met Chris McDermott.

He came to the show with three other fellows from the cathedral parish who marched in the parade. They met some of the boys from St. Malachi's who invited them out. The cast of the show and their guests all went to the club after the show for coffee and cake and sandwiches. Her mother was with her, naturally, but they got acquainted and Chris was calling at the house on Sunday nights for nearly a year before he asked her to marry him. Their families knew each other slightly, as all the Irish from Leitram did, and her father, "in the business" most of his life, liked the young man because he never took a drink.

"Ma," said Catherine fluffing her hair out when her mother came up to her, "Chris's coming out to supper tomorrow night and then I'm going with him to see his mother and father."

Katie Daly's hostility to young McDermott was as delicate as it was definite because there was too much of Catherine's father in the child to come right out and say she didn't like him and that she wished the daughter would find someone else on whom to throw her affections and the few dollars Joe Daly had saved up.

"Oh, yes," said Mrs. Daly. "Won't that be nice now. Well, he'll get the cold chicken, for I must roast it for your father's dinner. Cold chicken and whatever else there is will be all he'll get."

Torpedo Casey arrived at the McDermotts' after supper on Sunday night and Ned hustled him into the kitchen where he had a bottle of whisky.

"So Tim Lee told you I wanted to see you?" he said to his guest.

43

"Well, I do so. Haven't seen you for a hell of a long time. We missed you that day in Newport through no fault of our own or we'd have seen you long before this. How are you anyhow? How is things going with the Navy? There'll soon be war I suppose and that'll mean more money and a better job, won't it?"

"Ah, I suppose I'll be retiring in a few months anyhow," said Casey, "unless a war comes along in the meantime to stop it. Then it'll be no discharges for nobody. We'll have to train the young ones coming along, I suppose. . . ."

"Will you have a little drink for yourself now?"

"Ned, I hardly ever touch it nowadays," said Casey. "I did take a drop now and then, but late years I haven't touched it at all you might say except for a drop or two. . . ."

"What the hell, man," said Ned, "a drop won't hurt anyone. Here. . . ."

The front doorbell, bouncing on its coiled spring over the kitchen doorway, jangled.

"I'll go," said Nora from the dining room.

"It's Chris," said Nell, "with Catherine Daly, God bless her." She came out into the kitchen.

"You might come into the other room to say hello to the girl your own son's going to marry," she said to Ned, ignoring Casey.

"Don't mind me, Ned," said Casey, "go right ahead. I'll just have a smoke here while you're gone. Go ahead, now, don't bother about me at all."

Nell wanted them in the parlor as far as possible from Torpedo Casey, but Nora guided them right into the dining room. Catherine Daly bloomed like a fresh little flower in the heavy dreariness of the room. Her hair glistened in waves under her straw sailor hat; she was blushing, smiling and her blue eyes sang. With no embarrassment she put her hands on Nell's shoulders and kissed her on the cheek, Nell scrupulously cataloguing every detail of her clothing and puckering her lips into the trace of a smile. Chris McDermott set his soft hat on the table and fumbled with the Knights' emblem hanging from his watch chain. Nora hovered over them.

"You look just like your mother, red hair and all," she said, before anyone else had a chance to speak.

"Well, well," said Nell with the greatest restraint.

"How d'ye do, darling?" said Ned, shaking Catherine's hand. "How are ye, how are ye?"

"This is my Aunt Nora," said Chris, indicating her with a wave of his hand.

Nell tried to steer them around the table so Catherine wouldn't see Casey there in the kitchen with the bottle in front of him, but Catherine, glancing into a mirror that hung near the kitchen door, saw him and said:

"Oh, you're Mr. Casey, aren't you? How do you do. Chris never told me. . . ."

"Joe Daly's daughter from South Providence," said Nora.

"Father often speaks of you, Mr. Casey," Catherine said.

"I'll be damned," said Casey, resting his hand on the whisky bottle as he sat, "Joe Daly's daughter! I'll be damned! And a flaming redhead, too!"

They went into the parlor, and Catherine unpinned her hat and sat on the ponderous horsehair armchair with the arched and studded back. She felt like the hen in her mother's strawberry crate, waiting for the ax of their criticism to descend on her. She looked at the little gold watch that hung from a fleur-de-lis pin on her breast. Well, she thought, it's ten minutes past eight. She looked over at Chris sitting on the unyielding couch beside his unyielding mother, and half wished she hadn't come.

"Nora, put on a pot of tea," said Nell peremptorily. "Where is that boy?"

"Down in the street with the dog," Nora answered, starting for the kitchen. She cast an ugly look at Ned and Casey sitting there with the bottle between them and big murky water glasses beside them. Brushing by Ned, she looked out the window and saw Willie McDermott down in the blacksmith's yard throwing a stick for Peg. She called him.

"Wait till you see the boy," Ned was saying to Casey. "I have great schemes for him."

"The house is full of schemes," Nora said under her breath. "Schemes in the front and schemes in the back, it's all schemes and no. . . ."

"I want to make a doctor or a lawyer or something or other of him," Ned went on, paying no attention to his sister-in-law. "He has no father to do for him, you know. I thought I'd have a hand

45

from his nibs in there in the parlor, but now I guess he'll be off with that little pigeon of his. . . ."

"I'd put the lad in the Navy if it was me," said Casey, "where he'd learn a trade. . . ."

"That's what I don't want," Ned answered sharply. "I don't want him pounding sand in a foundry like the rest of us, nor I don't want him breaking his back over an anvil. . . ."

"No fear of that one breaking his back over anything," Nora interrupted him. She poured the boiling water into the teapot and set it on the side of the stove to draw while she carried the cups and saucers into the parlor.

Willie McDermott and Peg, both panting, burst into the kitchen. He was surprised to see Casey there; and the old man, with his rosy nose and his white hair, in a uniform Willie always thought of as being worn by young men, fascinated him. He examined the embroidered eagle over the chevrons that cut their red gashes into the left arm of the jacket and the long red slashes on the sleeve below.

"If it was me," said Casey, "I'd put the boy in the Navy when he came of age. It's the coming thing for a young fellow. That's what I'd do with him if it was me."

"Run along in to your grandmother," Ned told the boy. "Peg, stay here. D'ye see, Casey, I want to make something of him. I want to educate him. Pour yourself another drink, now, do. God knows in the old days we thought nothing of an education, but times is changing and it is the man with the schooling that gets anywhere today. . . ."

"There's no limit to what he could do in the Navy if he was to go in young enough," said Casey. "Why, he'd have a trade for himself or any damn thing and pension off when he was still a young man."

"Will you have a pension yourself, Casey, soon?" asked Ned.

"Oh," the sailor said, "I could pay off any time I wanted to, but I might as well be there and busy as outside with nothing to do for myself. I'm in so long now I'd miss it if I was to pay off for good."

"Ah, you have no family nor nothing to go home to," Ned shook his head sadly.

"A damn good thing it is, too," said Casey. "Nobody depending on me for nothing. . . ."

"I was thinking," said Ned, "that maybe later when the time comes and he's ready for it you might give me a hand with the boy there to see him through the school and all. I thought his nibs there in the parlor would lend a hand, but as I say he'll be flying off soon with his. . . ."

"When the time comes, Ned," said Casey slowly. . . .

"I could go to Pete Carron, that I know," Ned said, "but I don't want to be beholden to the son of a bitch, though many's the dollar I give him for Mick and Pete's bail. . . ."

"When the time comes," Casey began again.

"And it was my attic he stayed in when he first come out here," Ned said bitterly.

"If I have it, Ned," Casey cut in again, "you can count on me. . . ."

"I knew damn well I could," said Ned, overjoyed. "Knew damn well I could. On you and Tim Lee. Have another drink for yourself. There's plenty of it and more when that's gone. I knew damn well. . . ."

"But if it was me I'd put the boy in the Navy," Casey insisted.

"To hell with the Navy," Ned snorted. "I knew damn well I could count on Torpedo Casey. I says to Tim Lee. . . ."

Willie McDermott stared lingeringly at Catherine Daly, and the distance between the chair he sat on and the horsehair armchair where she was sitting seemed to expand and contract until it seemed that he was so close he could touch her. He had never seen anyone so beautiful. Not even Rose Riordan, not even the Jew's daughter all dressed in green (of whom he thought so often) was nearly so lovely. Catherine Daly was asking him about school, how he liked it and how he got along in his lessons.

"Speak up," Nora admonished.

"I like it pretty good," he stammered. "I get pretty good marks."

His grandmother decided enough time had been wasted with him and sent him out to his grandfather again.

"Hand me that album, Nora," said Nell. "I want to show Catherine some of the pictures of Chris when he was a little boy."

"I'd love to see them," said Catherine, watching Chris squirm uncomfortably on the couch.

Nell moved a chair over near Catherine's and began to thumb through the album that contained pictures of nearly everyone in her own family, cousins, brides, uncles, sons, boys and girls of all

47

ages and sizes, snub-nosed women with tight curls, one or two with crossed eyes, and nearly all of them with bosoms that seemed to explode or be ready to explode from the book. They found the small-sized picture of Chris in the curls and candy-striped stockings from which the enlargement that hung on the wall of the parlor had been made. He was standing alongside a conveniently formed rock that looked like the rear end of an elephant. Catherine looked long and quietly at this picture. She wondered, if she had a son, whether he would look like this little boy that seemed so serious, so firm and yet so very pretty. She looked into the other room where Willie McDermott was looking at the funny papers; she looked at his freckled face, his stubby nose and the straight black hair.

All the while Chris McDermott sat silently on the couch, smoking a cigar and knocking the ashes into a little glass tray that was resplendent with the bands from expensive cigars. It seemed to him that he could smell the whisky he knew his father and Casey were drinking in the kitchen and he groaned when he heard Ned saying "I knew damn well I could." He wondered what the old man was up to. He would be very glad to get away from this house, he decided, after he was married to Catherine Daly. That morning, like nearly every other Sunday morning, a tramp moulder had come to the house just as they were having breakfast. Ned sat the tramp down at the table with them. He had been to early mass himself with the boy and had nothing to do for the rest of the day. The tramp said he had been working with Ned's cousin Mick in Jersey but, God forgive him, he went on a bat and woke up only that morning in Providence. He asked if Ned had any tools he could lend him. Ned lent him the tools, a rammer, a slicker, and a pair of old brogans that never fit him quite right but just fit the tramp. Chris knew that when his father went downstairs with the tramp he must have given him some money. Yes, he was glad he was leaving all this and that he would set up housekeeping with Catherine Daly in some nice little place in South Providence where he wouldn't have to see these tramps at Sunday morning breakfasts.

"So this is the scholar," said Casey when Willie McDermott returned to the kitchen.

"This is the boyo," said Ned, clapping his grandson on the back.

48

"Can I take Peg out again?" the boy asked.

"How'd you like to be a sailor?" Casey asked him.

"All right," the boy said.

"To hell with the Navy," said Ned decisively.

The boy went out with the dog.

The visit was a bitter one for Nora from the moment when she realized that Catherine Daly, after kissing Nell, wasn't going to give her the same recognition. And now that the others had finished looking through the album of pictures she could have it. She knew every picture in it; many of them she had put there herself when they were given to the family. There was nearly everyone in the family, even to the most remote cousin, some of them dead and gone now, but most of them living, happy, with families and grandchildren, homes of their own, good or bad, homes of their own. Here they were on their wedding days, here they were on a trip here or there. Every picture marked for her some happy time, some happy time that she had never had; for Nora it was always marking another's happy time, never sharing it. She looked at Catherine Daly across the room from her, so young and lovely, and she thought of the many pictures there'd be made of Catherine Daly in the days to come, pictures with Chris when they would be married, pictures with a baby, a picture with a new dress, countless pictures. Catherine Daly was saying something about a photo album that she had been collecting ever since she went to high school, a great big one that her father had given her. Chris had seen it, of course, and as a matter of fact there were some pictures of Chris, too, in the last pages of it. Indeed there are, Nora thought. Nell was saying she would like to see some of the pictures of Catherine Daly and Chris, and Catherine answered that she must have some prints of them around the house that she would bring over sometime, or that she would give Chris to bring to his mother. Some of the snapshots that were taken at Block Island the summer before were really good, she said.

Nora found the last picture that had ever been taken of herself. It had been made about the time of Nell's wedding, that she remembered, but she couldn't remember the occasion on which it was taken, it had been so very very long since there had been an occasion in her life. She couldn't even remember the dress she was wearing in the picture. She closed the dusty red plush covers together and held the book in her lap. She'd never open the damn

49

thing again, she said, looking at Catherine Daly and feeling lonelier than she had in a long time. Dear God, she thought, even my prayers now are for someone else, for the speedy recovery or the happy death of him or her, for the repose of the soul of this one and that one. This chit of a girl sitting there was a schoolteacher, a station she had never even dared dream of achieving. Soon she'd be marrying and raising a family. Nora wanted to smile and say nice things to her, but she knew she'd break out crying if she even tried, and why should she cry her sorrow out in front of them, damn them. No, she wouldn't. She opened the plush covers again and whipped through the pages to the picture of Our May Mulvey.

"Well," she said, "here's Our May herself. Do·you mind the time, Nell, Our May's niece came out from the other side? That's a cousin of ours, Miss Daly. . . ."

"I do," said Nell, "but never mind Our May, Nora."

"Our May always lived in the country, you know, Miss Daly, and she has a little piece of land now out near Norwood, Mass. She has a cow or two and a few chickens, I suppose. The niece went to live with May on the farm but near drove her crazy with the airs she put on. . . ."

"Nora," Nell began. . . .

"May was telling us about her one day she came into town. It happened that Father Tierney was in the house when May got there and she was being as nice as pie telling about her niece in front of the priest and all. 'Dear me,' she says, 'she wouldn't do this and she wouldn't that and Lord knows what she would do. She wouldn't wash a dish and she wouldn't scrub a floor. Not a blessed thing. I'm sure I don't know what they're raising up for children at home these days at all. She was afraid the chickens would bite her and she couldn't milk a drop. I never seen the like of her. Anyway one day I was hard at it cleaning the house of a Saturday when I asked her to do some little thing or other and she says if you don't mind, she says to me, I'll take a stroll in the meadow. Well, do, I says, for there's not a blessed thing you'll do for me. So off she was for a stroll in the meadow and she hadn't gone ten yards from the house, I beg your pardon, Father,' says Our May, 'when she stepped in the cow's occasion.' "

"Nora!" said Nell.

"Well, Father Tierney laughed himself sick over it," Nora continued, "and kept saying to himself, 'the cow's occasion, the cow's occasion.' 'Yes,' says Our May, so pleased she made Father Tierney laugh so much, 'stepped right in the cow's occasion—and beshit her foot.'"

"Nora, I think you could find something else to talk about than Our May," said Chris McDermott.

Catherine Daly was laughing happily.

"Well," Nora said, "she might as well know the whole family is not bookkeepers and ladies and gentlemen. . . ."

"Oh, I think that's a very funny story about your cousin, Chris," Catherine said.

"You know how those old-fashioned people from Ireland are," he said. "Their talk and their ways are so different. Besides we hardly ever see her any more. I don't think I'd know her if I met her in the street."

"She was a very good-hearted woman in spite of the language she used," Nell declared.

"There was nothing fancy about her," Nora added, feeling that at least she had taken that damn little Chris down a peg or two. She thought Catherine Daly might be a nice girl after all, too nice for her nephew, maybe.

Ned was telling Torpedo Casey he'd walk him as far as the trolley car, and they both went into the parlor to say good night. Casey had put his cap on and saluted them grandly as he was leaving. They had to wait a while for the trolley which would take Casey to the center of the city where he would take his train down to Newport.

"Well, don't be a stranger, now, Casey," Ned said when they could see the light of the trolley bearing down on them. "Come and see us when you have the time. Any time will do, you know. . . ."

"I will, Ned, I will," said Casey. "And you can count on me for any old thing you need, but as I said before, Ned, if you want to do the best ever for the boy there—put him in the Navy. . . ."

"To hell with the Navy," Ned said as he waved Casey good-by. "I have your promise now and by God I'll hold you to it."

While they were gone Willie returned to the house with Peg. His grandmother and Nora had already gone to vespers at the cathedral and his uncle out to South Providence again with Catherine Daly. He left the dog in the kitchen at her water bowl and roamed through the house. The parlor door was open and the picture album on the horsehair sofa where Nora had dropped it. He opened it to the pages where his father and mother, who would always be young, looked fondly from page to page at each other. He had no recollection of either of them except in this book. His grandfather found him there and when he saw the pictures the boy was staring at, turned and started out of the room.

"My mother was pretty, wasn't she?" the boy asked him.

"What? Oh—yes, indeed she was, a very pretty girl, Kitty McDonough was. Yes. . . ."

"Was she—did she have hair like Catherine Daly's? Was she—did she sing? What did she sound like?"

"She—ah, put that damn book away, will you?" Ned said. "Yes, she sang and she danced, I suppose, with your father and all that. Whatever they did. Whatever they do. Like Chris, I suppose, and Catherine there."

"Did she come to your house, too?"

"Why don't you do as I tell you, Willie?" Ned was disturbed. "Why don't you put that damn book away? No, she didn't. She was never in the house once. Where is your grandmother and Lady Jane now? Did they go out?"

Willie said he thought they must have because they were not there when he came in with the dog.

"No," said Ned. "She was never in the house in her life. They were married very young, do you see, Willie. Your father was hardly out of his time and very young. It was Nora, of course, first heard they were running around together and she, God damn her soul, never could see anyone happy. Between them, between Nora and your grandmother, they raised hell for days about it until your father says, well, they might as well get used to her, for he was going to marry her. Dear God, your grandmother was crying in every ear she could find to cry in. 'My Will is just eighteen,' she'd say. 'Just eighteen and that one has him bewitched.' Why neither of them liked her, I don't know to this day. Anyhow, they were married in St. John's with none of the family there and they went to live in that house down the street that I showed you so many times. She never came here, though, or even passed the house on her way to the store or to church on Sunday. She'd walk all the way around to avoid it. I went in to see them one night, before you were born, and told her it was time bygones were bygones and to come to the house and see Nell and all. 'No,' she said, 'she didn't

52

want me and now I don't want her!' By God, she meant it, too, and never came. Nor your father never came while she lived, though after she died he did.

"It broke my heart to see them only a few doors down the street, but as far away as a stranger, and I used to stop there many a night on my way home from the foundry. I was there the night you were born. I'll always hear the two of them, 'Will is just eighteen . . . my Will is just eighteen.'—Now will you put that goddam book away and come out of there?"

Chapter Eight

NONE of the boys ever knew where he lived or where he went every Saturday morning, which was the only time they ever saw him, always walking alone down the avenue toward Jewtown, slowly and sedately as a priest in a procession. He was always in black, his coat as long as a cassock and his arms folded into the sleeves of it and held high on his chest as though he were carrying something sacred there. He appeared tall because he walked so proudly, his back smooth and straight and his head thrust ahead as if he were impatient to be wherever he was going. An abundant gray beard bushed out on his chest from one side to the other. When the dust blew up from the cobblestoned street he might draw his head down and into his chest, closing his large eyes and hold a long white-fingered hand on his black velour hat, but that was the only time he ever lowered his head. He never looked to the side of the street or spoke to anyone. When he reached a corner, he would pause so that if anything were coming he could wait until it had passed or turned and he would not have to hurry his steps. He had been coming down the street Saturday mornings for a long time, and everyone in the neighborhood expected him when they saw him but if, one Saturday, he had not come no one would have missed him or have even thought about it.

Joseph, because he was bigger and a year or so older, was the leader of the bunch and it was he who this morning led the boys against the Jew. Joseph never took a dare in his life and no blemish marred the bright shield of his courage. Young McDermott, though no more than any of the other kids in the neighborhood, held Joseph in great awe and esteem. It was Joseph who, the day they dumped a bucket of manure they had scraped up from the street into Goldstein's tailor shop, was the last one to run and dared Goldstein to throw the flatiron at him. When old man Flynn, the cop, chased them later that day and flung his club at them when he couldn't catch any of them, Joseph ran boldly back a few steps and kicked the club down a sewer.

Slats Maney, whose slanted eyelids were always inflamed and

crusted, had swiped six cigarettes that Saturday morning from his brother Step, and they had shared them in back of Kelly's drug-store, each of them peeking in now and then to see who was sitting in on the stud game Kelly ran. Besides Slats there were the two Canucks, the LaFlammes, Willie McDermott, Joseph, and his brother Eddie, and Runt Clay who always said he was Irish but he was a Protestant so no one ever believed him. Fred Kane, McDermott's cousin was there, too, but he went home when Slats passed out the cigarettes because he said he was going to confession that afternoon. They had wanted to play baseball but no one had had a ball anyway.

"Come on down Ocean Avenue," Joseph said.

They leaped back fences, slid through alleys and came out between Slattery's saloon and the hardware store.

"Here he comes," Joseph said. "Stump the leader!"

The old man, his hands thrust into his sleeves, was walking slowly toward them, ducking his head whenever a gust of the sharp October wind threw a puff of dust from the cobbled street into his face.

"Sink the Jew's skimmer," Joseph whispered. "I'll lead. Count ten and follow me. One at a time."

The old man was at the hardware store, he was passing them, looking neither to right or left. Joseph waited. The old man passed the saloon, he passed Goldstein's, he passed Dyer's grocery and was abreast of the high board fence that fronted the vacant lot.

Joseph rushed out and raced up the street after him. When he was just in back of the old man he leaped in the air with his arms swinging. His fist crushed into the old man's hat. Joseph sped on and vaulted up on the high board fence. The old man stopped still and looked at him, his arms still tucked into his sleeves. Runt Clay was next. He leaped, swung, and the hat went farther down on the old man's head. The LaFlammes were twins so they went together, screeching as they leaped and they each slapped the hat with the flat of their hands. Up on the fence they went.

The ones on the fence were nearly falling off from laughing but Eddie Riordan and McDermott, standing in the alley, were tense and frightened.

The old man was still standing where he had stopped when Joseph hit him. He was lifting the hat from his ears with both his hands. Eddie and Willie could see how slender and white they were.

"Go ahead," Eddie said. "My brother was first—I'll be last."

"You go ahead," McDermott said. "The Riordans want everything."

Eddie hurtled out of the alley and leaped as the others had, but in his excitement he hit only the old man's hand.

I've got to make sure I hit the hat, Willie McDermott thought, because if I miss he might grab me. He could see the others on the fence shrieking with delight and waiting for him. The old man was slowly walking toward them with his hands stretched before him, the hat battered now and rakishly perched on one side of his head.

When Willie looked at him it made him sick, and when, glancing across the street, he saw a woman with her shopping basket stop and shake her fist at them he was ashamed, but it was too late now for him to retreat; Joseph and the rest of them would laugh at him. He couldn't let them do that whatever happened. He was glad the old man's back was to him, not because he was afraid of him, but because he didn't want to see those eyes when he was hitting the hat. He darted out of the alley and bore down on his prey, but in front of Slattery's he tripped, it seemed over his own feet, pitched forward and fell to the sidewalk, the concrete burning and scraping the flesh from the palms of his hands. The boys on the fence saw him fall and forgot the old man coming toward them. Joseph boldly leaped down from the fence pointing at Willie and jeering. The old man turned to see what new assault was threatening him as Willie was getting to his feet. The old man was caught between them like a runner off second and Joseph, screaming as he went, whacked him on the back. Pressing his right hand pitifully against the side of his head the old man turned again toward Joseph and when he did Willie pounced on him, smashing his hat down over his ears. He flashed by and leaped up on the fence, breathless and frenzied even after they had all jumped down into the lot and out of sight from the street. They ran across the lot, stumbling over rusting tin cans and refuse to the fence at the rear.

"I thought Willie was cooked," Runt said, laughing.

Willie had flung himself down on the ground with his back against Kelly's wall, quivering all over him, his heart knocking furiously against his ribs. He could not quench the fire of shame that

56

burned in him. He felt as though they had all been pounding him instead of the old man, but, defying his conscience, he waved his hand contemptuously at Runt.

"He would of been," Joseph said striding toward the store. "If I hadn't saved him he would of been."

Eddie Riordan said them twins had no right to do it together.

"No," Joseph declared seriously. "They should of done it alone like everybody else."

"We done it, didn't we?" Joie LaFlamme countered.

Joseph said the old man came back along Ocean Avenue in the afternoon again and always came alone. He said they ought to get him again when he came back.

Willie trembled as though someone were shaking him. He couldn't go back again and hit the old man, but he couldn't say no to Joseph when he asked them all if they were game to do it all over again later. Before the time came, Willie thought, he would be able to find some reason for not coming back to Kelly's later in the day. He could say his grandmother made him stay at home or that he had to go to confession, or something; he would find some reason for not coming back until they had hit the old man again.

"He'll squeal," Runt said, worried. "He'll squeal or bring somebody back with him this afternoon. Maybe somebody saw us, too. Maybe they'll squeal on us."

"Ah," Joseph scoffed. "Suppose they did. Who cares about an old miser of a Jew, anyhow?"

"Why don't he go around by Water Street?" Runt asked. "Maybe that's the way he'll go on the way back."

"Water Street?" Joseph laughed. "He wouldn't dare go around that way."

"Where have you been?" his grandmother asked Willie when he went home for dinner.

"Just out," he answered.

"Were you down on Ocean Avenue this morning?" she asked him.

"No ma'am," he lied. "Just in the lots in back of Kelly's drugstore."

"Were the Riordans there with you?"

"They were all there," Willie said. "My cousin Fred and everybody was there."

"Helen Tracy says she saw the Riordans with that young Protestant and the French boys hitting an old man down on Ocean Avenue. Were you with them? An old Jew man, she says."

"I was with my cousin Fred," Willie said. "You can ask him. I was with him in back of Kelly's playing ball."

"Fred Kane wouldn't be doing a thing like that," said Nora.

"You'll go to confession this afternoon with your cousin," his grandmother decided.

Confession, Willie thought, escape. If he went to confession with his cousin he couldn't very well go back with Joseph and the others. They couldn't, they wouldn't dare say anything to him or laugh at him if he told them he had to go to confession. Perhaps Runt Clay, being a Protestant, would say something, but he didn't count anyhow. Willie began to eat heartily but when he began to think about going to confession he couldn't choke the food down his throat. He wondered what the priest would say when he told him he had been hitting an old Jew man in the morning, if it were a sin to hit an old Jew man, a mortal sin or a venial sin. If he could go to confession and not tell about hitting the old man he'd feel better but he couldn't do that because the sin would be on his soul and yes, he decided, it was some kind of a sin even if the old man was a Jew. He knew it must be some kind of a sin because he was so ashamed now. He could see the old man's white hands, his staggering step. Then he remembered that all during the attack the old man hadn't once spoken; not a single word had come out from the gray beard. He wished the old man had said something to them, almost anything.

Willie waited at Tanner's yard that afternoon until his cousin Fred Kane came along, and when the boy stopped to speak to him he grabbed his arm and pulled him behind a pile of lumber.

"If my grandmother says anything to you about where I was this morning or what we were doing," he threatened, "say that we were in back of Kelly's all morning. Say we were together all the time."

"Why should I have to lie for you?" Fred said. "You got in some kind of trouble and you want me to lie for you to get you out of it, don't you? Well, I won't."

Willie twisted his cousin's arm up behind his back until Fred cried out with the pain.

"Will you say it?" he asked.

"No."

58

Willie pressed the arm up until he could feel Fred's shoulder blade against his own hand.

"Will you?"

"No." Fred began to sob. "No."

Willie remorselessly pushed the arm higher.

"Stop. Stop!" Fred wailed.

"Will you say it now?" Willie asked, relaxing a little on the arm. "Will you?"

"You're making me commit a sin," Fred said hoarsely. "It's a sin on your soul. You're making me do it!"

"Say I was with you all morning. You'll be sorry if you don't!"

They went up into the house but his grandmother, telling him to come straight home after he went to confession, seemed to have forgotten about the incident of the morning. At any rate, she didn't say anything about it to his cousin. Nearing Kelly's, Willie began to think again about hitting the old man and about going to confession. He stopped for a moment, and while his cousin waited in the street he told Joseph that he would try to get out of going to confession somehow and come back there as soon as he got rid of Fred.

"I'm not going to go to confession," he told his cousin when they reached the corner where the church was.

"I won't lie to my grandmother about it," Fred warned him. "I won't lie about that for you no matter what you do to me. You'll have to lie for yourself. And what are you going to say if she asks you if you went to communion tomorrow?"

"Never mind what I'll say," Willie said. "Maybe I'll say I got up in the night and drank some water and broke my fast, then I couldn't go."

"You'll have to lie about going to confession, too. She'll ask you if you went to confession when you get home again."

"Mind your own business," Willie said, shoving his cousin in the back and running up the street again the way they had come.

He didn't want to go back to Kelly's or hit the old man again, but he was afraid to break his promise to Joseph and the others. Perhaps he could figure out some other way for them to spend the afternoon instead of going to Ocean Avenue to smash the Jew's hat again.

Joseph was stronger than he was, however, and even though Runt agreed with him that it might be too dangerous to go back to

59

Ocean Avenue, Joseph's will prevailed and back they went. While the others waited in the lot, kicking tin cans around, they posted Willie on the fence to watch for the old man, yelling to him as they played to ask if he were in sight yet. Willie wished one of the others were up on the fence, because on Saturday afternoons there were more people on the street and someone was likely to pass who knew him and might just happen to mention it to his grandmother or Nora. If Helen Tracy passed she would be certain to tell on him. He jumped down a couple of times, hoping that the old man would pass while he wasn't watching and that he could get out of hitting him again. Joseph said he'd better get back there where he could watch, and reluctantly each time Willie hoisted himself up again on the fence. He thought he might even let the old man pass without telling the other boys, but he knew if they caught him doing that they would give him his lumps, and besides they were all coming over to the fence and looking down the street every few minutes. He felt relieved in a way when the old man came into sight down the street. He called the boys, and they all sat brazenly on the fence waiting for their victim, who came slowly along and abreast of them without even glancing up, without even a hint that he recognized them as his assailants of a few short hours before. Joseph spat on the sidewalk in front of him as the man walked. He said to wait until the Jew got past the hardware store before they went after him. They all let themselves down into the street and bunched against the fence.

"Let's go!" Joseph cried, spurting down after the old man.

He had hardly hit the old man's hat, sending it flying into the gutter, when Gyp McGlinn, coming out of Slattery's, saw him and shouted:

"Shame! Shame on you to be hitting an old man like that!"

Joseph fled down the street. The others, not daring to follow, scrambled up on the fence again and retreated across the lot. The old man walked slowly to the gutter to retrieve his hat. He brushed the dirt from it with the long black sleeve of his coat, put it on and solemnly went his way.

Running along, Willie was glad he hadn't had to hit the old man again, but he wondered if Gyp McGlinn had seen him among the other boys standing by the fence waiting their turn to attack. He hoped not, not because he thought Gyp would tell his grandmother or his grandfather but because he liked Gyp and didn't want him to think he was the kind of kid that would do a thing like that. He wasn't that kind of kid, he thought. It wasn't his idea to go down there even the first time; he hadn't really wanted to hit the old man himself and he was sorry he had.

If he could only slip away from the others now and go to confession! But it was too late now, he realized; it was already getting dark and the priests would have left the confessionals. He would have to carry his sins home with him and hope no one asked him anything about what he had been doing during the afternoon. Fortunately Mr. Devine from North Attleboro was there at the house with his daughter Ann, a thin, crisp girl whose hazel eyes were smiling whenever she spoke ór listened to someone else speaking, a girl who seemed always to be pleasantly questioning everyone. His grandmother and Nora were rushing around the kitchen to get the beans and the brown bread on the table for supper while his grandfather talked to Mr. Devine and Ann. They stayed on after supper and Willie slipped away to bed before they left.

It was a frenzied rain for him that night. It whipped against the windows and howled down the street. The door to the dining room was open and he could hear the creaking of the rocker as his grandmother sat there saying her rosary and humming to herself as she frequently did. Her voice was like the banshee they told him about. She sang no tune but would break into the words of some song at intervals.

> Once I was young
> I could swing my shillelagh
> Or dance all the night
> With my brogues lined with straw.

She would hum again, hum and then suddenly—

> Oh my darlin' little cruiskeen lawn, lawn, lawn.

"What was that song about the Jews, Nell," Nora asked.
"Every nation has a flag but the Jews?"
"No," Nora said. "Not that."
"Oh, 'Little Harry Hughes. . . .'"
"Yes," Nora said, "that's the one. Helen Tracy put me in mind of it today telling about them Riordans and the old Jew man. . . ."
"I don't remember the words entirely," his grandmother said. "Let me see now. . . .

61

> *Little Harry Hughes*
> *And his schoolmates all*
> *Went out for to play ball*
> *And the very first ball*
>
> *And the very first ball*
> *Little Harry played*
> *Went right over*
> *The Jew's garden wall*
>
> *The Jew's garden wall*

For the life of me I can't remember how it goes. . . ."
She hummed again.

> *The Jew's garden wall*
> *Then out came the Jew's daughter*
> *And she all dressed in green*
> *And she all dressed*
> > *in green*
> > *in green*
> *Come back, come back*
> *My pretty little boy*
> *And play your ball again*
> *Oh, I can't come back*
> *Nor I shan't come back*
> *Without my schoolmates all. . . .*

"I don't know now what comes next but anyhow the Jew's daughter traps him there over the wall and leads him down a passage somewhere or other. Then it says:

> *Where none his cries could—*
> *Where none his cries could hear. . . ."*

"Yes, that's it," Nora said. "Then she out with a penknife and cuts his heart out. . . ."

"That's what happens," Nell said. "But I don't know the words of it."

Long after they had turned the gas down low so that Chris would have some light in the house when he got home, Willie McDermott lay awake on his bed. He wished he had gone to confession in the afternoon with his cousin Fred. He wished he could still go. He said an Act of Contrition. He writhed and plunged down a dark corridor of torment with Fred Kane jeering at him, an old man in the windy street picking his hat up and caressing it with his black sleeve, and the Jew's daughter singing sweetly and crying as she bent over him with a little silver penknife poised above his heart.

Chapter Nine

YOUR grandmother," Ned told Willie the next morning when they were walking home from early mass, "says you was not with the Riordans yesterday when they got after the old Jew man."

Willie mumbled that he was playing in the lots in back of Kelly's in the morning and in the afternoon he had been with his cousin Fred Kane.

"I'm glad you wasn't there," Ned said, "Gyp McGlinn was telling me about it in Deignan's last night too when I went there. He seen one of them, it seems, in the afternoon smash an old man's hat as he was coming out of Slattery's. Your grandmother says it was in the morning it happened."

"It was both times," Willie said.

"Oh, I see it was. What had the old gaffer done to them? Had he done them any harm? Had he ever?"

"No," Willie answered. "He was just a Jew."

"And what are the Riordans up to then, crusading around after Jews? Is it fighting they want? Why didn't they turn on Gyp, I wonder. He'd give them all the fight they wanted, wouldn't he? God damn a man, or a boy either, that lays a hand on a body that's weaker than himself. That can't hold his own with him. A fair fight's one thing and never run from it. D'you see old Loony Mulvaney across the street there?"

Old Loony, shrouded in an ulster that reached his heels, was always at mass, or vespers or benediction of the Blessed Sacrament. He attended all the funeral and wedding masses too, and would remember every month's mind for the repose of the soul of whomever the masses were being said for during the week. There wasn't a wake within miles he didn't attend, weeping bitterly when he prayed at the coffin and always sitting in the parlor with the women, sometimes all night long if someone didn't suggest it was time for him to go home. He was a tiny little man with a wreath of white hair and the voice of a little girl. Instead of just tipping his hat when he passed in front of the cathedral, as was the custom then, Loony would devoutly genuflect and bless himself. He was never silent, but he rarely ever spoke to anyone but a priest. He chattered his prayers hoarsely in whispers during mass, and when he was walking the street he might be almost dancing along, lilting an Irish song with his head thrown high, or walking dejectedly and mumbling his rosary. He lived in the back room of Austin McDonough's undertaking parlor and ran an errand or two for the undertaker when he could be found. When he did, Austin would give him a dime which he always brought into the cathedral and lit a candle in honor of the Blessed Virgin. Other people gave him money, too, but it had to be dimes that fitted into the box for the candles. He would not accept nickels or quarters that he had to change.

"That man," Ned said, "could walk the length and breadth of Jewtown, if he took it into his head, and never a hand would be turned against him. Not a hand. What is it makes the Riordans want to strike an old Jew, then? They must be braver lads than I thought them."

"Joseph says Jews will cheat you and they kidnap Catholic babies when there's no one looking and kill them right in their churches," Willie said.

"Indeed," said Ned, "wicked, ain't they?"

"He says they drink your blood, too, if they catch you and murder you."

"And where did he learn all these terrible things the Jews does? Has he seen them do it? Have they ever catched him to murder him? Willie, did you know years ago they used to say, the Yankees used to say years ago, that the priests was always after kidnaping Protestant girls on the streets in the dark of the night and carrying them off to a convent somewheres in the woods or something to make—to make baggages of them? Well that's what they said them days, though no priest was ever trapped at it. They used to say the priests would take the children that was born in the convents, babies that couldn't walk a step or defend themselves, babies the nuns had and didn't want, and bring them out into the woods at night and bury them alive, screaming and crying their hearts out on the way so they'd muffle them up in a priest's garments so no one would hear them and bury them alive in the dead of the night.

"I've seen me right here in this same street we're walking on now, after coming from a hard day's work at the foundry, marching around the convent with a club in my hand, me and a hundred or more when they threatened to burn it down. Threatened to burn it down and tear it apart stone by stone because there was some Protestant girl trapped in it, they said, and held prisoner by the nuns that was only doing the priest's bidding that kidnaped the girl. Dear God! Of course it was years ago when people was ignorant a damn sight more than they are today. So and they did burn them, too, in Boston, they say, years before when there was fewer Irish there than there is now. Yes, burned it to the ground and drove the good sisters out in the cold, rioting up and down all over the place.

"And what is it, our turn now to be savages? Is it our turn to? God damn it, Willie, is that what's to come of all the schools and the teaching? Sure we might have let the Yankees burn them down long ago and be done with it, if that all's to come out of it!

"Is that what the moiling and toiling of the old people is for, to raise up a litter of pups that runs wild striking a man down in the street? Damn strange things happens to the Irish in this country. Breaking their backs all day and their hearts all night for young ones that spits in their face—what are they going to grow up to, then, a band of thugs?

"Is the sisters teaching them in the schools that was built on pennies and nickels that might have bought bread to feed a hungry mouth to go out tearing and slashing at a man in the street because there's a beard hanging on his chin or he talks in a strange way to them? See that Boston bull, Willie. God, I'd love to mate my Peg with that one but your grandmother'd banish us all if I did. Wouldn't she? No, by God, such things was never preached in any pulpit where I heard a sermon. Thick as we are we're above that I hope, above raising a hand against a man because his faith is not our faith.

"Had I seen that yesterday I wouldn't have just yelled at them as Gyp told me he done. I'd have caught every last one of that crew and—and—and— How do you do, Mrs. Burns, lovely weather we have, ain't it?"

Willie could bear no more of it. He thought he was safe enough when his grandfather first began to talk because he was certain neither Helen Tracy nor Gyp had seen him with Joseph and the others. Now he was wretched because of the very fact that his grandfather, from the way he spoke, was convinced that he had not been in the attack. The Jew's daughter and she all dressed in green, walked between him and his grandfather, accusing him, accusing him and accusing him every step of the way. His grandfather was not walking swiftly, never did, but it made Willie gasp a little trying to keep pace with him. He was stifled with his own wickedness.

"I hit him," Willie said low, almost inaudibly, glancing into Tanner's yard as though he expected to find Fred Kane hiding there to accuse him, too. "I hit him, too."

"Yes," Ned said putting his hand on the boy's shoulder at the gate and looking up at Peg standing at the window above them with her paws on the sill. "I know you did."

Chapter Ten

NORA timidly drew the yellow envelope of the telegram from under her shawl and put it beside Ned's plate. Nothing could have been worse on Christmas Eve than a telegram, and Ned looked quickly away from it.

"Why don't you open it, then?" Nell said.

"Some mistake," Ned said. "Some mistake the boy made in the dark down there at the door."

"It says your name right on it, there," Nora defended herself.

"Open it," Nell said anxiously.

"Open it you," Ned roared.

With palsied hands she picked it up and slit the flap of the envelope with her knife. She extracted the message carefully and looked at Ned inquiringly before she started to read. . . .

"Edward T. McDermott," she started. "426 Hester Street . . ."

"I know all that," said Ned angrily. "What else does it say?"

"MEET MOUNT HOPE TONIGHT. PURSER HAS PACKAGE. MERRY CHRISTMAS. KIT SOMERVILLE."

"Well, I be damned," Ned breathed, a smile slipping over his lips. "What in the hell can it be?"

"Whatever it is, you'd think the man could find some way of telling you about it without scaring people out of their skins." Nora was nettled. "For the life of me I couldn't think what it could be and the boy there, I asked him, and he says. . . ."

"What time is it now?" Ned asked. "What time does that boat dock?"

"You know more about the boats than I do," said Nell.

"Merry Christmas, all," said Ned's Pat, opening the door and shaking the snow from his hat. He kissed his mother.

"God, Pat, you're just in time," Ned said happily. "Come along with me down to the *Mount Hope*. Kit Somerville has sent me a Christmas present."

"What do you need me with you for?" Pat asked.

"Go along with your father," Nell ordered him.

Ned was already getting into his coat. He told Willie to get his things on and come along, too. They hurried through a lightly falling snow and took a streetcar to the other side of the city where the boats docked. Willie remembered the wharf shed where they waited impatiently until the little steamer came out of the storm, huffing and blowing off her excess steam while the Bravas made the lines fast to the wharf. Ned and Pat were aboard as soon as the gangway was ashore and they found the purser, wrapped in a heavy ulster and answering them through a haze of alcohol. Ned handed him the telegram from Kit Somerville.

"Oh, sure," the purser said. "Have you got an express wagon or something with you?"

"What the hell do I want with a wagon? Sure I can carry a package as well as the next. . . ."

"Not this one you can't," the purser said, leading them to the cargo that was piled forward.

"What the hell can it be, then?" Ned asked Pat.

The purser pointed to a large crate of clucking, screaming, flapping fowl. It was knee-high, nearly three feet wide and quite long.

"Mother of God," said Ned in dismay. "It's a whole flock of birds. Are you sure this is the one for me?"

The purser said Kit Somerville had brought it down to the boat himself and told him to be sure that it was delivered to Ned McDermott in Providence. Kit said to be sure and keep the birds warm, that was why he stowed them alongside the bulkhead next to the engine room.

"We can take it between us," Pat said. "We can get it as far as the trolley car. It won't be so heavy, I don't think. I can only see four hens in there. It's going to be clumsy to handle, though."

They tried lifting the crate between them and found it was not heavy. Willie McDermott was transported with delight at the prospect of having four hens that would lay eggs. No one else in the neighborhood had any hens. His grandfather and his uncle started for the freight gangway with the crate.

"Wait a minute," the purser said. "What are you going to do with the sack of oysters. The boy can't carry them."

"Oysters?" cried Ned.

"Yes," the purser said. "There's a sack of oysters here, too."

"From Kit? For me?" his grandfather was really bewildered now. The purser showed them a soggy, bursting potato sack with the sharp edges of the oyster shells pushing its sides out. He said again that he couldn't see how they'd manage them both unless they lived right near by, adding that if they wanted to he would hold the oysters until they got the crate of hens home and they could return for them. But they had too far to go, and if they left the sack there overnight they would have to pay for handling. Pat said if his father and the boy could manage the crate, he would take the sack of oysters. Ned helped him hoist the sack to his back, and with Willie at one end of the crate they started out in the snow for the streetcar line a street away. The wind whipping along the water front made a thousand little cyclones of the snow, and they stopped every little while for the boy to warm his hands. They were all tired when they reached the streetcar stop on South Main Street and set their burdens down in the snow at the tracks.

Two cars slowed up and spurted away from them when the motormen saw the freight they were carrying, Ned cursing them as they drew away. The third stopped and between them Ned and Pat managed to get the sack on the rear platform before the conductor pulled the starting bell.

"Would you leave four poor hens to perish in the snow, you son of a bitch?" Ned yelled at him.

"Try to get on the next one," Pat shouted from the doorway. "I'll get the oysters home for you."

The birds were caroling in the crate, and Ned told Willie they must be dying of the cold for he never in his life heard a hen make that kind of a noise when it was well and healthy. They lugged the crate to the sidewalk and put it in the shelter of a doorway. Ned commented bitterly to the boy that it was the same with every goddam thing in the country; the oysters that must be kept cold was boiling there on a hot streetcar and the poor hens that must be kept warm was freezing to death in the snow. They made two more unsuccessful attempts to board cars with the crate, walking each time to the next stop when they were refused.

People stared at them plodding through the snow with the box of screaming fowl, and a drunk, lurching out of a barroom, asked them for an egg for his breakfast.

"Pay no attention to him, the goddam fool," Ned said to the boy. "Don't let him bother you now."

Hopeless when another conductor refused them, Ned decided to break open the crate and carry the birds under their coats. He asked the boy if he could carry one. Crashing his foot through the thin slat on the top of the box and bending the broken board back, he released a beautiful speckled guinea hen that whirred up into his face and screamed as she sped away over the snowdrifts. The boy ran after her. A block away she lighted on the blanketed back of a delivery horse standing in front of a tenement house. Unable to reach her, the boy stood throwing snowballs at her. She took shelter in the back of the covered grocery wagon and the boy crawled in after her. He trapped her at last in a dark corner, and with one hand around her neck and the other holding her wing he started back to his grandfather.

"By the feet," the old man yelled to him. "Hold her by the feet!"

He was sitting on the broken crate and took the hen from the boy, telling him to run into a grocery near by and fetch a length of string or something so he could tie the feet of the birds together.

The prisoners finally bound, Ned with three of them stuffed under his coat and Willie with the remaining one tucked away beneath his, they managed to get aboard a car for home, the warm birds quiet at last. They stood on the rear platform, pushed into a corner by the crowd of late holiday shoppers who boarded the car as it passed through the center of the city.

"There's always a way to overcome your troubles if you have the patience," Ned was saying half to himself as the car rolled along. "Damn thoughtful of Kit Somerville. Damn thoughtful."

A cup of tea in his hands, Pat was sitting beside the stove laughing when they reached home. Ned opened his coat and dropped the flopping birds on the floor. Willie reached under his coat and held a guinea hen up for his grandmother to see.

"Where's the sack of oysters?" Ned asked.

"In the kitchen and they must be taken out of there with the fishy smell of them," said Nell. "I won't have them stinking up the whole place. And take them chickens off that carpet."

"Did you have much trouble getting them home?" Pat smiled.

"Not a bit," Ned answered. "Have you opened any of the oysters?"

"We're waiting for you to open them," Pat said. "I don't know how."

"I'll be at them in a minute," said Ned. "First, we'll put these

71

birds into the cellar for the night, and then I'll have a nice drink if there's a drop of whisky in the house, Nell."

"There is," she said. "Get them chickens off the carpet now before they make a mess on it."

Ned took the heel of a loaf of bread in his hand and he and the boy carried the chickens down the stairs to the cellar. They cut the bonds and the birds, two lovely white Wyandottes and two guinea hens, hopped around in the candlelight for a minute and then flew up, one after the other, to perch on the top of the coalbin. Ned threw the bread on the floor near them and went upstairs with the boy. Gyp McGlinn was in the kitchen jabbing at an oyster with a carving knife when they reached there.

"They're not like a clam," he was telling Nell and Nora. "There's a way to open these damn things if you know the trick of it. The shell flies right open for you when you know the trick of it."

"A smaller knife's the thing," Ned said. "Here, let me have a try at it."

"Ah," said Gyp as he snapped the end of the blade off, "damn poor piece of steel you have here, Nell. I'll try it with the smaller knife, as Ned says."

"Try it on another oyster, Gyp," Ned said. "Try a smaller one; it might not be so tight closed or as strong of a shell as the big ones."

Gyp tried a paring knife on the rim of a smaller oyster, but no matter how he tried to cut it open or send the point of the knife between the shells, he made no impression. Ned gave him his jackknife that he used for cutting up his plug tobacco, but Gyp still could not get the shell open. Pat tried it and sent the point of a paring knife into the flesh of his hand, the oyster still defying any attempts to open it. Ned tried to drive the sharp end of a file into one with the hammer but he could not hold the oyster up on its end long enough to get in a good blow. Gyp put a flatiron between his knees and hammered around the edge of one until he banged his thumb with the hammer and gave it up. He said that was the only way it could be done finally; set the damn things on top of the flatiron and hammer away at them until you shattered the shell. Ned objected that it would make damn bad eating in that case, with the shells all splintered through the oysters. He said there must be some way to get the damn things open, though, if you only knew the trick and had the patience to do it right. Nell asked if she couldn't take a handful of the things and steam them open in a pot. Gyp told her the steam would spoil the flavor of the oysters if she did.

"And how do you eat them, then?" she asked.

"Raw," he said.

"Well, I'll want to see what they look like first before I'll eat any of them raw," said Nell.

Ned and Gyp, with the boy pulling fresh oysters out of the sack until they were spread all over the kitchen, on the table, the end of the stove and on the floor, beat the shells and sliced futilely at them with knives for half an hour more. Ned told Nell at last that they might get something done if she and Nora would get out of the kitchen and leave them alone for a while. Their hands were cut and bruised from the sharp edges of the shells and tiny slivers were strewn over the room. Only one of the shells that Gyp hammered relentlessly at was open and that one on the end, with the succulent fish leaking out of it. It was hardly a triumph, though. Joe Tracy came upstairs to ask what all the hammering was about and he was pressed into service, although he said he didn't know a damn thing about opening oysters. He brought a cold chisel up he said might be some good, but that didn't work, either. Fran O'Keefe dropped in from Luke Eagan's and laughed at their efforts. With the aid of a small paring knife, now blunted and dulled, he opened three dozen of them in a few minutes and showed Ned how it was done. No one could eat them, though. Joe Tracy said he might take a plateful down to his wife since they had so many of them there.

"Slimy damn things, ain't they?" his wife asked him. "Where do you suppose the McDermotts got hold of them?"

"How in the hell would I know?" he answered.

"I hope to God they get those damn hens out of the cellar soon, or whatever they are, squawking and messing all over it," she said, tired, dumping the oysters into the garbage pan.

"I would not eat one of them damn things if I never et," said her husband.

"Nor I," said his wife sadly.

Chapter Eleven

FIRST up in the morning, Willie found in the spot where the sun had flung a little rectangle of light at the foot of the round stove, packages marked with his name. One from Catherine Daly he ran to the kitchen and opened. There were three books in it, *Poor but Proud*, *Best Foot Forward*, and *With Clive in India*. There were in the house, besides the two huge volumes of Mick's Civil War books, only two other books, Moore's *Poems*, with golden shamrocks clustering on its cover, and Burns's *Poems*, which had, instead of the shamrocks, sprigs of golden thistle bristling on its boards. The pages of the books were adorned with drawings of ruined castles, bridges that spanned slivers of unhappy little streams, and the print was very fine and hard to read. Moore's poems he was allowed to read when he liked, but they were all so sad they did not hold him. There was something immoral, dark and forbidding—word of all words—about the Scotch, his uncle said, something loose and immoral especially about Robert Burns, so though the poems were always there his grandmother did not permit him to read them. When he did read them, in the cold secrecy of the parlor at times they thought he was looking at Mick's Civil War books, the words were spelled so differently mostly that he was never quite clear about what he was reading. There was no one but his grandfather to ask what immoral meant, and Ned had said it was just something no good Catholic could ever be.

Willie opened the drafts and the oven door of the kitchen stove and brought his grandfather's rocker up to it. His feet warm in the new long black stockings, and the new long underwear he had found beside his bed itching him, he sat comfortably in the chair and opened the books one after the other. All of them had his name inside them with a Merry Christmas from Catherine Daly. He was sitting there trying to devour all of them at one great feast when Ned came into the kitchen wearing his Sunday pants, but no shoes or shirt over his underwear. He stood beside the boy for a few minutes before Willie noticed him. He shielded the books with his hands so that Peg would not paw them. Ned moved around behind the rocker and put his hands on its back, rocking the chair slowly.

"Can't keep the scholars away from the books, can we?" he said, looking at Emmet. "First thing in the morning and last thing at night, I suppose. Forever at it. Ah, it's no more than we can expect with scholars in the family."

Willie told him the books were from Catherine Daly.

"I know," Ned smiled. "Scholars and teachers in the family is a grand thing. Or soon will be in the family, I suppose, if that one in the bed there will ever make up his mind. . . ."

They heard wild screams that seemed to fill the back hallway.

"In the name of God!" Ned yelled, "what is that?"

The screams continued, shriller, and they were joined in a moment by the deep shouting of Joe Tracy downstairs. They heard little Helen Tracy calling:

"Mamma! Mamma!"

"The chickens!" Ned cried rushing out of the kitchen. Willie followed him in his underwear, pelting down the stairs to the first floor where he saw Mrs. Tracy trembling against her kitchen door with the coal scuttle in her hand. The lumps of coal were strewn over the floor and parading among them were the two gray speckled guinea hens.

"Ah, 'tis nothing, nothing at all," Ned was saying as he booted the hens down the stairs into the darkness of the cellar.

"Nothing? Nothing at all?" Mrs. Tracy's face was a blister of rage and terror. "I'm after being set upon—set upon and—and clawed to shreds by wild birds pecking at me in the cellar and it's nothing at all, he says. . . ."

" 'Tis nothing," Ned reassured her. "I'll drive them down in the cellar again— I'll shoo them away into the cellar. . . ."

Joe Tracy, hauling his belt together around his middle, opened the door. Helen peeked out from behind him.

"Joe Tracy," his wife said, braver now, "Joe, I've been attacked in the cellar by McDermott's animals. Pecked at, Joe, and bit. Pecked at and bit on Christmas morning. Make him get them out of the cellar, Joe. 'Tis not safe to go down there with them."

"Why, Joe, it's only a couple chickens that never hurt a soul in their life," Ned said apologetically.

"Out, Joe," his wife insisted. "Make him get them out, Joe."

Tracy hesitated, but much as he did not want to quarrel with

Ned, he knew if he didn't see to it that the chickens were taken out of the cellar his wife would give him no peace. Ned declared they couldn't be cruel enough to send the poor birds out in a blinding blizzard itself to freeze to death, no matter what. Mrs. Tracy said he could kill them and save them the suffering, but Ned said they couldn't ask him to kill a Christmas present, not that, by God. Tracy said he didn't care what was done with them as long as they were got the hell out of the cellar. The whole house was up now and Nell, spying Willie clad only in his underwear, sent him upstairs to dress himself and not shame the whole family. As last they compromised, Ned agreeing to kill the two guinea hens, for they might be a little wild, if the Tracys would let the Wyandottes stay until he found a place for them. He promised to kill the guinea hens as soon as he came home from mass.

After mass Ned and Willie said a prayer under the electric Star of Bethlehem that glittered above the crib where the Christ child lay in the yellow straw. Willie whispered to his grandfather that he wished they might have some of that straw for the chickens and Ned, remembering his promise to Joe Tracy, hurried him away home. He did not seem so anxious to reach there, however, as they neared the corner of the house. They stopped in Kelly's drugstore, where Ned sat in the back room and had three whiskies before they started on their way again.

It was good to have Tim Lee there to talk with while Nell and Nora went to late mass. Chris had gone out to South Providence to mass at St. Malachi's with Catherine Daly and he would stay a while with her.

If it was him, Tim said, when Ned told him about the trouble with the chickens, he would just catch hold of them and wring their necks the same as they did with the chickens that was licked in a fight.

"If it was any day but Christmas Day," said Ned, who wanted to delay the execution as long as he could. "Any other day but this I'd do it. But not on Christmas Day."

He sent Willie down to the cellar with a handful of bread for the birds.

There was damn little choice about the killing of a bird, Tim reminded Ned. You could wring their necks, or slit their throats or chop their heads off, if you liked.

"I know it," Ned admitted. "I know it. But—well, let them have a good meal anyhow before I do."

76

Tim opened the bottle he had brought Ned from McGarraghan's and Ned said he might as well have one since he had the kind of a job to do that he did have. He wondered, after the second one, if Joe Tracy might not change his mind about it if he went down and talked to him. But no, he said, any man was that mean he'd send his wife into the cellar for a scuttle of coal on a Christmas morning would never change his mind about nothing on the face of the earth. Tim said he didn't think so either. No, any man that mean would never spare the lives of two innocent chickens.

Perhaps, Tim suggested, Mrs. Tracy wanted the birds killed so she'd have one of them. Ned said he'd see them rot first before he'd give them even the part that went last over the fence. They talked on the rest of the morning until at last Tim said he had to rush away home, for Annie would be expecting him to his dinner. No amount of urging by Ned would change his decision. He said if he had more time he would give Ned a hand with the chickens. Well, it was so late now Ned would wait until after he had had his dinner, anyhow, before he killed them. Nora, who had come in with Nell in the meantime, said all he had to do was to go into the cellar itself and the smell of his breath would lay them out.

When Chris arrived from South Providence they sat at the table, Willie reluctant to close the book about the boy who was poor but proud. Afterward Ned said he thought he would lie down for a while and rest before he went into the cellar to get at the chickens, but Nell demanded he go at once and get the job done, because they had to go to South Providence to see Pat and his family and she didn't want to hear Mrs. Tracy still jabbering about the birds when she got home.

Willie caught one of the chattering birds and gave it to his grandfather, who had armed himself with an old rusted carpenter's hatchet. With shaking hands Ned held the guinea hen's head on the edge of the chopping block and swung the hatchet. The head was not severed until he had struck it several times. Then he flung the twitching corpse on the floor and Willie caught the second one. When the fowl were finally hanging from a nail they went upstairs again where Nell was sitting with Gyp McGlinn. Ned told him it was a sad day when a man had to kill his own Christmas present and explained to him the trouble he had in the morning with the Tracys.

"Sure, why didn't you tell me, then?" Gyp asked. "No need to kill them. We might have brought them across the street to the

shop where you might keep them as long as you like in the old stalls
there in the back. What a shame you killed them."

"See that, now," Ned was angry. "How things is. Well, what's
done's done. Would you take the white ones over, Gyp?"

"And glad to," Gyp said.

The birds safely out of Tracy's way, Ned started for South
Providence with Nell. Willie went upstairs again. He didn't like
to visit his cousins, where there were always two against one and
where old Tessie Butler, an aunt of Pat's wife, Mollie, was forever
asking him questions and trying to see whether he was smarter than
young Pat or Johnnie. His Uncle Pat, he had more than once heard
his grandmother telling his grandfather, didn't go to mass and
something must be done about him. Nora stayed at home with
Willie.

Never before had Willie stayed so long reading. He read a little
in Father Finn's book about the boys in the parochial school and
a little about the poor boy who worked so hard for his widowed
mother. With Clive in India was the thickest of the three books
and he was fascinated by the adventures of the young subaltern
who went out with the troops to wrest the rich land of India from
the treacherous French. He had gone far into the book despite the
small print when he realized he was reading about British soldiers.
He closed the covers in amazement that the British could be brave,
or honest, or good. Something was wrong, very wrong, he thought,
in reading books about British soldiers however brave they were.
Catherine Daly must not know very much about the Irish to have
given him the book, yet he could not believe that about her, a
schoolteacher. There wasn't much difference between the British
conquering India and the redcoats invading Ireland, except that the
people in India were natives. He resolved not to tell his grandfather
about the book but to ask him more about natives. He heard the
Riordans and the LaFlammes in the street, and went down with
Peg to join them. They threw snowballs for a while; then tiring of
that, began to hunt rats with the dog, first in among the snow-
covered piles of Tanner's lumber and then across the street in the
yard of the blacksmith shop. They cornered one peering out from
a manure pile and Peg had it in a second.

Holding the rat in her teeth, the dog spread herself out on the
snow and let it try to squirm itself loose from her jaws, jerking
her head quickly when it seemed almost free. She leaped to her

78

feet suddenly and lowered her head to the snow, the rattail cutting sharp lines on the surface, then threw her head back and flung the rat high in the air. It fell silently head over tip and she caught it in her mouth again, snapping her jaws tightly and growling fiercely. The boys could see the rat go limp in her mouth, and she dropped it on the ground, sniffing it over and walking around it. Willie kicked its corpse back onto the manure pile. He was very proud of Peg and said no one ever taught her to do that trick of throwing a rat in the air and catching it again and that she learned all by herself. She was probably the best ratter in the whole city, he said. He looked in on the white hens before he went home and in the hallway he smelled Peg over to make sure she wouldn't smell too much of manure, which his grandmother didn't like. To make certain of it he took her outside again and rubbed snow up and down her back and over her legs.

Chapter Twelve

WHAT made Ireland so dear to them—Gyp McGlinn, Pete, Pat, old Carroll from Fall River or Devine from North Attleboro, and there was never a Saturday or a Sunday when there were not two or three of them there at the house—Willie could not determine. None of them ever said anything about being very happy in Ireland. People were always coming from Ireland, too, and someone had to help them when they arrived and look for a job for them; and, it seemed, no one in Ireland ever had any money except what someone was sending him—often enough the money to pay for the trip to come here. He heard about landlords driving people out of their houses, how wretched the people were in Dublin during the great streetcar strike there only a little while ago, and how they had to send money and something for them to eat from England. That puzzled him more than almost anything else, except sending so many children to England during that strike to keep them from starving. He could not understand why they all loved it so very much if so many of the people starved there. None of the great men he heard about, and many were admitted to the company of the illustrious Emmet though none ever attained such stature, were ever winning; they were all hunted, shot, beaten, tortured, robbed of their homes, arrested, imprisoned, hungry, ragged, hung or sentenced to exile far away in Australia. His grandfather could never tell him and he never quite dared ask any of the people who came to visit. His Uncle Chris he felt, wouldn't know the answers anyhow, and he could never satisfy himself by trying to make any sense of the answers his grandmother or Nora would give him. It was as mystical and beautiful to him for many years of his childhood as it was to know God was good and dwelt in heaven; England was evil and Ireland was good. Ireland someday would be free; and that freedom itself was cloudy and obscure to him. The war they spoke about that Mick fought in freed the slaves. He knew that, and wondered if, when the Irish were freed from England, they would be like the colored people that were free and equal but lived all around the place in houses no one else wanted to live in and did all the dirty work and could never work in the foundry where his grandfather did.

If it weren't for the British Army, Ireland would be free to-morrow morning; that was clear enough to him. Why, oh why, then, did so many of them talk about their cousins that had been in the British Army, or the Navy. Someone said one night there were more Irishmen in the British Navy than ever there were in the Army. True, it's true enough, his grandfather had answered. He wanted desperately for someone to tell him why so many Irishmen were in the war against the Huns, too, though it seemed everyone was against the Huns. All the schoolteachers, everyone he heard speak of anything outside the house, was against them and said "we'd soon be in it, too, along with the rest of the civilized world." Generally, though, at home it was agreed that Wilson "will keep us out of it," and his grandfather said it was a damn good thing, too, that he would, and he would vote for him.

Always carefully listening for hints of answers to these questions which bothered him Willie, for whom school would have been a delight, were it not that he could never shake off the feeling of being crowded, cramped and nearly in prison, created for himself a world into which everything he knew about fitted nicely except himself. He could never find a place for himself in it because there was this strange person in the reaches of the future that his grandfather was determined he should one day become. Willie could not define just what this person was to be or how he himself was going to become this person. He doubted his own capacity to become the man his grandfather hoped he would. He was like one of his own little kites lifted just over the housetops, suspended between reality and the wide blue sky above with only a slender line to hold him from drifting away.

The Easter of the year he made his confirmation there was a late snow on the Sunday, but he wore the new blue suit with nothing over it anyhow, proud to show all the kids who had fathers that his grandfather would do everything for him that their fathers would or could do for them. In the afternoon he went to the drugstore with the Riordans, Joseph, Eddie, Margaret and Rose, dark, fragile Rose whose little new hat was a garden of pink and blue flowers in the black loam of her hair. Joseph wanted to go somewhere when they left the drugstore, but a rain spattered over them and they all went into Riordans' house where they sat in the chilly parlor with the Riordans' Bible open on the carpeted floor in front of them. Willie had never seen a Bible, and he thought of it as something the Protestants used in their churches, nothing so sacred as the large black book the priest read and sang from on the altar at mass. All the Riordans' names were written on pages in the back of the Bible, with the dates they were born, baptized, confirmed, married and, Willie was astonished to see, would die. Rose, who was turning the pages with agile, scampering fingers, showed Willie the name of a Martin Riordan, born simply "Ireland," married on a date and died on a date but not credited with ever having received his first Holy Communion or his confirmation. She said somebody must have known the dates but they must have just forgotten to write it down in the Bible. Joseph and Eddie tired of looking at the book and began to cuff each other around the room, their father yelling at them from the kitchen where he was having a holiday bottle of beer with Mrs. Riordan.

"There's pictures, too," Margaret said. "Turn to the pictures, Rose."

The pictures were few. In the front of the book was the *Ecce Homo* crowned with the black mocking thorns of the sins of man. Rose passed swiftly to a page with a picture of two women standing with large jars in their hands at a well, then she flipped the page over before Willie had time to read what was written underneath the picture. He, too, was tired now of looking through the book and started to get up from the floor, but Rose, saying nothing, laid a restraining hand on his arm. She drew the closed book in toward her crossed legs until its corner touched the buttons of her shoes, opening it then with a sure hand and a sweep of her arm to the picture of an abandoned, despairing school of swimmers, who vainly were reaching their hands and arms out of a tempest of the wildest seas toward a jagged rock which rose above them in the water. Some of them clung to a point of it while the relentless waves washed over them; others had been swept away in the current. There were boys and girls and babies, one of them clinging in terror to the white roundness of its mother. All of them were nude. Their faces were tormented, lashed with pain beyond words; they seemed to be snarling and tearing at one another, pushing one another away from the rock of refuge. They were mad, doomed, perishing without hope, tortured, terrified, even thirsting, but unbelievably beautiful in their agony. Willie could not lift his eyes from the page. They crept with an unquenchable delight that he had never known over the damned voluptuousness of the serrated thighs, the arms of the women, and fixed in horror and fascination on the faces of the men. He put his hand on the corner of the page, absorbed and absorbing it.

A sudden loud hiss sounded in the kitchen, startling him, and Rose closed the book saying that she guessed her mother was starting to get the supper ready and that he better go home. There were no more pictures, anyway, she said, especially no more pictures like that one. Willie's mind clutched her meaning and he was drenched with shame and anger when he saw that Joseph and Eddie were standing behind him.

He thought of nothing but the picture, its women, the men, the rock and the fury of the sea, until the next night just before suppertime when Gyp McGlinn, the powdery coal dusted over his hairy arms, his face and the V of his chest that showed under his opened gloomy undershirt, broke into the kitchen yelling:

"Nell, Nell! Great God, Nell, there's a rebellion on in Dublin. Where's Ned? The rebels has wiped out the British garrison and seized the city!"

"Oh, my God!"

"I must tell Ned," Gyp roared. "Where's himself?"

Willie ran to the window to see if his grandfather was coming along the street. Hatless, beside himself with joy, he let Peg out ahead of him and ran down into the street. He had the feeling he was hardly moving as he sped over the soggy mud of the sidewalk after the dog. He would be the first to tell his grandfather!

Peg reached Ned first, yelping and leaping up on him, as he rounded the corner of the eight-cornered house where the doctor lived. Willie sprang up on the old man and anchored himself to the handle of the silvery dinner pail when his grandfather set him down after brushing his mustache over the boy's forehead in a kiss. Willie fired the news at his grandfather in happy salvos. Ned put his other hand over his grandson's on the handle of the dinner pail and bent slightly over to him, the tears rising in his eyes. He hardly dared believe what he was hearing.

"God bless them," he said fervently, starting ahead. He stopped again and fixed his eyes sharply on the boy. "How do you know all this?"

"Gyp!" Willie shouted. "Gyp told us. Gyp ran up from the blacksmith shop all dirty and told us!"

"Greatest thing ever happened," Ned said half to himself. "Is Gyp at the shop still? Where is he now?"

"Home. He's up in our house."

They trotted as fast as Ned's legs would carry him, swinging the dinner pail between them, its tea flask ringing out gladly against it. Peg made the shortening distance to the gate twice before they reached it. Trooping up the stairs, their steps thundered like drums.

"Is it true?" Ned asked when he saw Gyp.

"True? True as the word of God," Gyp answered him.

Street by street, building by building, the bitter losing fight was fought every night from every newspaper they could get, even the raucous Boston paper with the flaming red headlines, the paper his grandmother said shouldn't be let into the house but that was brought there every day by his uncle, who said he got it because it told the truth.

Every night the McDermotts had more visitors than ever before. Tim Lee and Gyp McGlinn were in several times, always with a new story, a new interpretation of what was going on. Joe Tracy came up from downstairs and nearly got into a fist fight with Chris McDermott, who said that the uprising was doomed to certain failure, and that it was criminal of the leaders. This Pearse and this Connolly the papers spoke about, not to mention this McDermott —and you can be sure, he said, that he's no kin of ours—were a wild and rabid gang of crazy idealists who were sending their men to certain death with nothing to be gained from it. His grandfather had gone over to Deignan's and Willie, listening to his uncle quarreling with Tracy, was astonished at his opposition to the men his grandfather said were heroes, and silently prayed that Tracy would punch his uncle. As the week drew to its tragic close for the rebels, Ned was wearied with staying up late at night listening and talking. Mr. Devine from North Attleboro, his brogue so buttery it seemed to spread his words out flatly before him, dropped in for supper, and before it was finished Jim Ryan, a dear friend of Tim's, Ned's brother Pat and Tom McGlinn, Gyp's brother, had gathered.

Ned wanted to sit and talk with them but he had stumbled with the ladle in the foundry that afternoon and he was worn out. He stretched himself out on the couch when he finished eating, and

Peg crawled up behind him with her chin resting on his knees. Willie sat with his back against his grandfather's chest to listen to them.

The rebels, said Mr. Devine—of course, he was simply repeating he said, what he had seen in the papers, that is, what they were saying editorially—were undoubtedly in league with the Huns.

"More power to them, then," said Tom McGlinn. "I don't care who they're in league with or without. England's difficulty's Ireland's opportunity. England's enemy's Ireland's friend—or should be, be God. . . ."

"I'd far sooner have a Hun at my throat than an Englishman at my back," Ned muttered without taking the pipe from his mouth. He closed his eyes.

"There's been news of German troops as well as arms landing on the west coast of Ireland," said Mr. Devine. "Seems they landed them by submarine."

"They'd better watch out," Jim Ryan declared, "if they're dealing with that devil in Berlin. They'd better keep an eye on him for he'd turn on his own mother!"

"Sure them fellows is all alike," said Nora, who was clearing away the dishes from the table. "Ain't he the cousin or something of the King of England?"

She left the teacup in front of Mr. Devine and the sugar bowl with its crust of brown candy around the rim. Mr. Devine measured his words carefully and measured the ash on his Saturday cigar, letting the gray coins fall hissing into the teacup.

"For the life of me I can't see them in cahoots with Kaiser Bill," he said slowly. "The madman of Europe. No, not that butcher of the innocents, as they say. It's bad enough to have them stabbing their own lads in the back and them dying there in the trenches of France."

Nell had settled herself in a rocker beside the stove and, after a futile attempt to send Willie off to his bed, sailed along the smooth channel of her rosary as she listened. Nora, in the most comfortable rocker as usual, rode in her wake.

"Their own lads," said Tom McGlinn acidly, "have no damned business in the trenches of France fighting England's wars. I don't care a damn who they're fighting, either. Not a tinker's damn."

"Right," said Ned, rousing himself a little and clapping his hand on Willie's shoulder. "Let them stay at home if they want

85

fighting. Wasn't there enough trouble there with the conscription and all? With Redmond and Dillon making the Irish all kinds of promises that had been made and broken every year for eight hundred years. Let them stay at home if they want to fight."

Nell thought there had been enough talk around the house about Ireland for a while and she didn't like the heat that was beginning to arise from the talk.

"Well," said Mr. Devine, "isn't it democracy they're fighting for anyway and the rights of small nations? Isn't that what they're fighting for? The right of a small nation like Belgium and its people?"

Willie could hear his grandfather breathing heavily as he did when he was asleep. He wished the old man would stay awake for a while and talk, but, watching him, the boy saw the bowl of the pipe turn itself upside down as it frequently did when Ned dozed off, and he knew it was no use.

"Did you ever see the picture of Paddy Fahey?" Nell asked, "when he was with the British Army in India. He was a long time in the British Army, you know."

Paddy Fahey was a cousin of hers who, like many others they knew, had a day's work with the pick and shovel when he could get it and didn't worry much if he didn't. Like the others, too, he raised a large family only because his wife worked herself into an early grave, cleaning the cars on the New York, New Haven and Hartford railway. They said Kate Fahey fed her family with what she took from the dining cars when she was cleaning them nights, wearing an extra petticoat that had a pocket in it where she carried her money and the bread she pilfered; they said too that she used to stuff steaks and slices of cold ham or lamb in between stockings and her underdrawers, but she couldn't put the bread or cake there because it crumbled and the crumbs itched her. Ned McDermott didn't like Paddy Fahey, or any other man who drank what he made and let his wife feed him when he was out of work.

"We have the picture of him in the other room," Nell said. "Fetch it out here, will you, Nora? Fetch us the picture of Paddy Fahey."

"What about Paddy Fahey?" Ned asked stirring himself again. "What the hell does he want this time?"

"Nothing from you," said Nell. "Anyhow it's only his picture I was talking about."

"The hell with him and his picture," Ned mumbled, righting the pipe before he dozed off again.

Nora glared at her sister, knowing that fetching the picture from the other room meant she was going to lose the comfortable rocker. However, she went obediently to search for it among the dozens of pictures Nell had stored there.

"The Butcher of Berlin," said Pat McDermott who had been quietly smoking his pipe up to this, "is overshooting the mark like the Little Corporal did before him, I'm afraid."

Jim Ryan said the difference was that the kaiser was fighting on what a military man would call an inside line whereas Napoleon had the disadvantage. . . .

"The French are on the seas again, boys," said Tom McGlinn. "Don't you ever weary of talking about Frenchy?"

"You wouldn't dispute the genius of the man, I hope," said Jim, twirling Mr. Devine's teaspoon in his hand like a baton.

"Here's Paddy Fahey," said Nora brightly, bounding in from the front room.

"What the hell," growled Ned from the couch, "does the son of a bitch want now?"

"Nothing you have to give," said Nell sharply.

"No," Nora said. "It's Paddy in India."

"Let the son of a bitch stay there," said Ned dozing off again.

"Furthermore," said Jim Ryan, "the lad in Berlin is little better than a goddam heathen while Bonaparte, you know, was a great Catholic. Great friend of the Pope himself. I heard Father Tom Tierney tell the story years ago how some high muckamucks was talking to him there on St. Helena. What, says one of them, was the greatest day of your life? They thought he'd tell them of some great victory like crossing the Alps in the dead of the winter or something of the kind. But he had the answer for them, all right. The greatest day of my life, says he, standing there with the arm across his chest, the happiest day of my life was the day I received my first Holy Communion. Think of that now. The man was an emperor, the maker of kings and princes whenever or wherever he damn pleased but, says he, the greatest day of my life was the day I received the first Holy Communion. Father Tom used to love to tell that one, Lord have mercy on him. Great thing for the Church and all, Father Tom used to say."

"Wasn't there something about switching wives or something of the kind?" Mr. Devine asked.

"I believe there was a dispensation from Rome took care of the matter," Pat said.

"How did it come about then," Mr. Devine asked quietly, "if he was such a great Catholic and all, he saw fit to drive the Pope out of Rome and shut him up in a dungeon? Oh, yes, he did, too, Jim. Yes, he did."

"The man was no more nor less than a goddam tyrant," Pat said. "A goddam tyrant and the worst kind of an adulterer to boot. Cared no more for the Church than for what he would get out of it. Fought the British all his life and never lifted a finger for Ireland."

"Paddy Fahey was a fine looking man in those days," said Nora, passing the picture to Mr. Devine.

"Queer looking kind of a damn uniform they wore, wasn't it?" Mr. Devine asked, passing the picture to Pat.

Pat skimmed it across the table to Jim without even glancing at it.

"By God, Nell," said Jim, "you must be damn proud of a redcoat to keep his picture around the house all these years."

"Here the paper says, the British commander declares the revolt is no more than the last desperate sally of a treacherous and mutinous minority. He states that it will shortly be put down, order restored to the country and the guilty punished," said Mr. Devine. "However, I suppose it's hard to judge the matter so many miles from the scene of action."

"Well," said Pat, "I hope they drive the goddam British out of the country, kaiser or no kaiser. I hope they drive every damn one of them into the sea. Let Ireland be the mistress of her own destiny. Kaiser Bill and Napoleon be damned. I hope they drive them into the sea."

"Oh, indeed, I want to see Ireland free as much as the next one," said Mr. Devine. "But I don't want to see her hand in glove with the Huns."

"There's a fine bit of poetry, you know, about Frenchy," said Pat. "Fits Kaiser Bill to a T. Shelley wrote it."

"Able was I ere I saw Elba," smiled Mr. Devine. "I suppose that's the one you mean. Goes the same written forward or backward, you see. Able was I ere I saw Elba. Quite a thing. He couldn't get away from it one way or the other."

"That," said Pat, "is not what I mean. The lines of the poem are called the 'Feelings of a Republican on the Fall of Bonaparte.' I could give it to you . . ."

"Do," said Nell. "Do recite us the poem, Pat, if you remember it."

"Oh, I remember it, all right," said Pat. "Every word of it."

Willie couldn't see that Napoleon had very much to do with Ireland, but he hoped that his grandfather would stay asleep now for a while, at least until Pat finished with the poem, because if his grandfather heard it and liked it he was sure to order Willie to learn it all by heart and recite it to him sometimes, especially when Tim Lee, or someone came to the house.

"I don't seem to remember this Shelley at all," said Jim. "Was he a poet now?"

"Indeed he was," said Pat. "Indeed he was a poet."

"Doesn't matter a damn one way or the other," said Mr. Devine.

Pat clasped his hands in front of him on the table, looked down, rubbed a forefinger across his mustache two or three times and cleared his throat. He looked up suddenly and fixed his gaze on the Alpine Hunter who stood heroically on the top of the stove.

I hated thee, fallen tyrant, he roared
I did groan
To think that a most unambitious slave,
Like thou shouldst dance and revel on the grave
Of Liberty. . . .

He jabbed a forefinger accusingly at Jim.

Thou mightest have built thy throne
Where it has stood even now: Thou didst prefer
A frail and bloody pomp which time has swept
Into fragments toward Oblivion.

Nell rattled away in the rocker, nodding her head in approval. Ned stirred on the couch and the dog blinked at him expectantly. Pat cleared his throat and went on. . . .

Massacre, for this I prayed,
Would on thy sleep have crept,
Treason and slavery, rapine, fear and lust

89

And stifled thee, their minister. I know
Too late, since thou and France are in the dust
That virtue owns a more eternal foe
Than force or fraud; old custom, legal crime
And bloody faith, the foulest birth of time.

Ned raised himself up on an elbow and watched them, his pipe still drooping upside down from his mouth.

"God, Pat," said Mr. Devine, "that's a grand thing. Where did you come across it?"

"Shelley wrote it, you say?" asked Jim grudgingly.

"P. B. Shelley," said Pat.

"And who in the hell is he?" asked Ned, taking the pipe from his mouth. "What the hell is he up to? Freeing Ireland with a jingle is he?"

"Shelley was the finest flower of British poetry," said Pat. "He was cut down in the bloom of his youth, you might say. He was drownded there in a foreign land. His living heart defied the flames of the funeral pyre. Defiant to the last, the living heart of him contemptible to the fire."

"Faugh," Ned snorted. "I thought so. A British jingle maker . . . what's this you were saying about Paddy Fahey?"

Chapter Thirteen

THE river, sluicing in and out of the spavined pilings of the old coal piers, its banks scabbed with city dumping grounds where it began to broaden out a little farther down to the bay, was as dirty and mysterious to Willie McDermott as many of the things he was beginning to learn about from Joseph Riordan. Beneath the green, oily, smelly surface of the stream was a wicked garden that sprouted a crop of rusty tin cans, broken bottles, sharp and slimy stones that lacerated his feet when he first began to wade into its depths. He would hop along on one foot, thrashing wildly with his thin arms as though he were swimming. He never remembered the hour or the day even when the great secret was revealed to him and he first lifted both feet from the bottom to begin to swim, but as soon as he was doing it, the mystery dissolved for him. He prowled under the water, eyes closed but smarting, and somehow let himself up again to spew the bitter drink from his mouth. It was not long, scattered and harassed as they always were by the workmen along the waterfront, before the boys were boldly walking out to the end of an abandoned pier and diving into a real depth. Even at low water the river was deep enough at the end of the pier for the river boats to dock. They sent their thin bodies sounding down, down to the bottom, fetched handfuls of the heavy mud to the surface again to prove their prowess, and treading water while they showed their prizes to those who might be still on the pier, would see the mud melt away in their hands.

Many times during the summer Willie would slip away from the house in the morning with Peg, meet Joseph and Eddie at a hideaway in Tanner's yard behind the piles of old doors, lintels, window frames and mouldings, and head for the river. Among themselves they would usually contrive to scare up a nickel from the pennies they were learning to steal when they were sent to the store. Perhaps Ned might have given Willie two or three the night before, sometimes even the whole nickel. These were rare days, because they would be able to buy perhaps four cigarettes and still have enough to go to the bakery for the broken cake they could buy when the baking was done.

The bakery, where thousands of loaves of bread were piled into the wagons every day, was only a street away from the river, a huge yellow brick building whose sweet smell of bread, cakes and pies never left the streets around it. At one of the doors they would fill a whole large bag with the warm cakes that were split or broken when they were taken from the huge ovens. The price was a nickel. The boys would bring their bags, still warm and sometimes a little greasy, down into the shadows of the coal pockets and eat themselves full. Sometimes, when they had eaten all they could, they threw the remaining cake at each other; at other times, they battled for the last delicious piece.

They made excursions to the dump, a landfill on the shore which was humped with refuse, decaying and putrid. With long sticks from broom handles, the boys prodded and poked among the piles of rotting trash for whisky bottles, bits of brass, copper or perhaps a length of lead pipe which they could sell to the junkmen. They had a clever tactic with the junkmen; Willie would be making the sale to one of them while Joseph, sneaking up to the wagon from the other side of the street, would be plundering it for what he could lug away with him to sell to the next one who came along. The junk yards where the wagons all pulled in at night were not far from the dump.

They were always careful to avoid getting too near the cadaverous old men who roamed the dump every day prospecting its beds. The two old men lived in a little shack, bandaged with tin signs, not far from the dump itself. One of them was very tall and as thin as the shadow of a picket fence, and the other one was very short, hardly taller than the boys were. No one ever knew their names or where they came from and no one cared. They were never seen anywhere except at the dump or sitting in front of their shack. Peg nosed her way into the shack one day and the little one, screaming unintelligibly, drove her away. Peg enjoyed it and the boys did, jeering at the old man until, noticing Peg scoot off again as though she were frightened anew, they turned and saw the big one storming up behind them. They fled. Eddie said he had seen a scapular swinging from the little one's neck when he was chasing Peg away from the shack. Willie never told his grandmother or his grandfather when they went dump-picking, and before they went into the house they would stop at the horses' drinking tub in the yard at old man Edwards' blacksmith shop and wash off the filth from the river that clung in oily dots to their skin.

Even after school started, they made trips to the dump on Saturdays until the weather got so cold the mounds of refuse froze solid and they couldn't pick their way into them with their broomsticks. They built fires in the lots in back of Kelly's drugstore and roasted potatoes there and sometimes a chop if they could filch one from the pantry.

Joseph, ever restless, always exploring, told his brother and Willie one Saturday afternoon, as they huddled around the fire in the lots after the other boys had gone home, that he'd bet he knew something about Kelly's that they didn't. He said he'd bet that he knew something about Kelly's cellar they didn't. It couldn't be the card games Kelly had in the back room and it couldn't be the whisky selling on Sundays when the barrooms were closed because everybody in the neighborhood knew that. They asked him to tell them what he knew about the cellar that they didn't.

"I know how you can get in it," Joseph said. "I could get in it any time I wanted to and Kelly would never know it. I could take anything I wanted to and Kelly would never know it. There's a way you can get in by the alley."

"Suppose you did get in the cellar, what good would that do you?" Willie asked him.

"You could get anything you wanted," Eddie said.

"How would you get out again?" Willie asked.

"Same way you go in," Joseph answered. "I could get in and out any time without Kelly knowing a thing about it."

"You'd get pinched if you got caught," Willie said cautiously.

"Who's going to get caught?" Joseph laughed.

"Who's even going in?" his brother said.

"I am," Joseph declared.

Willie was speechless.

"When?" Eddie said, never doubting that if his brother said he was going into the cellar he would do it.

Joseph said he didn't know, but some night after Kelly closed the drugstore for the night he was going to slip into the cellar and help himself to whatever he wanted. He asked them if either one of them dared to come with him some night. Willie was terrified at the suggestion. Joseph was laughing at him and asked him what he was so scared about; he wasn't even in there yet, Joseph said. He took them down the alley between Kelly's store and the house next to it. There was a small cellar window, about a foot and a half high with three dirty panes of glass in a row. Joseph, leaning against the wall of the frame building, pressed his foot against the bottom of the window and gently pushed it open about an inch, then, bending over, he put his hands on the narrow ridge at the bottom of the sash and carefully pulled it closed again. They walked slowly home, Willie, feeling very guilty, fearing every moment that Kelly himself would come up in back of them and grab them. Joseph said again that he didn't know when he was going to do it, but some night when Kelly closed up the store for the night he was going to push that window open and get in.

He talked for weeks about it, telling them how easy it would be with three of them. One of them could watch on the outside, he said, in case anybody should happen to come along, but no one ever went in that alley at night anyway. Joseph talked so much and so confidently about it, describing just how they would slip in and out of the window that the other two boys began to feel themselves a part of the enterprise. There was no use trying it while there was snow on the ground, Joseph said, because they would be able to trail you through the snow wherever you went. They would find your tracks and hunt you down with the stuff you took. The snow was never cleaned out of the alley between Kelly's and the next house, he reminded them, because no one ever went down it. That would make it all the easier to get in and out, he said, when the snow was off the ground. He led them deftly along with him until the idea, at first so fearful and fraught with danger to Willie, became almost an obligation he felt he owed to Joseph.

By the time the snow had gone, permanently it seemed, toward the end of February, Willie, schooled carefully in his role, was ready, even anxious to get into the cellar and get it over with. He was to accompany Joseph in and Eddie was chosen to stay outside to watch for anyone who might come around. They arranged that when they did it Willie was to tell his grandmother he was going over to Riordans' house and they would tell their mother they were going to his house. Joseph explained that they would all be home again before anyone had a chance to find out where they were.

Kelly closed at eleven o'clock, leaving one light burning in the front window, shining through the large oval jars of red and blue liquid. The boys shivered in the streets, running over to the front of the store every few minutes during the long evening until at last they saw the bright lights inside the store go out and Kelly himself locking the front door. He always went out the side door at night, Joseph said, and they watched for him there, because sometimes, after locking the door for the night, he went into the back room with the cardplayers and they stayed there a long time. Willie wondered how Joseph knew so much about what Kelly did when he locked up the store at night. They had to make sure, Joseph warned, that Kelly really went home, and they hid behind a fence to watch him go up the street.

Willie wanted to retreat, but it was too late for that. He followed the Riordan brothers up the street and over the fence into the alley alongside Kelly's. He was shaking and his mouth was hot as he blinked in the darkness of the alley. Joseph was on his knees already pushing against the window with his hands while Eddie crouched beside him. Joseph whispered that he would go in first and that when Willie got in they would let the window close down again. If everything went all right when they got inside they were going to tap twice on the panes and Eddie would push it in again and hold it open for them until they got out. Eddie was to whistle and run if he saw anybody coming. Joseph slipped his feet in first and let himself slowly into the darkness. Willie was cast, unable to move until he heard Joseph's rasping whisper to "come on." He followed him into the cellar and the window closed softly behind him.

They groped their way to the stairs and up them to the door that led into the store, not daring to light a match for fear the light might be seen outside. Willie thought, as they moved away from the window, that even if Eddie did whistle now if someone came they would never be able to hear him. The door leading into the store was locked when they tried to open it, and silently they crept down the stairs again to the cellar.

"There must be something here," Joseph whispered. "Come on."

He led the way, groping around wooden boxes whose contents were mysteries to them and barrels that smelled of alcohol. Willie, his hand on Joseph's back, moved with him, swallowing his spit so loudly it seemed to him that his own ears were ringing with the sound. There was a damp smell of medicine everywhere that he could almost taste and it began to make him sick; he felt almost like vomiting. Joseph hit his head against a shelf in the dark and

95

said, "Jesus." Willie wished that he wouldn't swear now above all times. Joseph stumbled, knocking a cardboard box over from a pile of them and it landed with the thud of a cannon on the cement floor. There were cigarettes in it, hundreds and hundreds of cigarettes, Joseph found when he got down on his knees to examine it. He began to stuff packages of cigarettes into his blouse and his pockets and told Willie to do the same. Willie did and then whispered that they must have been in there an hour already and that they better get out while they could before someone came.

"Shut up," Joseph hissed.

He explored further, but Willie knelt where they had stopped, too fearful to move another inch. He didn't even dare move toward the window a few feet away, where he could see against the light of the moon that was pouring down a small motionless round form that might have been Eddie's knee. At last he started to creep toward the window. Suddenly he felt Joseph's hand tighten on his leg.

He stopped and Joseph crept away again. Willie could hear him as he poked at boxes and cartons. The shadow against the moon shifted and grew larger, coming to rest again only when it had blocked out nearly half the window. Eddie couldn't be that big, Willie thought; someone must have come, and they didn't hear Eddie whistle to them. He supposed that Eddie got away from whoever it was but perhaps he had been caught.

"Joseph," he whispered. When Joseph crept back to him Willie pointed to the shadow at the window.

" 'S Eddie," Joseph muttered.

"Let's get out," Willie gasped.

Joseph stood boldly up and tiptoed to the window, beckoning Willie to follow him. Their eyes were becoming used to the darkness now and they found the way back easier than the way in. Joseph shoved a heavy wooden box under the window; it grated on the floor. He stood on it and tapped twice on the pane with his fingernail. Standing beside him, Willie watched the sash move slowly and noiselessly in toward them and he reached up to start climbing out. Joseph pushed him away quickly.

"Me first," he snarled, hauling himself up on the ledge and slowly disappearing.

Willie followed, the boxes of cigarettes he had stuffed into his shirt cutting against his belly when he moved himself over the ledge. Just as he was getting his legs out, Eddie let the window go and it dropped, pinning him there. The more he struggled to free himself the tighter the window held him. He moved his arms back and inch by inch squirmed himself out. By this time both Joseph and Eddie were over the fence and he stood there afraid to move. He didn't catch up with them until they were going into Tanner's yard where they had decided they would hide the loot.

"You bastard, Eddie," he said, almost crying. "You skipped me. So did you, Joseph. Why didn't you wait for me?"

"Shut up," Joseph said. "You got away all right, didn't you?"

They squatted on the ground near the old doors and window frames after they had stowed their booty, wrapped in an old length of rag, behind some doors where the rain couldn't wet it. Joseph had held on to a box of the cigarettes and they each lit one. Then Joseph hauled a box of candy from under his jacket and they began to eat. Joseph swore them each to secrecy, even if they were caught later. No one would squeal on the others. They smoked and ate contentedly until the Mediator bell boomed once. It had all happened within half an hour, the most daring thing any of them had ever done, and none of them thought of anything more than that.

Willie realized that he would have to get home before his uncle did or he would have to answer questions about where he had been and what he had been doing. He went over the fence and into the house by the cellarway, groping his way to the stairs and quietly going up them. The gas was turned low for his uncle, and Willie could see, as he undressed in the length of light it threw into his room, that his hands were dirty and scratched. They shook like shingles in the wind when he held them up. He started to kneel as he always did to say his prayers before he got into the bed, but he couldn't. He was more frightened than he had been in Kelly's cellar, and with a frantic jerk he hauled the covers back and buried himself under them, not daring even think. He lay awake long after his uncle came home and turned the gas out in the other room. He hoped, as he watched his uncle kneel to say his prayers, that the smell of the cigarette smoke wasn't too strong. Then slowly his strength evaporated, his fear of being caught bellowed and shrieked in his mind wildly. He felt nauseated and thought he could still smell the medicines in Kelly's cellar. He could feel his arms and legs quivering under the blanket and his eyes were like coals burning

97

in his head. The bed itself seemed aflame and he dared not stir an inch lest he wake his uncle. When morning came, he decided, if morning came, he would tell his grandfather what he had done and beg him to forgive him, beg him to. Then he remembered his pledge to Joseph and Eddie, realizing that he could not betray them to his grandfather because then his grandfather would surely hate him more than ever. There's nothing, he could hear his grandfather telling Tim Lee, that I hate worse than a man that'll betray another. Nothing I hate worse than a man'll betray another man to save his own skin. At least, Tim, he was saying, a man can take his punishment and keep his tongue in his head. Wretchedly, he combed his mind for a reason within the scope of his grandfather's rules that would permit him to unburden himself, but he could find none.

Chapter Fourteen

"WELL, Larry!" said Ned McDermott as his cousin Lieutenant Larry McDermott of the Providence police department walked into the dining room, "it's months since we've seen you. How are you now, and all the family?"

Ordinarily when someone knocked at the back door Nora would sit wherever she was and let someone else go to the door. Only when the front doorbell rang and it might be someone of importance would she answer. But when Larry knocked she was going into the dining room with the teapot, anyhow, so she paused and let him in.

"Don't bother with any supper for me, Nell," Larry said. "I just dropped in on my way home from the station house to see how you were all getting along . . ."

"Ah, Larry, you might as well have a bite to eat," said Ned. Nell set a place for the lieutenant beside Willie, and the big man, grunting a little as he packed his weight into a chair beside the boy, blessed himself with a huge freckled hand.

Hot and palsied, the boy watched the policeman's hand with its red hair make the sign of the cross. A diamond ring, the stone as large as a bird's egg sparkled under the gaslight; the flesh around the wide yellow band seemed to swell out. There could be only one reason for Larry McDermott coming to the house, the boy knew; they had been discovered. Someone had found out; perhaps some of the kids to whom they had been giving cigarettes had told old man Kelly; perhaps the loot so carefully hidden had been uncovered by the searching policemen. What about Joseph and Eddie? Had they been trapped? Was there a policeman at their house now? He trembled to think of their oath never to squeal on each other. He wanted to get up and leave the house, but he knew his grandmother would know there was something wrong if he went out without eating some of the pie she had on the table in front of her. Eddie Riordan, perhaps, had been caught and had squealed; Joseph would never, no matter what they did to him. He was certain of Joseph's loyalty. Who could have told on them? No, it couldn't have been Eddie because he was more afraid of

99

Joseph than of all the cops in the world. Some other kid must have done it. . . .

Lieutenant McDermott ate slowly and with apparent enjoyment, answering Ned's questions about his family with single words. They were "fine," "good."

"Things are quiet enough these days, Larry," said Ned.

"Uh-huh," said the lieutenant, stuffing potato into the tight mouth, that seemed too small for his huge jowls. "Uh-huh. . . ."

"Nothing like days gone by," Ned went on, "when the dagos was raising hell on the hill. . . ."

"Nope," said the policeman, slanting his piggy eyes down at the boy beside him.

"They raised hell them days," said Ned.

The lieutenant wiped his hand across his mouth and stirred sugar into his tea.

"Seen John Kelly this afternoon, Ned," he declared. "Had a great robbery at the drugstore a few nights ago, it seems. . . ."

"No!" said Ned amazed.

"Things goes right on under your nose and you never know a word of it sometimes," Nora said, shaking her head. "Was there much stolen, Larry?"

"Well, we're investigating," said the policeman. "It's a pretty serious affair in a way, breaking into a store you know, next thing to highway robbery. . . ."

"Desperate criminals in the neighborhood and you never even think about it," said Nora. "We might all be murdered in our beds for all you know. . . ."

"Some of the booty has been recovered," said the lieutenant. "They didn't have time to dispose of it all. . . ."

"Who was the thieves, then?" Nora asked.

"Ah, that we're not sure about," said Larry. "We have rounded up several suspects, though—the Riordans across the street there is being questioned in the matter . . ."

"The Riordans!" Nell gasped. "Why—Willie is only after leaving them to come in to his supper. . . ."

"Is that so?" Larry McDermott was smiling. "Pretty bad companions for a boy his age. That Joseph is a bad one. Bad all the way through. Do you run around with them much, Willie? Did you notice them smoking a lot of cigarettes lately?"

"I—they don't smoke," he said sullenly, looking up at his questioner and shifting his eyes away quickly again so that he would not have to face his grandfather.

"Well, they admitted their part in the crime," said Larry. "But it seems they weren't alone. Seems there was someone else with them. . . ."

"Was it you?" his grandmother screamed. "Was it you with them?"

"No," he declared, determined to brazen it out now in spite of any of them.

"They say it was," Larry McDermott said very deliberately. "They say it was you with them when they broke into Kelly's."

"Oh, God," his grandfather moaned.

"You wicked boy!" His grandmother was enraged, crying. "Oh, you wicked. . . . oh, in my own house, a thief in my own house. . . ."

His grandfather, tortured, his eyes red with tears, turned to his wife with fury and hatred pounding in his words:

"What thief?" he cried. "Who's the thief? How the hell do you know there's a thief in your house? The Riordans says it, do they . . . the Riordans . . . God damn the Riordans!"

Wailing, Nell ran from the room, snatching up her apron and hiding her face in its folds. Nora ran after her.

"There, Nell," she soothed. "There, Nell."

The boy, so powerless, so guilty, sat hopelessly between his grandfather and Larry.

"Well, Willie," said the lieutenant in a wheedling, kindly way, "you're breaking your poor grandmother's heart. Tell us about it now. Tell us all about it. Was it the Riordans put you up to it? Was it them put you up to it? Was it the Riordans, Willie?"

The boy couldn't speak. He sat in a flaming torment. If he only knew! If he only knew whether it was Joseph or Eddie that squealed. Perhaps neither one of them had. Perhaps the cops were just guessing about who it was. . . .

"Don't be shielding the Riordans, Willie," the lieutenant persisted. "Don't try to protect that riffraff. They'd tell on you in a minute. It was them told on you in the first place."

"Did you," his grandfather was saying with his hand crushing the boy's arm. "Did you?"

The boy buried his face in his arms on the table and wept.

"Well, Ned," the lieutenant said kindly. "I hate to see one of my own people mixed up in a thing like this. That's why I come over myself. We'll go over to the station house now, the three of us and see what's to be done about it. They picked the Riordan boys up this afternoon; caught them red-handed with some of the stolen cigarettes in their pockets. That Joseph's a tough little customer, though; couldn't get a word out of him all this time."

There was no use trying to run away. Willie was happy that he hadn't brought any of the cigarettes into the house with him that night as he had intended. They got ready to leave. Peg, wildly running from the boy to his grandfather, was scratching at the door in front of them when they were dressed.

"No, Peg," the old man said. "No, Peg . . ."

In a scrubbed and barren room, on a long bench underneath glass cases of pistols, handcuffs, butcher knives, cleavers, baseball bats with spikes driven through at their thick ends, short lengths of iron and lead pipe, and brass knuckles sat two dirty-faced boys. Joseph was at the end of the bench, his hands clasped between his knees, belligerently staring at an old sergeant who was pacing up and down the length of the heavily disinfected room. When the sergeant passed along so that his back was to Joseph, the boy would grimace at him and stick out his tongue in derision. Eddie's cheeks were splotches of gray dirt where he had been rubbing away the tears. Larry McDermott went behind a desk and sat down. In a chair at one side of the desk sat Mr. John Kelly, the druggist, looking very pure of heart and long-suffering. On the other side, his bloodshot eyes breathing out his hatred at the boys on the bench, sat Mr. Martin Riordan.

"Go ahead and smoke if you want to, Martin," said Larry McDermott, trying to put the older persons all at ease. "Well, Mr. Kelly, it seems we have all the culprits collared now. . . ."

Ned, standing as near the door as he could and still be in the room, glared at Kelly.

"Well, I didn't accuse the McDermott boy," said Kelly, "I only said that where the Riordans was, there was McDermott. I see them forever playing together in the lots in back of the store. . . ."

So Eddie hadn't squealed on him after all. Neither had Joseph. But how did they catch them?

"Well, they all admit their guilt," said Lieutenant McDermott. "All more or less admit their guilt. There's a complaint to be made out against them. Sergeant, will you get one of the complaints for

Mr. Kelly? Unless, of course, there's some other way. Unless there's some other way the matter could be straightened out to the satisfaction of Mr. Kelly. Unless Mr. Kelly would be ready to accept restitution for the loss of his property. How much was the loss, Mr. Kelly? In case there might be some way the matter could be straightened out to your satisfaction . . . in view of the age of the boys. Of course if there was to be no complaint made out against the boys, the police would be ready to drop the matter. That is, the police will not proceed further until there is a complaint made out. Now if Mr. McDermott and Mr. Riordan here was to make good the loss, say, and take care of the punishment of the boys in their own way, of course, there would be nothing for the police to. . . ."

"The loss is substantial," Mr. Kelly said, smoothing the hair back over his baldness. "Substantial, indeed. Couldn't be worse no matter what age they were. And who's to say if they're not punished for this they won't indulge in something worse later. The loss would be in the neighborhood of one hundred dollars, more or less. . . ."

"In that case," said the lieutenant, "I think the fathers of the boys would be willing to make proper restitution. Am I right, Martin? Ned?"

Martin Riordan and Ned said they would be ready and willing to make the loss good if there were no further action taken against the boys. They said it was the least they could do under the circumstances. Yes, they were ready and willing to make good the loss and the boys would be punished properly, the lieutenant could be sure of that. Neither of them, however, had the money with them and it was agreed that they should call at Kelly's later in the evening and pay him. The lieutenant said Martin and Ned might as well go along home now and leave the criminals there with him.

When he was alone with them he told them how lucky they were to have such fine parents, and how very lucky it was that Mr. Kelly had been so lenient with them after robbing his store. Joseph said the stuff they took wasn't worth nowheres near the hundred dollars Kelly said it was.

"Come over here, you," said the lieutenant. He slapped the boy in the mouth with his maul of a hand. "You speak when you're asked to speak, you little bastard. D'you hear? If it wasn't that young McDermott here is mixed up in this you'd all be on your way to reform school in the morning. . . ."

He stood up and walked over to Willie McDermott, grabbing

the boy by the arm and hauling him to his feet. He held him and slapped him viciously across the face, then flung him off again, the boy's head hitting against the wall. Willie slumped down on the bench. Joseph reached down to the floor and handed him his cap.

"Stand up, you little bastards," the policeman roared. He pulled Willie and Joseph to him and knocked their heads together. Joseph's nose was bleeding and Eddie, quavering on the bench, burst out crying. He slapped the two repeatedly with the back of his hand, then turned his attention to Eddie, pushing him and slapping him around the room as the boy retreated from his blows.

"Think you got away easy this time, don't you? . . . got away easy this time, hey? . . . dirty little thieves," he grunted.

The boys were bruised and exhausted. Eddie was sobbing and with each slap cried out. Breathless and dazed, Joseph and Willie leaned against the wall, their heads drooping but their eyes, simmering with hatred, watching every move the policeman made. At last he hauled Eddie toward the door and slapped him once more; then he opened the door and flung the boy out:

"Get home," he ordered.

Joseph was next and received the same treatment. Willie was too weak to retreat when the policeman stormed across the room to him. He pinioned the boy against the wall, thumping his shoulders and head on the plaster.

"You bastard," he snarled. "You little bastard. This is the last time you'll get off so easy. If you're brought here again, if I ever hear of you raising hell, I'll break every goddam bone in your body. Following Pat's Eddie, are you? Going to be a tough guy, are you? I'll show you who's tough in this family. . . ."

The boy was choking. He could see only the flaming red face above him, the green little eyes in it and the tight mouth opening and closing. The policeman let go and he fell on the floor. He was jerked to his feet and thrown toward the door. Stumbling, he put his hand on the knob and the policeman knocked it away.

"Where the hell are you going, you little thief? Get away from that door . . ."

Once more the policeman grabbed him, this time at the throat, holding him so that he could only gasp.

"Dirty little thief," he sneered. Flinging the door suddenly open he jerked the boy down the corridor toward the entrance. He pushed him into the street.

His grandfather and Martin Riordan were standing under the elm across the street, Joseph and Eddie hiding in the shadows near them. As he came up, they all started silently down the street toward home, the old men walking together and the lagging boys trailing behind them. Joseph held the others back and let the distance between the old men widen. Martin Riordan, big and heavy, strode along swinging his arms, but Ned McDermott, short and bent beside him, was dragging his feet and his head was down.

"Who squealed?" Joseph Riordan was muttering. "I wonder who squealed . . ."

"Not me," Eddie said. "Not me, Joseph . . ."

Willie McDermott, still breathless and aching, stared ahead at the sagging form of his grandfather. He was sick, penitent, and he wanted to run away from them all. He hated Joseph Riordan. He thought of all the people he hated: Joseph Riordan, his cousin Fred Kane, his Uncle Larry McDermott, his Uncle Chris.

"Some son of a bitch must have squealed," Joseph repeated. "I'm going to find out what son of a bitch squealed on us. . . ."

Nearing home, they stopped talking and narrowed the gap between themselves and the old men reluctantly, realizing that no matter how severely Larry McDermott had beaten them, their worst punishment was only about to begin. They agreed to meet in Tanner's yard in the morning if they could sneak away.

Chapter Fifteen

FROM the dark refuge of his room Willie listened to the storm of his grandmother's anger flooding the house and his grandfather's low voice answering her. He couldn't distinguish all they were saying, but he trembled to realize that his grandmother was insisting that they put him away somewhere. He could not imagine where they might put him except in the reform school or an orphanage. While the tempest raged in the other rooms his penitence for his sins was smothered by his terror of being separated from his grandfather. No punishment could be worse than that. He wanted to go into the other room to plead with his grandmother not to do it, wanted to assure her that he would never, never steal anything again, but he didn't dare. The fury of the storm subsided for awhile, and after he heard the front doorbell ringing he could hear a deep voice that he thought was Martin Riordan's talking with his grandfather. He listened carefully but still couldn't make out what they were saying, and he was afraid to open the door even a crack because he knew it creaked. The talk had not been long in progress when he heard his grandfather and someone else going down the front steps and he knew it must be Martin Riordan with him. They would be going to Kelly's to pay him, as they had promised in the police station, and he knew they would stop for a while at Deignan's before returning.

Exhausted, and beginning to feel the pain of the beating Larry McDermott had given him, he knelt beside the narrow bed and prayed earnestly for God's help in resisting his temptations to steal. He asked God's forgiveness for having hurt his grandfather so grievously and begged in the name of every saint whose name he had ever heard that he would not be sent away to the reform school or to an orphanage. He was in a daze of fear and sorrow when he took his clothes off and got into the bed. He could not sleep and lay there listening for his grandfather to come home, expecting that any moment his grandmother would come into the room and snatch him out of bed to pack him away to wherever it was she wanted to send him. He got up and peered out the window across the street to Riordans' house, wondering what was happening to Joseph and Eddie and if they, too, were going to be sent away. He wished, before he had to face his grandfather again, that there might be some way in which he could escape the guilt of his thievery, but the boy knew he could not lay the blame on Joseph or Eddie or anyone but himself. He knew that if he hadn't been afraid of what Joseph would say about him he might never have gone into Kelly's in the first place. He wanted to hate Joseph, but when he remembered how bravely his friend had stood before the blows Larry showered on them and how contemptuous he was of the policeman's threats, he could only admire him. Joseph wouldn't care, he decided, who came to know about the affair, but he did. He didn't want his uncle to know about it or Catherine Daly, but he knew they would learn of it somehow from his grandmother. If that cousin of his, Fred Kane, ever mentioned it or told anyone about it he would slug him. Fred Kane or his cousins in South Providence, Pat and Johnnie, would never even dare break into a place like Kelly's. But these tangents were no consolation to the boy. His grandfather would be coming home soon and he was guilty; there was no escape for him and he dreaded to face the old man. If his grandfather would beat him it would be easy; he could stand all of that they wanted to give him, but the old man had never done it yet and Willie knew he wouldn't begin now, no matter who wanted him to—Larry McDermott, his grandmother, or anyone else. Yes, if his grandfather would beat him and get it over with, it would be lots better.

Gradually his weariness blunted the knives of torment that cut him and he slipped away into a doze, his face buried in the pillow. He woke up in terror with someone's hand on his shoulder and sat up to see his grandfather sitting beside him. The gaslight from the other room dribbled in like a yellow haze, and Peg stood with her forepaws on the edge of the bed ready to spring up if he said the word. His grandfather had his back to what light there was and Willie was glad that he didn't have to look at the old man's eyes. The grandfather put his head into his hands and began to talk. . . .

"Whatever made you? . . ." he was almost whispering. "Christ, boy, you didn't have to. Well, that son of a bitch Kelly is paid every cent and that's the end of it as far as he is concerned, but why did you ever go there in the first place with all the things that's being . . . all the things that's going to be done for you? How will we ever be able to do them at all if you carry on this way breaking into stores like a thief?

"What is it you want that you don't have, then? Why, I could take you, God forgive me, I could take you and break you into two, God damn you. Why, the shame of it, the shame of it for a boy like yourself that's going to . . . that's going to be educated and all. And why would you go breaking my heart like that, then, after what I'm planning and scheming for you? Why would you do that to me?

"Ah, there's nothing on God's earth you couldn't have and willing. Nothing . . . don't you see? It's only a little while now and you'll be in the high school and then the first thing you know up and away to a college or something of the kind where they'll make . . . how in the name of God could you ever have done it?

"Quiet now! *Listen* to me!

"This is the, this is the last time, d'you hear? This is the last time."

"I won't," Willie said from a throat that was as dry as the cobbled gutters in August, "I won't ever do anything like that. I promise I won't. I promise."

"Only tell me what it is you want. Only tell me," the old man said. "Whatever on God's earth it is I'll see to it somehow."

"Nothing," the boy whispered. "There's nothing I want."

"I'll have to see," his grandfather murmured. "I'll have to see what's to be done."

"Send me away?" the terrified boy asked.

"No, not send you away. No. I'll not send you away. You'll go to school as I've always said you'd go and you'll go on from that, too, as far as you like. . . ."

"My grandmother wants to send me away," Willie persisted.

"Faugh! She wants nothing of the kind. You're breaking her heart, though, with stealing like that."

"I heard her say so," Willie went on.

"She'll not," his grandfather asserted. "Not now, nor never."

"She said so, though."

"Never you mind, there's no sending away unless I do the sending," Ned declared. "In the name of God where would she send you, then? What would happen if she sent you away and what would you grow up to? Be quiet now and don't wake up the house. I'll have to see what's to be done here. I'll have to see. . . ."

Chapter Sixteen

THERE was no use trying to hide it from Catherine, Chris McDermott told his mother and father; Willie had become a little thief, and it made no difference whether it was evil companions or what it was, steps had to be taken before it was too late or he would turn out a real disgrace to the whole family, no good to himself or anyone else. He had brought Catherine to the house—"though God knows I hate to bring you into this, dear"—because she was a schoolteacher and knew something about boys. Oh, they could have had the boy go down to have a talk with Father Scanlan, but he didn't want to ask Father Scanlan, chaplain of the council, to have to take his time from other and much more important things to spend on the boy. He didn't want to seem too stern, he told Catherine, but, if it were up to him he'd put the boy into a home or something of the kind for his own good where he'd get a good Catholic upbringing and probably make something of himself in later years. If the boy was going to go on like this, he concluded sadly, there wasn't anything else they could do to spare his grandmother more sorrow. Nell, shaking her head sorrowfully in agreement as he talked, looked to Ned for approbation.

The old man, sitting at the table with his elbows on it and his chin resting in the cup of his hands, neither looked at his son nor thought very much about what he was saying. To him it was becoming a conspiracy to rob him of the boy and strip him ruthlessly of his dignity and authority as the head of the house.

Enraged at his son's boldness, knowing that he must have talked about his sly plan with Nell, Ned's few words failed him; he could not talk to them in terms of halfway measures and he wasn't clever enough to shunt them off the track. He had been so utterly astounded by the whole affair that he had not yet been able to decide what was to be done, though he knew something drastic must be. The shock had been so severe he had not even realized that when Larry McDermott sent him and Martin Riordan out of the police station, he had done it so that he could punish the boys. Even then he had not understood they had been beaten; it had not become clear to him until the next day, when he saw the swollen lips and the puffed eyes on the boy, and he knew that it hadn't been from weeping they were bruised so.

"Let there be no more talk of a 'home,' " he said without looking up from the table. "While I'm here this is his home—and that'll be a hell of a long time, too, please God. . . ."

"Oh, dear," Nell whined, "God knows what he'll do next. I have no control over him at all, no more than the man in the moon. I never thought. . . ."

"Now, Ma," Chris said, "don't plague yourself any more about it. Something can be done. . . ."

"It *is* done," said Ned abruptly.

"Willie will have to . . ." Chris started to say—

"I'll take care of the boy," Ned declared. "I'm damned if he's beyond redemption, you know, if he did steal a handful of cigarettes."

Catherine Daly toyed with her spoon, tapping it on the edge of the teacup. She was uncertain of what to say, but she knew she was learning something about Chris McDermott which she had only suspected the first Sunday she had come to his house with him and watched him with his mother. There was a righteous chill to him that she hadn't known, that she had never seen in her father, in spite of his slightly avaricious and grubbing nature, and that she was sure old Mr. McDermott didn't have. It was not, she thought, that Chris was cruel himself, but it would be cruel to old Mr. McDermott and to the boy if they were separated and the boy put into a "home." The fact that Willie McDermott actually broke into a store appalled her and was frightening. She taught a grade in school where the children were much younger than Willie, and boys who stole things, who were "bad," were boys of a dark remote world she heard about, but which had never been closer to her than her father's saloon.

"This is not the first time, Catherine," Chris was saying. "Of course, the other things were not so serious as this, but time and again mother's had to punish Willie for little things. Perhaps if she'd been sterner with him then. . . ."

"I've tried, Chris. Oh, I've tried to do my best for that boy," his mother wept.

"Nell's more than a mother to him," Nora said. "More than a mother to him. But Ned here lets him run away with him. . . ."

"Ah, sssh," Ned warned her. "There's a damn sight worse than Willie in this family. If Christ on the cross could forgive a thief it's little less than you could do—all of you. He never tricked a man out of his house, did he? Nor he never drove a family into the street that couldn't pay him his rent, did he?"

"Ned McDermott, you well know Pete Carron came by all he has in an honest way. . . ."

"Ah, sssh . . ."

"And he sheltered the good sisters that was driven out of France, God bless him; built an orphanage for the poor children. . . ."

"Buying his way into heaven," Ned sneered at her. "Faugh. And who in the hell is Kelly to throw stones? With his card games in the back room and selling whisky on Sunday. Who the hell's he to throw stones?"

"I don't see what Pete Carron or John Kelly have got to do with it," Chris interposed. "My mother is at her wit's end with what to do about Willie. We've done everything we could for him. . . ."

"Everything we could and more too," Nell echoed.

"After all, Chris." Catherine Daly couldn't remain silent any longer. "Willie's only a little boy, Chris. I'm sure he's not a hardened criminal. There must be some way you could . . . well, there must be some way to help him break these bad habits of his. He seems like a nice boy. Chris told me," she turned to Ned, "that Willie was very smart in school."

"Bright's a dollar," Ned said, regarding her carefully and trying to determine whether she was neutral in this or whether she might possibly be on his side, the side of justice and mercy.

"Sister Esmerelda—she's at St. Anthony's and teaches a fifth grade class there—tells me that no matter how the sisters try, the children are terribly unhappy there when they first come, no matter if their own homes have been of the worst possible kind," Catherine said.

"You see, Miss Daly," Ned began cautiously, "I have great schemes for that boy. I have great schemes that would be a shame to spoil them now for a handful of cigarettes, wouldn't it? Wouldn't that be a shame? What'd happen to his education if they was to put him away in a home or an orphanage? I'm not saying a word against the good sisters now, but there's things they don't know about boys, you see. Things a boy needs they would never think about."

111

"Yes, it would be a shame, Mr. McDermott," Catherine said. "It would be a shame if he didn't have an education."

"The cigarettes is bad," Ned continued judiciously. "I think that's the worst part of the whole thing—smoking them damn cigarette. I've seen Skinny Byer—that's one of the young fellows in the shop that's just out of his time—why the man is crazy if he don't ahev a cigarette. Regular fiend. Cigarette fiend. It's the curse of the younger generation."

"It's too bad there aren't some nicer boys for Willie to play with," Catherine said.

"There's his cousin, Fred Kane," Nora snapped. "Why don't he play with Fred Kane? Sure, every time they're together Fred is running home with a bloody nose or a cut lip. Oh, there's a plenty of fine young boys in the neighborhood, but they won't play with Willie."

"Little you know," Ned answered. "That's the trouble with the world today, Miss Daly. People that has neither chick nor child is forever telling them that do how they should bring them up, you see. . . ."

"He fights with Pat's boys, that's Patrick and John," Nora was reveling in bedeviling the old man. She knew what he was trying to do, turn the talk away from Willie McDermott.

"Perhaps there's some work he could do after school to keep him off the streets and away from bad associates," Catherine suggested.

"Who'd hire a little thief?" Nell asked very sadly. "Who'd trust the boy now?"

"I'll do the working in this house," Ned said. "When the day comes I can't work then it'll be time to think of his working."

"It might be a good idea to let him quit school altogether and get a job somewhere. Probably he could get a job learning a trade, a machinist, there's always work for a good machinist," Chris was serious, conscious he was trampling his father's cherished hopes under foot.

"When you were his age there was no one thought of finding a trade for you to learn," Ned whipped at him. "You done what you wanted. You wanted to go to the Brothers' school to learn your bookkeeping, and you done it. Willie, Lord have mercy on him, wanted to go into the foundry after me, and Pat done what he pleased, though it's never amounted to much and he has no trade today. But you all done what you wanted and this one will, too, the same as the rest."

112

"Chris," Catherine Daly said, "if your father wants to educate Willie I think we ought to help him find some way of helping Willie to break his bad habits and keep on with school. I don't think we should keep insisting on things your father doesn't want to do. After all it's your own brother's boy, Chris; it's not a stranger you're talking about. . . ."

"Oh, poor Will," Nell sighed. "It would break his heart if ever he knew his own son was a thief."

"Well, he really isn't, Mrs. McDermott," Catherine said. "He made a terrible mistake, but I'm sure he's sorry now that he did it, and if we can only help him I don't think it will happen again."

"Faugh! Happen again? Of course it won't happen again," Ned assured her. "The boy promised me."

"If you only lived in St. Malachi's I know things might be lots different for Willie. Father McCaffrey is out there. He's a young priest and the boys all idolize him. He plays ball with them and he's in charge of the altar boys. Willie could be with boys like that. . . .".

"By God, you've struck it there," Ned cried. "Remove the occasions of sin! The good influence of the priest is what the boy needs. That's what he lacks. If we lived in St. Malachi's? Well, by God, we can move to St. Malachi's, can't we?"

"Move to St. Malachi's?" Christ McDermott protested. "Why—why we always lived in the cathedral. We . . ."

"Why, yes," Catherine said happily. "He'd go to a different school and he'd meet new boys. He'd probably never even see the boys he knows now."

"What the hell's to stop us from moving to South Providence?" Ned demanded.

But for Chris McDermott, reluctant fundamentally to inconvenience himself for the boy because he was always jealously aware of his father's affection for him, there was something to stop them. All his plans were centered within the indefinite confines of the cathedral parish where he had already become known as one of the most promising young men, where he had become president of the Catholic Club and was well on his way, having held several minor offices, to being elected grand knight of his council. Although St. Malachi's was a scant three miles away, he viewed the idea of moving there, now, with all the family, as though someone had suggested moving to Australia.

"No one in South Providence would know a thing about what

happened to him." Catherine was sailing brightly along in the idea she had launched.

"Not till after Nora went to mass once," Ned said.

" 'Twasn't me broke into Kelly's," Nora asserted quickly.

"I hate to think of moving in with strangers after living here so long," Nell said. "We've been a long time here. I don't like to think of moving."

"We'll move to South Providence," Ned announced finally. "Come Peg, we'll go for a walk."

The criminal sat alone with his sins in the bedroom, unable to hear what they were saying although he knew they must be talking about what they were going to do with him. Every day after school he had to stay in the house and when he had eaten his supper he was banished to the little room. When people came to the house the door was shut; only when they shouted at each other could he hear what was being said, and even then not much of it. When he thought of his grandfather he was unhappy because he had caused the old man so much pain, but when he thought of his uncle a mutinous fury boiled in him and he plotted even greater crimes. He would watch his uncle dressing at the mirror under the flickering gaslight, hating him. He would stare at him sleeping in the morning, his mouth open and his white teeth grinding endlessly as he breathed. The boy, sitting on the edge of his own narrow bed to dress himself, quietly so that he would not disturb his uncle, would measure the man's length there beneath the swells of the covers and estimate the strength of the arms. When his uncle went out for the evening, the light was put out and he was told to say the rosary on the black beads with the silver crucifix that had been his father's. Sometimes he would say them sitting at the window and sometimes he would get into the bed before he began them. No one spoke to him in the long evenings, but before he went to his own bed every night his grandfather would come into the room and stand there looking at him, patting him on the head before he left. These nights the old man did not speak to him nor did he speak to him in the morning when they were up before any others, but sometimes he would clap him on the back with his hand when his grandmother wasn't in the room, reassuring the boy that salvation was near.

Ned's warning to her notwithstanding, Nora could not resist the temptation of telling everyone who came to the house about Willie McDermott's being arrested for the robbery at Kelly's drugstore as she called it. Nothing worse had happened in the family since Pat's Eddie, Ned's nephew, got the girl in trouble, some Protestant girl, and ran away to the Army the day after he had married her. She was the first to tell Ned's Pat one night, when, as he often did, he dropped in the house after supper on his way home from the brewery. His mother, always happy when he came, even if it were to borrow money, ran to the pantry to get him something to eat and make him a cup of tea. Ned was at Deignan's when Pat arrived.

The way Pat took it disappointed Nora. He was neither startled nor angry. She went on to describe the visit of Larry McDermott and to tell how good he was to get them out of trouble.

"It wouldn't look very good, would it," Pat said, "for him to be arresting one of his own family? Did he cuff the kid around? He's fond of that, I hear."

His mother said Larry McDermott had certainly gone out of his way to be nice to them in their trouble, and she didn't like to hear Pat making remarks about his father's cousin.

"He's no worse than any other kid, I guess," Pat said. "Why the hell don't you get him out of this goddam neighborhood?"

"Pat, don't swear and curse so," his mother urged. "The neighborhood was good enough for you and Chris and Will, and I should think it would be good enough for him."

Ned came in from Deignan's and sat on the couch to take his shoes off, asking Pat how his boys were and how Mollie was. He said he might drop out to see them all on Sunday because they were thinking of moving to South Providence.

"Damn good idea," Pat said. He told his father the house across the street from him, the corner house at the end of the street on Melrose Avenue, was for rent. The second-floor tenement that Tom Slattery used to live in was empty.

"D'you see, Nell?" Ned cried elatedly. "D'you see how nice that'd be, now? No strangers at all. You'd be right next door to Mollie and Tessie Butler and all, and you'd see Pat and his boys any time you wanted. Why the hell didn't you say something about it before this, Pat?"

"I wonder how them boys would get along together." Nora looked troubled.

"Sssh! Do you wonder, too, how the Irish saints gets along in heaven itself with the French saints, if there is any. Are you worried about that, Nora?" Ned asked in derision.

"There's an English family downstairs," Pat began.

"Oh," said Ned, his enthusiasm wilting.

Pat added that they were English Catholics. Mr. Reed, the old Yankee that had the henyard in back of his house, owned the place, and if they wanted him to he'd speak to the old man and have him hold the place open until they had a look at it, anyway.

"Do that," Ned ordered him. "English or no English we'll have a look at it. Tell him your mother will be out to look at it."

"Sure," said Pat. "I hear you had a visitor since I was here last."

"Who's that?" Ned knew, but thought if Pat hadn't heard about Willie's trouble he wouldn't mention it.

"Your cousin Larry."

"Nora, your tongue is that goddam big it's a wonder you don't choke from it," said Ned bitterly. "Yes, he was here. Why?"

"Did he beat the kid?"

"He deserved it," said Nell.

"Larry McDermott," Pat mumbled. "He's the only cop in the family, ain't he?"

"I think so," Ned admitted. "Tell the old Yankee your mother will be out there someday soon to look at the house. Is it much rent? I suppose not or Tom Slattery wouldn't have been living there all these years and raising the large family he has."

"How is Chris these days?" Pat asked casually. "I hear he's running around with Joe Daly's daughter."

Nora's cue again. She told Pat it was serious between Chris and Catherine Daly and that they were going to be married soon. Where she had gathered the details no one knew, but she was able to tell Pat, after she finished describing what a beauty Catherine Daly was and how smart she was, just about how much money Joe Daly was worth and what the Daly's house had cost them.

Slipping his suspenders down from his worn shoulders, Ned started for his bedroom, pausing in the doorway to caution Pat not to say anything about Willie's trouble to anyone in South Providence, especially the boys, because he wanted the boy to start off there in the new house with a clean slate and nothing held against him.

Chapter Seventeen

NOTHING had ever been so welcome to Willie McDermott as this great upheaval in their lives, moving to South Providence. His grandmother went to see the house where Tom Slattery had lived, and pronounced it satisfactory in all ways. Even the Englishwoman downstairs, she said, was a nice old lady that seemed to be one that would mind her own affairs. Nora who had tagged along with her sister to inspect the tenement, gave Ned the additional information that they were a Catholic family, all right, because one of the woman's sons, the oldest one she thought, was the superintendent of St. Anthony's Orphanage and lived in the little brown cottage just across the street on the orphanage grounds.

Luke Eagan provided the barrels and boxes for them to pack the few sticks and rags they had been a lifetime collecting. The pictures were taken down from the walls, leaving rectangles on the wallpaper. Mick's Civil War books were stowed in a crate; and the huge chamber pot with the oak leaf and acorn design in blue bloomed with the crooked stems of old umbrellas, curtain rods which sprouted onionlike corrugated bulbs at their ends, and several odd green and white roller curtains, whose tassels drooped over the sides of the pot. Trunks were loaded with clothing, faded pictures, blankets, comforters wrapped around the best set of dishes, and the lace curtains from the parlor, as gritty to the touch as a handful of cinders. For three whole days they were packing and piling the results in the parlor. Peg was bouncing from one room to another, sniffing at everything that she could. Chairs whose cane seats sagged from years and were torn away from their frames were brought down from the attic. Willie McDermott worked frantically with his grandmother and Nora. He labored like a paroled convict hoping for an eventual pardon, and the old women, forgetting his crimes in the great and general excitement, were more pleasant to him than they had been for many months. Meals were hastily scraped together and they all ate in the kitchen, counting the hours before the great step would be taken, wondering what the new house would be like, discussing what a phenomenon it was to encounter English Catholics. There was no impatience; they were all so happy to break the deadly routine and the tiresome schedule of their lives that they would have been glad to go on living just as they were for weeks more, although Nell said it was no more than camping out like a band of gypsies.

Monday the moving man was to be there first thing in the morning.

The day before they moved, the pace of the activities rose to new and even more frantic speed. Willie McDermott bounded from the attic to the cellar and up again, with Peg scooting in front of him, dodging between his legs, barking, whining when he closed the door on her, and pouncing wickedly on old rags when she found them on the floors of the rooms. Toward noon, winded, she stretched her length out on the wide steps at the foot of the back stairs and was contentedly dozing there when Helen Tracy went out to hang some things on the line in the back yard. When Helen returned, she sat down beside Peg, pulled her into her arms, and stroked her ears. The dog submitted petulantly to her caresses, twitching nervously when Helen's breath swept warmly into her ears. From the attic came the sound of Willie McDermott's voice, calling the dog. Peg tried to squirm herself free, but the girl clung to her tightly.

"No, Peggy, no," she said, circling the dog's shoulders with her arms. "No, Peggy, stay here with me."

Willie McDermott called again from the attic and the dog twisted her head in a frenzy and began to growl a warning as she tried to spurt ahead through the circle of the girl's arms. Helen held on with all her strength. Once more the boy called and the captive, lurching through her bonds, leaped down on the floor and spun sharply around, tensing her muscles to spring up the stairs. She growled threateningly, but Helen, reaching quickly down, snatched the dog's collar in her hand and held her. Peg panted hoarsely, pulling with spasms of all her strength, but the grip was too much for her.

"She's all right, Willie," Helen called up the stairs. "Peggy's here with me."

"Let her go," Willie shouted. "Here, Peg!"

Yelping, baring her teeth as she snarled, the dog wrenched herself suddenly to one side and snapped at the hand that held her, the teeth cutting deeply into the soft flesh of Helen's hand. Helen screamed and the dog sprang up the stairs to the attic, prostrating herself on the floor in front of the boy.

"My God, what's that?" Nell cried running into the hallway.

Helen ran wailing into her own house, terrified when she felt the warm blood drip from the throbbing wound. Mrs. Tracy began to scream, too, louder than her daughter when she saw the bite. She gathered the girl into her arms and rushed her to the kitchen sink where she thrust the injured hand under the cold water faucet. Nell ran downstairs to find out what had happened and Nora stood at the top, calling to her sister to tell her what had happened. Willie McDermott, ever cautious now, and suspecting that Peg had something to do with this tempest, put his finger to his lips to warn the dog to be quiet and went to the head of the attic stairs to hear, if he could, what the trouble was.

"Peggy bit me, Peggy bit me," Helen Tracy was crying.

He could hear calls about a doctor, a doctor, for God's sake get a doctor quick. His grandmother's voice, Nora's voice, Mrs. Tracy's and above them all Helen's cries of pain. He tiptoed back into the room where the dog was and sat down on the floor beside her. The panting little animal blinked her eyes at him as he trembled his hand over her head. Then he heard his grandmother's voice again, calling him, and he shut the dog in the room before he started down the stairs. Peg, now completely bewildered, whined piteously and flung herself against the door, scratching at it feverishly.

His grandmother sent Willie for old Dr. Hall, the Protestant doctor on the corner who hardly practiced at all these days. By the time the boy reached the street he could hear them saying Ned McDermott's dog went mad and others saying something about shooting the dog. He ran down the street to the doctor's office, hoping that Peg wouldn't make too much noise in the attic while he was gone. It palsied his hopes, though, when he remembered that they always shot mad dogs. He reasoned to himself that Peg wasn't mad; but she had bitten Helen Tracy and it would be enough for them to want her shot. If he could only keep Peg hidden in the attic until his grandfather got home at night he thought he might save her from their wrath.

When he reached the house again they were saying Ned's dog was on the rampage and bit everyone in the house. Mrs. Riordan, Rose and Margaret were in the hallway with his grandmother and

Nora. They were restless, crying, and Helen Tracy's moans could be heard from the kitchen. He could hear Peg, too, crying in the attic. Telling his grandmother the doctor would be right over, he ran up to the dog, quieting her and reassuring her that she wouldn't be shot, no matter what happened. He wouldn't let them shoot her, he told her; he'd hide her until his grandfather got home and he wouldn't let them shoot her either. He wished, though, that his grandfather would get there quickly.

The shadow of death itself, it seemed from Nora, hung over Helen Tracy. That mad beast, his grandmother said, must be kept in the attic until they came to take her away and shoot her. The boy pleaded with her, trying to convince her that the dog was not mad, she hadn't meant to bite Helen at all, Helen must have been teasing her. His grandmother was adamant; the man from the dog-catcher's would be there any minute to take her away. They could get a policeman to come in the yard and shoot her, but the dog-catcher would take her away. She said to keep Peg locked up in the attic until the man came. Then she went downstairs again with Nora to see if there wasn't something they could do for Mrs. Tracy.

Willie wondered if he could get Gyp McGlinn to hide Peg in the blacksmith shop until his grandfather got home, but he was afraid that someone would see him sneaking her over there. When they all went downstairs, he went to the attic and opened the door for Peg. She was overjoyed, and he brought her down to the kitchen and slipped her out the front way. They slipped through the break in the fence of the house next door and went into Tanner's yard. He took her to the corner where Joseph Riordan and he hid out sometimes and told her to stay there, but when he started back to the house the dog followed him. He took her back twice, begging her each time to stay where she was until he came back for her. The third time he beat her, holding her by the collar and slapping her on the snout. That time Peg stayed and he went around to the other side of the house to find the dogcatcher's wagon standing at the gate.

"Where is that dog?" his grandmother asked when he went into the kitchen. The dogcatcher, stolid and seemingly disinterested in the proceedings, was standing beside the stove, a pair of canvas gloves on his big hands.

Willie said she must be in the attic where he had left her. The dogcatcher said he'd been up there but there wasn't any mad dog there. Willie said she must have got out of the room where he had put her. His grandmother knew he was lying; she told him to get the dog. Willie said that if she wasn't upstairs he didn't know where she could be. Nell hit him in the face with the back of her hand, her heavy wedding band raising a little lump on his forehead. She warned him that his grandfather would punish him when he came home if the dog was not produced at once.

"You better get that dog, kid," the dogcatcher said, "before she bites somebody else."

"I don't know where she's gone," Willie lied again.

"You've brought enough trouble to this house," his grandmother declared. "Remember, now."

He defied them, certain his grandfather, when he came home, would protect him. The dogcatcher said he couldn't wait there all day and asked Willie if he knew he was breaking the law by hiding the dog. Would he have to go and get a policeman to help him get the dog, he asked the boy.

Willie didn't care. Nora was calling the dog out the window. Let her call. Peg would never come to her, anyway, Willie knew. Let her call. It seemed forever, with every moment of it a new torture as they threatened and cajoled him. In the midst of it they heard Peg's joyful bark at the back door.

"There," his grandmother said. "Go let her in."

"That's all right, lady, I'll go get her myself," the dogcatcher said, stepping into the hallway.

Willie followed him.

"She'll bite you," he cried. "She'll rip your legs! Peg! Go 'way!"

Too late. The dogcatcher opened the door and Peg leaped inside.

"C'mere, pup," the dogcatcher said, gathering the dog into his arms. He clamped his gloved hand over her black snout, stifling her cries, and marched out to the wagon with her.

Willie ran after him, kicking at his ankles and tearing at his arms as he went through the gate and opened the mesh door in the rear of his wagon. The man hurled Peg into the wagon and slammed the door shut. Pushing Willie away from him he took a padlock from his pocket and snapped it on the hasp of the door. Peg stood on her hind legs, barking.

"You son of a bitch," Willie screamed, kicking the man again as he went to the front of the wagon. "You black Protestant. Let that dog out!"

"God damn you!" The dogcatcher slapped Willie in the face and knocked him against Tanner's high board fence; then he stepped onto the wagon and flipped the reins on the horse's back.

Willie ran after it, clinging to the mesh, as long as he could run.

In the confusion of the moving, Ned McDermott didn't notice Peg's absence when he first came home. When they sat down to supper, though, and she wasn't there, he asked Nell where the dog was. He looked from Willie's surly, sullen face to his wife's flaming red cheeks. Nora got up from the table and went to the pantry, coughing.

"I said where the hell is the dog?"

Nell's words tripped and stumbled over each other as she started to tell him about the dog foaming at the mouth and rushing around the house biting everyone in sight of her. She had to send her away with the dogcatcher, she said.

"She's dead," Willie said. "Peg's dead and you know it."

"Dead?" His grandfather was stunned.

"I had to have her shot after she bit Helen Tracy," Nell defended herself, glaring at the boy as though he had been the agent of the trouble.

"Shot? Helen Tracy? What in the hell is this?"

"She bit Helen this morning and I had her taken off to be shot," said Nell, her courage rising now that he had been told.

"You had her shot?" he roared. "God damn you! You had her shot?"

"The dog was mad," said Nell with finality.

"Mad? How the hell d'you know Helen Tracy wasn't mad?" Ned cried. "Why the hell didn't you have Helen Tracy shot? God damn Helen Tracy and—God damn you!"

"I think it's probably a good thing," Chris McDermott said quietly. "The dog was a nuisance."

"Who in the hell asked you what you thought?" his father rasped.

His knife and fork clattered down on the plate and he left the table, bumping into a barrel of dishes as he reached for his hat.

"You have a heart like a clod," he said bitterly to his wife as he went out.

Once the dishes were cleared away and washed, dried, and packed into a barrel, Nell sat in a rocker to say a rosary. The last one she would ever say in this house, she thought wearily, skimming tiredly in her mind over the joys and sorrows that had been theirs while they were living there. She sent the boy to bed after his uncle went out—to visit the Dalys in South Providence, he said. Nora slipped away to her room and Nell sat a long time asking God's blessing on the new house with every Our Father and the intercession of the Blessed Virgin with each Hail Mary. Ned was staying out a long time, she noticed, going to her bed. She lay in the darkness waiting for him, and soon she heard him at the front door. She heard him go to the kitchen and draw a glass of water; then he came into the bedroom and quietly undressed. He sat down in the rocker, smoking a last few puffs of his pipe. Nell could see the red coal glowing under his nose.

"Ned," she said, "I'm sorry about the dog—I'll miss her."

"Yes," he said. "She was a darling."

"Ned."

"Yes," he answered. "What is it?"

"My heart's not a clod. I'll miss the dog, Ned."

"She was a darling," he said unforgiving.

The fiery coal of the pipe swung out at her and back again as he rocked. The rocker quieted down soon and she heard him scraping the ashes from the bowl with his knife. The back of the rocker hit once dully against the wall when he got up and sat on the edge of the bed.

"Ah, well," his voice was low and she could hardly hear what he was saying. "Ah, there's no great undertaking ever was done without suffering and sacrifice. Poor Peg. Go to sleep, now, Nell, and rest yourself. You have a hard day before you tomorrow."

Chapter Eighteen

THE elms, swaying their lower branches perilously close above the trolley wire that was strung along on the west side of Melrose Avenue marked off a verdant little Vatican from the secular city across the street. The heavy trunks, so thick a man could not circle them with his arms, were that close to one another, beginning at the corner of Cambridge Street, that the branches overhead were mingled like vines. St. Malachi's rectory was at the corner of Cambridge Street and next to it on the south side was the "old church," a low brick building with a spread of granite steps that were worn away enough in the center for rain to gather in the depressions and stay for days during the springtime. Set farther back from the street than the church was St. Anthony's Orphanage, a building so heavy it seemed to be crushing the green bosom of lawn that rolled out in front of it and extended all the way to the high board fence separating the orphanage itself from the caretaker's cottage. The last elm was at the corner of Colfax Street where there was another cottage, smaller than the caretaker's. There old Mrs. Daly, whose husband had been caretaker of the asylum grounds and garden years ago, was dreaming out the days of her widowhood with only a small black and white fox terrier to keep her company.

Dwarfed by the elms, a row of telegraph poles and lampposts grew across the street. Opposite the rectory was the three-story barracks of a house where Quinn had his undertaker's establishment. From there to the corner of Sayles Street, where the mansard roof of old man Reed's house reached clumsily up above them, stretched a row of haggard frame houses, all painted different colors but each looking just like the next one. There were picket fences in front of the houses, some with gates that sagged and limped and some with gates lying on the ground. The houses themselves were set back from the sidewalk and in front of them, between the bay windows and the picket fences, were wastes of dirt where mangy patches of colorless grass grew, or slopes of sun-baked and frost-cracked blue-gray concrete. Only Mr. Simmons' house, a catechism-cover gray next to old man Reed's, had a gate that opened and closed on its hinges and a latch that worked. Mr. Simmons never allowed families with children to live in his house and there was no grass in his yard, a gray plain of concrete, empty and barren except for four clothes poles that bloomed briefly on Monday.

The moving van rolled ponderously off Melrose Avenue into the lane of rutted sand that separated old man Reed's house from the one in which Pat McDermott and his family lived with Tessie Butler. A battalion of children soon gathered. Patrick and John McDermott, because it was their grandmother moving in, were the important members of it. The movers had hardly begun to carry the furniture into the house when a clanging streetcar pulled up at the corner and their grandmother, Aunt Nora and Willie McDermott got off. Willie sized up the kids as he went into the house.

His grandmother carried a bottle of holy water, and the first thing she did was to sprinkle every room with it, going even up into the attic where Willie, to his great joy, was to have a room to himself. From the window between the sweep of the elms he could see the orphanage, the slate roof of St. Malachi's "old church," the caretakers' cottages, and beyond them the billboards on the corner with a picture of a policeman pointing to a bottle of whisky. The policeman, except that the wings of his mustache were white instead of red, looked like Larry McDermott. From the window on the side of the house he could see the carbarn, its gaping wide doors swallowing the ends of countless trolley lines.

The walls of the room careened in with the pitch of the mansard, and their rough plaster was cracked on the side where the white enameled bed was put. Trunks which might never be opened again were stowed in the room; and a tiny commode that had a painting of a lake scene on its doors, a relic that had never been used in the other house, was set against the wall opposite the bed. There was no going out, his grandmother told Willie McDermott, until the work was done.

The boy hadn't asked her about it, but it was clear to him that the confinement of the other house was ending. He spent the whole day pushing chairs and tables around the rooms, fitting the stovepipe together and unpacking the sugar barrels of dishes for Nora to put away in the pantry. There was a bathroom at one end of the kitchen; the tub was freshly painted white, its galvanized belly modestly skirted with cherry-colored tongue and groove boards. It was every bit as elegant as the Kanes had in their house.

During the afternoon his grandmother called a halt in the work when Pat's wife, Agnes Sheridan, one of their neighbors, and Catherine Daly sat down with her to have a cup of tea. She said Willie could go out with his cousin if he wanted to, but to stay near the house for fear she'd want him to run an errand or something.

"I know you'll like it here," Catherine Daly said. "It's so much better than the other side of the city. Our house is just down at the end of the lane. You can see the back fence from your kitchen windows, I think. Chris could just jump over the back fence to come home if he wanted to—but I know Chris wouldn't do it."

"God, no," said Nora, "not Chris."

Red-haired Frannie O'Toole was in the back yard with Willie's cousins when Willie climbed the high board fence on the lane and looked down at them. Frannie's eyes were grape-green and on his forehead ran the pink scar of ringworm. One of his front teeth was broken off. They guided Willie over the fences into the barnyard of Dyer's store, leaped the manure pit in front of it, and went out on Ash Street. Standing under the billboard on Melrose Avenue, they threw rocks at the picture of the policeman pointing to the bottle of whisky. Willie liked this and his aim was very good. While they were hurling the rocks they noticed a bony length of a man pedaling slowly toward them on a bicycle, a saw wrapped in blue striped overalls lashed to its handle bars. Patrick said it was Spider and they ran in behind the billboards. Willie didn't know why they ran, but he did, too. When the man came abreast of them the boys began to shout "Spider" at him. The man dragged his big foot on the ground to stop the bicycle at the corner of Melrose Avenue and turned to them. He spat on the ground angrily before he pumped away.

"He hates to be called Spider," Patrick said. "He'll give you a chase sometimes."

"Why do you call him Spider?" Willie asked.

"He looks like one," Frannie O'Toole said.

"He looks like a spider crawling over the roof of a new house. He's a carpenter," Patrick added.

Facing the billboards on Melrose Avenue was a row of store fronts; Mike Tally the bald-headed barber on the corner, Tony Testa, the cobbler next to him, then Mr. Shapiro the tailor, whose kids were very tough and used to bring him his lunch and suppers up from Jewtown, and last with double doors, Fontaine's grocery and market.

At home, his grandfather asked him if he liked living in South Providence and how he liked having a room all to himself. When he went up to it, carrying the sheets and covers for his bed, Willie McDermott saw old man Reed for the first time, a thin old man, bent over like his grandfather, with a round, white, neatly trimmed beard. The old man was silhouetted against the lamplight that shone from the half-opened door at the head of the stairs.

"You're the McDermott boy, I suppose," he said in a high quaking voice. "Are you a nice quiet boy? Or are you one of the noisy skittish boys? My Mattie can't have no noise up here. No noise up here, my Mattie don't like it. Makes her terrible nervous."

Willie didn't know which question to answer first.

"No noise in the night, no noise in the day."

"He talks like old man Tanner or old man Edwards," Willie thought.

"Remember, now," the old man cautioned him, and closed the door.

Willie went softly down the hallway to his room and quietly shut the door. He lit the stub of a candle his grandmother had given him and set it on the commode. He made the bed as neatly as he could, because he knew his grandmother or his grandfather certainly would come up to inspect it before they went to bed. He knelt beside the bed to say his prayers and then stood looking out the window, listening to the monody of the elms and the bass rumbling of the streetcars below. Kneeling on the bed, he looked out the other window at the yellow lamps shining out from the front of the cars in the carbarn. He was sleepy and crept under the covers, happy for the first time in many weeks. This was so far from Larry McDermott, so far from Kelly's and Joseph Riordan that it seemed that he had never even lived in the other house, that he had never been punished for stealing or swearing or lying to his grandmother and Nora. Suddenly the thought of Peg assailed him. Poor Peg. He longed to reach his hand out along the side of the bed, as he had in the other house when the lights were out and everyone was asleep, and feel her wet nose, scratch her warm head. No more Peg. Willie thought he heard someone singing very low and softly. He could not blot from his mind the old Jew man;

that was who old man Reed looked like, the old Jew man they whacked on Ocean Avenue. The song he thought he could hear was swallowed in the rumbling of the streetcar as he fell asleep wondering who old man Reed's Mattie was.

Chapter Nineteen

THEIR first Sunday breakfast in the new house began happily, with the sun so bright it streamed through the kitchen doorway and bathed the somber carpet of the dining room in a light that brought out deep red flowers that hadn't been seen for a long time in the other house. Willie McDermott stepped out of the bathtub with tiny flecks of the newly dried paint sticking to him where he had sat on it, but very proud to be in a house at last that had its own tub. His grandmother was at the stove frying dough and his grandfather was polishing his shoes, having decided that in the new parish he might as well wait for the late mass instead of dragging himself out of bed at the crack of dawn as he had done so many years. The children's mass was at half past eight and his grandmother said Willie wasn't too big to go to that for a while.

At the table even his uncle, still sleepy-eyed and in his bathrobe, was pleasant. Nora was humming: *Brian O'Linn had no coat to put on so he went and he got an old potato sack* as she spun in and out of the kitchen with the "doughboys," the tea and the fat round little sausages, so full and heavy the succulent meat was bursting out of the skins at the ends.

His grandfather, ruby cheeks glistening, silver mustache clipped the night before at the barber's and hair cropped close, sat in a collarless white shirt open at the neck with a shiny brass collar button waiting only for him to bend a clean white collar to it. But that would be after breakfast. God, you don't want a man to choke himself to death, do you, before he has even a cup of tea in the morning?

They were startled when the front doorbell jangled; it was the first time it had rung since they had moved into the house. They were all pleased but not a little worried, for who could be ringing the bell at this time of a Sunday morning when they had hardly moved into the house? So occupied with their own speculations were they that no one thought of going downstairs to see who was there or even looking out the bay window in the parlor. At last Nell said, irritably:

"Willie, run down and answer the bell. Don't sit there as if you were cast in the chair! See who it is now!"

"By God," said Chris, "if that's a tramp moulder. . . ."

"Sure how would a tramp moulder find me way out here?" his father said.

But it was.

Willie opened the big door to look into the bearded dirty face of a green-eyed man wearing a cap over his black hair; a tall man with a very dirty shirt under his loose jacket. The thick lips parted, revealing large tobaccoy teeth.

"Hello, young fellow," the man said. "Is your daddy home?"

"Who do you want?" Willie asked.

"Your daddy. He's home, ain't he? Ain't this where Ned McDermott lives?"

"Yes," Willie said. "This is where he lives. What do you want?"

"Why I want to see him, kiddo," the man said. "I have to tell him something from his brother Joe. I come all the way from Brooklyn, kiddo."

There was only one thing to do about it, so Willie closed the door after the man and led him upstairs. The man flashed ahead of him as soon as they were in the room and clapped Ned on the back.

"You don't have to tell me you're Joe's brother, Ned. I can see it written all over you; you look just alike. I been working with Joe in Brooklyn, Ned, and he told me if ever I was in Providence to drop in and see his brother Ned," the man's talk flowed like the froth running off a newly tapped keg.

"Hello, mother," he said affably as Nora came into the room.

It made even Chris laugh, but only for a moment. He had thought they would escape these Sunday morning visits when they moved from the old house, and he was determined if at all possible, to put an end to this sponging on his father.

"Now then, what's your name?" Ned began. . . .

"Hourihan," the tramp moulder said. "Ha, Joe, I mean Ned, they call me Necktie Hourihan. Ha, no matter how bad the battle goes Hourihan is always on deck with the necktie."

"Well, Hourihan, then," Ned said, "you'll have something to eat."

Scowling, Nora had already set a place for him at the table and was heaping the plate with the fried dough cakes and bacon and pouring a cup of tea.

"Now," Hourihan said, "I been real sick, Ned. Real sick. Don't know I can eat a thing. . . ."

"Put that into you," Ned said, "And talk afterwards. How is Joe?"

Nell scrutinized this strange creature, strange, but still the same man, in a way, that had been coming to the house for years. She wondered why Ned was always so good to them; if he himself—and she knew he was as good a moulder as there was around—had ever thought he might like to light out the way they did, striking town of a Sunday morning and finding it made no difference what town it was, some moulder like Ned would give them a breakfast, probably a couple dollars and the tools to strike in the shop in the morning. He that came home every night of his life and saw to it that there was a full table—she wondered if he ever wanted to travel around that way. She knew that he gave them money for she had seen him do it more than once, and he had told her that he had never yet found one that didn't give it back to him later or send it to him if he moved along.

The tramp moulders always interested Willie McDermott. He had been meeting them at breakfast as long as he could remember anything. He had seen them coming to the house at night—not too late at night for they wouldn't get in if they did—or coming even on a Saturday or a Sunday afternoon. There was something alike about all of them and something different about every one of them. This one was different from any of the others. He was no dirtier than many of them, but he talked more than most of them.

"Joe is fine and dandy," the tramp said. "Fine and dandy, Ned, and his boy Joe is serving his time in the foundry with him now. I suppose this young fellow is serving his time with you, too."

"No," Ned said. "He's not and won't."

"Well he's certainly a fine husky-looking kid and'll make a fine moulder someday when he starts to serve his time. Fine husky-looking kid, Ned."

"Yes," Ned said. "Hourihan, eat your breakfast now and go in there and shave yourself so you go to mass looking like a decent man. . . ."

"Went to early mass this morning, Ned," the tramp said. "I had a hell of, beg your pardon, mother, I had a hard time finding you, Ned. I went to the wrong address and the people there told me you moved. I found it though, because I promised Joe I'd drop in and see Ned if I ever hit Providence."

Chris, clapping the teacup into his saucer, stalked to the bathroom before the tramp moulder should get in there. He didn't like having his razor used by them anyhow, and he was determined to use it before this one did.

The man's green eyes whittled away at Willie McDermott. Eating or talking or drinking his tea with the spoon sprouting from the side of the cup as he held it, the man seemed to be directing all his words to the boy. Willie was perplexed by the man and his eyes. He was glad when, looking at the clock, he saw that he had just about time to race down the street and get to St. Malachi's in time for the half past eight mass.

It was stranger to him to be going to mass alone, without his grandfather, he thought when he got to the church, than it was to be going here to St. Malachi's instead of the cathedral. Mass was held in the basement of the church, the chapel, since the "upstairs" of St. Malachi's was not yet finished. The low ceiling and the low altar were foreign to him after the high vaulted ceilings of the cathedral, but he saw his cousins, Patrick and John, serving mass and the sight dispelled his worries about it. The boys—he was as big as almost any one of them he saw—were on St. Joseph's side of the chapel and the girls to their left, on the side of the Blessed Virgin's altar. Willie lingered on the corner, hoping that his cousins might come along after mass, but he didn't see them until later in the day when they asked him if he wanted to go to the park with them. His grandmother said that he might, and with a dime each from his grandfather they started.

Chapter Twenty

ST. MALACHI'S was not a new parish and it had never been a
large or rich one. Consequently, although it had been the
fondest dream of Father Walsh, when he was pastor there, to have
a parochial school built on the lot at Cambridge Street and Melrose
Avenue, there had never been money enough to put up the building. Ned wanted Willie to go to a parochial school—"God knows
we struggled hard and long enough to build them"—but it was too
far for him to go to the cathedral grammar. Cambridge grammar
would have to do him, then, the same as it did many another.

The way there was a long one for Willie, not because of the
distance but because there were so many new things for him to
see. The first day he started out with his cousins, but they left him
staring into the windows of a jewelry shop. Huge stamp presses
ceaselessly punched out piles and piles of shiny brass coins the size
of a quarter, and at the windows on the corner of Cambridge,
hunched-over little men, gas lights flaring beside their ears, worked
at the benches and squinted at tiny objects like his grandmother
did when she was threading a needle. Little heaps of bright stones
that looked like diamonds and emeralds and rubies flashed on the
benches. In the adjoining building was the printing shop where
the giant arm reached up to pluck the papers from the press and
the perfume of the inks filled his nose. At the corner of Burnside
was Engine 10; and the big dappled Belgians, muscles of bunched
power rounding out under their sleek clean coats were being curry-
combed in the yard. Willie was watching the firemen groom them
when he heard someone call him. From the splintered crate of the
gray house across the street he saw two boys running, a tall skinny
one who looked as though his arms and legs would fly away from
him if he weren't held together by his clothes, and a shorter,
husky one with a chubby smile. They yelled that he would be
late for school unless he hurried up. They were late already, they
shouted happily. They were Johnny and Billie O'Connel, he learned
later from his cousins.

Reuben Crandall, the principal of Cambridge grammar school,

wore immaculate batwing collars, and when he listened to someone talking to him dropped his chin into the space between the wings and pouted his thick lips under the sweeping gray mustache he wore. Though he was bald, the bushes of his eyebrows were full and the eyes themselves seemed always gasping behind his thick glasses. He was so nearsighted he wore a second pair, which he clamped over the first ones with a great swing of his arm, when he read. He always appeared perplexed and about to solve some unfathomable question or expound some new and miraculous truth. A massive Masonic emblem hung majestically from the cable of gold chain that rode over his swollen belly. The click of the second pair of glasses when he clamped them on was terrifying. Willie was surprised that his voice was so soft and high.

Willie followed him to Miss Grant's room where they were just finishing the recital of the 23rd Psalm. Emma Grant was a sturdy little woman with tawny hair piled high on her head and large teeth that seemed to be constantly nibbling at something. Her face was square and her eyes were blue. While she spoke she fingered a dainty jabot which was lacy and scented.

She gave Willie a seat in back of his cousin Patrick and in front of a Swedish boy with a harsh bronchial voice. Frannie O'Toole sat on one side of him and on the other was a slender eager Negro girl whose black hair showered down in waves on her shoulders. Her eyes, wide and dark, seemed to be holding things no one else could see, and her hands, held out in front of her on the desk, were constantly moving, the long fingers playing lightly over the thumbs as though they were trying to touch something or hold something they couldn't reach. The names of many of the girls seemed strange to Willie: Aratheusa, Leonore, Sigrid, Hermine. The Negro girl's name was Celia. The boy's names sounded odd, too: Bertil, Millard, Clarence, Horace, Ernest, Curtis. Willie had never been in a room with so many Protestants in his life. It was strange to him to look up to the teacher's desk and see Miss Grant's soft hair and lacy jabot instead of the somber habit of the nuns.

During the morning, he noticed, whenever Miss Grant asked a question, Celia would start to get up from her seat as though only she had heard it, as though only she could answer it. Neither his cousin Patrick nor Frannie O'Toole, Willie saw, volunteered to answer any questions Miss Grant didn't ask them directly.

Willie was happy Miss Grant didn't ask him any questions about the rivers of New England or where they rose and emptied, or anything about Rhode Island's representatives in the Continental Congress, although he knew the answers.

At recess he clung to the scaly brown high board fence rather than dive into the stream of rushing boys. A boy, shorter than he was, with jigging eyes and a polished snubby nose, and a slight, hesitant pout which pushed his mouth in and out when he spoke, asked him if Patrick McDermott was his cousin or something. Yes, Willie answered, Patrick was. The boy asked in a kind of a detached way, as though he were going to leave before he heard the answer, how Willie liked Miss Grant. Then he came nearer and took a picture from his pocket which he handed to Willie, saying that the one on the right was his brother. The picture showed two young men in straw hats, wide striped coats and white trousers. Under the picture it said Murray and Mort. Willie looked and handed the picture back to the boy without commenting.

"*Morris*, my *brother* Morris," the boy said, as if he were taking Willie to task for not having known it himself all the time. "Keith circuit. Moish makes up the songs and Morty does the dancing, soft shoe. They travel all over the country, New York, Detroit, Cleveland, everywhere. My father don't like it after spending so much money on Moish's violin lessons. He says it's a waste and he don't care how much Moish makes a week, it's a waste. So now I have to."

"Have to what?" Willie inquired, trying to seem not much interested.

"Take violin," the boy said, again appearing impatient that Willie didn't know. "Do you take anything, piano or violin or anything?"

The boy said his name was Sam Weinberg. He said it was a wonder Willie hadn't seen him in Miss Grant's room in the front seat in the last row. Miss Grant was all right, he said, but gave lots of homework and he had to practice violin an hour and a half every night. Willie was very lucky he didn't have to take violin and practice an hour and a half every night with his father sitting in the kitchen and no way of telling the time until his father said it was enough practicing.

Patrick hardly spoke to him all day and Willie was somehow glad of that, too. Nothing was new or different about it, he decided at the end of the day when he stopped to look in at the jewelers' again, except the faces and the names of the boys and girls, nothing but the fact that they didn't have to recite Christian doctrine, as he had had to in parochial school. He took as long as he could getting home, because when he was in the house alone with his grandmother and Nora they were like the sparrows in the blacksmith's yard, ready to spin down and peck at him. Once his grandfather was home from the foundry, it was different; they let him alone. There was no Peg to run in the street with, no Joseph or Eddie Riordan to talk with, no foundry where he could watch the moulders pouring off. There were only the pinch-backed little men bending over their narrow benches with tiny tweezers in their hands. The fire horses were too far from the house, and besides they were out in the yard only in the morning, he learned from his cousins.

Chapter Twenty-One

H IS grandmother said often she was tired of seeing his head forever buried in a book and it was a long walk to the marble tomb of a library where he found little to welcome or interest him and where sprung and yellowing little women looked at him from their desks as though he were taking something that didn't belong to him. Their whispers were strident in the stony quiet. He resented the way they scrutinized him when he carried books to them to be marked with those bold black angular marks that were so heavy for such little women they seemed to be glad to get them down on the cards. None of them ever spoke to him but there were always pricking questions in their sour eyes. He never told them the new address because he had the feeling they would smother him with the suspicion which they appeared to spread over everyone who entered the library. Yet, when he could he went there, hooking a ride on a truck when he could get one, and walking the whole way back and forth when he couldn't. He wanted to read as many of the thousands of books he saw on the shelves in front of him as he could before the cold whipping eyes of the librarians drove him away entirely, which they did before he had graduated from grammar school. In his haste to escape them he would rush in, careful not to let his heels click on the marble floors, because that brought nasty looks, too, and drop the books he was returning on the desks in front of the women. When he had his card again he would hurry to the shelves and snatch three books, all he was permitted to take home at one time, and timidly offer them with his card to another one of the women. The books marked with the number of his card, he would run out again, not slowing his speed until he had bounded down the large flight of stone steps. He was careful in selecting the books he chose only to see that he hadn't read them before and that none of the pages in them were torn or missing. He marveled at how his grandfather, who he now realized couldn't read, would notice each new volume he brought home, at how sharp the old man's questions about the books were and how quick he was to remember, when Willie would tell him stories, that this one he was reading today was almost, not quite, mind you, like the one he had been reading a month or even two months before. It seemed damn queer to him, Ned said once, that every Irishman in the books Willie got from the library was a damned fool or a drunk and there never seemed to be a Catholic born into the world except perhaps a Frenchman and what the hell did they amount to after all, anyhow.

But go ahead, he said, and read them, read them all for the more you read the more you'll want to read and God knows there must be an Irishman hidden away in them somewhere that walked on his hind legs and had learned to speak more English than "whisht" and "begorra." Surely there must be some books in that big marble barn of a place about Emmet, or Tone, Lord Edward or Michael Davitt and the Land Leaguers. Was there nothing about the Fenians, or the Catalpa that brought the felons all the way from Australia to Boston and John Boyle O'Reilly? Them men wrote books themselves, he cried, dozens of them. Wouldn't there be a book about Father McGlynn, either? About how he was excommunicated and the Pope of Rome himself had to back down on it? If there was no books about the O'Neill, God damn him, that kissed the arse of Queen Bess, nor nothing about Malachi that wore the collar of gold, he could understand that, it was a long time ago and far away. But surely to God a great man like Father McGlynn himself that had a parish of his own right in the heart of New York ought to have some kind of a book written about him. Well, he said sadly, Father McGlynn's a long time dead now, God rest his soul, and there's few enough that wrote books would speak up for him when he was alive and fewer than that remember him today that he's dead and gone. He wished to God he knew where them kind of books was to be found because there must be some of them somewhere. Nora said she thought Kate Reagan had the book about Charles O'Malley, the Irish dragoon, somewhere around her house if it was Irish books he wanted the boy to read.

"Dragoon be damned!" Ned cried.

Nora declared she had read the book years before and it was one of the grandest things she ever seen, full of fun and a pleasure to read from cover to cover.

"I wouldn't doubt it a damned bit," Ned said. "I laugh myself sick whenever I think of Easter Week! Never mind your dragoons —I'll find the books—I'll find them."

Chapter Twenty-Two

HESITANT, more conscious of his sins than he had been since they moved to South Providence, Willie McDermott went up the concrete path to the door of St. Malachi's rectory. It was a two-story square frame house, painted the color of the bruised strawberries at the bottom of the box. On his left was the brick wall of the old church, smothered with ivy, and before him the white curtained windows, a light burning in the ones to the right. He went reluctantly up the steps and pulled the silver bell handle.

His grandfather had not been wholly in agreement with Catherine Daly's proposal that Willie should go on the altar, but after a long talk she convinced him that the influence of Father James McCaffrey, who was in charge of the altar boys, would be the making of the boy. Ned gave his consent and Willie was sent to join. The boy himself was skeptical. His cousin Fred Kane was on the altar in the cathedral and his McDermott cousins were serving mass in St. Malachi's. Willie detested Fred Kane and neither Patrick nor John McDermott were companions of his own choosing. Since the incident at Kelly's, however, his own wishes were the last thing to be considered, and he was afraid that if he opposed the project it would confirm him as a "little thief." Still, waiting for an answer to the bell, he wished they had not sent him. If it had been only his uncle who wanted him to go he could, with the support of his grandfather he suspected, have resisted. But it was Catherine Daly's plan and Catherine Daly, next to his grandfather, probably, he thought, was the best friend he had.

Father O'Farrell's own sister, Nora, who was the housekeeper and who looked just like the women in his grandmother's picture album, her hair rolled into a tight bun on the top of her head, came to open the door. He told her he had come to see Father McCaffrey. She let him into the fresh, clean-smelling hallway and knocked on the door to the right.

"In there," she said in a syrupy alto brogue, "take off your cap and bless yourself."

He dipped his fingers into the tiny bowl of the holy water font in the corner, blessed himself and knocked again at the door where the housekeeper had tapped.

"Come on *in*," said a pleasant voice.

Five boys his own age sat in spoked armchairs facing a desk over which hung a single electric bulb shielded only by a bulky scalloped shade. At the desk sat Father James McCaffrey, a short black haired young priest whose keen brown eyes Willie could hardly see behind the glitter of the nose glasses. He wore his cassock, and the black buttons of it gleamed brightly, too. Everything about him looked husky and strong to Willie; his shoulders, his jaw and the white teeth that shone when he smiled.

"Ah, ha," the priest said, "McDermott, isn't it? What's the first name—William? I'll bet Patrick and John don't call you that, do they? Sit down there, make yourself comfortable. What do Patrick and John call you, what do they call you at home?"

"Willie, Father."

"Good, that's what we'll call you," the priest said cheerfully. "This is Stevie Ganley, Byron Searles, Joe Treanor, and that guy underneath the pompadour over there on the end is Paul Dougherty. Sit over there between Paul and Joe if you want to. Now, I was just asking if everybody here knew his catechism, as far as you've gone, you know. How about the catechism?"

"All right," the priest said when Willie delayed his answer. "We'll take it for granted they teach the catechism in the cathedral. Patrick and John are not authorities on it, either. Anyhow, we'll begin all over again because you were late getting here."

"I came at half past seven, Father," said Willie.

"I don't like to repeat things once I've started," the priest said. "You're altar boys now and you're expected to conduct yourselves like altar boys. That is, you are altar boys if we can persuade you to remember a few prayers in Latin. We're going to learn a few prayers first, the 'Our Father,' 'Hail Mary,' the 'Apostles' Creed' and the 'Confiteor.' I suppose we all know them in English, don't we? Don't we, Stevie?"

"Yes, Father," Stevie said, pursing his lips over his big buck teeth.

"Good. I hope so," Father McCaffrey said. "Then we'll study the responses of the mass, the responses you're supposed to know without looking at the cards that are on the altar steps beside you. Monday nights for the rest of the summer we'll meet here and

Friday nights we'll meet in the sacristy of the new church basement. We'll learn how to walk on and off the altar at mass and serve the priest. All right, we'll begin with the 'Our Father.' You repeat the phrases after me. Find it on your cards there. Now, *Pater Noster . . .*"

For an hour they repeated the phrases of the prayer after the priest until they had gone through it a dozen times. Each time Father McCaffrey would repeat a longer phrase, slowly, carefully pronouncing the words for them. Then he asked if anyone, with the help of the card, could read the whole prayer through. Byron Searles said he could.

"I mean I can try," he corrected himself.

"Let's hear you try, then," said the priest. "We'll help out if you get stuck."

Confidently the boy started to read the prayer.

"Wait a minute," said the priest. "What have you got in your mouth there besides your tongue and your teeth? Gum? Get rid of it."

The boy went out and threw the chewing gum on the grass. He returned to read the prayer through and did very well with it. Father McCaffrey told them to take the cards home and study them. He expected each of them to know the "Our Father" in Latin by Friday night and if they didn't know it, they'd better stay at home until they did know it. They were all going to have to recite it to him, he said, without any help, and it wouldn't be like a lesson in school where they could get away with knowing half of it or three quarters of it; they'd have to know every single word of it. He told them they could go home and he didn't want them racing through the streets or battling each other when they got outside the door.

"All right, then, fellows, Friday night at seven-thirty. Everyone on time and everyone prepared to recite the 'Our Father' in Latin. McDermott," he said as an afterthought, "I wish you'd stay a couple of minutes after the others go—there's something I want you to take to your grandmother. Good night boys, God bless you."

"Well, McDermott," said Father McCaffrey when the others had gone out, "how do you like St. Malachi's? Think you're going to like us out here in the woods?"

"Yes, Father."

"Good. That's good. There's some great boys on the altar out here. You're going to like them. You and I are going to get along all right, too. I can see that. It won't be hard for you to learn the Latin, will it? Catherine Daly says you're a good smart boy. . . ."

Willie wondered how much Catherine Daly had told the priest about him.

"She says you're quite a scrapper, too. That right?"

"I don't know, Father."

"Well, we don't want any . . . say, what's the matter, there? You look as though you were sore at the world in general. Are you?"

"No, Father," Willie said.

"Well, that's better. You look as though you had something on your mind, though. Got something on your mind that's bothering you? Have you? Got something you want to get off your chest? Ah, ha! Tell me, is it that thing Catherine Daly told me about that happened a few weeks ago? Is that still bothering you?"

She *had* betrayed him!

"Why, I thought that was wiped off the slate," Father McCaffrey laughed. "That's past history. The slate's clean out here. All you have to do is keep it clean. No one out here knows a thing about it. Not a thing. Well, *I* do. Do you think *I'm* going to ever mention it? I'll tell you what I'll do. I'll make a bargain with you, how's that? You forget it and I'll forget it, how's that?"

The boy tried to speak but couldn't.

"Do you know the Gospel about the stray lamb? No? Look it up when you get home. Tell your grandmother to tell you about it. You're no lamb, though, are you?" He pointed to Willie's head. "You've got an awful crop of wool there, though, haven't you? Why don't you get a haircut? Run along home now."

"You said you wanted me to bring something. . . ."

"Oh, that's right, I almost forgot," Father McCaffrey said, starting to write on a piece of paper in front of him on the desk. When he finished he handed Willie the sheet of paper, folded in the center. "I'm not going to seal it; I think you can take it home without reading it, can't you? I'll take a chance. Don't forget Friday night, now."

"Yes, Father. Good night."

Willie sped out the door without stopping to bless himself at the holy water font. He was consumed with a desire to know what was written on the paper Father McCaffrey had given him for his grandmother. What had the priest written? Was it about him?

Of course it was. He walked in the shadow of the elms debating with himself whether or not he should read the note. All he had to do was turn the page back and there it was; no envelope to open; no one would ever know that he did it. He had to know. But if he opened it he would be starting in all over again getting himself into trouble. He held his hand over the note in his trousers pocket. In the light of the street lamp he stopped and took the note from his pocket, turning it over and over in his hands. If he did read it no one would ever know, but how could he go back there Friday night and look at Father McCaffrey again, even if the priest didn't ask him about it? He was so tired of hanging his head and running out of rooms when people came to the house, so ashamed of avoiding his grandfather's eyes, so afraid of shattering the fragile frame of his new freedom he thrust the paper into his pocket again and ran furiously home to get the paper out of his hands.

His grandmother, flattered that a priest was paying her the attention, woke his grandfather up to read it to him after she had read it through herself several times and let Nora read it over once.

"Dear Mrs. McDermott," the note said. "Thank you for sending Willie to the rectory. He has the makings of a fine altar boy and I'm sure he will prove a credit to you all. James McCaffrey."

"Man of sense," his grandfather commented. "Fine judge of character I can see that. McCaffrey? Kerry I suppose."

"There's two brothers priests," Nora said.

"I do hope things is on the mend for that boy," said Nell.

"You read what the priest wrote, didn't you?" asked Ned.

Willie heard. He believed, too, that the priest meant it when he said Kelly's was past history that was wiped off the slate. Still, if Catherine Daly had said nothing at all about it he might have wiped the slate clean all by himself. This way it was like going to confession in broad daylight instead of in the gloomy sheltering anonymity of the confessional where you yourself were the only one who really knew what you had done and you were just another penitent voice to the priest, shielded by the darkness and your Act of Contrition. Surprisingly, Father McCaffrey, knowing all about his adventure with Joseph and Eddie, had not seemed angry or yet even very much disturbed by it. His welcome had been genuine, and the note to his grandmother surely proved he had held nothing back when he was talking. Willie's wretchedness had been so complete he expected everyone who knew about his thievery to shun him or berate him and those who didn't to suspect him, everyone but his grandfather and Catherine Daly. He retrieved every word he could that the priest had said during the time he was in the rectory and it all seemed friendly. Perhaps, after all, he hadn't fallen so far from grace he couldn't recapture it. Nothing would stop him from trying to, he resolved, *nothing*.

Chapter Twenty-Three

IN THE parched patches of the mill lots near St. Malachi's new church there was plenty of room for two diamonds, and between the outfields was an abandoned shack, its sides plastered with Bull Durham signs and the scrawls the boys had chalked there. Its door was broken down by the boys and nailed up by the fireman at the mill a dozen times a year and hung crookedly with one of its planks loose so that they could get in without smashing it entirely. It was the one lot from which old man Finn, the cop, wouldn't chase them, probably because it was half a block up from the avenue where his beat went, and Finn took no steps he didn't find necessary. A foul might roll up on the church lawn once in a while but never as far as the building itself, and the windows of the mill were all screened with a heavy galvanized net.

Father O'Farrell didn't like them playing and shouting so near the church, but there were several Protestants among the boys who played there and he didn't like to complain for that reason, for one thing. Another reason was that whenever Father McCaffrey was passing he would stop and knock risers out for them or get behind the plate if a regular game were going on and umpire. They always knew when Father McCaffrey was going on a sick call because then he would be carrying the sacred Host with him and only nod to them in answer to their greetings.

Patsy Gray, the cigar salesman who played for Villanova when he was younger and drank himself out of the big leagues later, would always stop with them, too, and Bill Cudahy, the plumber, would set his clanging leather tool bag down and pitch for them, a tireless lefthander, graceful as a dancer for all his two hundred pounds plus and with speed to burn. Bill had been in the big leagues, too, but couldn't last. He would say, laughing a little disgustedly when they asked him about it, that there was nothing big league about the goddam town or anybody in it. They may shine when they're young and go away for a while, but they always come back, he would smile; they always come back. Some of them come back with no sand left in them and some of them come back with a big thirst, but they all come back! The men would watch the boys carefully every time they threw, or fielded a ball, or swung a bat, and tell them if they ever wanted to make the big time they'd better not let the side-arm throw, or the choppy swing get the best of them. Neither of them ever talked about anything but baseball, or horses or prizefighters, and the only places they ever went, except on the job and that was for the most part to barrooms, was to the ball-grounds, the fight club and St. Malachi's to mass on Sunday morning.

From the first day he saw them, Patsy pitching for one side and Bill for the other, they were kind to Willie McDermott, recognizing him as a new boy in the neighborhood, and greeting him on the street after that as though they had known him all their lives. About the same age as his uncle, they were freer and happier than he was. They spent as much time, probably more, at Joe Daly's "store" where the baseball scores and the race results were chalked up as they did working. Sometimes Patsy, who lived with his mother in a white cottage near the Cambridge school, would come through the lane by McDermotts' house late at night staggering a little and singing, the words usually blunted because he would not take the cigar out of his mouth.

Willie's admiration for them brought his uncle's wrath down on him in a torrent one day, and he had to defend them alone because his grandfather was not there to lend him a hand. Ordinarily, if his uncle wanted to flatten his enthusiasm, he would spit out a bitter little squirt of a phrase that would be passed quickly by or swamped by the waves of what his grandfather might be saying. This time he didn't stop after telling Willie there were better men in the parish to model himself on, but angrily went on to say that the two of them were worthless and a pair of rumpots that, if they ever might have amounted to anything, had long since lost what hope there was of it. About all either one of them was good for, he said contemptuously, was to lean against a bar somewhere, filling their bellies with beer and the air with low foul talk. An honest day's work would kill either one of them if they could be trapped into it, but he supposed there wasn't much chance of that happening.

Willie said they were both good friends of Father McCaffrey's, and *he* didn't seem to think they were bums. He said he knew they spent lots of their time in Joe Daly's bar, but, he added with as nasty a sneer as he could fry on his lips, you do too, don't you; you spend plenty of time at Joe Daly's.

"I could slap your face for that!" his uncle roared.

"You have my permission, pet," said Nell hotly.

Willie knew his uncle wouldn't hit him because his grandfather, who didn't count the many raps on the forehead the boy got from his grandmother's heavy gold wedding ring, would not let any of them strike him. Reserving, he insisted, *that* right for himself if need be.

"But you do, don't you?" the boy taunted, skipping out of reach of his grandmother's arm.

"Mother," Chris McDermott asked, catching Willie by the shoulder and shaking him a little, "Mother do I have to listen to this kind of talk from this little—this little?—"

Willie pulled himself free and made for the door, where he turned and laughed at his uncle.

"They made the big leagues one time," he crowed. "But you never will—you'll always be in the bushes. That's the best you'll ever do, the bush leagues."

He skipped over to Patrick's, although he didn't feel much like seeing him or John or Frannie O'Toole, but he had to be somewhere safe until his grandfather got home.

Chapter Twenty-Four

IT WAS damn nice of Tessie Butler, his grandfather said, to make the surplice for Willie. Tessie said it was nothing, nothing at all and she had made the surplices for his two cousins Patrick and Johnnie, only wishing them good health to wear them.

No one in St. Malachi's was more devout than Tessie Butler, who went to mass every morning rain or shine and to Holy Communion the first Friday of every month. People said Barney Butler must have left her a good bit of money before he died, she was always so well dressed, a black satin in the summer and sealskin in the winter. She let them think so, although she had lost it all but the house Pat McDermott lived in with her niece Mollie. The house was not a palace, she admitted, but although Tom Feeley, the bald-headed barber with the crook in his neck, had swindled her in a real estate deal just after Barney died, Tessie always managed to keep it well painted and neat on the few dollars the Deignans, who lived on the second floor, paid her for rent. Pat McDermott paid her no rent but she ate with them, living in a room in the attic, and her needs were few.

She was never idle a minute. She was a member of half a dozen sodalities in the church and dressed the three altars in St. Malachi's new church every week, carrying the altar cloths home to wash and iron on the same day she washed and ironed the surplices she had made for the boys. She attended every meeting of the sodalities, and when vespers were said she went to vespers. Friendless, she was friendly to everyone and always a lady, especially in the morning. Every morning except Sunday when there wasn't much use anyhow, she would go into the cellar and pull an old apron over whatever she was wearing, the satin or the sealskin, put on an old pair of gloves and take a seasoned old butter tub and a tiny tin shovel to gather up the manure in the street. All summer long she would gather it and pile it in the back yard to spread over her garden. Then when fall came she spaded it up. On the side of the house between the street and the lattice at the back door was a bed of lawn hardly big enough to lie down in and roll over twice where Tessie spread her fertilizer over the snow during the winter. She had a ring of fragrant mint in the center of the grass and at the kitchen door was a lilac which also got its share of the fertilizer and which threw its slender branches over the high board fence into Mulvey's yard next door. Tessie grew no flowers, but in the springtime she carried bunch after bunch of the lilacs to St. Malachi's to put on the altars. She had her greens, which she dearly loved, all summer from the garden.

Tessie didn't want Nell to think, she said, that because the surplice she made for Willie was not quite as nice as the ones she made for Patrick and John that she meant to slight the boy, him an orphan boy and all. It was just that she had a bit of lawn and batiste in the drawer when the other two went on the altar. She was intending someday, if ever she got around to it, to make the goods up into petticoats for herself; and there it was now put to good use in the honor and glory of God instead of a petticoat, not stuck away in a drawer there to rot forever.

The brothers always served mass together and the neighbors said they were lucky to have an Aunt Tessie to do for them. Father O'Farrell was always after them to remember their Aunt Tessie in their prayers. If they served early mass Tessie would wait for them at the corner, usually with old Mrs. Walsh, and tell them how pleased she was with the way they behaved at mass.

One morning Father O'Farrell gulped down his wine and one drop of water all at once, shuddered and coughed. Young Pat winked at his brother and mimicked the priest. Tessie was near crying when they saw her on the corner after mass. She screamed at them all the way up the street and swiped at them with her silk umbrella. She kept it up in the house while they were eating breakfast until Mollie couldn't stand it any longer.

"For the love of God," she screamed, "Will you let those two eat, Tessie?"

"God bless us, Mollie," said Tessie, "you don't want them making sport of the priest, do you, and himself standing at the altar of God."

"I want them to eat their breakfast," Mollie said. "Leave them alone."

"It's a sad day," Tessie moaned.

"Listen, Tessie Butler," Mollie cried, "I'm damn sick of you trying to rule this roost. There's no peace with you and your nuns and priests and sodalities. You got the two boys on the altar and that ought to be enough for you. Go up to your room and get out of my sight."

"God bless me," Tessie sighed, "ordered around my own house like a servant."

"I wish I never seen the damn house," said Mollie.

"You were glad enough to slip into it when the lazy ..usband you have was out of work," said Tessie calmly.

"And where would you be for your tea and egg in the morning when the Deignans don't pay their rent?" Mollie was coughing she was that angry.

"I'd be where a cup of tea is not begrudged me," said Tessie. "I'd be with Agnes Sheridan that's asked me manys a time to come and stay with her."

The brothers were serving early mass. John told his mother they hadn't seen Aunt Tessie all week in church.

"Run over to Sheridans' after you come from school," Mollie told them, "and see if she's sick."

Patrick had to go because John said he didn't like the smell of rooms where sick people were if Aunt Tessie was sick.

"Oh, dear, dear," cried Aunt Tessie when he went into her room. "Patrick darlin'. Oh, dear, dear, dear. He's come to see poor old Aunt Tessie. Oh dear. I suppose your mother sent you?"

"No," he lied. "We—I mean I just came in from school."

"Oh dear yes," sobbed the old woman. "And you're serving early mass this week. I wish the dear Lord would give me strength to go to mass, but that fool of a doctor says I must stay in my bed. Och, Patrick darlin', it's a terrible thing to be old and unwanted. . . ."

"She's sicker than you think," said Agnes Sheridan as he was going out the kitchen door. "You better tell Mollie if she wants to see her alive she'd better come over. Dr. Monaghan says it's hardening of the arteries and she may go any time. She may live a week or a day."

Patrick had to go over to Sheridans' again that night with his mother. There was an oil lamp burning in Tessie's bedroom, right off the kitchen, and the old woman was sleeping, propped high on pillows and with her white hair streaming down over a flannel nightgown. They sat in the kitchen talking with Agnes Sheridan until Tessie woke up and heard Mollie's voice.

"Mollie," she called, "Mollie come here to me."

Mollie ran into the room and flung her arms around the old woman. They both sobbed violently.

"Oh, Aunt Tessie," Mollie kept saying over and over.

"Mollie, Mollie," wept Aunt Tessie. "I'm old and unwanted. I'm afraid I'm dying Mollie, dear, and I want to come home and die with you."

"You're far from dying, Aunt Tessie," Mollie said, "but come home if you want to, though I don't know what I can do for you that Agnes Sheridan can't."

"Like my own daughter, Mollie. Agnes nurses me day and night like my own daughter, but I want to come home and die with you in my own house."

"Come home, then," said Mollie. "But how in the name of God will we get you there? Can you walk?"

"If God gives me strength I could walk," said Tessie. "I could walk there with you now."

"I think she's too weak to walk, Mollie," said Agnes.

They talked over how they would get her to the house and Agnes said the only way she knew was to hire a hack from McDonough, the undertaker, but Tessie said she'd give McDonough not a penny except to bury her. Mollie said she would ask her cousin Fran O'Keefe, who drove Frank Quinn's grocery wagon, if he couldn't call around at Sheridans' the next night. She said that God knows the family paid for the damn nag over and over again with the grocery bills.

The trouble began again as soon as Aunt Tessie arrived home. Pat and Fran O'Keefe carried her into the kitchen, but she said she wanted to go right upstairs to her own room.

"Not in that cold icebox," said Mollie. "You'll sleep in the boys' room there right off the kitchen where I can hear you if you want anything at night."

Tessie protested but at last permitted Fran and Pat to carry her into the boys' room. Mollie brought her in a cup of mutton broth which she drank greedily while Fran and Pat sat in the kitchen having a bottle of porter.

It seemed that they were hardly in bed when they heard the crash. Aunt Tessie got up for something and knocked over the little table which Mollie had put beside the bed. She was groaning on the floor when the boys got there and turned the lamp up. Her thin wasted legs, laced with blue veins, were jerking frantically beneath the nightgown. John and Patrick were trying to get her back into bed when their father and mother came running in. Pat got her under the arms and the boys each took a leg to lift her back into bed. She was as light to lift as one of the surplices.

"I suppose you were after the rosary," said Mollie.

Tessie was screaming with pain.

"Och, Mollie, I only wanted to make water," she sobbed. "Only to make water. I have the rosary on the pillow."

She began screaming again, and Mollie said Pat had better go to the carbarn where they were open all night and call Dr. Monaghan. They couldn't find a nickel at first but he finally got under way. When Dr. Monaghan came and examined her he said Mollie certainly had a job on her hands now, because the old woman had broken her hip.

They quarreled again from the moment they saw each other in the morning, which was before anyone else was up. The tea was too cold, the egg stiff as a potato or the gruel too thick. Nothing pleased the old woman. The kindest thing she said to Mollie was the day Mollie got Nell Fennessey to kill one of her pullets and boiled it for Aunt Tessie.

"Well, thank God for that snack," said Tessie after tearing at the little carcass and wiping her hands on the bedcover. "Some folk would call it a meal."

That, Mollie said, finished her. They were at it again when the boys got home from school and even when Pat came in from the brewery, tired and dirty. Mollie would call Tessie an old bitch and Tessie in turn would snarl that it was a sorry day she ever came back to be cursed and insulted in her last hours by a damn little narrowback.

They damned and goddamned each other (God forgive us both) until suppertime. Pat was just sitting at the table when Tessie screamed that the tea was so hot it scalded her poor throat, and Mollie shrieked that she wished to God it was hot enough to scald the tongue out of her.

"Now, by Jesus," Pat said. "I had enough of this. By Jesus I had enough. Either you two shut up, both of you shut up, or I'll get the hell out. I'll go across the street to my mother's to stay. Where I'll get some peace."

"Och, Pat darling," said Tessie, "I don't blame you, poor man. I'll go along with you, Pat darling."

Chapter Twenty-Five

GLORIOUS apostle, dear saint of our isle, upon whom the poor children bestow a sweet smile. . . .

Father Hanlon's bronchial tenor rang out defiantly in St. Malachi's after mass on St. Patrick's morning that came rainy and blustery as it always did in the middle of Lent. There was time to go home, Willie McDermott thought as he stood in the sacristy taking off his cassock and surplice after serving mass, time to go home and eat a great breakfast and still get downtown in time to see the parade. Father Hanlon's voice pealed out over the organ while Willie was putting his coat on, and he waited there listening to the song which, as far as he knew, no one else in the world ever sang except Father Hanlon, and he sang it only on St. Patrick's morning.

It was a greater day, almost, than Fourth of July or Christmas. His grandfather never worked that day and although he did not march in the parades, he always took Willie to see them and the boy never knew what great adventure might be waiting. They might meet Tim Lee on the street and go with him to the harbor master's; they might even go out in the country to a cockfight later in the day; there was no telling what they might do.

Ned was waiting impatiently for him when Willie went home.

"Hurry, now," his grandfather said. "We don't want to miss a thing, you know."

Willie shoveled away a breakfast his grandmother served him on the kitchen table and soon they were on the streetcar bound downtown. His grandfather asked him where he thought would be the best place to watch the parade, over at the Statehouse where the line of march was forming or at the cathedral, where the bishop would come out on the steps to review "the troops." Willie, thinking Joseph or Eddie, or perhaps Rose Riordan might be in the crowd near the cathedral, said he thought it would be better to watch it from there because then they would be sure not to miss anything.

Dragging his grandfather with him, he found a place at the foot of the statue of Mayor Tilden in the middle of the square by the church, across from the steps. From there they could see everything, the bishop and his train, as well as the whole of the parade. Willie searched among the crowd for Joseph or his brother or sister, but until it was nearly time for the vanguard of the marchers to appear he couldn't see any of them. Then, with the rain that dripped steadily now shining on her saucy nose and sprinkled into her black hair, he saw Rose waving to him across the square. He waved to her and beckoned to her to come over. He told his grandfather he had seen Rose Riordan but his grandfather didn't answer. Willie sat in the wet on the granite step at the base of the statue, his grandfather standing behind him and holding a hand on his shoulder. He cautioned the boy that when the crowd broke up after the march he was to cling tightly to him and not get himself lost in the rush. Willie assured him he would stay close by all the time. He wished Rose would come over because he wanted to ask her about Joseph and Eddie and he wanted to be near Rose. She had disappeared into the crowd again.

People were straining to look down the street where the bands could now be heard. At last, in a line that swept across the whole of the street, their horses dancing wildly, came the mounted police led by Pete Carron, grand marshal, in a stovepipe hat and a cutaway black coat with a green silk sash bound in front of him. The bishop had barely time to raise his hand in a blessing for the parade and Pete hardly time to raise the little baton tied with green ribbon in salute, before the horse, a dappled gray that was almost white, reared up nobly and spurted ahead in a gallop. Pete, clapping one hand on his hat, the hand that held the baton, rose in his stirrups and hauled mightily on the reins. The horse plunged and reared across the square and the crowd drew back. Then, with both hands straining, Pete reined the horse in and trotted on.

"God," Ned muttered aloud, "that's a grand horse, that."

The flags came along, the Stars and Stripes on the right and the green flag of Erin on the left, its golden harp bright and glittering with raindrops. Leading one of the platoons of policemen on foot was Larry McDermott, his big feet shooting out at angles. Willie turned away and looked into the crowd again for Rose Riordan, but couldn't find her. The AOH division was the first in line and their leader, McGovern, the contractor, was also mounted, on a finer looking animal than Pete Carron rode, too, Ned said. Their silken banner was carried by a huge man who towered over the man who carried the American flag on his right and the one who carried the Irish flag on his other side, and they were not small men. The front rank all wore silk hats and carried canes, most of them heavy blackthorn sticks.

Willie felt someone touch his shoulder and looked up to his grandfather. He turned and saw Rose Riordan. He pulled her down with him on the granite step and asked her if Joseph or Eddie were with her. She told him they were around somewhere, but she didn't know where they had gone. They had left her before she saw him, she said, or she would have brought them along. She asked him why he never came around the old house any more, and said that they were going to move soon, too, she thought, and probably out near the park, or somewhere in St. Malachi's.

It was cold on the granite and they stood up as the AOH division ended and the blue-coated band with horsehair plumes flying from their white helmets came along in front of the first section of the Knights. Ah, but here was a great display. Not only the marshal of the Knights division was mounted, but also the color bearers and the whole first four ranks of the marchers.

"Well, one trying to outdo the other," Ned said. He noticed Rose for the first time. "Hello, child," he said, "how are you? How is all the family, God bless them?"

"Hello, Mr. McDermott," Rose said shyly. She was wedged tightly in between Willie and his grandfather.

The Knights had more bands than any other division in the line of march, too. Women's divisions followed, Holy Name societies, the Catholic Foresters, all with their bands and with flags and ribbons of green. When the last contingent had appeared, straggling along, and the bishop, gathering the folds of his cassock in his hand, turned to give the crowd his blessing and go into the cathedral, the crowd, most of them blessing themselves, exploded in a thousand directions. Willie grabbed Rose's hand and, following his grandfather through the tumult of people, took her along with them. They broke free at last and he had to let her hand go again. His grandfather, unasked, went into the Greek's candy store next to the shoe store and ordered ice cream for them. While they were deciding what kind they would have his grandfather pressed a quarter into Willie's hand and told him that he would be back in a minute. Willie knew that he would be going into Flannagan's next door for a drink, but he didn't say so to Rose. Rose knew it, too, but she didn't say anything to Willie.

"Why don't you ever come to play with Joseph?" Rose asked him when his grandfather had gone. "Don't they want you to?"

"I—well, it's so far from where we live now," he stammered.

"That's not why," Rose shook her head, closing her eyes and pursing her lips. "Your uncle doesn't want you to, does he? Your grandmother doesn't either. That's why you don't come to our house. They think we're all *bad*, don't they? They don't like us."

"No," he lied. "No, Rose, I can come if I want to."

"Why don't you then?" she said tartly.

"Well, I told you. It's so far from where we live now."

"You're an altar boy now in St. Malachi's, aren't you? I know you are because Fred Kane told Joseph you are."

"Yes," he said, feeling somehow that he had betrayed the Riordans.

"Do you want my shamrock, Willie?" Rose asked him.

"Yes."

She took it from her coat and pinned it below the button he wore.

"There," she said, taking his button off and pinning it on her own coat.

"Thanks for the shamrock," he said.

"I never thought *you'd* be an altar boy, Willie," she said.

"Why?" he asked.

"Oh," she shrugged her shoulders daintily. "I just didn't."

She made him promise he would come to see Joseph soon because, she said Joseph and Eddie both missed him since he moved away. They finished their ice cream and went into the street again where crowds with green neckties, little green silk flags and green ribbons on their coats were still plodding up the hill after watching the parade. Rose said she saw her sister across the street, and, pressing his hand in hers, she ran away into the crowd. Willie waited outside Flannagan's until his grandfather came out and they walked down the hill again, past the cathedral and the statue to the streetcar.

157

"Pete Carron on a horse!" his grandfather exclaimed shaking his head merrily. "That's the goddamdest thing I ever see in my life. Pete Carron on a horse leading the Patrick's Day parade. And a stick with green bows tied to it, bowing to the bishop!"

Willie said it was a great parade, though, and he was certainly glad they went to the cathedral to watch it because they had seen the whole thing, even the bishop and the people reviewing it from the steps. His grandfather told him that someday he might be leading the parade himself with a stovepipe hat and all. He said it was a great honor, after all was said and done to be leading a Patrick's Day parade, with half the city tagging along behind you on foot while you were riding along on a white horse, at least a dappled gray. He said there wasn't any need of going right home, that's to say getting off the car right in front of the house; they might as well ride up to the carbarn and he'd stop for a minute or two in Fitzpatrick's there just to tell them about the parade and all, in case any of them might not have gone to see it themselves. They rode to the end of the line, and Willie watched the men shooting pool at the parlor on the corner while his grandfather went down the street a few doors to Fitzpatrick's. When the old man reappeared his walk was determined and his step very precise.

"Yes, it was a great turnout," he said. "A great march indeed in spite of Pete Carron making a fool of himself on that white horse in front of the bishop and all. It damn near throwed him, did you see that, Willie? Damn near dumped him off right in front of the bishop. Wouldn't that have been the disgrace, though? Well, the family was well represented there, wasn't it? Pete Carron at the head of the line of march and Larry McDermott leading the squad of police . . . ah, Larry's all right, too, I suppose, in his way."

Willie asked his grandfather if he could go to the play at St. Malachi's old church that afternoon; he said it was an Irish play they were giving. His grandfather declared it didn't seem right to be going to a play or entertainment of that kind during Lent itself, but that if it was given in the church it must be all right; the church wouldn't allow it to be given if it wasn't all right. If his grandmother said yes he could go, his grandfather said.

Chapter Twenty-Six

THE restlessness subsided when the lights went down and only the pale March light seeped through the diamonds of colored glass that had never been removed from the old church, although mass hadn't been said there for a long time. There was a slight shifting and scraping of the undertaker's chairs and then Professor Flannigan beat out a medley of Irish airs on the grand piano just under the stage, "The Wearin' of the Green," "O'Donnell Abu," "The Boys of Wexford," and slid off into a dreamy rendition of "Believe Me, If All Those Endearing Young Charms."

Willie McDermott found a seat in the front row, not too good a seat because the floor of the old church naturally had no pitch and he had to tilt his head far back to see what was happening on the stage, which was a good six feet higher than the floor. Professor Flannagan's' medley stopped abruptly in the middle of the "Wearin' of the Green" as he played it for the third time. The curtain rose, slowly at first and then with a sharp, wild ascent. . . .

EVENING. Old Phelim is sitting before the peat fire of his cottage warming his hands at the fire (at right). He stands up and looks at the sun declining through the window (center) on the other wall of the room. It is a simple cottage, only a rough table with a couple stools and a cupboard with a few dishes in it serve for furniture. A black crucifix is hung over the fireplace. There is tremendous applause for old Phelim (Mr. James Walsh, the plumber). A knock at the door (left) and it comes the gombeen man, Murphy (Mr. Owen Galligan) wafer-thin and his voice is high-pitched. He is everything evil—landlord's agent, tax collector and it is at once clear, a spy. But a *caed mille faelte* for him, anyhow, from old Phelim, Murphy is peering around the room as though he were boring holes in every corner. He supposes Phelim will have his back rent before the sun is high on the hills tomorrow. The sun declines very rapidly out the window (center) as he talks and night shuts down. No, Phelim sadly shakes his head, he has neither pence nor pound for Sir Reginald Ashby-Ponsonworth

(Mr. Peter Cahill) the landlord. Then out you go, threatens Murphy, when the shadow of the sun crosses the stile below, the eviction papers will be served. Dear God, no, cries Phelim; the little cottage and the few acres of land are all that he has for him and his darling Kathleen. Surely Sir Reginald could never be so cruel. Wait! Murphy sidles up to Phelim furtively, glancing around the room, running to the window and looking out and running to the door to open it and peer out into the black night. Wait! If Phelim could tell Murphy the whereabouts of that rascally Rory O'Dea that is stirring the tenants up against Sir Reginald perhaps Sir Reginald may be lenient. Come now, Phelim, this is your one chance to save your home. You don't want your darling Kathleen cast out into the wild storms of the winter, do you? Phelim hangs his head and Murphy, conscious of his guilty role, again tiptoes to the window and the door. This time he goes to the door first and when he is at the window stands there holding one of the trim little white curtains in his hand. He starts; someone is coming along the road. He skips over to Phelim. Quick, man, what's your answer? He must know before he goes to the manse to report. Snatches of "Danny Boy" are heard approaching off stage; the door is opened. Enter Kathleen (Catherine Daly). The applause is unrestrained; there is stamping of feet, whistling, cheers, hand-clapping. Kathleen starts to break into a dash across stage to embrace her father but stops; she cannot speak her lines over the tempest of applause.

She pauses, blushing through the grease paint and rouge. An exquisite cape of emerald green lined with white satin covers her, and her golden-red hair bursts like sunlight on a cloud upon the soft lining of the hood. She is trembling with joy, though it's really only a dress rehearsal for the evening performance, and lowers her eyes to the silver buckles on her black pumps. Kathleen throws the hood back from her head and goes to her father. They embrace. Chagrined, bitter, Murphy stands at the door, his shifty eyes wickedly looking from the father and daughter out into the night.

MURPHY: Come, O'Leary, what is your answer?
PHELIM: The answer is—
KATHLEEN: The answer—is—no! (He goes out.)
Brave Kathleen, the audience loves you! There is a tapping at

the door, a cautious, but persistent tapping that sounds like a Morse code. Kathleen hastily blows out the candle and the footlights go down. Now the moon cascades into the room and Kathleen opens the door a crack to see who knocks. Enter Rory (Mr. Jack Gilmartin), his ringlets of black hair spiraling down on his forehead. He is wearing a shirt open at the throat and corduroy breeches with gray woolen stockings and black pumps with bulldog toes.

RORY: Kathleen! Asthore!

KATHLEEN: Rory!

She closes the door and they embrace. Old Phelim, happy in his sadness, nods his white head in blessing. Kathleen pours out their trials in a rich and resonant alto. Rory clenches his fists in anger and strides across stage clasping and unclasping his hands as he listens. She pours tea for him and they sit at the table and plan what they will do to circumvent Sir Reginald. Never fear, Kathleen, Rory will find the way. He must go now for he is a hunted man, but he will be back before the sun reaches the stile tomorrow. Yes, Rory, you will, we know you will. But what is that devil's face leering in at you from the window? Murphy! He has heard all! Rory, beware! Exit Rory. Kathleen rushes to the window to watch her lover go down the path as CURTAIN!

Willie McDermott's throat was dry and hot as the house lights, a series of brass circles suspended from the high ceiling, a dim bulb here and there, came up again. The spell was not broken. The stagehands created a thunder of hammering and stamping behind the curtain that was hardly noticeable with the applause. Fathers McCaffrey and Hanlon, patroling the aisles, were hardly able to keep order in the house.

MORNING. O'Leary's cottage. Kathleen is making more tea as Phelim enters, depressed and his old head drooping. He takes off a nondescript soft hat and crushes it in his hands, sighing loudly. But Kathleen is bright as the morning itself for she knows Rory will soon be there to save them. She tells her father never to worry about a thing. She is almost gay and hums a little tune as she moves about the room. Enter Rory himself, very whipped-looking because he has not been able to solve their dilemma. If he had a thousand pounds of gold he would give every last farthing of it to save them, that they know full well. But he is a hunted man, an outcast man. Who knocks? Tim, faithful Tim (it's only Johnnie McKinnon) come to warn Rory that someone is coming. The clatter of the horses is heard. Tim disappears and Kathleen tells Rory to fly. Rory will not fly. The horses come nearer and nearer as Kathleen looks out the window. Sir Reginald she tells Rory, with that scoundrel of a Murphy. Fly, Rory. Never! The horses stop and in strides Sir Reginald clad in riding boots of patent leather, breeches, a plum-colored coat and a silk hat. He carries a riding crop in his gloved hand and swishes it. Rory had hidden himself behind the open door, a large pistol ready in hand. Murphy brings up in the shadow of his master. Kathleen stands defiantly before Sir Reginald. Not a penny have they! She knows the alternative, my pretty Kathleen! Do your worst, then, says Phelim, shielding his daughter with his arm. Sir Reginald walks to the window and is about to signal with his riding crop. Stay! Not so fast, Sir Reginald, says Rory, leveling the pistol. Sir Reginald halts in his tracks, but the wily Murphy has slipped away.

Rory's words as he orders Sir Reginald away from the window are drowned by the joyous shouts of the audience again. He is telling the landlord that he dare not evict these gentle souls. The Britisher sneers at him. Kathleen begs Rory to save himself. The tramp of marching feet is heard off stage and Kathleen tells Rory the redcoats are coming. Rory is trapped and Sir Reginald is mocking him. Fly, Rory, says Kathleen, they are surrounding the house. Gladly would Rory surrender, but he has a secret message to deliver. Fly he must. He embraces his colleen bawn. The marching men are coming closer, they pass the window (without looking in it) and the tips of their muskets can be seen. Rory retreats to a position near the casement. He passes the pistol to Kathleen, may God protect her! The British captain (Mr. Robert Day), sword drawn, storms into the cottage as Rory leaps out the window. Glass crashes off stage violently although the window is open. The soldiers march in (Tom Curran, Frank Hennessey, Walter McGuinnis, Leo Ganley). They are followed by the unscrupulous Murphy. The redcoats are standing stiffly at attention. The captain points his sword out the window and he is saying something to his troopers but it cannot be heard for the audience is in an uproar. The muskets are lifted to the shoulders of the redcoats and pointed out the window in the direction Rory has fled. Aim, cries the captain. He lashes his sword down, fire! The muskets click and thunder off stage. Distraught Kathleen, wilted and weeping, is gazing out the window as CURTAIN!

SAME EVENING. Night has fallen over the glen. Impatient, her green hood drawn up to mask her face Kathleen looks to the far-off hills where she knows her Rory is hiding and she comes to the footlights, her eyes downcast and sad. She is looking directly at Willie McDermott, he thinks. A hoarse whisper is heard and from behind the hummock of rock (right) Rory raises his head. She flies into his arms. She lingers while he tells her to keep the courage burning in her heart and put her trust in almighty God who will see justice and mercy triumph and the wicked punished. She is sobbing bitterly. Good Father O'Neill is sheltering her poor aged father and she has taken refuge in the hut of a peasant. Rory has come back to give himself up to the British for their sakes, but now it is too late, he fears. Too late, yes, Rory, too late, for now they have been driven from their little cottage.

Damnable Murphy has tracked them down. Crouching behind the same rocks where Rory was hidden he listens to all they have to say. Away he goes, but he'll return. He does, with the same British soldiers from whom Rory escaped only a few minutes ago, and as the lovers are parting the muzzles of their muskets bristle from every crag. Surrounded Rory surrenders to them as the captain and Sir Reginald appear. Handcuffs are snapped on Rory's wrists and he is led off. Kathleen, desolate and inconsolable, sits on a rock. She is alone, wringing her hands, weeping. Sir Reginald appears again, stealthily approaching her and tapping her on the shoulder with the riding crop. She springs to her feet.

You, Sir Reginald, have come to mock her in her hour of sadness. Devil take you, sir, you will never bend us to your will. Ah, Kathleen, you wrong him, he pleads, you know not that his heart is really yours, that he wants to take you from the crude cabin and make you the mistress of the manor with servants to wait upon your every whim and coach and four to ride in. A word from you and he will free Rory. A word, Kathleen. He drops on one knee, his hat in his hand. Save Rory from the felon's death, Kathleen! No never. Sir Reginald rises in fury and claps his hat upon his head again, striking the rock with his riding crop. Very well, then! Wait, oh wait, Sir Reginald, she beseeches. Spare him from the gallows, spare an innocent man! But the decision is yours to make, Kathleen. You have but to say the word and Rory is a free man. He steps toward her, arms outstretched. Oh, wretched Kathleen, what are manor houses or servants to wait upon her or coaches and four to ride in? What are all the jewels and finery? But she cannot see her Rory go to his death. Take her then, Sir Reginald, take a brokenhearted girl who will never love you. Yes, take her! Forgive her, Rory! It is for you, Rory, that she makes the sacrifice. Rory! Rory! CURTAIN.

The audience was groaning, hissing Sir Reginald and some of the little girls, when the lights came up, were wiping tears from their eyes. Willie McDermott hated to see the curtain fall and shut Catherine Daly off from him for even a moment. He sat hunched in his seat and spun furiously around when Pete McNally, sitting directly in back of him, smacked him on the head with the flat of his hand. He would have punched Pete then and there if Father Hanlon hadn't come along.

A FEW DAYS LATER. The bars of the cold prison cell (left) held Rory fast and in the grim corridor the British sentry paced. Rory O'Dea sat in a green spotlight on a rude wooden bench in the cell, one arm drooping between his legs and the other holding up his head. A pair of rosary beads hung from the hand between his legs. He is condemned. Father O'Neill (Mr. Joseph Foley) is heard off stage, demanding to see the prisoner. Enter Father O'Neill. With him is the jailer, lugging a huge ring of clanking keys. Rory shakes Father O'Neill's hand and they sit on the bench together. The jailer locks the cell door on them again and exits. The good priest comforts the condemned man. Rory wants nothing more than to see his darling Kathleen once more before he walks to the gallows. The priest assures him he will see her and calls to the jailer to let him out. Exit priest. Locking the door again the jailer sneers at his prisoner and tells him to listen to the sound of the carpenters building the gallows in the prison yard. Hammering is heard off stage and the muffled voices of the workers building the gallows. Rory goes to the bars in the front of the cell and tries their strength. The sentry is at the far end of the corridor when—hssst! Faithful Tim's voice is heard. He reassures Rory. They talk in whispers while the stupid sentry continues his marching in front of the cell.

Again Rory is sitting on the bench. Wait until night falls and Tim will have him free.

The off-stage voice ceases and Kathleen's lovely alto is heard. Enter Kathleen with jailer. The hood is thrown back from the cape and her radiant hair flies free and proudly as she walks to the cell bars. The lovers clasp hands through the bars and Kathleen stands with her head hung and her voice low as she tells Rory of the sacrifice she is about to make. She weds Sir Reginald in the morning. Rory forbids her; he would go to his death rather than see her wed to the scoundrel! Her word is given, Rory, she cannot break her promise even to the despicable Sir Reginald. Think of her, Rory, think of Kathleen! She presses his hand in a last farewell and dashes away, turning as she gets to the wings. Remember Kathleen, Rory. CURTAIN.

Willie McDermott would remember her. He would long remember her sweet voice and her golden-red hair, the green cape and tender rosebuds on her dress. Proud that he knew her, grateful beyond measure to her for what she had done for him, he was beside himself with envy of his uncle that so soon would marry her. His eyes were fixed on the laurel that entwined the painted lyre on the curtain, but he neither saw it nor heard Pete McNally whispering to him.

MORNING AGAIN. O'Leary's cottage. Kathleen sits at the window in her wedding gown, the purest white batiste billowing about her, laced at its round neck with green velvet ribbon and her shoulders nearly bare. The friends of her childhood, the girls from the village are grouped around her. Shawled and forlorn, three old women of the town stand near the fireplace whispering to each other. Unhappy Phelim stands in the doorway looking out into the sunlight. The fiddler stands ready to play and Father O'Neill restlessly paces the floor.

Kathleen turns her head from the window as the sound of horses approaching is heard off stage. The bridegroom is coming. Young men of the village enter and begin to talk to the young girls. Enter faithful Tim, who at once begins a hurried and secret talk with Kathleen. She brightens. Hope rises in Willie's heart. Enter Sir Reginald followed as ever by the treacherous Murphy. Phelim has stepped aside and drops his head. Murmurs arise from the village people and the audience.

The sounds of a harp are heard off stage. Seumas, the blind minstrel, appears at the open window and sings: *Well may the men of Erin weep, for Connacht lies in slumber. The West asleep,* Seumas mourns, *the West asleep.* Only the haughty Sir Reginald is pleased, only he and his crony Murphy. Let Connacht lie in slumber deep for all they care. The minstrel ends his verse with Ireland prostrate. But what sound is that now, rising above the harp? Horses! The harper lifts his blind eyes to the sky and the music swells as Rory enters. He has escaped! Kathleen rushes to his arms while Sir Reginald cringes. Rory deftly disengages one arm and pointing to the landlord, cries "Seize that man!" The harper's voice rises to the next verse—*The West's awake, The West's awake!* The village youths, members of Rory's rebel band, seize Sir Reginald. Rory announces to all that his lads have driven the British garrison from the town, the nation is in arms, the English barracks in flames! Kathleen is saved, she rejoices and the harper lustily cries his song again: *The West's awake!* CURTAIN.

The enraptured audience began to shout and whistle as the curtain rose again on the whole company stretched out in a line across the stage, bowing and smiling. It fell, and when it was lifted again there stood Catherine Daly with Peter Cahill on one side of her and Jack Gilmartin on the other. A second time the curtain fell, and was lifted to reveal Catherine standing there alone. The audience was standing on its seats and crowding down to the front rows to cheer her. There was no stopping them. Willie McDermott was still cheering when the curtain fell and the lights came up. There was a scramble for the doors and he lost himself in it. It was the first time he had ever seen a play. It was the most beautiful thing he had ever seen in his life, more wonderful than a solemn high mass! He ran all the way home.

"Well, then, how was the show?" his grandfather asked.

"She was beau—it was great," Will said excitedly. "Oh, it was great! Great!"

"What was it then, dancers doing jigs, or hornpipes or reels or something like that, I suppose?"

"No, no," Willie cried. "It was a play, a play about a British landlord that tried. . . ."

"My God!" his uncle said, "must I listen to that for the few minutes I'm home? I've been listening to every line of it Catherine recites. I have to go and see it all over again tonight . . . do I have to listen? . . ."

"You do," said Ned very curtly. "What's this about the British landlord, Willie?"

Willie began a feverish description of the peaceful cottage, the infamous proposal of the gombeen man as his grandfather, pipe laid aside, crashed his elbows on the dining room table and, thrusting his chin into the palms of his hands, stared at the boy like a child. There had been a couple short jaunts to Fitzpatrick's during the afternoon and Ned was very receptive.

"Wants the good man to turn informer," he snorted. "Heh, d'you see. See, see, see. That's how they do it. Wouldn't do it, hey—heh I thought not. Go on, go on, Willie, go on."

"No," Willie told him, explaining how Kathleen ("that's Catherine Daley," he said, "she was beautiful") came in and drove the spy out just before Rory entered.

"The rebel!" cried Ned joyfully. He jerked his hand from under his chin and pointed at the boy as much as to ask him if he weren't right.

Willie described how later the landlord himself came and Rory escaped out the window when the British soldiers came. . . .

"Sure he couldn't fight the whole British Army, could he?" Ned said indignantly. "And what'd they do then, shoot the man in the back did they? Ptu! Go on, Willie."

The boy skipped quickly over the scene in the glen except for the part where the traitor Murphy spied on the couple and brought the British soldiers again to arrest Rory.

"Ah, it's the disgrace of the Irish," Ned groaned. "There's forever a traitor amongst them. He is always a turncoat to the Church too—though not always, God forgive them. Yes, and the landlord is there, too, is he, watching the proceedings?"

"Yes," Willie answered, "and he says he'll get Rory out of jail if Kathleen will marry him."

"Ah, he's after her is he? He might as well get *that* out of his mind. She'll never do it, never in God's world. She didn't, did she?"

"My God, no," said Chris McDermott testily. "Are you satisfied now? No, she don't marry him. . . ."

"I know that anyhow—who in the hell asked you? Be quiet till I hear what happened to the poor girl. Tell us the rest of it, Willie. Go on. And you be quiet!"

"Well, she almost does," Willie continued, "but Rory escapes from jail and the rebels drive the British out of the town and the West's awake then so she doesn't have to marry the Englishman."

"Ah, good, yes, the West's awake. Indeed it's awake. Good for them," Ned sat straight up, folded his arms across his chest and slowly shook. "It's a grand tale, Will. It is, yes."

"And then Rory comes in at the end and I guess he's the one that marries Catherine." Will ended his report.

"Oh—oh, yes," said Ned. "And the landlord what happens to him and his informer?"

"The rebels seize them both," Willie answered.

"Aaah, d'you see! That's it. And they sing it, too? 'The West's awake'?" Ned was jubilant. "Hah, do they?"

"Sure they do," Willie said.

"Aaah! Grand song. Nell," Ned shouted, "Put on your hat and coat till we go hear them sing 'The West's awake' at the Patrick's Day show. Tell the mother superior there to come along, too."

Nell and Nora were bewildered, since neither of them had been anywhere except to mass and an occasional wake or a funeral for many many months, and neither of them ever thought of going anywhere else.

"Come," Ned said, going out to the kitchen to them and reaching for his derby, "get on your things, both of you."

"Ned," his wife said. "How can we—why, Ned it's hours before the show—I—"

"Put on your things," he repeated.

"Yes. Yes I will Ned," she stammered. "But it's hours before the play starts again."

"Well, well," he began.

"And you'll put a collar and tie on you, I hope," said Nell

"Yes," he said. "I'll put a collar and tie on me for the show. Now get yourself ready. And you, Mother Superior, you, too, you know." He was struggling into his overcoat. "I'll just step out whilst you get ready—for a drop—of fresh air."

Nell and Nora were waiting when Ned came in to put on the collar and tie. Nell said she hated to go out and leave Willie there all alone and it was much too early to send him to bed. Ned said he saw no reason the boy shouldn't come with them; he couldn't learn too much about the Irish on Patrick's Day. The four of them, Ned and his grandson walking together ahead of the women, went to the hall. It was too late for seats on the main floor and they had to be satisfied with the front row in the organ loft. Willie wanted to tell them as the play went on what was going to happen next, but his grandfather would restrain him. At the end of the piece the ushers ran down the aisles with armfuls of flowers for the girls in the cast, all of them. But Catherine Daly got more than anyone else. Roses were piled high around her feet when she took her last curtain call.

"What the Irish can't do," said Ned as they were going home. "What scholars and poets they are! What scholars, Willie! Ah, that was a grand thing! My boy, the talents the Irish has is—is unspeakable!"

Chapter Twenty-Seven

THE brook of Father McCaffrey's friendship sprang down the parched rut of Willie's spirit, bounding and brightly splashing over the dark stones of doubt in its course, soon covered and forgotten beneath its clear waters. Patiently, the young priest taught the group Willie was in to pronounce the Latin responses at the mass and carefully translated the meanings of the words for them into English, so that by the time the schools were closing every one of them, at least with the help of a glance at the card now and then, knew them.

Of all the group Willie liked Byron Searles, the pallid, alert boy who read at the first meeting and whom Father McCaffrey had told to throw his chewing gum away. Byron, it appeared, was more than casually acquainted with Father McCaffrey. Willie learned that Byron's father was a Protestant, who had no objection, however, to his son's being brought up a Catholic by his devout, florid mother, a woman whose maiden name had been Maggie Donovan and who even now had trouble getting her husband to call her Margaret. Willie met her one night after a meeting when he went home with Byron. The Searles' lived in the Slater mansion, an apartment hotel and the most pretentious place Willie had ever been in, on the fringe of the parish.

There was a scrawny-legged girl, Byron's sister, sitting with Mrs. Searles in a large bow-windowed room when the boys went in. The girl snapped a forefinger against her nose and made a face at them to greet them; then she got up and, clasping her hands together, marched with bowed head to a near-by dresser, where she picked up a box of candy. She marched with the candy to her brother and, dipping her fingers in it as the priest does into his chalice at mass, took a chocolate out and dropped it into his mouth. She did the same for Willie, and was just dropping the chocolate in when her mother, heavy-breasted and very short, sprang from her chair and made for the girl, brandishing a book at her. The girl thrust the box of candy into Willie's hands and fled from the room. As soon as she started to run her mother stopped.

"Well, go ahead," she said testily, "have some candy. That damn child drives me crazy with her actions. She's always making fun of things that are sacred. She's been making fun of Byron ever since he became an altar boy. She don't mean any harm though. She only does it in fun. She's really a good little girl, just flighty. What's your name?"

Willie told her and soon discovered that Mrs. Searles knew his family better than he did himself. She knew his grandfather and all his brothers and she knew his own mother. There wasn't much about the McDermotts Mrs. Searles didn't know, he discovered. Oh, yes, Mrs. Searles said, she was well acquainted in Providence, but she had lost touch with many of the people she used to know because they had been living in New York for several years. Willie said his grandfather's brother Joe lived in Brooklyn, but Mrs. Searles said she never happened to know him very well.

She gave the boys milk and a large, imposing piece of cake, fully as large as the one she ate herself. The girl came back into the room meanwhile and perched on a window seat in back of her mother and ate her cake, mimicking every word and gesture Mrs. Searles made. Willie discovered that the Searles' not only knew Father McCaffrey very well, but that they visited his family's house and were very fond of Father Joseph McCaffrey, his younger brother, a teacher in the university in Washington. Byron said Father Joe—it surprised Willie to hear anyone speak so familiarly of a priest—would be coming home from the university soon and Willie must be sure to meet him. Byron grandly told Willie to ride his bicycle home and they went into the cellar where an old Negro dressed in carpenter-striped overalls dragged out his bike.

It was a corking Iver Johnson, red, with shining handle bars, a chime bell that rang when you pulled a cord and it dipped its rim on the front tire, and mudguards. Byron rode it around the circular driveway in front of the mansion before Willie left. Willie rode silently across town, hardly jingling the bell when he came to the corners of streets. When he rode it over the next day to return it, Byron said Father Joe McCaffrey was in town and he was going down to see him. He told Willie to get on the handle bars and he would ride him down to the McCaffreys' house, too.

A tall, thin young man with lustrous black eyes gleaming and a lock of black hair swooping down like a scimitar on his pale forehead stood smiling with bloodless lips and large teeth in the far corner of the cool front room at McCaffreys' when the boys went in, Willie trailing Byron somewhat reluctantly. The young man was dressed in a white shirt, opened at the throat, and creamy flannel trousers. He held a long-fingered hand out to Byron and clapped him on the back as they shook hands. He gravely smiled again when Byron introduced Willie to him. It was the first time Willie had ever seen a priest clad in anything except his vestments at mass, the cassock and biretta in the rectory or the Roman collar and black suit and hat on the street. He wondered at first if Byron hadn't made a mistake.

He was reassured when Father Joe asked Byron how he was getting along learning Latin and whether Father Jim was a severe teacher. Byron bubbled with self-assurance and said they both knew the Latin so well by this time he didn't see why Father Jim didn't let them serve mass once in a while. He said he was sure they knew the Latin as well as anyone on the altar. Father Joe said he was sure they did, too, and asked Byron how he would like it if he asked Father Jim if they might both serve mass for him while he was in St. Malachi's. He said he wouldn't mind if they made a mistake once in a while; in a week's time they would both be letter-perfect.

The priest asked Byron if he were still reading those trashy Henty and Alger books as much as he used to, or whether he was really going to grow up some day and read some books that were worth spending his time on. Byron said right now he was reading about history an awful lot. The priest asked Willie if he did much reading and the boy started to say he read the newspaper every night when Byron laughed wickedly. After that Willie found it impossible to go on and tell the priest any more about his reading.

Well, I brought a few books home with me and there are plenty more in the house here," Father Joe said. "We'll all have to get together often during the summer and see if we can't get some good reading done. We'll have to see if we can't find a few books to read that they don't give you in school. You go to the public school, too, I suppose, Willie?"

Willie said he did.

"What a shame there isn't a parochial school in this parish after all these years," the priest declared. "It certainly could support one now."

The priest's father and mother came in, both very thin quiet people, and shook hands with the boys. Father Joe told his mother he would have two guests for supper and she said it was good because Father Jim would be there, too. She said it was too bad none of the people from Pawtucket could get over to see him but that they would probably be there the next day.

Father Joe went into the grassy back yard with the boys. He said he hadn't meant there was anything wrong about either of them going to the public schools; as a matter of fact there had been many disputes among the clergy themselves concerning Catholic schools and public schools, many disputes. Some contended, he said, that a Catholic, facing a hostile world of business and politics and religion, ought to educate himself among these very people, providing, of course, his faith was strong enough to withstand it. He meant higher education, he said, more than just schooling. Personally, Father Joe said, he would like to see every Catholic boy and girl educated in Catholic schools from the time they first began to learn their ABC's. He told the boys they would have to do some reading about Rome and the ancient world. Byron said he had read most of Ben-Hur. That, the priest said, was not a bad beginning, not a bad beginning, but hardly scratched the surface; there was more, so very much more to read and know, so much to know about the struggles of the ancient Christians, the founding of the orders, the building of the Church itself.

Willie thought how happy his grandfather would be if he could really learn and know about so many, many beautiful things before he was even out of school, and thinking of his grandfather he realized he would have to cut himself away from this house and be at home in time for supper. He told them he would have to go and was just leaving when Father Jim McCaffrey, hatless, came out into the yard. He wouldn't hear of Willie's leaving and said he would personally see to it that his grandmother wasn't upset. He was leaving right after supper he said, and would stop at McDermotts' house on his way to the rectory to tell his grandmother Willie would be a little late getting home.

When they went in the house again at suppertime, Willie met Theresa and Frances McCaffrey, sisters of the priest. Theresa, the older one, had a sharp hooked nose like her mother and was very thin, too. She wore rimless, sparkling nose glasses that she squeezed every few minutes, took away from her nose and pinched back on again after she blinked her eyes a few times. Frances, the baby of the family, closely resembled Father Joe, but her rosy face was rounder, her lips full and red, and her black eyes alive with passion far different from that which glowed in her brother's. Looking at all their faces as they sat at the table, Willie thought she was the only one he could see sitting at his grandfather's table sharing his evening onions with him.

After supper, Theresa went to the upright piano and ran over a few bars of a piece of sheet music she said she had bought in the Boston Store on her way home. Father Jim warned Father Joe that practically the only music he would hear while he was at home would be ragtime and, laughing, said he might as well get used to it now as at any other time. Nothing classical in that house, he warned. When she had played the music through once she started the chorus over again and began to sing in a voice as harsh as wagon wheels scraping the curbstone: *I found a rose in the devil's garden.*

"What is that? What is that song?" Mrs. McCaffrey cried, running in to the piano.

"Why, Mother, it's only a song," Theresa said. "It's only a popular song."

Mrs. McCaffrey snatched the sheet of music from the piano and crushed its length in her bony hands, declaring no such song as that would ever be sung in her house. She turned in amazement to the young priests, who were both smiling. Then she upbraided them both for not interfering when their own sister brought music like that into the house. Well, perhaps Father Joe, shut up in the university with his books all the year long, might not know the wickedness that went on around him, but there was certainly no excuse for Father Jim, curate in a parish, permitting songs about roses in the garden of the devil himself to be sung in his presence. Yes, Father Joe might be excused, she supposed, the Sulpicians were not as strict as the Jesuits or some of the other orders. Sadly shaking her head she went to the kitchen, saying she was going to burn the music or throw it into the garbage pail where it belonged. She cautioned Theresa from the doorway never to bring such songs into the house again.

Promising to come again to see Father Joe, Byron and Willie started home in the warm June night. Walking with Byron's bike between them, each with a hand on the handle bars, Byron asked Willie if he wasn't glad he had gone to McCaffreys' house and if Father Joe wasn't the greatest priest he had ever known in his life. Willie said he was, and wished that he knew even half as much as the priest did about things. Byron inquired whether Willie had ever thought of becoming a priest himself, adding that *he* had and had even talked it all over with his mother.

Willie never had, but he said it must be a great thing to be a priest and a teacher as Father Joe was. Byron said, of course, he hadn't made up his mind that the priesthood was really his vocation; it was much too soon for him to know yet. When he got as far as college, he said, he was going to go to Holy Cross, and by that time he would be able to make up his mind better.

"You're going to go to college, aren't you?" he asked Willie.

Willie said he was pretty sure of going because his grandfather wanted him to. He said his grandfather didn't care whether he became a priest or not; they never talked about it at home; but there were many things to be besides a priest if you went to college.

"Sure there is," Byron assented. "There's a great future in politics, too. My father would like me to get into politics when I grow up. I might, I don't know. It all depends."

Ashamed of his own uncertainty about his future, a little repelled by Byron's almost boastful attitude and more than a little distrustful of him, Willie was glad when they reached the Slater mansion. When they parted Byron let the bicycle go into Willie's hands. He said Willie could use it if he wanted to for the whole of the coming week, because he was going down the river with his mother and sister to visit some people his father knew. He said when they came back to town again he and Willie could go to visit Father Joe again. His mother was very anxious for him to know Father Joe as well as he could, Byron added, on account of his father being a Protestant. He shouted from the steps of the house, as Willie pedaled away down the drive, that Willie would have 'to pay for any punctures.

Chapter Twenty-Eight

FATHER JOE said mass at the side altar, St. Joseph's, at six o'clock in the morning while the damp that had rolled up from the river during the night would be still silvered over the green ivy. His congregation was usually only the old sexton, whose false teeth seemed to whir in unison with the clicking of his beads as he prayed in the half-light of the front pew. Father Jim agreed that Willie and Byron Searles could begin serving mass for his brother, warning him, however, that he would have to train them both.

It was easy for Willie to get to the church on time because his grandfather would be leaving for the foundry about that same time and was more than pleased to call him for a breakfast at which there would be only the two of them. If Willie happened to be a little late getting to church he would find old Stephen lighting the altar candles. One morning, when neither he nor Byron had appeared before Father Joe was ready to leave the sacristy, Stephen, grumbling and scowling, was serving mass himself.

There was fervor and frightening supplication in the manner in which Father Joe said the prayers at the foot of the altar steps when he began the mass, and he would wait, head bowed and hands clasped, for the boys to say a response that might have fled them in their sleepiness. Any of the other priests, Willie noticed, would say the response himself and continue the ritual. Father Joe's tall reed of a body seemed to break in half, almost, when he would bend to kiss the altar and he never hurried a word or gesture. Every word of the Latin flowed from his thin lips, from his first blessing and "Introibo," with the music of poetry renewing itself each morning. Humbly, with his eyes averted as though he were accepting the services for someone else, he would let the boys pour the wine and water into his chalice and take the small linen towel to dry his fingers, after Pilate has washed his hands, with a shadow of pain on his face for a moment as though he, and he alone, bore that ever-recurring guilt. Each of his prayers through the mass was an entreaty so eloquent it reached through

the Latin into Willie's understanding, sadly, or with such exalta-
tion and joy even the deaf could hear it. When he repeated,
Domine, non sum dignus ("I am not worthy") he smote Willie's
spirit, yet he tore away the victories from the hands of Willie's
enemies, too, the pride and arrogance from Larry McDermott, the
insufferable pretentions and shoddy little cruelties of his Uncle
Chris, the sting from the slaps of his grandmother and the jibes Nora
leveled at him and his grandfather, for, if Father Joe were not
worthy, what were they? Reading the last Gospel on the left side
of the altar near the end of the mass, he was like a tired man
who has left his heart in a far country and is refreshed again, reading a letter from the land where his spirit still dwells. When the
prayers after mass had been said, "Oh, clement, oh loving, oh, sweet
Virgin Mary! Pray for us, oh Holy Mother of God! . . . That we may
be worthy of the promises of Christ . . ." he would turn to Willie,
serving on the right side of the altar, and take his biretta from
the boy's hand with an almost imperceptible smile of thanks moving
his lips.

One morning, when a summer storm had been thundering itself
out during the mass and Stephen hurried around with his long
stick to close the windows just at the Consecration of the Host,
they returned to the sacristy to find Father O'Farrell pacing the
floor there and reading his breviary, his gold-rimmed nose glasses
so near the tip of the nose he could look straight at them without
lifting his head from the little book. Stephen told Willie and
Byron, when they went to take off their cassocks and surplices, that
Father O'Farrell had to go away out of town that morning and was
going to say an early mass. He wanted them to stay and serve him.
If they were starved to death for the want of a breakfast or
prostrate with piety, Stephen said, he would stay and serve Father
O'Farrell himself, but he had other things to do that must be
done and he hoped they had enough zeal left in them to spend
another half an hour in the service of Almighty God. They might
as well, anyhow, Stephen said, as though he were protecting them
from some disaster, because they'd both get wringing, soaking wet
if they tried to get home in the storm anyhow, or *drownded*, like
rats in a trap. The boys said they would stay and Stephen went
home to his breakfast.

Father O'Farrell's brogue was so heavy and his voice so harsh it
made everything he said an almost unintelligible mutter. He

rasped the Latin with the sound of McDermott's worn shovel scraping the floor of the coalbin. The boys missed their responses and made him irritable. He made them nervous and hastened along so that the Latin scratched Willie's ears. Willie got a drop too much water into the wine to suit him and Father O'Farrell bumped the sharp lip of his jeweled chalice against the spout of the cruet, glaring at him. Willie and Byron, relieved when the prayers after mass were said, raced away, leaving the bewildered priest to pick his biretta up from the altar steps himself and follow them into the sacristy. Well, he had to hurry away and catch his train, but he made a mental note to speak to Father McCaffrey about the new altar boys and let him give them both a good talking to about the dignity of serving a priest at mass and a little more training at least, Father, before sending them out on the altar. He asked them both their names to help him remember it and forgot them again as he hurried through the rain to the rectory.

Mornings when he was invited to spend the afternoon at McCaffreys' house would crawl with clubbed feet for Willie, impatient to get there and sit under the maple with Byron and listen to Father Joe talk. Several times Father Joe asked them to come and have lunch, but Nell would never let Willie go because she wanted no one, *especially* not the McCaffreys with two sons priests, to think the boy wasn't properly fed at home, or there wasn't always enough for everyone at all times. Nora agreed with her; it was not the right thing for Willie to do. They were both very proud, though, that the young priest had taken such an interest in Willie. His uncle told Catherine Daly about it, too, and she said she was as glad for Ned's sake as she was for Willie's, because Ned loved the boy so very much. "Oh, Chris," she said, "isn't he a lucky boy to have someone like your father, to have Father McCaffrey's brother interested in him?"

Poor Tessie Butler, though, in her bed across the lane, heard about it, as she did, inexplicably, all the news of the parish, before Nora or Nell came over to tell her. Now, Nell's boasting she didn't mind too much. After all, the woman was the boy's grandmother, practically his mother, and it was only to be expected she would have great pride in him. But that Nora! That damn Nora—you'd think she was there at McCaffreys' house herself, to hear her talking about it. "Keep her out, Mollie, tell her I'm sleeping." Tessie begged her niece, "for I can't stand to hear her boasting."

It irked Tessie, it wounded her, that all the time she spent dressing the altar at St. Malachi's church and as long as Patrick and John had been on the altar, they had never once been asked to McCaffreys' house. Good boys, the best of boys, and here this Willie, God knows the stories they told about him! He's traipsing over there every other day! Tessie prodded Patrick and John about it, trying to find some way they could edge themselves into the McCaffrey home. She had to give that up; there wasn't any. One morning when Father Jim McCaffrey stopped in to see her on his sick calls she slyly tried to turn the conversation in that direction, but, when she had nearly reached the turn, she grew ashamed of her own trickery and stopped. She ended up by praising Willie, for what she didn't know. Still, it gnawed at her heart to hear Nora talk about it, Nora who was no more than herself, a grand-aunt, living on Ned's bounty all these years, raised up to heights she had not climbed.

The bitterness of it! And she had no help at all from Pat McDermott, who didn't care whether his boys went to McCaffreys' house or not; in fact, he would just as soon they didn't because he didn't want either of them to be priests, if he could help it, and that seemed to be where Willie McDermott was headed. Tessie thought he had no pride whatever in his sons. He laughed at her. Nothing would have made Tessie happier than to have been able to make either young Pat or John a priest.

In the foundry, Ned would tell his brother Pat he hardly ever saw Willie at all this summer, what with him spending so much time at the priest's house, no, not the rectory at all, the house where the McCaffrey family lived. Well, deprecatingly, better than running wild on the streets as he used to, yes, far better than running the streets and picking up with all sorts. Of course, if the boy wasn't as smart as a whip himself, the priest would soon discover that and lose interest in him, but no fear on that score.

In Father Joe's words, the life of Jesus and the vivid symbols cf it in the mass, the miracles, the sufferings, the betrayals, the trial before Pilate, the Passion and ultimate triumph, cried with reality for Willie and Byron Searles. The priest brought Rome and Judea as close to them as Olneyville and Pawtucket and the cedars of Lebanon as near as the trees in Roger Williams Park, Galilee spilled into Narragansett Bay. From Galilee, the story strode the waters, came Simon Peter, Kepha (Father Joe hoped that some day they would both study Greek and Hebrew) the Rock. Yet even he denied Him, three times in the yard of the high priest. He slept, as the unawakened sleep today, cool under the olives during the agony of His Gethsemane. But later, when the Saviour asked the disciples, Simon Peter answering said: "Thou art Christ the son of the Living God." And Jesus answering said to him: "Blessed art thou, Simon Bar-Jonah, because flesh and blood have not revealed it to thee, but my Father, who is in Heaven. And I say to thee, thou art Peter; and upon this rock I will build my church and the gates of hell shall not prevail against it. And I will give to thee the keys of the kingdom of heaven. And whatsoever thou shalt bind upon earth, it shall be bound also in heaven; and whatsoever thou shalt loose upon earth it shall be loosed also in Heaven."

"There is the divine authority for the Holy Mother Church," said the priest. "Someday soon we'll talk more about it. And someday we'll talk about Catholics in this country. I'll bet neither of you can tell me very much about that. Now, I'll just bet both of you there isn't very much you can tell me. There's too much, too many, many things to talk about in the little time we have to do it in, but we'll do what we can, won't we?"

But, no matter where he began (it might have been to show them that fierce and hostile as the trackless new world was to the nameless Jesuits who carried the faith into its forests and mountains, the world *they* lived in, when it denied God and shunned or persecuted His Church, was no less savage) Father Joe would return always, before he stopped talking, to bring Cyprian or Augustine out of Africa's glorious antiquity or Origen's prophetic words to them. Then he would realize, unhappily, that they were still boys and had still many long miles to travel before he could discuss these holy men and their ideas with them, before they would know or remember what he said.

Soon Willie could tell his grandfather about the great saints of Ireland itself, of Brendan, the navigator, sailing west, always west, over seas no man walked before, who had come at last to a land there; and who knew whether he hadn't built the great stone mill in Newport with its spans of arches that led now only into the void of its past, arches that Irish hands might have raised for eternity in the rolling fog of the years? "Ah. God damn the English," Ned cried, "who knows, who knows we didn't do it? But there would have been a cairn or a cross of some kind somewhere around, wouldn't there, Willie? Well, the seas, as the saying was, only join the lands they separate." Nora said she never heard that one before, though if the priest said it was so, she supposed it must be. She had never heard of St. Ferdiad, either, the missioner who went from Ireland to Europe and was the patron of Lucca in the Tuscan hills where they called him San Frediano.

"That'll be St. Fred, I suppose," Ned pondered. "Well, now, I never heard tell of him, either. And them changing his name to a dago name, now! What the hell do you think of that. They had a hell of a crust, didn't they, and him a saint!"

Nora informed them that saints were never canonized until long after they were dead, but Ned said, no matter, he must have been a saint when he was on earth for them to know he was a saint, for he certainly did none of his good works after he died, did he? Well, they did, Nora insisted, maybe the most of their good works was done after they were dead, the martyrs and all.

"Well, the inside track in heaven and that, I suppose," Ned couldn't let her steal this from him. "But what they was made saints for was what they done whilst they was here below, wasn't it? That's what I mean, the good works that they done here below, teaching the heathen the word of God. They didn't have to teach the word of God for the holy angels in heaven, did they? Nor do miracles for them, I hope, to convert them? Faugh, Nora, there's a hell of a lot you don't know about such matters."

Oh, she didn't say the Irish wasn't the greatest of scholars! True enough, they educated half Europe in days gone by when there was no one else to do it. "Sure they were all saints and scholars, yourself included, Ned."

The ignorance of a woman, the old man told his grandson, was the stone she sharpened the horns of her spite upon.

With all the learning and knowledge Willie carried home to him, Ned was quite a little troubled because it began to appear that Father Joe, from whom it all flowed, was beginning to supplant himself in Willie's heart. It irked him that there were so many things, even about Ireland itself, that the priest knew that he had never even heard about. Columbanus was a name to him, but a damn strange one; and he didn't care whether the Jesuits went to Asia or Africa or whether or not they had ten houses or four hundred houses in Japan or India. He was ever on the watch to see where, if possible, he could trip the priest up, not on matters of religion, for there he dared not even venture to dispute him. His great chance came when Willie told him about Daniel O'Connell and the Catholic Emancipation for the poor of Ireland, way back in 1829.

"Oh, that was a great man," Nell said. "I was sure the priest would speak of him. Oh, my, there's no one like Daniel O'Connell. No, indeed, he was a great Irishman!"

"Indeed he was," Nora added.

"Yes," Ned's voice came very slowly. "I suppose he was, after all, a great man. He was—well, God damn it, he was the kind of a great man it seems only the Irish are—two parts saint and two parts son of a bitch. Why, God damn him, I heard tell years ago that he was after poor Emmet there, a greater man than O'Connell would ever be, I heard tell he was after Emmet, hunting him down with a blunderbuss. They said when he sat in the English Parliament—whatever the hell he wanted there—he voted along with the British lords and dukes that thought daylight to dark wasn't enough for the little children to be moiling and toiling away in their factories and mills. Well, that's what I was told years ago. And that, if a union man raised his voice in Dublin, the great Dan would shove a fist down his throat, and a big fist he had, too. But as you say, Will, there was Catholic Emancipation and it was a great thing that the Irish could go to mass again without a British gun stuck in their backs. No denying it. Then, with all that again, they had a right to own the cow, or the horse or the ass they hadn't the money to buy in the first place.

"The great Dan didn't give a damn whether the farmer had enough land to grow a dish of potatoes in or not. And why in the hell should he? Sure the O'Connells owned half of Kerry. They clung to it through thick and thin, too, though God knows how, when no one else had a spoonful of it to call his own. Why, there wasn't a wave would dare creep up on the shores of Kerry without first tipping its hat to an O'Connell; nor a blade of grass would dare push its little head up into a meadow without first it asked an O'Connell.

"Ha! That was your great Dan for you, traipsing off to London and Rome when he damn pleased. That was your great Dan for you, with his fine great house. Oh, yes, and running off with this trollop and that one, the son of a bitch, worse than Parnell ever did. At least *he* stuck to the one, didn't he? Yes, that's the worst they could ever say about him, but the trouble was, I guess, he was of the wrong persuasion and he would see to it that a farmer wouldn't have to send his children and his grandchildren, too, maybe, out here to this country to earn enough money to pay his taxes with, or his rent. But my great Dan can do as he damn pleases and then, when he's worn out and too tired to raise any more hell, he can slip away to Rome and say he's sorry he did it in the first place and never meant to at all; it was maybe the drink did it and he never knew a thing about it until he woke up in the morning. Well, the cardinal or the bishop or was it the Pope himself, I can't recall now, gives him a pat on the back and says, 'Never mind, Dan, that's all water under the bridge now and forgiven. Think no more about it, all's forgiven.'

"Oh, he was a learned man and a great Catholic. And learning is a great thing, too. A man must free himself of his own ignorance before he'll free anything. But more than learning is needed to free Ireland and always was. Emmet had the right way for that, see; Emmet was for the sword and the gun and the hell with them all. Now O'Connell there had his chance, they say, that Emmet never had. But he was always for palavering with them—and God knows some of it had its place, too—but the sword is what's needed in the last run. They can talk and talk, but it's the sword will have the loudest voice in the end.

"Them poor lads that was murdered in Dublin there only a while ago, does the priest ever talk about them? Has he ever mentioned them to you?"

Willie's mind quivered with indecision. He had barely time to say Father Joe hadn't spoken to them about the Sinn Feiners, and start to think of reasons why he hadn't before his grandfather began to talk again.

"That's it, see, a man must be up on all things. But I suppose it's best for a young priest to keep his nose out of them things entirely. Let him stick to religion itself and be on the safe side. The line's drawn very fine sometimes between it and politics. Let him—it was the great Dan himself said it—take his religion from Rome, as he does, and you take your politics, if it's politics you want, from them that knows more about it."

It was the first time in a long long while that his grandfather had mentioned the name of Emmet. Willie had never forgotten the words of Emmet's speech to the British judges as he stood in the dock, though; and Emmet's picture, the cream of the tight pants he wore curdling a little with the passing years and the horrid brown of the judges robes corroded now, still hung in its oaken frame over the table in the kitchen as it had hung always in the old house.

The words below the slight defiant figure were Willie's first words of learning and he wished there were some way he could tell this to Father Joe without having Byron Searles riddle them as he knew Byron would be likely to do, with the scorn the other boy had for the defeated, the vanquished. Willie was proud of Emmet's words and he knew they rode on the waves of great and unconquerable seas, but he knew, too, that Byron was clever enough with a sharp word or two, to make them appear almost ridiculous, the words of an obscure romantic failure, unless Willie could beat him down with facts and facts and facts about what Emmet had done, or tried to do, and that, Willie knew, he didn't have the knowledge to say. Byron was like that, proud, tremendously proud he was a Catholic, but always careful, without actually hiding the fact, not to mention that his mother was Irish and always giving the impression of being, because of his Protestant father, unassailably American.

Chapter Twenty-Nine

NED lay with the gas turned low as it always was left when Chris was out. The pipe did not capsize, though, because Ned was troubled and far from drowsy. He was afraid that in his talk he might have said something that would discourage Willie from seeing more of the young priest and listening to him talk, or that the boy might say less about it at home. He didn't want that, but he was nearly an hour puzzling out what he could say to the boy that would reassure him. He went quietly upstairs to Willie's room and asked:

"Asleep, Will?"

The boy stirred in the bed and sat up. Ned went to the window, looking out into the dark surf of the elm-tops across the street.

"It was only that I thought you might—well, not understand, you know, what it was I was saying about the priests and politics. Only that I didn't want you to think I was disputing the man in matters where I'd no right to speak, or something."

"He doesn't talk to us about politics," the boy said, still not fully alert.

"There's politics in things where you think there's no politics, Will, and many a priest has stubbed his toe over it. I want a priest, d'you see, I want a priest for to tell me what's good or bad for my immortal soul and I'll take care of the rest of it."

"That's really what he talks to us about," said Willie, somewhat feebly trying to find the words that would give his grandfather some deeper understanding of the meaning Father Joe's talks had for him.

"When it comes to politics," Ned said carefully, "a priest can blunder and blunder on the wrong side, see, or the Church itself can, and has, more times than you could count. They, well, they want to keep things as they are and not upset them, see? And that's not always what's best for people, Will. There's times when —the Church condemned the Fenians, you see, excommunicated them right and left—"

"Was Emmet a Fenian?" Willie asked.

"Same thing, though he come before them—excommunicated

them right and left, but they wouldn't give up though it broke their hearts. They had nothing to do with Emmet for he was a Protestant like Tone. They blundered then and they blundered again when it come to the Knights of Labor. Every time on the wrong side, the Molly Maguires."

"Not on doctrine," Willie was awake now and stirred.

"Doctrine, no. That's what I'm saying, Will. They're right every time on doctrine, but when it comes to other things they might overstep the line, see, and say it was doctrine when it wasn't at all, when it was no more than politics that had nothing to do with doctrine or doctrine with it."

"But the priest knows what is doctrine better than we do," Willie argued. "We can't tell the priest what is doctrine—"

"No and we can't trample on it, either, when it is doctrine. But sometimes we can tell the priest when it's not doctrine—when it has to do with things that—when it has to do with the things— things that's not religious things."

"Well, what Father Joe talks about are all religious things. He doesn't talk about those other things. When he told us about Daniel O'Connell it was about what he did for Catholics."

"I know it was. I know it was, Will. What I mean is there's lots he couldn't tell you about them things, for he wouldn't know himself. I want a priest," Ned said now, seeing that he was tangling himself in talk about things he felt better than he knew, and wanting to end it before he said something he might not intend saying, "I want a priest to bring me the sacraments when I need them and the doctrine. Yes, to preach the doctrine of the Church to me. I want him to help me to keep myself out of hell everlasting. That's what I want the priest for. Or least—at least, if I stumble around the fiery edges of it to give me a hand that I'll get out before I'm singed around my own edges, before I'm scorched beyond recognition. That's what I want him for, Will."

These were the first sweet fruits of Ned's long schemes for the boy's education. He never lost an opportunity to tell Tim Lee of the great strides the boy was making and they would walk sometimes to Owen Tegue's harbor master's shack on the bridge, where Ned would sit and repeat proudly what he had just told Tim.

"What are you up to, Ned?" Tegue asked one day, "Are you going to make a priest of the boy?"

"Oh, I don't think the twig is bent in that direction," said Ned. "Though you never can tell; he might turn in that direction. The wildest of them sometimes does, you know. I suppose Father McCaffrey would like to see him a priest, he's that interested in him. Whatever's to be will be, of course."

"Is there a priest in the family, at all?" Tegue asked.

"None I know," said Ned, "Though Nell's cousins in Fall River there, the Casey's, one of them's a priest and there's nuns galore of them."

"I know the Caseys," said Tegue. "There's more of them in the mills than the convents, God knows."

"One of them, not the father of the priests, but the uncle, I think he is, is very proud of them boys," Ned said. "He come to the house one time when we lived in the other house. Him with a jag on and bragging about the priests in the family, wearing a sealskin cap that he never took off all the time he was there and it was Fourth of July Day, so the mills was closed down. Hot as the flames of hell itself, it was that day. I'll never forget him in the sealskin cap, and he says a dozen times before he went away, 'Now yez must all come to Fall River before the snow flies.' God, and going out the door he says it again, 'before the snow flies again,' he says, 'yez must all come to Fall River now.'"

"Hell of a fine time to be talking about priests with a half a jag on," Tim commented.

"Well, the old codger worked hard for them ¹oys to educate them," Ned went on, "and he was proud of them. He never was married, you know, and the only times he ever took a sneak for himself was to come here once in a while. But wasn't that a hell of a thing, now, sitting there with a sealskin cap on Fourth of July Day? I says to Nell it's a hell of a funny family she's related to, the Caseys."

"I'm related to the Caseys myself, you know," Tegue said a little belligerently.

"So you are, Owen," Ned said. "So you are."

He walked back to Tim's house with him when Tegue closed the shack for the day.

"He's touchy about the Casey's, ain't he?" Tim said.

"Ah, sure," Ned laughed. "Pat Casey is all right, you know, but when he has a jag on he's forever bragging and boasting about his family. You couldn't pry him loose from that sealskin for love nor money. It's the finest cap he ever had on his head and he'd wear it to bed if they'd let him, I suppose. He was damn good, too, to the brother's family when they was growing up and studying."

Well, Tim said, he supposed there'd be no stopping Willie now with the priest helping him and teaching him things all summer long. He said it was damn lucky for the boy to have the priest that interested in him.

"Tim," Ned said, "my schemes for that boy is only begun. With God's help there's no limit to where he'll go in this world. Ain't it a great country, Tim, with the young teaching the old about things they never knew a damn about in their lives?"

"Yes, Ned!" Tim said. "It's a grand country for that."

Chapter Thirty

A SANDY payday quarter from his grandfather in his pocket, Willie McDermott started from the house just before dusk for Father Joe McCaffrey's house. Byron Searles would be there and they would listen again to the priest read them wondrous stories like the letter that was stolen by the wily ambassador or hear him tell part of another one like the heroic race of the charioteer, Ben-Hur. He cut through the break in the fence by the lumberyard and sped along, looking in the windows of the tobacco store at the magazines when he came to the car tracks. The grim table of the ball field, pebbly and flat, spread out before him along the side of the rubber factory. He stood at home plate, in front of the high diamond-meshed backstop ready to clout out a homer, at least a triple.

Christy Mathewson was pitching, but he could hit him and he swung the bat sharply at the twirler warming up for the first pitch. Wide, high and wide, that first pitch and he let it go, swinging the bat again while Christy warmed up for the second. Too low, but the umpire called it a strike. One and one. He wasn't worried yet even if it were Christy Mathewson pitching; he knew he could hit him. He swung at an inside curve, an in-curve that broke too fast for him and it was two and one. The next one was too low and he let it go, knowing the umpire would see it. Two and two and the best one coming up. Oh, yes, looking out in the field he remembered there were three on bases and two out and the score was tied in the last half of the ninth. He took a chance and let the next one go too, way outside. Three and two and his last chance. He fouled one. Then Christy put it just where he wanted it and—crack! He sent it out to left field and started down to first base.

He slowed up halfway to the base. He had plenty of time; it was a long drive, and he put his hand into his pocket for the quarter. You could never tell, he might have to slide into third or home and that quarter might fall out. Clutching the coin in his hand he rounded first and picked up some speed going to second.

189

He was watching that left fielder who might try to throw to the plate to catch him. When he passed third he dug his spikes in hard and streamed for the plate, not looking for the outfielder again. He slid in, scratching himself on the pebbles. What a clout. Drove in three runs beside himself and won the game in spite of Christy Mathewson.

Slapping his legs to dust himself off afterward, he looked at his opened hands, realizing that the quarter was gone. He must have lost it when he slid into the plate, but it might have been when he was rounding second or even third. He was afraid dark would fall before he would be able to find the coin among the gravelly sands of the ball field. He went down on his knees around home plate first, moving slowly around in a circle and groping with his hands in the dirt. He tried to grope every inch of the sand where he was before moving ahead, and wound himself back into the home plate without finding it.

Although he knew he had taken it out of his pocket on the way to first base he walked the whole way peering along the base line. He couldn't remember how widely he had circled first when he was cutting down to second, so he cut twice into the arc there before he continued. Then he thought, anywhere along there he might have let it fly out of his hand and he went down on his knees again, crawling to the imaginary spot where second base was. He had sliced it short he recollected, and didn't bother creeping out toward center field. He couldn't determine how far the coin would fly out of his hand if it had, though, and retraced his course.

His eyes were weary with searching when he reached third again, but he continued frantically on to home plate, kneeling there a moment to decide it must have been when he slid in for the winning run that the quarter had fled his fist. The daylight was fading fast now. He swept the palm of his hand carefully over every inch of the ground around him, sifting it through his fingers and trying to plot the next tiny area he would explore. He thought of coming over to the field early in the morning when it got light, but if it rained during the night, and it might because it was getting dark so fast, the silver piece would be driven into the sand.

He continued to grope and sift, grope and sift, casting the small pebbles away from himself in anger when they yielded nothing. When he thought he had covered every inch of the ground where the money might have fallen he began all over again. He was sure now that it couldn't have been lost at first or second or third; it must be right here somewhere. Suddenly he heard a vaguely familiar voice:

"What's the matter, kid, lose something there?"

He looked up at the backstop and saw, coming slowly around it toward the first base side a tall man whose walk he obscurely remembered. The man walked to the end of the backstop and stood there leaning against its steel frame, tugging nervously at his cap with his free hand.

"Lose something there, kid?" the man repeated.

"Yes," he said. "I lost a quarter."

"It's getting pretty dark, kid. How are you going to find it now? It's getting dark fast now."

Willie said nothing, but continued his probing into the gravel. Maybe he wouldn't find it, but he would keep on looking until it got so dark he couldn't see anything.

"You ought to have a light there, kid, if you're going to see anything in the dark. Do you want a match?"

The man sauntered over to him and put his hand on the boy's shoulder holding matches down to him.

"Want me to help you?" the man asked.

"If you want to," Willie answered. "I can't find it."

"Sure you lost a quarter, kid?"

"Am I sure?" Willie straightened up and looked at the man. "I ought to know."

"Sure," the man said, striking a match and kneeling down beside the boy.

Willie looked into the light and the green eyes of the tramp moulder who had come to the house the first Sunday they were living in South Providence. The man recognized him, too.

"I'll be damned; it's the McDermott kid," the man said. "Well we certainly got to find that two bits now, kid. I certainly have to help any relative of Joe McDermott's."

He asked the boy how he had lost the money. Willie tried to tell him how he had been running around the bases for practice and that the coin must have flown out of his hand when he slid into home plate. The man crawled away from him then toward the shin-high bench, still lighting his matches and looking in the dirt.

191

"What's this?" he called suddenly. "Is this it?"

He held a coin up in his hand with the flame of the little match lighting its silver surface. Willie got up off his knees and went toward him. The man sat himself down on the bench and the match flickered out. He still held the coin in his hand. When Willie came over he handed it to him.

"It's not my quarter," Willie said. "It's a half dollar."

"It is," the man said. "Well, keep it anyway. Somebody must have dropped it. You might as well keep it; you'll never find that quarter, kid."

About to put it in his pocket, Willie reconsidered. It wasn't his and the man hadn't found it, he knew. He had given it to him. Much as he wanted the quarter and twice as welcome as the half dollar would be, he held it out to the man:

"No," he said. "I don't want it."

"Why, look, kid, you might as well keep it. You lost a two-bit piece and I'm making it up to you. Joe McDermott was good to me when I hit town and I'm just paying him back in a way. That's all, I'm just paying back in a way what Joe done for me, that's all. You might as well keep the half a buck, kid."

Willie wanted it, but could not put it in his pocket. He flipped it in the air and caught it again, proffering it once more to the moulder.

"Sit down, kid, take it easy," the man said. "You're all excited about losing the two bits. Sit down and catch your breath. What are you running around the bases all alone for? Nobody to play with? Seems funny for a kid like you to be running around the bases all alone at night. Was you just practicing?

"Where's your pals? Why wasn't they here playing with you? They could have helped you look for the quarter. I bet you're quite a ball player at that. What do you play, pitch? Was you just running bases while you waited for your friends to come?"

"No," Willie said. "I was—I was going someplace."

"Oh, just practicing all alone, hey? I bet you're quite a ball player at that. You're pretty husky for a kid, I can see that. That's funny, you're here all alone running around the bases not waiting for anybody and I'm walking along the outside of the field all alone not waiting for anybody either. Funny how things happen like that ain't it?

"I bet you're a kid that likes to go alone sometimes with none of his pals around waiting for him or not expecting anybody. I do, too. Sometimes I just walk around here about this time all alone after work like that, not waiting for anybody and not supposed to meet anybody."

Why he distrusted the man, Willie didn't know. He thought of Father Joe and Byron Searles waiting for him and wanted to go. The man put his arm on Willie's shoulder, pulling the boy to him.

"Funny. Funny, that's awful funny when you come to think of it. When you come to think, I hardly know anybody in town at all." The man seemed to be talking to himself.

"I have to go someplace," Willie said.

"Not yet," the tramp moulder was half whining and yet there was a threat in his words. "You don't have to go anywhere yet. Stay here with me for a while."

Willie tried to shake the clawing hand from his shoulder, but the man pinned him and slipped the arm around his neck. The boy was terrified and powerless to move for a minute. Suddenly the man's other hand descended on his thigh, gripping it fiercely. He was laughing a high, gleeful little sound.

Willie ducked his head quickly, scraping his forehead on the buttons of his captor's vest, and jerked himself to his feet and started to run. The man was on his feet almost as soon as the boy, and nailed him against the heavy wire mesh of the backstop. Frantically the boy strained at the man's grip, trying to think of tricks he used when he was fighting with other boys, but his mind seemed to have vanished; he could think of nothing. The man was bending over him, over, his laugh bubbling behind his lips that were slipping back and forth over each other.

"You don't have to go nowhere yet, kid," the man was saying. "Why don't you be nice and stay with me for a while? I ain't going to hurt you, kid. We can have some fun."

Looking up into the laughing face, Willie saw the man lift his head, close the drifting eyes briefly, and then look down again at him swiftly and savagely. He squirmed, trying to kick at the man's shins, but the man skipped back a step and then closed in on him again. With all the strength he could summon up, Willie lifted a leg that spurted up like a piston and his knee caught the man squarely in the groin.

The man groaned and, doubling over, let go his hold on the

boy to grasp himself in the groin, moaning and cursing. As soon as he let go, Willie broke into a terrified run down the street. He could hear the man cursing at him as he ran, but he did not look back until he had reached the next corner and then only a second, running on until he came to the car tracks and there were people walking on the street.

Remembering weird things Joseph Riordan had told him about sometimes and sometimes hinted at, Willie understood what had been happening to him, what the man had been trying to do, and he was even more terrified. In his fright, though, he was fascinated, wickedly fascinated, and he felt degraded, when he came near the McCaffreys' house, not by what had happened to him but by what had not, except in his own mind. He crossed the street where there were no street lamps and continued on home.

Chapter Thirty-One

STRIP me, Nell," cried Kate Reagan, dropping into a rocker, "these corsets have me strangled."

"Why, Kate," said Nell, "You're looking fine."

"Let me catch my breath, Nell," Kate gasped, "I'm worn out with these damn things. I must get them off me, or loosen them before they choke the daylights out of me. Oh dear, Nell, what a time I had with them sitting there with Mrs. Murtaugh herself and the girls. Up and down on hands and knees measuring them—"

"The Murtaughs!"

Kate fumbled with her skirt and squirmed in the rocker. At last she stood up and lifted her dress high, reaching under it with one hand while she rolled her hips like a dancer.

"Yes, the Murtaughs," said she. "I have the sewing to do for them all—God what a relief—I had the samples with me and I measured them. The dear knows how I'll have it all done in time for them with the fittings and all, but that's the least of my troubles now."

Kate let herself down into the chair again with a sigh of content. She sewed for many of the Irish families who had a little money, but, among them all, the Murtaughs were the richest. Who wouldn't envy her running back and forth to the Murtaughs' great mansion on the East Side with its cook and maids and chauffeur now to drive old man Murtaugh to the brewery every day? And it wasn't as a servant she went to them, either. She sat in the grand rooms with them and the maid brought her a cup of tea while she was there.

"And from there I went to the Boston Store," Kate told Nell and Nora as though she had not interrupted what she was saying, "from there to the Boston Store to order the material, yards and yards of it that I should be working at this minute, and it measured and cut for me ready to wrap up and take away, when old Cameron, the floorwalker, comes along feeling and feeling it and says It's a large amount of goods you have there, Miss Reagan. It is, I said, and I'm charging it for the Murtaughs. For the Murtaughs, he says, charging it to the Murtaughs, Miss Reagan? No, said I, I'm charging it to my own bill, Mr. Cameron. I'm sorry, said he, Miss Reagan, but I'm afraid we can't do that. I'm afraid we can't do that for you."

"Not for the Murtaughs?" Nell was astounded. It had always seemed to her there was nothing the Murtaughs wanted done wouldn't be done. It did please her a little, though, that Kate Reagan, so thick with the Murtaughs and all she drank tea with them a maid brought her, was coming to her with her tale of woe.

Ah, she couldn't charge the material to the Murtaughs, Kate explained; it would injure her reputation with them and besides, when you sewed for the Murtaughs you gave them the bill when the work was done and that was all there was to it. It was a terrible pickle to be in for only last Monday she put out every last penny she had in the house on the mortgage; and there was Joseph, her nephew at Georgetown, forever needing money at the medical school; and indeed if she lost the Murtaughs' work now, God knows she'd never get it again. She didn't know *what* she was going to do.

And why bring me your troubles, Nell thought, when every other time you come it's Joseph this and Joseph that, or the house is this or the house is that. When every time you come you have something to boast about and brag about to me. Yet she was pleased and flattered, too, that Kate had come to her.

"I only dropped in for a minute," Kate said, "I thought I'd drop in on the way home."

Now that was strange, indeed, for Kate lived in the Assumption parish halfway across town and there was no reason for her to pass through South Providence on her way home, unless, unless she did have a reason.

"You'd think," Nell said slyly, "there wouldn't be enough they could do for the Murtaughs with all their money and the trade they bring. You'd think they'd go out of their way once in a while to do something for the Murtaughs."

"I know it, Nell. I know it," Kate answered distractedly. She had told old Cameron the money was as good as gold, the bill would be paid as soon as ever the Murtaughs paid her for the work, but there was nothing she could do with him, nothing at all.

Couldn't she borrow the money somewhere, Nell asked her. She could go to Pete Carron, now, and tell him what the trouble was and she'd have the money to buy the material in no time at all. Nell was sure Pete Carron would understand the matter and let her have what she wanted. He surely trusted the Murtaughs if the Boston Store didn't.

Kate knew that, too. Sure Pete Carron and old Murtaugh were thick as thieves and that was just why she didn't want to go to Pete with her troubles. How would it look going to Pete Carron for the money and then he'd bump into old Murtaugh somewhere and sooner or later the story'd be out; she'd had to borrow the money to buy the materials for the Murtaughs' dresses and that above all she didn't want the Murtaughs to know. How would old Murtaugh feel if Pete Carron was to say he lent the money to Kate Reagan to buy the materials for the Murtaughs' dresses? No, that was one she couldn't go to, though she well knew he'd let her have it in a minute. The money was as good as gold the minute the Murtaughs paid her and God knows the Murtaughs had more than enough to pay their bills, no matter what they were.

Nell wanted to know what the bill would come to, then.

Well, with the linings, and the Murtaughs had to have the best of everything, with the linings and the paddings for the coats and the material for the gowns the girls were going to wear to the ball, with the braid and facings, the silk and the velvet and the lace that would go into the yoke of Mrs. Murtaugh's dress—it would all come to about three hundred dollars, more or less. Three hundred and some odd dollars, but what was that, after all to what the Murtaughs were worth.

Nell was stunned at the huge sum, so stunned she forgot for a minute or two the satisfaction she was getting out of hearing about Kate's predicament. It was more money, it was as much, or nearly as much, as Ned had been able to save in his whole life. Why with that much money you could almost buy a house and lot, it seemed to her. Three hundred dollars for dresses!

"To you or me it's a fortune," Kate said bitterly, "but to the Murtaughs it's nothing at all."

Nell was excited beyond her few words, not so disturbed she didn't see now why Kate Reagan had come all the way out to South Providence; that was clear enough. Kate wanted her to lend her the money. The idea elated her; first, that Kate would think she had that much to lend out, and then that it would be for the Murtaughs themselves she would really be lending the money. Kate watched her closely, not sure that it was yet the right moment to ask for it and hoping Nell might offer the loan of her own doing.

But Nell had no such intention. If Kate wanted her to lend the money she would have to ask for it, and what a moment it would be! Kate Reagan, that owned her own house, that hobnobbed with the Murtaughs, that had a nephew in Georgetown, borrowing money from her! She told Nora to make a pot of tea for them and she asked Kate if she would like a pinch of snuff. Kate said the tea would be all she wanted, thanks.

If the amount was less, Nell would have felt better about it. Three hundred would take nearly every penny of Ned's savings that she had neatly rolled up and tucked away in the base of the plaster statue of St. Anthony that stood always on her bureau. She had never taken it to a bank because she felt safer with it there in the house beside her under the rigid folds of St. Anthony's brown robe. It grew slowly, except when the shop was shut down, and never once had Ned asked her to account for how much she had. She never counted it, never touched it except to add to it, or when there was sickness in the house or she ran short near the end of the week. But that was rare, because she could always get a dollar or two from Chris. The only time Ned had ever asked her for any of it was when Willie was in the trouble with Kelly, and she would never forget how painful it had been to turn St. Anthony up on his ear and pluck the money from his insides. She always thought of it as Anthony's money, more or less, and when she put another bill to the roll she would say, not without a certain touch of piety, "Another one (or perhaps it might be two, or three) for you, Anthony, darlin'. Mind it for me, now." No one had ever seen her put anything in and no one had ever seen her take anything out. It was a secret with her and Anthony and the little child the saint held in his arms, inviolate as her own confession.

While she waited for Nora to bring in the tea, she asked Kate what kind of dresses the Murtaughs were having that cost so much money and Kate described the patterns to her, spreading the sections out before her on the table and fondling them as though they were the silks and the broadcloths themselves, showing her where they were flared and where the gores would come, holding the tissue paper pieces, stuck through with pins, against her own sides and bosom to let her see how they'd hang and where the pleats would come. The table was heaped with the wispy forms and Nora was careful to move one of them before she put the tea things down. It was as though Kate were laying them out for Nell herself, and Nell, studying the designs carefully, selected one model she said she liked above all the others, and declared she wouldn't mind having a dress like it herself. Kate took the samples from her bag to let Nell feel the softness of the material. When Nell asked her how much it would cost to make the dress, she answered that, of course, it depended on the material, but that she could make her up one, after she finished with the Murtaughs' sewing, of course, for half the price she'd charge the Murtaughs, providing she had some of the material left over or if Nell wanted to get a little cheaper material. She might even, she said, if she weren't rushed too much, cut the material and fit it for her, just for old times' sake, if Nell wanted to finish up the sewing herself. Nell didn't see any reason why she couldn't do that.

Kate saw now that Nell wasn't going to give her the money unless she asked for it and just how to do it was a problem. She asked first if Nell had any idea at all how much the Murtaughs spent on such things. Nell hadn't. Kate told her it was a small fortune and soon as the work was delivered to them they paid for it without so much as a single question. Of course, they might want an alteration here or there, but that made no difference to them. As soon as the work was delivered it was paid for in full. Nell said that was the only way to do. Now she'll ask me, Nell thought. But Kate didn't. She assured Nell again that whoever lent her the money would have it back the very day she got it from the Murtaughs and that, she might be sure, would be the day she delivered the work to them.

"Well, I don't know where to turn," Kate wailed, taking a sip of the tea. "If I thought you had it, Nell, I'd ask you to lend it to me. I know you wouldn't see me lose the Murtaughs' trade—if you had it to lend."

"Oh," Nell chirped, narrowing her eyes and lowering them to the rim of the cup. "I have it, Kate, put away, but—"

"You do, Nell?" Kate shut the trap. "Oh, thank God!"

"But it's such a lot—"

"Only until I'm paid, Nell," said Kate feverishly. "Not a day longer than that. Oh, thank God I dropped in this house, Nell, for I was at my wits' end to know what to do."

"I ought to ask Ned," Nell realized she had already halfway committed herself to the loan.

"Don't bother the poor man about it at all," Kate urged. "Sure it'll be paid back and done before he knows a thing about it, Nell.

Sure what does a man know about the Murtaughs' dresses and all, anyhow?"

"You're sure of that, Kate?" Nell asked carefully, her eyes fastened on the visitor. "You're sure I'll have it the minute you're paid by the Murtaughs?"

"May I never stir a step from this chair, Nell—"

In Nell went, reluctantly, to the bedroom and the little statue. Now that she was letting Kate have the money she wasn't sure it was Kate had asked for it or she had suggested the loan. No matter, it was she lending it and it was Kate would be beholden to her however soon it was repaid. Her hands shook a little as she turned Anthony on his ear and she said a bit of a prayer to him, too, since he was the patron of all adventures and the getting of work and things like that, that Kate would keep her promise to return the money the very day she herself got paid by the Murtaughs. You may say what you like about Kate Reagan, though, she's as honest as the day is long and she'd bring back the money. In ones and twos, it took a long time to count out to three hundred. There were so many bills. Yet when she had counted the three hundred there was so little to stuff back into Anthony's pouch under the robes she was a little ashamed and frightened. She had the feeling it was the saint himself she was taking the money from, and she thought of Ned and what he might say if he ever knew she had loaned the money to Kate, whom he never liked anyhow, any more than any of the other relatives she had, and often said so in his own way—a withering look. She put the money in her apron pocket and went out to Kate again, counting it over slowly while Kate sat looking not at her, or listening to her, but at the green sandy bills Ned brought home from the foundry, sandy as the greens before they were washed. Kate scooped the money up at once and put it away in her bag with the samples and the patterns.

"Now, Kate," Nell began.

"I know," Kate said, "And you know, too, Nell. You'll have it back again as soon, as soon as ever I have a penny from the Murtaughs. God bless you, Nell. God save you and bless you, Nell. I wonder if I've time to get down to the Boston Store again now before they close it for the night?"

"Oh, yes," said Nora. "Sure you could be down there and back again before Ned got home from the foundry."

"Then I'll hurry along," Kate said, "so that I can start first thing in the morning."

"Another cup of tea," Nora said tartly. "Another cup of tea. Sure Ned won't be home for a long time yet."

Nell looked at her sister. No, Ned wouldn't be home for a while yet and she wouldn't have to face him. She saw at once that though she had Kate Reagan under obligation to her forever and a day, Nora had herself under the same sentence until the money was paid back. Not that Nora would tell Ned; she wasn't afraid of that; and besides if Ned could use the money to pay back Kelly for what Willie had stolen, why couldn't she use it for Kate Reagan; at least Kate would pay it back.

"No," said Kate rising, "No, I've had all the tea I could drink."

Chapter Thirty-Two

NED McDERMOTT, grunting and mumbling to himself as he always did working, pounded the sand around the pattern with the head of the brass rammer, its sounds muffled in the dampness like the beating of faraway drums. Carelessly, without straightening his back or looking around after it, he tossed the rammer over his shoulder when Skinny Byer, the shop chairman, called "heads up" for the midday half hour lunch. The rammer landed in the hump of his sand pile and Ned walked away from it to his locker where he took his dinner pail and sat down on a flask near his brother Pat's floor. His weary bones and his shriveling muscles welcomed Skinny's call, but he begrudged himself the half hour away from the flasks because the floor these days never had the crop of moulds it used to have at pouring-off time. His hands shook now lifting the pattern out of the sand, the cope was heavier to lay over, the ladle would splash and drip when he trotted with it and he spattered the stream of iron sometimes when he dipped into it. More of his castings came back than before, and although he had devised a cunning scheme with the timekeeper by which they raised the count of good ones and split even the money they cheated the company by doing it, he wasn't carrying home the wages he used to. Pat wasn't either, that he knew. He looked at Pat's shrinking arms and his blue eyes, sagging with care, and watched him fumble into the dinner pail, grope on his bench for the plug of tobacco. Pat's talk these days had lost its edge, it seemed. There was a day when Pat would spend the whole time they were eating shouting blasphemous, bitter jibes at the other moulders, goading them sometimes even to fighting with each other. Pat's floor at the end of the day hadn't as large a harvest of castings either. Still, Pat had only himself and his wife to look after. The girl was working and the boy—Pat didn't know where the hell he was, in the Army somewhere, Texas, Panama, out West, he didn't know; he didn't care a hell of a lot either as long as the son of a bitch stayed away and let his poor mother have some peace.

Ah, it was a step and a half now, not a leap, when they would strike in again, to get up on top of the flask and jump the sand down hard on the pattern, a painful stretching of the short legs, a lash of torture. The blast of the wind going on in the cupola would scream into his ears and make him dizzy. He would be panting, almost exhausted, when it came time to get the iron and his eye unsure when he poured it into the moulds. He would scamper tiredly to the chill of the whitewashed washroom where the hot streams of the showers, pouring into the coldness of the room sent up clouds of vapor out of which arms, hairy legs and black wet heads would jab and retreat. It would revive him momentarily, bring the blood to his cheeks, parboil him. He would feel weakened and hungry when he stepped out into the alley and started his walk home.

He almost bumped into Larry McDermott, majestically walking down the hill, before he looked up into the policeman's ruby scruff of mustache. There was nothing casual about Larry McDermott, Ned knew. If he wanted to see you he did, and if he didn't have something on his mind to see you about you might not run into him for months at a time. Ned had never forgiven him for beating the boy in the police station and when he had seen him in the meantime, at wakes or the like, he had had as few words as possible with him. Thank God they were out of Larry's precinct now in South Providence. Larry's hulk towered above him, eclipsing the street lamp.

"What brings you down this way, Larry?" Ned asked.

"Walking home, Ned. When I'm working days I walk home now and then."

He's a damn liar, Ned thought, what the hell's on his mind. It can't be the boy for he's in no trouble these days, that I'm sure of. But there's something on his mind and I must find out what the hell it is. I wish he'd say.

"Step across the bridge with me, Ned, to McGarraghan's and we'll have a nice drink," Larry said.

"I will," said Ned. "But only the one for I must get home to my supper."

Crossing the span Larry asked him how the boy was doing these days since they moved to South Providence, if he was behaving himself. Ned was happy for the chance to talk about Willie, although he would never have mentioned the boy's name to Larry if the policeman hadn't mentioned it first. Larry said he was very glad to hear that the boy was doing well and reminded Ned how fortunate it was that he, not some other lieutenant at the station, had been able to clear up the matter at Kelly's, because it was a serious thing, breaking into a store like that. If it had been anyone else but Kelly, he declared, willing to accept payment for his losses without pressing the matter further, even a lieutenant might not have been able to straighten it out. Ned said he wouldn't give a damn for a boy that didn't raise hell once in a while, though he was glad that Willie seemed to have sown the last of his wild oats for a while, anyhow. They went into the little front office at McGarraghan's instead of into the bar itself and Ned knew damn well then that Larry had something on his chest. Looking out behind the bar they could see Owen Tegue leaning against it at the far end.

Larry waited until the drink was in front of them before he started to talk.

"Ned," he said slowly, "What's your Pat doing these days?"

"My Pat or his Uncle Pat? Which do you mean?" Ned asked, sparring carefully.

"Your Pat, Ned. What's he doing these days?"

"Ah, he's firing in the brewery out there near Olneyville. Working steady right along. Lives next door to us, you know, just the other side of the lane in Tessie Butler's house. Why?"

Larry looked worriedly at the whisky glass in his hairy, freckled fist.

"Why," Ned asked again. "Why did you ask about Pat?"

"Well, Ned, we had some trouble out there in Olneyville a couple days ago. Trouble with that son of a bitch Jim Trenn. . . ."

"Who the hell's Jim Trenn?"

"A young doctor out there, Ned. A Socialist. He's raising hell up there at the Algonquin mills."

"I never heard the name," said Ned.

"He's out there night after night in the square raising hell. It'll lead to trouble sooner or later, Ned. I can tell you that. They won't stand for it."

"What's he raising hell about?"

"I tell you, Ned. We had complaints from up there and I went up with a detail of men to see what the hell was going on. What the hell does any Socialist raise hell about? Everything's wrong with them. Nothing suits them. The banks is robbers and the mills is thieves and the priests is liars to a Socialist. They're after organizing a union out there."

"Thought Tom McCann was the head of the union in the mills out there," said Ned.

"So he is, Ned. So he is," Larry said. "That's the hell of it, do you see. If this goddam Trenn'd leave Tom alone things would be all right. There's no trouble with Tom and his union, but this young Trenn is out there stirring them Polacks and all up against Tom and his union. No good can come of that, Ned. There's anarchists and every other damn thing mixed up with him. You wouldn't want your Pat running around with a crowd like that, I hope."

Thefts, rapes, sluggings, sometimes a murder, desertions of families, arson, violence of any and every kind were the lieutenant's daily fare, and he had encountered among the people of his own family almost every crime among them, but for him Socialism was the cardinal sin, except for denying God himself, there was nothing in the calendar worse than Socialism. If your brother's boy was in trouble and you couldn't "straighten it out" you hunted around until you got him a smart lawyer like Fitzgerald that could. But to sit in the station house and have the man on the beat tell you your cousin's boy was running around with the Socialist agitator was a blow you couldn't dodge. To see the fool there himself lapping up every word of what the agitator was spouting was more terrible still.

"Is my Pat running around with them?" Ned distrusted Larry since the beating of the boy and wanted to get the whole thing out of him before he committed himself.

"God, Ned, I seen him with my own eyes out there in the square Saturday night."

"Well, Pat's a grown man, you know, with a family of his own now. He can run where he likes without let or hindrance from me, Larry."

"Family?" Larry was aghast. "Why them sons of bitches is breaking up the family. What the hell does the sacred family mean to them, or the Church, either?"

"Pat has two fine boys," said Ned.

"Owen," Larry called out loudly. "Owen Tegue, come in here, will you?"

"Who, me?" Tegue called from his place at the bar outside.

"Yes, come in here, Owen," Larry repeated.

Tegue loped slowly into the little room and McGarraghan, curious about what had been going on in his office, though he didn't like to ask the lieutenant, took a stand in the doorway that led to the bar.

"Owen," said Larry, "What would you do if you was to find out one of your boys was running around with that goddam Socialist Trenn out in Olneyville? What would you do, Owen?"

"Do?" Tegue said. "I'd break his goddam neck and send him home."

"Do you see, Ned?" Larry spread himself out in the chest.

Ned was caught. Socialism was a vague and foreign word to him. He had heard it from the moulders and from Mick at home, but its meaning was as obscure to him as the meaning of many of the other words people were using nowadays. When they talked about democracy he was bewildered, only half sure what they meant. Democracy for small nations. When he thought of small nations he thought of Ireland, and when he thought of Ireland he didn't think of democracy, he thought of freedom.

"Sunday after Sunday, Father Tierney is up in the pulpit in St. Mary's warning the people against having anything to do with Jim Trenn," Larry declared. "They say one Sunday he told them anyone connected with him in any fashion would never receive absolution from him anyhow. . . ."

"What's this?" Ned asked. "What has the priest to do with them organizing a union, then?"

"A union?" Tegue was indignant. "Sure it's not a union they're after—they want to tear down and smash up the Church itself."

"If that's what they're after," Ned said, feeling that he must defend Pat at all cost, "If that's it, what do they bother about the mills at all for? Why don't they go after the Church the same way as the French did some years ago? Anyhow I'm damn sure my Pat is not after that at all."

"Well, if I was you, Ned," Larry warned, "I'd speak to Pat and tell him to drop them. Sure what the hell has he to do with them in the mills, anyways? He's working there in the brewery, ain't he? What the hell does he bother with them at all for?"

Ned was sorely troubled. To think of his own son involved in anything which might even remotely raise a banner of opposition to the Church pained him, but he resented Larry McDermott, though he was a lieutenant, setting himself up as the head of the family, so to speak, and telling the rest of them what they might and mightn't do. He decided to have a talk with Tim Lee at the first opportunity and to ask Pat when he went into the foundry in the morning. He was certain there was more to be said about the matter than Larry had told him. No sense waiting until the morning; he would go around the corner to Tim's now since he was so near by. To extricate himself from Larry and Tegue without capitulating to them was another matter. He said he'd speak to Pat about it the first time he got a chance.

"Do, Ned," said Larry. "Have a talk with him before it's too late to do anything with him."

"Is Pat running around with that Trenn up there?" Tegue asked.

Ned went out without answering him and was soon knocking at Tim Lee's door on Water Street.

"It's a damn hard thing to say, Ned," Tim Lee was saying. "They tell me this young Trenn is as smart as a whip and don't care a damn what they say about him. Sure he could let well enough alone if he wanted to and just run that dentist office of his, but he has the bug in his head, do you see. He's a Socialist, all right."

"That's what Larry says," Ned recounted. "Swears up and down they're out to tear down the Church and the banks and all."

"Sure ain't that what they said about Father McGlynn, God bless him, years ago? Said he was out to ruin the country with his wild ideas." Tim's allegiance to the New York priest had never waned over the years and his fervor was undiminished. "Rome excommunicated him without so much as how d'ye do. Think of excommunicating a priest no less! Took the archbishop, Rome and all to do it, but they did it at last. Refused to be silenced by any of them and fought right down the line. Never recanted and was restored to his holy offices before he died, too."

"But Father McGlynn was no Socialist, surely," Ned was happy Tim was bringing a priest into the discussion.

"Next thing to it, though," Tim ruled. "Single taxer. Caused a hell of a stir. Cardinal Gibbons interceded for him in Rome, they say, along with some Molly Maguire or somebody that was excommunicated at the time. Molly Maguire or Knights of Labor, some such thing—I don't remember. Got them both off, too."

"Is this Trenn a Catholic, then?"

207

"Born and bred one like you and me," Tim said. "There was many a Fenian excommunicated, too, you know, Ned, many a one."

"But, Tim," said Ned, "it's a far cry from a Fenian to a Socialist."

"True, it is. But it's the politics of it, Ned, I'm speaking of. Now I don't hold for a minute with a Socialist like that son of a bitch Larkin tearing the children out of good Catholic homes and shipping them off to Liverpool as they say he did during the car strike there. Shipped them off to God knows what kind of a Protestant hovel in Liverpool."

"What the hell did he do that for? You see, Tim, that's what Larry was saying—they want to break up the homes and tear down the Church. . . ."

"Did it to feed them, God knows. They were starving in Dublin, hadn't a crust to eat. And Connolly was there with him in it all. Still the man was a patriot. Died for his country in front of the firing squad; still he was a Socialist, too, they say. Agitating far and wide in this country at one time till he went back home again."

"God, I can't make head or tail of it," Ned shook his head.

"What the hell's all this got to do with your Pat?" Tim asked.

"Why, Larry says Pat is running around with Trenn and them Socialists up there in Olneyville raising hell."

"Smashing up his own home, too, I suppose," Tim laughed.

"God, no," Ned answered.

Chapter Thirty-Three

WILLIE had begun to swim slowly out of the bottomless
whirlpool of frustration in which he had been trying frantically to keep himself from being sucked under ever since the night
at Kelly's. His grandfather, if anything, was kinder than he had ever
been to him. Every night now they shared a raw onion and the
newspaper. The onion was sliced into the saucer of a huge teacup
that had been broken in the moving. Around the saucers' rim on
one side was printed *A Cup of Kindnesse* and on the other, *For
Auld Lang Syne*. Whatever else there was to eat that night, the
onion was always there, a big Berumda when Ned could find them
in the store near the foundry, that would have shadows of faint
Lenten purple sprayed over the white discs, or a heap of small-
change slices of Spanish ones, as Ned called them. Whenever he
happened to think of it Ned would take the saucer up daintily and
hold it past Willie's place toward Chris who would refuse them
with a frown of impatience. Great things for the kidneys, Ned
would laugh, and a damn nice thing to eat, too, if he only knew it.
Chris's discomfort made the onions more savory for Willie and his
grandfather seemed to know and enjoy it, for the gesture slowly
grew to have a deeper meaning for the old man; it spoke his scorn
for the ways and manners of the breed of small men he found in
his son. A man of Pete Carron's size, now, would lash into an onion
and be damned, or a man like Kit Somerville would, or Davitt or
one of them would. It was what he wanted to tell Willie but he
never knew just how to say it to him and he didn't want the boy
to think that was all there was to it; there was lots more to it, God
knows, that wasn't in all the books.

There was always a race to get the newspaper before Nell got
at it, and Nora would hide it for her sister out of spite when she
could. When Nell got it first she turned always to the deaths and
obituaries. However remotely, she seemed to know every person
with an Irish name who was listed there. Surely Nora would if Nell
didn't. Between them they knew when this one or that one came
out to this country, when they were married, how many children

there were, and if one of them had died or got married; and they would speculate on how much money they might have had put by or whether the mortgage on the house was paid. It tormented Ned to hear them forever rolling corpses around the house, as he told them once, and picking the pockets of their poor souls to see how many mortal or venial sins was in them. There was always at least one name listed that would bring a gasp of horror to Nell's lips when she read it aloud, as she did the whole column, skipping, naturally, the Protestants and Jews or the few Italians that were beginning to be printed these days. Her gasp would sting Ned with the realization that every time he listened to her reading, his own days were that many less than the last time he heard her. Often he would snatch his hat from the nail on the door and tramp to O'Leary's for a glass of beer, or across the lane to Pat's house. But O'Leary's was farther away than Deignan's had been for him and he was weary at night.

If he got the paper before the rest did he would tuck it under his arm while he filled and lit his pipe; then he would stretch out on the couch and scan the front page with a grunt or two before he handed it to the boy. Willie would read the headlines, large and small, and when his grandfather said, "Ah-*ha*" or "Well *now*" would read the story that followed. If there were a grunt or a snort he would skip that piece and read the next headline. Sometimes, though rarely, Ned would bring him back to a story he had skipped. When they encountered a word neither of them understood, Ned would have the boy copy it down there on a bit of paper or something and find out in the school what the meaning of it was and the next night they would read it over again and again. He said that the book that had the meanings of all them words in it must be one of the greatest ones ever written, and one night, the night the word "peremptory" halted the reading, he pulled a red-covered pocket dictionary from his pocket and told Willie to find what it meant. He said he bought it in the paper store, and there was more of them like it when they needed them, that had the meaning of more words in them but that this would do until they knew what all the words in it meant. By that time, he said, there couldn't be a hell of a lot of words they wouldn't know as soon as they clapped eyes on them.

If, during the reading, there were no comments from his grandfather Willie would know he was falling asleep. Nell and Nora usually would be watching, too, to see if Ned's pipe had turned its bowl down on his chest, the sure sign of it. Then one or the other would snatch the newspaper from him and send him away to the kitchen to study his lessons. It might happen soon after he had started to read or it might take an hour or more, depending on how hard the day had been in the foundry.

The paragraph ADMITTED TO BAR announcing that William Clancey, son of John Clancey, plumbing contractor of South Providence, had been admitted to practice law in the Federal District Court, might end the reading for the night while Ned told the boy of how long he had known John Clancey and how he struggled to educate his family, girls and all, and what a great satisfaction it must be to him now to see his son practicing law in the highest court there was. It would bring more discussion than whole columns on the war, perhaps, or the fire at the Eastern Coal Company's wharf. When Gahagan was caught profiteering and cheating on the weight of oleomargarine, Ned hoped that he would be sent to prison for all it was worth. Yes, Nell said, missing a Hail Mary, but it must be hard on the family; his wife was one of the Higgins girls. There was nothing worse a man could do, Ned declared, than steal the food from another man's table whatever tricks he used to do it.

Willie shared his grandfather's joy now when Tim Lee, always a great reader himself, came to the house. All their lives Tim was the one who first mentioned the things they talked about, imparting his knowledge of events with great gusto and intimacy.

"I see," Ned would be careful to say before Tim had a chance to speak. "I see there's hell to pay in the coal mines."

Since Ned was careful to put out the facts, the details, the possibilities with indisputable clearness and always to preface what he said with "I see," Tim could only assume Ned had his wealth of information from the newspaper, and he decided finally that somehow over the years Ned had taught himself to read without ever saying a word to anyone about it. His grandfather's memory was infallible, Willie saw, deadly accurate and left nothing out. Nora, tempted several times, never quite dared expose Ned.

Never hesitant to speak his mind on any matters that interested him, Ned was talking now to visitors about things they never thought entered his head and some, Mr. Devine and Gyp McGlinn among them, began to wonder if Ned hadn't been conning them all these years and if they hadn't been wrong in thinking he couldn't read or write. Mr. Devine told Ann Nell must have taught Ned long ago and they were both that shy neither of them ever said a thing about it. He certainly was a well-informed man in many matters, Mr. Devine said.

The reward Willie had, and he could have had no greater, was to be asked, very casually, by his grandfather to corroborate a date or place or a name, then to be encouraged to tell some bit more of the story that had, it seemed, slipped his grandfather's mind at the moment.

"So it is, so it is," Ned would say, picking up the story.

War bellowed its coming for weeks and Willie, reading it every night to his grandfather, was feverish with it. Ned was not. He didn't know Germans and he didn't hate them; there was nothing atrocious the paper was ascribing to them that he didn't know more bitterly about the English. The Germans sacked and burned Louvain; he thought of Drogheda, he thought of Limerick, of Vinegar Hill, and Easter Week was yesterday afternoon. Time was never pocketed into carefully laid-out years and it was not closed between the covers of books for him. He didn't think of 1690 as farther or nearer than 1811, nor any more remote than Parnell. If the Germans won the war and that would free Ireland, he would be happy, not because the Germans would win but because the British would lose. He doubted that the Germans cared whether or not Ireland was ever free; he distrusted them, but not more or less than he hated and distrusted the English.

When the day in April came at last though, and the war was declared, he saw things he had never seen so clearly. He saw the great land where he lived attacked. He saw the foundries and the mills, the shops and the farms; he saw the grandeur of the churches and all that was dear to him attacked. For the first time he knew his heart was not all Ireland's; it was half there and half here. It pained him, and when there was talk in the shop about this man's boy going into the Navy and that one's into the Army he thought of Willie and was glad the boy was still too young to have to go into the war whatever happened. Chris's eyes would keep him out; Pat had his family. None of them would have to go.

Mick, sober as a lake of milk, hobbled solemnly into the house the day after the war was declared.

"God damn them, Ned," he said, "they're in for it now. It's all up with them when they think they can tackle America."

"Yes," Ned said, "it's all up with them, but there's a war to fight, ain't there, Mick? There's a war will cost the life of many a young fellow before it's over and done, and that's something you're not thinking about. . . ."

"I done—I fought. . . ."

"Ah, be damned, Mick, that's so far away and so long ago. . . ."

"Not to me," Mick said. "Christ, I can see us there, hundreds and hundreds of us on the horses riding down on. . . ."

"Mick, you have damn good eyes to see that, haven't you? Where was you riding down? Now don't tell me, for I know damn well you'll drag out every damn lie them old bucks down there in Bristol is telling every day in the week and the first thing you know you'll have the rebels licked with your own hands, won't you, Mick? . . ."

"I was three years in it, Ned. Three years is a long time, a damn long time, Ned. This one will be over and done with long before that was."

"I hope it will, Mick. Yes, I hope it will—and god damn it, I wish there was some other way of going about it instead of teaming up with the damn English. I don't trust them. I don't trust the Germans, but by God I don't trust the English either. . . ."

"Will Chris go into it?"

"Chris? No. He can't see across the street. . . ."

"Ah, they could put him up closer to them, couldn't they? Close enough he could see to shoot three or four of them. . . ."

"No," Ned said. "They wouldn't take Chris in the Army and they won't take Pat either. . . ."

"Willie there is a big lad—I suppose he'll want to be into it before long, won't he?"

"No!" Ned cried. "No, he won't, and they won't take him into it either if I have anything to say about it. Look here! They won't take that boy into it, do you hear? Joe's boys'll be in it, I suppose, and Pat's Eddie is in the Army anyhow and damn good thing for his poor mother at that. But they won't take this boy. They won't take the one I have left to me old days from me. No, by Christ, that's one McDermott they won't take. There's enough McDermotts will be in it, God knows. There's always enough McDermotts—there's always McDermotts enough when there's a war on. But there's one McDermott they won't take!"

Chapter Thirty-Four

TESSIE BUTLER'S hip didn't mend; it could not be expected to in one her age, the doctor said, and she weakened every passing day. She weakened, and the sharpness of her tongue, the hard bitter edges of her words, seemed to be wearing smooth and soft. She wheedled where once she spat, she begged where once she commanded with Mollie. Every day there was someone from one of her sodalities in to see her, or two, or three and almost every day one of the priests from St. Malachi's dropped by, frequently to bring her communion. Her own oak communion set, candles in silver holders on each side of the crucifix, a frosted jar of holy water with the glass cross on its cover, nested in the purple velvet lining of the box. Mollie was very proud of her and every day, after tirelessly running in and out of the room to bring Tessie the things she asked for all morning, would wash the fading face and gently pile the lovely white drifts of Tessie's hair high in a pompadour on her head, careful always to tuck the gray celluloid side combs in where the old woman had always worn them, even the one that went in back, though no one could see it. It was hard for Mollie, because Tessie lost all control of herself, and Mollie had to change her bed a dozen times in a day. Light as Tessie was, Mollie found it almost more than she could do alone to lift her. When Pat or the boys were at home they could help her, but Mollie couldn't leave her aunt unchanged while she waited for them to get home from school, or from work. Nell and Nora didn't know, at first, how very wearing it was for Mollie, but when they found out how much she had to do they insisted on coming over to help her. Mollie must call one or both of them, Nell said, whenever she had to change Tessie, or there was any heavy lifting or anything of the kind to do. Mollie was grateful and did call them, perhaps twice in the morning and usually once in the afternoon after the sodality members had left. Their attentions were not lost on Tessie. She would pat their hands when they came into her room or when they had finished changing her, and she would say:

"God bless you, Nellie, you will have your reward for this day's work. Nora, Nora, you're all so good to me." Or, simply, "God bless you, both," and near the last end of it all only, "Bless you. God and Mary bless you."

The weaker she grew the longer the sodality members stayed, hoping, as Pat McDermott said, to be in on the last end. Not hearing Mollie call them one afternoon, Nell and Nora went over while Agnes Sheridan was still there and she and Mrs. Joe Daly were just leaving. Tessie smiled when they came into the room and asked them all to stay a little longer, only a little longer. She asked Mollie if she would send Johnnie in to her.

"Go up, Johnnie," she said, "go up to my room and bring down my sealskin coat and my best satin dress. . . ."

"Oh, Tessie, now," Mollie objected, humoring her with a knowing smile, "how will he know where to look for those things —I'll get them for you later. . . ."

"Mollie, dear," Tessie said, "It's now I want them. I want them now, dear."

"Oh, dear, I'll get them for you, Tessie," Mollie said.

"And while you're there, darling, bring down the second best satin and the Paisley shawl and the gray wool one. Look in the bottom of the tin trunk for them. Bring the vici kid shoes with you, the ones with the arch supporters in them, and the other ones, too. Bring down the Spanish fan I have there and the lace, the Irish lace I have, and the French lace, too. In the right-hand drawer, Mollie, of the dresser is a prayer book Barney gave to me years ago. Bring that with you. . . ."

"Oh, Tessie," Mollie patiently said, "how will I ever carry all those things downstairs?"

"John, dear," Tessie said, "go with Mummy, darling, and help the poor thing with all she has to carry. Take the postcards on the rack for yourself, Johnnie, to share and share alike with Patrick and some for little Willie McDermott, too, God bless him. The little lacquer matchbox with the picture of the heathen church in Japan painted in gold on the cover you may have for yourself, Johnnie, for you was always partial to that from a little boy. That you may have for yourself. Mollie, fetch the best and the second best alpaca along, too, and down in the wood trunk, not the tin one, you'll find a gray alpaca shirtwaist I had Kate Reagan make for me years ago and never put on. Bring all them things down to me, Mollie. I had that shirtwaist made before Barney died, and I never could bear to wear it after he died. Some would, I suppose, but I could never bear to see myself in anything as giddy as that with its white lace yoke in it and all, after he died. . . ."

While they were gone Nell said the rest of them might as well say a rosary together, and she began it.

"Now, Nora," Tessie said when Mollie and John returned, their arms heaped high with the clothing. "Nora, when I'm dead and gone, I want you to have the sealskin. Your old bones will never be chilled in that, Nora. . . ."

"Tessie, no," Nora said, looking at Mrs. Joe Daly and Agnes Sheridan. "No, I couldn't. . . ."

"If Tess wants you to have it, Nora," said Nell, looking also at the other two with a gleam of great satisfaction leaping from her eyes, "if she wants you to have it you'll take it. Try it on you, now. Hmmmmmmm," she shook her head, "it'd cover two like you. No matter, I'll soon fix that. Oh, Tessie, it's the grandest coat ever— It's the grandest thing she ever had on her back. . . ."

"Nell will take care of it, I'm sure," Agnes Sheridan said, meaning to mean almost anything they wanted to take from what she said.

"Yes," sighed Tessie, "well, that's done. Now, the best satin, that's what I'm to be laid out in, Mollie. . . ."

"Oh, Aunt Tessie!" Mollie gasped, really pained.

"Whisht!" said Tessie. "In that and I want the gold watch pinned to my breast, but you may have it after. Don't bury the watch with me. Bury my beads and my wedding ring with me, Mollie, and the beads and my wedding ring on my hand. Mollie, give it to Pat, for he has none, and a man has a right to wear a watch to mass on a Sunday. I would have had Barney's gold watch to give him, but I never did know what became of it after one time I—ah, never mind, give Pat the watch to wear on a chain. I want to be laid out with the combs in my hair as they are now, Mollie and the beads and my wedding ring on my hand. Agnes, the second best satin and the best alpaca is both yours. Take them, Agnes, and God give you health to wear them. The shirtwaists is for you, Mrs. Joe, and the gray alpaca would become you very well indeed, I think. Yes, it would, too, with your gray hair . . . very well. . . ."

. . . Tessie was weary and stopped talking, her thin fingers crawling in and out around the folds of the black satin around her. . . .

"Oh, dear," she said, "won't the boys have a grand time looking at all the pictures on the cards of faraway places all over the world, some I seen myself and some I never seen. In among them is a card from County Leitram, Mrs. Joe, a picture of Fenach Abbey, the ruins of it, you know, near where I was born. Think of it, Nell, still standing there after all these long years. They were ruins when I was a little girl and when we'd pass by, mind you, we'd make the sign of the cross and bless ourselves, and there they are, still standing in ruins. It's so long ago, Mrs. Joe, and it only seems it was yesterday morning I was going that way past the ruins. I wouldn't know a soul, now, I'd meet on the road going past the abbey. Not a soul, but still, I suppose, they bless themselves when they go past and always will. I would like to see it once again, only once.

"Nell, I want you to take the vici kid shoes, both pairs of them, Nell, for I know they'll fit you to a T. Mollie, take the arch supporters out of them and give them to Kate Reagan, for I know she has trouble with her feet. Nell as many times as I passed the ruins there at the abbey, I never had shoes on my feet until the last time I passed by and then I never saw it again, except in the little picture postcard that was sent Barney one time by a brother of his. Nell, those vici kid are like gloves on your feet."

She held out lengths of lace in her hands to each of them, some of whom received longer lengths than the others.

"Now that's all I have to give," Tessie said. "That's the whole of it. All but the little house and my bedroom set that's upstairs, the walnut bed and the bureau with its marble top pieces and the commode—and that's for Mollie. That's all for Mollie herself so there'll always be a roof over her head and the boys' forever. Yes, the house will be Mollie's."

Agnes Sheridan and Mrs. Joe Daly kissed her on the cheek when they went out of the room, weeping and carrying with them the dresses and shirtwaists she had given them. Nell and Nora stayed to help Mollie change the bed things once again under the old woman. Nora said on the way home that Tessie looked weaker that day.

Mollie wearily sat down for a cup of tea after they had gone and she was sipping it when Tessie called her into the room again. Only Tessie's hair, her nose and her wide blue eyes looked like herself, and in the eyes Mollie thought she saw snatches of pain and trouble.

"The house, Mollie," Tessie whispered, "mortgaged to the last

217

shingle on the roof. They're after me now for months about it, threatening me. Water bills is not paid these two years. Money is owed on all sides of it. They didn't know a thing about that, did they, when they were here today? Did they, Mollie? I don't know what you'll have out of it, Mollie. I've been cheated right and left since Barney died—among the Irish are the most pious thieves in America; you never know with *them*. But if it was a mansion I had, Mollie, it would be yours all the same. It would all be yours."

"Oh, my God," Mollie moaned.

"Yes, I'm a poor woman," Tessie whispered again. "God bless you, Mollie, you were good to me. . . ."

She fell asleep then with the beads laced over her hands and the combs still set in their places. Mollie looked in on her later, when she was going to bed, and she found her dead in the morning.

Chapter Thirty-Five

NOT a sliver of doubt about it, Willie would win the medal when the readings took place in springtime in the school. Why, not even the priest preaching a sermon could stand up to the boy when it came to that, Ned knew. And hadn't they practiced night after night as soon as the date of the readings was announced in the paper, the boy standing like a soldier with the book held out a little in front of him in the left hand and turning the pages of it slowly with the right when he finished one, carefully raising his eyes from the page every few lines and throwing his voice out clearly to pronounce each word distinctly and strike the emphasis where it should be though he had never seen the page before in his life. That would be the test for the medal reading in the school, too. Each of those chosen to read would be given a passage he had not seen before to read before the judges, teachers themselves from other schools with perhaps a minister with them to lend dignity to the occasion. Ned counted on this, deciding to himself that if he could only get the boy to read enough at home to him there would never be a thing they could find for him in the school that the boy hadn't already been reading. Willie wanted to win the medal more than he had ever desired anything before, and could lose himself in an ecstasy of words when he was reading, but though he was never shy or nervous about it, he began to be embarrassed by the determination all the McDermotts centered on his winning the prize. His grandmother and Nora would sit rapt in attention while he read, and his Uncle Chris had Catherine Daly drop in to give the boy a few points, because she had won the medal herself when she went to school and was considered to be an elocutionist of great talent. Ned said that was a fine thing, too, and she would be a great help; but of course the boy was a natural born orator, as he himself had known all along. His cousin Patrick reluctantly admitted that Willie was the best reader in the graduating class and there wasn't any doubt about his copping the medal; everybody in the class including the teacher and even Mr. Crandall himself expected Willie would win, Patrick said. Naturally Ned told Tim Lee that the boy was up to read for the medal at the head of the class and would undoubtedly win it for himself.

Willie read to himself aloud in front of the mirror, looking up from the page at the proper places at his own freckled reflection in the rusted, spotted glass that stood on his dresser. The most difficulty he had was in getting the books from which to read, for he could not overcome his dread of entering the library and confronting the weird sisters behind the desks who never spoke or smiled when he went there. Catherine Daly had given him the list of authors from which he selected the books—Scott, Defoe, Cooper, Mark Twain, Dickens, Stevenson, Dumas—and he found a collection of short pieces that contained a story about a man who had brought his dreams to America, and that, his grandfather said, was a handsome way to put it. His uncle brought home the *Saturday Evening Post* in which there was a continued story about John Barleycorn, written by Jack London.

In the paper one night he read to his grandfather the story of a raid on a gambling house connected with the fight club in Blackstone. Among the names of those who were arrested was that of Warren Searles, allegedly, the paper said, the manager of the establishment, although not the owner. It was the name of Byron Searles's father and Willie stopped reading. His uncle, who was still in the house, said, yes, it was young Searles's father, all right, he had known for some time all about it though he had never said anything at home. Willie's hands holding the paper began to tremble. He liked Byron Searles and he could not believe the happy, fat little man who was always so kind to him when he went to Byron's house was a criminal.

Ned was infuriated when Nell said that perhaps it would be better for Willie if he didn't go running around with that boy any longer. She said these mixed marriages never worked out in the long run and something was bound to happen to the children of them sooner or later. Ned sat up, waving his pipe like a club to point up his words. Where, he asked, in the whole of the Ten Commandments, or anything else for that matter, was there anything said about its being a sin, mortal or venial, to bet on a horse race or play a game of cards for sociability's sake? He never was a worse Catholic, he said, because he put a five spot, or a ten, or more if he had it in his younger days, on a chicken. He was damned if he could see the difference, either, between gambling with cards or what at the fight club or winning a ton of coal or a set of dishes at St. Malachi's lawn party on Decoration Day. He told Willie to think no more about it and stick to the books. How the man made a living, if his family never wanted, was no one else's damn business. Willie was disturbed by it, though, until he saw Byron the next time at one of the altar boys' meetings. Byron was as gay as he ever was. During the meeting, while Father McCaffrey was writing down the assignments for the boys to serve mass during the coming week—two wedding masses, three funerals and the weekday masses in addition to the Sunday services—Byron stuck his wad of chewing gum into the red hair of Leo Dion, the French Canadian boy whom, because of his flaming hair and the piety of his brown eyes, Father McCaffrey always chose to carry the crucifix in the church processions. Leo could scrap better than any of the other boys and it was a daring thing for Byron to have done. Willie admired Byron for it and, with the rest of the boys who sat in the back row, enjoyed Leo's painful struggles to remove it from his hair. Ganley whispered that Leo was lucky to have a barber for a father who would clip his hair for nothing.

"I'll clip more than that for you, Ganley," Father Jim said, starting to read the assignments for the week, "if you don't keep quiet. Come up here and say what you have to say."

"I only said Leo's father would cut his hair for nothing," Ganley said, suppressing a laugh.

"Was there anything funny about that, McDermott?" Father Jim asked.

"No, Father," Willie said.

"Searles, did you think that was funny? No? That's fine. Now, Dion, stop combing your golden locks there for a while and I'll read the assignments over."

Out on the lawn Byron said he was sorry he had stuck the gum in Leo's hair and they made it up after he removed what he could, taking a bunch of hair along in one last quick pull. Willie decided that Byron either didn't know about his father's having been arrested or just didn't care. Either way it was all right with him if it was with Byron and he never revealed to anyone that he knew Byron's father was a gambler.

The time was drawing near for the reading in the school and for his graduation. Willie prayed ardently, at the suggestion of both his grandmother and Nora, to St. Anthony for aid and assistance in winning the medal. That was the right saint, his grand-father said, reminding Willie of the little blue book which the St. Anthony on his grandmother's dresser held in his arm. Anthony was the boy would see him through.

They were chosen a week in advance—Fred Horton, Sammie Weinberg and Willie—to read for the boy's medal, and Celia, Hazel Carey, whose father was a fireman, and Anna Conroy, a buoyant dark girl whose cough was so violent it seemed to shake her big teeth loose in her wide mouth, which would certainly count against her in the reading if it should happen. Miss Horne, a tall bulging Englishwoman who taught the graduating class, wished them all success but reminded them that there would be only two winners, one boy and one girl and that the four who did not win should not be too disappointed. It was a distinct honor, she said, even to be chosen to read for the medal.

Sammie told Willie there was nothing for him to worry about and the medal was his already. Fred Horton, always excitable and bursting, stuttered a little bit when he was spoken to by the teacher or had to recite in the classroom. His voice was as loud and un-restrained as Freddie himself. Sammie couldn't understand why Miss Horne had picked him to read because he never did it without stuttering. Willie had no misgivings in the matter. He had been reading so much to his grandfather, and everyone in the house was so sure he'd win, he was convinced of it himself. He knew he didn't hesitate at any of the words he encountered in the newspaper, the magazines or the books, and although many of the meanings were obscure to him even after he had tracked them down in the dictionary, he did not falter about pronouncing them as well as if he had written them there himself.

The afternoon was bright, and the lazy spring day smelling of the fresh tar they were putting on the road near by rolled in the open windows. Willie looked through a course of dusty sunbeams at the judges sitting on the dais in the front of the room, the Reverend Mr. Norcross wearing a Roman collar like a priest, his hands folded on his lap in front of him. He wore a coke gray suit, not quite black. On one side of him was Miss Olive Fraser and on the other Miss Marian Otis. Both of them were high school teachers and looked to Willie like the women in the library except, perhaps, better fed. They both wore their hats and both of them were unsmilingly nibbling at the students with their eyes. Mr.

Crandall's voice clogged up a little while he was announcing that the girls would read first; each reader would read the passage marked for him in the book and shown him, or her, by Miss Horne when it came his turn. The principal appeared to be making an effort to be pleasant and free, but he had always been so distant from the boys and girls, so irritable and brusque with them, that the effort was futile.

Celia read first, her voice kissing each word, almost, before her lips let it go. Hazel Carey read as though she were saying a penance out loud and couldn't get it finished quickly enough. Anna Conroy coughed horribly twice while she was reading and tears were ready to drop from her eyes as she walked to her seat again. Fred Horton stalked to his place in the rear of the room and with a gay, firm voice read every word of the passage marked for him without stuttering once. He closed the book with an authoritative slapping together of its pages and walked confidently to his seat, his lips drawn away from his teeth in a smile of happy accomplishment.

Willie couldn't see the place where the book was marked when Miss Horne showed it to him and she pointed at it again as he held it up to her. The floor boards creaked raucously under his feet as he walked to his place and the hand holding the book shook so much the words on the page were leaping up and falling away again from his eyes, black grasshoppers he couldn't catch. He chased them despairingly, hardly knowing what he was reading, and continued a few phrases beyond where the book was marked before he realized it. The high·school teachers, each of whom had a copy of the book, looked at him wonderingly as if to ask if the book from which he was reading was marked differently from the ones they held. He closed the book at the end of the sentence and hurried to his seat, ashamed of himself and shaking. He heard Sammie Weinberg reading over again the last sentence he had read in a clear resonant voice. He thought how like feeble quavering his own voice must have sounded as he sought the fleeing words, like Tessie Butler's probably, when she was nervous and excited. Suddenly Sammie's voice stopped and Willie saw the teachers and the minister filing slowly out of the room to make their decision in Mr. Crandall's office. The class was given permission to talk while the judges were out of the room and someone was telling Willie how well he had done. He couldn't tell from the low tone whether it was a girl's or a boy's voice and he did not try to answer. His eyes were lost with his pride in a glittering spot on the desk where the sunlight now was reflected from the varnish.

The unanimous opinion of the judges, the Reverend Mr. Norcross said when they came back to the room, was that the medals should be awarded to the first girl who read and to the third boy. He held them, large silver discs dangling from wide lavender ribbons, in his big smooth hands. Calling Celia and Sammie to the front of the room, he placed the ribbons around their necks and shook hands with them. The class applauded and the teachers shook hands with the winners. From the pit of his disappointment Willie saw Celia, clutching the medal in her hand, walk to her seat, her shoulders, her arms and her slender hips swinging as she walked. Sammie, blushing and looking down at the medal, seemed confused and sat quickly in his front seat. The applause died down and Willie could hear the pavers in the street pounding their rammers on the stones, painfully as though they were striking his heart. When the class was dismissed he rushed out into the street, and as he went he heard someone say he should have won the medal because he was the best reader in the class. It was no comfort, because he knew that although there might have been indecision in the minds of the judges about whether Fred or Sammie should have won, he had not deserved the prize, and that hurt him worse than if one of the others had won without deserving it. The boys gathered around Sammie at the gate and on the sidewalk the girls ringed Celia, stroking her ribbon, praising her. Anna Conroy said Celia was the first colored girl ever to win the medal. Willie didn't stop with either group. He turned to look back at them when he had taken a few steps and saw Celia breaking away, running toward him. She repeated as she flew by him that she was the first Negro girl to win the medal and she was saying, as he watched her foal's legs slashing happily on ahead of him, that she was happy, so-o-o happy.

If his grandmother were feeling kindly toward him she would say, "Ah, poor boy. Well, try, try again," and that would be worse than if she were angry. There was no trying again or again. There was only the bitterness of not winning, disappointing his grandfather and facing all the people who were so certain he would be the winner, his Uncle Chris, Catherine Daly, his cousins and all the old people who came to the house and his grandfather had told he would surely win. Blistered and stung, he hurried along the

224

street but he didn't want to go home and admit his defeat to his grandmother and Nora, no matter what either of them might say. If he waited long enough he knew his cousin would go up to the house and tell them, so that much shame he could escape, anyway. But there seemed to be no place where he could go for the rest of the long afternoon, and he couldn't hide away all the other afternoons. Backtracking at the corner, he found his way down toward the river to the dump where he had gone so many times with Joseph and Eddie Riordan and where the warmth of the spring was already lifting the stench of the refuse over the streets. The two old men, bent over their sticks, were poking and prodding into freshly heaped mounds of stinking debris. He tramped along the waterfront for a while and then cut up again past the screw machine factory to the Willows where the slit of stagnant water gleamed in the sun and he threw stones into its flatness.

He walked into streets that were flat and barren, where the houses were shaggy with rotting shingles loose and flopping in the little wind that crept unfragrantly up from the river and the dump, where outhouses lined the back yards like frightened shivering old men, where windows were cracked and stuffed with bits of cloth; and when he saw the Negro children running in the yards he knew, although he had never been there before, that he was in Coon Hollow.

Celia, happy, so happy, must have brought her shining medal, its satin lavender ribbon soft on her brown neck, into the dark squalor of one of these houses, as in Jewtown, among the crooked streets where bloody feathers flew like snow and bakeries with murky windows of black pillared loaves seemed to hold the rickety houses above them, Sammie Weinberg proudly was showing his medal to a twisted, stammering old man who owned the junk yard, or to his father with his black skullcap. He despised them both, hated them, hated them beyond saying. He hated that Sammie for deceiving him, telling him so many times there was no doubt about who was going to win the medal and scheming, scheming all the time to win it himself if he could in his sly, smiling way. Why had he even listened to him, why had he let himself be taken in, why had he been friendly with the little Jew bastard when the others in the class would hardly speak to him?

His hands on the crook of his crozier, the rusty shaft of an umbrella plucked of its ribs long ago, a black and feebler Loony

Mulvaney sat on the steps of the Abyssinia Baptist Church and sang, beating with his staff on the wooden stairs, *nnnn I feel the Spirit mov-innnnnn m'heart, I pray . . . when I feel th' Spirit mov-innnnnnnn my heart, I pray.* He slid his hands down along the stem of the umbrella and raised it, bowing, to his miter, a moulding derby on the curls of snow, as Willie passed by. Black Loony the length and breadth of Jewtown and a ribbon of green soft on the Jew's daughter's neck for we are the savages now who come out of the schools they didn't burn down. Not his hand, his heart is raised to strike them down in the street and his grandfather knows it, his grandfather knows he hit the old man, too, because Sammie *is* the old man and Celia, so happy, the Jew's daughter in lavender, accusing him and accusing and accusing him with a scalding song of the Spirit moving in her heart while the rammer of the old man's crozier is pounding on the stone of his own.

Willie rested sitting on the anchor posts in back of the billboards to which the diagonal supports were pinned. Old Mrs. Daley's lumpy black and white terrier smelled and wet the posts near him and came over to nose Willie's shoes and his legs, confidently, and the boy scratching the dog's back and his ears, said hello to him, hello boy, hello boy. The dog stayed where he was until the voice of old Mrs. Daley called him home.

"Come, Tip! Here, Tip!"

His grandfather was asking if there wasn't an onion left in the house to have with his supper, a good strong Bermuda if there was one with the purple skin on it, for they were a prettier thing to see than one of them with the brown dry leaves wrapped around it and no tang to them. No tang or taste to them. Willie sat beside him and they shared the Bermuda without offering it, in its blue saucer, to Chris. There was nothing said about the medal or about anything except the big purple Bermuda and the tea that Nora brewed so strong it tasted like *titanic* acid in your mouth, black as sin and bitter as titanic acid. She might have brewed that same tea, said Ned, with the water of the Providence River and leaves of dark mayo. He got up and tucked the paper under his arm while he filled his pipe and when the gas was lit in the fluted bowls he handed the paper to Willie.

"Let's see," he said, "what's going on in the world around us, the big wide world around us. I was thinking, Nell, of the time the shop was shut down. Do you remember the time just after Will was born. Lord have mercy on him, that I took the job with the pick and shovel, the only time in my life ever I did, too. It was digging the foundation of that bank downtown there and they struck water so that you were mud to your hips. Oh and the weather was mean and nasty all the time I was there. Too mean, it was, to snow right out or rain right out, but drip, drip, drip all day long.

"But down we dug and dug till they'd get rock or something they could build on, for that was the biggest building in its day there was in the city. The skies dripped and the walls of the hole dripped. There was a greenhorn alongside of me, a Galway man, and he telling me between drops all day as we went down deeper and deeper into the muck, wet to the skin every day, how grand it was at home. He was a fisherman and out in the curragh every day when it was fair and sometimes not, with his brothers. And, oh, the size of the fish they got and the colors of them and prices they fetched in the market, fresh, or salted down and dried. Dried? I'd say. Dried, was they? Ah, yes, he'd say, never once catching on, fresh or dried they had always the best price in the market.

"He had the ear talked off me and I wasn't long on the job, though it seemed a creeping century to me then. 'The more fool, you,' I says to him one dirty day, 'for ever leaving that place and coming out here. Why,' I says, 'how could you ever do that?' I says. 'I'll tell you,' he says, with a cold rain showering down on us and he sweeping the shovel around at the walls of the pit. It was forever out and in over the same waves and in and out again the next day over them and I grew tired of it, I suppose. And whacking the shovel against the wall of the pit he says, 'so then and there one day I made up my mind I'd see the world and all that was in it!'

" 'Well,' I says, 'it's a cold one and a deep one and a wet and muddy one, ain't it?' I says. 'Do you think you'll ever go back?' I says. 'I will, says he, one day I will.' "

"Oh, dear, oh, dear," said Nell, "he said he'd see the world and all in it and there he was—"

"I think of him manys a time," Ned laughed, "buried to his ears in the muck of that pit while he was seeing the world. How much of it he saw or whether he ever got out of that wet hole, I don't know for I've never seen the man again to this day. But I often think of him."

"You never told about him before," Nell said shaking her head. "But I remember well when you worked with the pick and shovel and how it was, you said, on your back. Whatever made you think of him now?"

"God, I don't know," he answered, "unless it was me seeing the world myself from the couch here—and that with Willie's eyes. I don't know what made me think of him."

Listening, Willie had forgotten the paper and the medal and everything but the wet Galway man in the pit, forgotten the shame of his hatred of Sammie and Celia because they had won. But now all of it rose up like vomit in his mouth. He pushed the paper toward his grandfather, his heart sagging.

"I didn't win," he said. "I didn't get the medal."

Ned pushed the paper back at him again.

"Oh, the medal!" He casually flipped the words out. "So they told me. Well, it was not a piece of the True Cross, was it, they gave for a prize? Read us what's in the news tonight."

Chapter Thirty-Six

INTO such bright basilicas of thought as Father Joe led them
before the next summer ended and he had sprung the horizons
of the back yard across the centuries for him and Byron Searles,
Willie knew neither his grandfather, nor any of the other McDermotts, had ever entered. The three of them sat on the grass under
the dark shower of the maple tree and the young priest's words
were blinding flashes of sunlight tearing through the shadows of
their perplexities. Willie struggled with all the strength of his
heart to see and know, beyond the mystical splendor of Jesus of
Nazareth and the words of his disciples, the awful authority of the
Church eternal which was not of this world, but so jealous of its
power in it. Vainly he tried to reconcile this Church of Father
Jim, devout and reverent in its chasuble and alb, beautiful above
the reaches of his own thoughts in the magnificence of its cere-
monies and its symbols, which he now was beginning to understand in some measure of the depth of their poetry and ecstasy, this
Church which was so vigorous and militant in the streets, the life
and affairs of the city, and that immutable Church of Father Joe,
agelessly alive in all time, so potent in its very humility, so sublime
in its rejection of all that is not of the heart, the spirit, the immortal soul.

When they would sit out in the yard again after supper, perhaps,
while the crickets cried in the darkness around them and the
tinkling bells of the ice-cream man's wagon coming slowly down
the street would sound like the bells of the Sanctus, the restless
stars wrote hope and faith for them across the black heavens.
Father Joe read to them, passionately and devoutly, from the sermons of Newman, sermons of spring, a second spring, of death and
rebirth, of one death which was the parent of a thousand lives. It
was stately writing in long, fragrant sentences that made Willie feel
the same indefinable conflict of pain and joy within himself that
he did sometimes when, at Benediction of the Blessed Sacrament,
they swung the silver thurible, the chains in the altar boy's hands
gently touching the sides of the vessel with the sound of tiny cym-

bals and the sweet blue smoke rising, rising, rising to their cadence to lift itself high above the carved lace of the main altar's yellow marble and vanish when it reached the violet, the green, red, blue and purple lights pouring into the sanctuary from the garments of the figures in the rose window.

The young priest unchained the lightning and thunder of the inspired voices of Egypt for them, swept the clouds away from the sun of Africa. The boys listened to the passionate Augustine, sinful, heretical, tell of his long, thirsty journeys and his finding at last and drinking the sweet, intoxicating waters of the fountain of Faith and their hearts were "inebriated," as his was. The heresies, and it was almost more than they could grasp to hear that men who seemed so holy and pious were heretics, were shriveled, damned and shriveled before them. Still the voices rang through the summer days until Willie could hear no other voices; they exalted and terrified him; he heard them cry to him when he was alone, when the iridescent images of Catherine Daly, of Rose Riordan, of Celia, sometimes of Hazel danced in the waves and the flames of his sleep. They would not be denied, returning to him always lovelier no matter how loudly sang the chorus of Augustine, Origen, Aquinas, Chrysostom or any of the other great singers of the Church about whom the priest might have been talking to them that day.

Willie walked with frightened feet on narrow girders of hope that spanned the craters of a thousand hells, hells where joy and sin and wickedness, where pain and torment shrieked and where Catherine and Celia and Rose trampled him. He dared not mention his thoughts to Father Joe or to his grandfather, either when they were good or when they were evil.

Lions and tigers, giraffes towering over them, were prowling the billboards everywhere in the city. Father Jim, laughing with teeth whiter than the trim sailor straw he was wearing, came out in the yard one afternoon while Father Joe was telling Willie and Byron about the first monasteries peopled by small bands of pious men who withdrew from the world and went out into the sands of the desert, consecrating their lives to God. He didn't want to interrupt the lecturer, Father Jim said, but he was wondering if the professor and his class couldn't adjourn the next day and go to the circus with him. Byron said he was going anyway, but if they could all go together he would like that better and go with them instead of his mother and sister. Willie had been planning to go with his cousins out to the tracks when the circus pulled in on the spur near the park and help the men carry water and hay to the animals, which his cousins said you could always do and get into the tents for nothing. He had said nothing about it to either Byron or Father Joe, because he didn't want either of them to think he would rather go and watch some animals and acrobats or jugglers and elephants instead of going to Father Joe's house. This settled it for him, but he wondered if his grandmother would let him go. His grandfather would not give him money to go, he knew, because in such things it was share and share alike with his cousins and the price of admission for the three of them would be more than Ned would have to spend on a circus. Father Joe suggested at first that his brother take only the boys and he would stay at home and rest. He said he wasn't feeling any too well. Father Jim told him it was nonsense, he ought to go and furthermore someday, when there was a double-header, he was going to take them all out to see the Grays play. They had a couple of new twirlers, he said; one of them was from Baltimore and came from one of the boy's schools there, a Catholic boys' school. Ruth, his name was, Father Jim said. Byron, laughing, said it was the first time he had ever heard of a boy named Ruth, or a man. Ruth was his last name, Father Jim said, and he was supposed to be a great twirler.

Father Jim sat on the grass and took his religion off, as he always said (bringing a frown skidding momentarily across Father Joe's face), his Roman collar, his jacket, the little black bib and his white starched cuffs. He loosened the collar of his shirt tucking the ends inside.

"Well, go ahead with the lecture, Father," he said to his brother. "Perhaps I can profit from it myself. There isn't much time you know, for intellectual discourse when you're head over heels in the work of a parish. You're going to make a pair of theologians out of these two, I can see that. In the fall I won't be able to teach them anything about Christian doctrine they won't know as well as I do myself. How do you like them, anyhow, Father? Do you think either of them could hold his own on Aquinas?"

"There are many things we haven't gone into, Father," said Father Joe smiling but slightly irritated by his brother's apparent nonchalance before the boys.

And the spell was broken for the day. They talked about schools and colleges for the rest of the afternoon and Byron said that he was certain he was going to Holy Cross because his father, thought it would be a very good idea for him to be away from home for a while when he was studying. Both the priests had studied there and it pleased them to hear that Byron, self-sure and cocky as he sounded, had decided at this early stage to go there, too. Father Jim asked Willie if he had thought about going to Holy Cross, but Willie, who always found such questions of the future puzzling, could only say that he thought his grandfather would send him there, yes, he probably would go to Holy Cross. There were great teachers there, Father Jim said, and he asked them if they remembered Father McCarthy the Jesuit priest who con- conducted the mission at St. Malachi's the year before. Father Mc- Carthy had been a star football player at the Cross when he went there, Father Jim said. When it was suppertime Willie went home.

Patrick and John, sitting on the high board fence watching old man Reed giving his chickens their evening feed, called him as he was going in the gate and asked him if he were going with them to see the circus come in and carry hay and water to the animals. Willie wanted to tell them that he was going to see the circus with the priests and Byron Searles, but he thought it would be better not to, so he said he would go out to see it come in. His cousins said their father had told them they might go and their mother would wake them up when it was time. They would have to be out at the park about two o'clock in the morning or they wouldn't see it. They agreed that Willie, whose grandmother was sure to oppose his going out in the middle of the night, would slip downstairs when he was going to bed and take the hook off the screen door so that one of the others could sneak up to his room and call him. They didn't think about his getting back into the house or what would happen if his grandmother called him in the morning and he was still out at the park carrying water to the animals.

The best thing to do, it seemed to Willie, would be to carry water with his cousins and slip away from the grounds while the parade was on. Then he could come home and clean up before he went down to McCaffreys' house to go out to the grounds again with Byron and the priests.

It was very still when they hurried along the path in the woods that led to the spur. Johnnie ran on ahead of them, hiding every once in a while in the bushes to snap the branch of a tree on them as they came up to him. A little rain had fallen earlier in the night and they were soon wet from the showers Johnnie splashed on them. Halfway through the woods they could hear the clanging of the cars as the circus train pulled into the long siding where it would unload. They ran toward the tracks where there was already a chaos of horses, men, wagons. Before they reached the tracks a huge black mast rose majestically into the night with long, reluctant vines dripping from it. Four and six horse hitches groaned through the sand and whips cracked. Beacons of hissing yellow flares began to leap out of the darkness around them, avenues of them, circles of them, diamonds of light. Men grunted, swinging giant mauls, one-two-three, grunt, one-two-three, grunt, at stakes in the ground and told them to run home and keep the hell out of the way. They walked endlessly looking for someone who would give them jobs helping take care of the animals, but none of them knew where to go or who, among the hundreds of men they saw, would be the man to ask. They were chased away from the animal cars.

Toward daybreak they were all tired, dirty and very hungry, but Patrick found a sawed-off, hammered-down man wearing a spotted scarlet jacket frogged with gold braid at the collar and cuffs and spotted with grease who said he would let them all in to see the show if they wanted to help out feeding and watering the animals. He said he would show them where they could get a cup of coffee later if they wanted it. The fire hydrant at the end of the bicycle bowl was opened and lines were running from it. They filled canvas troughs that were rigged for the horses to drink from, and lugged pails that grew heavier and heavier to the men who were cleaning up the animal cages, until the parade formed and pulled out of the lot.

The sawed-off man, when they found him again, looked very different in the daylight; he had shaved, leaving a sharply outlined gray neck that was about the same color as the undershirt he wore. Patrick asked him when they would get the tickets to see the show, and he told them to be around when it was time for the show and he would slip them into the main tent. They didn't need tickets, he said, just make themselves handy until the time came and he would see to it that they saw the show. They soldiered while the parade was returning and dispersing its glittering stream of wagons, and were glad to see that a hose had been rigged up and that a man was playing it over the elephants, playing countless pails of it over their leathery gray sides. They clung to their pails tenaciously.

At noon they caught the sound of the mill whistles blowing over the tumult and Willie gave his cousins the slip shortly afterward, hurrying home to clean himself up before he went to McCaffreys' house. His grandmother scolded him for slipping out of the house in the morning without telling her where he was going, and he imagined how much worse it might have been for him if she ever knew he had gone at midnight instead of just before she got up, as he told her. She sent him to the store, telling him to stop at Mollie's and see if they wanted anything, too, since those boys had been away from the house all morning long. Although he ran as fast as he could, it took him longer than he thought it would, and when he had done the errands his grandmother insisted on his eating before she would let him out of the house again. Then she made him clean his shoes because he smelled like a stable. Time was slipping like sand through his fingers and he still had a long way to go to get to the McCaffreys' in time to meet Byron and Father Jim.

Free at last, Willie sprinted and dogtrotted until his tired legs were snarled with pain and his breath was coming so short he had to walk. His clean shirt stuck to his chest. Walking revived him a little, and he ran again until he came to the corner of the street where the McCaffreys lived and it wouldn't look right to be seen running. He listened, when he pressed the bell on the porch, for the sound of Father Joe or Father Jim talking, but the house was as quiet as though it were empty. He heard a slow step and creaking of shoes on the stairs inside and Mrs. McCaffrey, looking annoyed and impatient, opened the door. They had gone, she said, just a little while ago and she asked him, feeling of his wet shirt, why he hadn't been there on time. If he hurried he might be able to catch them at the streetcar. Willie bounded away again, leaving her standing there shaking her head after him. They were not at the car stop, nor at the next one, nor the one after that and it was a long walk, even cutting through the woods to the circus grounds. He hoped against hope he might reach the circus as soon as they did—probably they would wait around at the entrance before going in to see if he would come—and hurried along as fast as he could. There was no speed left in his legs and the pain that knifed his side under his heart was stabbing his spirit, too, it seemed.

Nearing the grounds his eyes hunted feverishly among the groups of people for Byron and the priests, but he knew he wouldn't see them. They would think, when he hadn't arrived at the house on time, that he didn't want to go with them, or that his grandfather wouldn't let him go. Either way was unbearable. He dove into the crowds at the entrance to the main tent, searching every face, every straw hat vainly for them. The crowd swelled and thinned; it bunched in front of the side show tent and dribbled away again; it moved sluggishly and almost ran. Willie moved with the current for a while and then swam back against it, across it until, it seemed an eternity, he was so weary he couldn't push his way any longer and he went around by the side of the big tent where they had been carrying water in the morning to look for the man with the scarlet jacket.

He couldn't find him, but there were other men, unshaven, patrolling in and out of the taut ropes, carrying clubs in their hands and they wouldn't let him near the tent itself. Exhausted he went into the woods again where it was cool and where there were crap games going, and groups of men, and sometimes young women with colored balloons, drinking from bottles of whisky. He cut away from the path itself and, finding a spot behind some bushes that grew among the elms, he stretched himself out on the grass. He could see the spread of the big top with pennants flying over the tips of the birches below and he could hear the bands, and the roars of the animals. He could hear the people applauding until he fell asleep.

When he woke up, bewildered an instant by the bushes around him, he could hear no bands playing nor any sound of people applauding. There was only a strident voice reaching from the tents, a sharp, shrill unintelligible cry that repeated and repeated itself, cutting through the trees. He walked through the woods again to the now nearly deserted main entrance. A few people were straggling there and the barkers at the side show tent were lashing themselves into raucous spasms trying to wheedle or drive them into the show. At the stands the men were spinning their wheels—wheels with the numbers on them like boys rolling hoops alone in the dusk.

Willie scuffed toward home through the woods again, trampling broken balloons, paper bags and torn Crackerjack boxes, meeting a few people on the way who were going to the night show or perhaps only to wander around the grounds. What a long, miserable day it had been, filled with scalding disappointment on every side. He wanted so heartily to become fast friends with Father Joe, and Father Jim, too, but Father Joe was even more important to him; he was envious of every minute Byron spent with the priest when he was not there because he suspected vaguely that there was a bond growing between them that he had not achieved. Byron would have spent the whole afternoon with him, probably was having his supper at the McCaffreys' even now. Facile, clever Byron who understood everything without ever asking any questions and who always snickered a little when Willie asked them. Clever Byron, whom nothing prevented from doing just what he wanted to when he wanted to do it.

When Byron wanted to go to the circus he told his father and he went; he went with his mother and sister or he changed his mind the day before and went with Father Joe; no lugging water, no running home, no skipping his cousins, just going to the circus. It would be so good if once he could sit and listen to Father Joe, asking him whatever disturbed his mind, without Byron there to smirk at him. He painfully decided he wouldn't go to McCaffreys' house for a few days, to avoid having to explain why he missed meeting them and seeing the circus until Byron had forgotten a little about it. Perhaps he could see Father Jim or Father Joe at mass and tell them why he had been late.

Chapter Thirty-Seven

IF HE wanted to, Nora said, he could go around to Martin McShane, the milkman, and see about helping him on the wagon. Poor Martin, she said, had the worst luck; if it wasn't one thing it was another and this time the horse trod on his foot in the stable and near crippled him, and him with a regiment at home to support. Worst of all that damned Dyer, with money to burn what with the hothouses and the milk business, told the poor man he could get out and rest up for the day but to be back at work in the morning or there'd be another to take his place. Hobbling around he was, with a stick, and screaming with pain and nothing would help him but a drop of whisky. As though Cassie McShane hadn't enough worries without this on her hands and she ready any day now to bring another soul into the world besides the six she had.

Ned pleaded with her to stop and catch her breath before she strangled herself to death with the worries of the McShanes and tell them, for the love of God, what the hell she was trying to say.

Well, only that she had seen Cassie when she went out to the store in the afternoon because Willie wasn't home or forgot to go, and Cassie told her that Martin had his foot crushed under the hoof of a horse in Dyer's stable that morning and that he had to have someone to help him on the wagon for he couldn't jump up and down from it and run into a house with an armful of bottles and she thought Willie might as well go over and see the man at least and earn a few dollars while school was closed for the summer and Martin laid up, or almost flat on his back and still expected to work. The pay was half a dollar a day, that was three and seventy-five cents for the Sunday, and good wages indeed for a boy his age to be earning. Besides, Martin was finished with the route before noon every day and Willie could have the rest of the day to himself after the horse was put up, of course, and taken care of.

"Why the hell didn't you say so?" Ned asked. "You have me kicked to ribbons with all the horses. What about that, Will, do you want to go traveling around on a milk wagon with McShane?"

Willie was elated and surprised that his grandfather would consider letting him, because several times when there had been a chance to carry papers at the cigar store he had asked and Ned had refused to "have him out on the streets cadging pennies like an orphan."

"He'll have all the milk he can drink," Nora added, nettled that her part in the enterprise was ended with a few words. "And Martin sure won't work him to death."

"Where does Martin live, anyhow?" Ned asked clipping her off again.

Dyer's lane was a few narrow yards of gravel between his greenhouse and creamery, barely wide enough for one of the wagons to pass down without scraping the sides of the buildings. Moonlight glistened on the glass roof and side walls of the greenhouse, and the flowers, all blooming white and colorless, sent their fragrance into the alley to mingle with ripe ammoniac from the stable which stood with its doors facing the street. Willie could hear the stomping of the impatient horses in their stalls, the rumbling of the heavy cans, their clanking covers, and the rattling bells of the bottles. Where the wall of the creamery ended there was a loading platform and a small yard where he saw Martin McShane, stiff in a starchy gray jacket sitting with one leg drawn up on the white shafts of a wagon. Without saying good morning to him, Martin told him to squat while he finished his pipe (never smoke in the stable), and they would go in together and say good morning to Boxer, the finest beast in the stable, if the son of a bitch did step on his feet yesterday.

"Ha! Boxer, y'old rebel, you," Martin said, limping into the stall of a full-fleshed, lusty black gelding whose coat, under the fly-spotted electric light, looked sifted over with grain dust. Martin leaned against the feedbox and directed Willie to bring the oats, clean the stall while the horse was eating, brush and curry him and not forget to comb out the tail. Then he could wipe down the harness, and make sure he had the brass knobs on the hames shining like the sun itself.

The harnessing was easy with a hand from Martin, and Boxer was soon out in the yard backing into the shafts of the wagon where Martin had been sitting. Loading the cans and racks of bottles was not so easy, but Martin stood with his red pad checking everything Willie did and assured him all was going fine, a little slow and he would have to set a faster pace once he got used to it, but well and good for the first morning. They rolled out of the alley, Martin driving, into the quiet streets. When they stopped at houses Martin would announce what went in—"a quart of the brew for Mrs. Horton's crew." "A pint for Mrs. Norcross—she starves her brood." "Two here for the Callahans, God bless them and help them pay that bill, it's three weeks owing now." "One here for Kelly with the cast-iron belly—you should see this one when she comes to the door; never mind, skip!" "A nice, sweet, fresh one now, for little Tessie in the rear house—I wish she took boarders! Tessie'll make some man happy one day, but not the one she's married to! Put the bottle well on the side of the door so she won't trip and fall over it when she comes out." "You're doing fine, McGee! Keep it up! In here, now with a drop·for the Whiteheads." "Two weeks owed here, too, but bring the Williams two anyhow." Martin got down himself and helped with the cans that went to the groceries and the first streaks of the morning were coloring the sky when they arrived at the all-night restaurant across the street from the carbarn. Martin went in himself, telling Willie to follow him, because here he had a different order every day. He sat at the sticky marble counter and there was a cup of hot coffee and powdered crullers waiting for Willie when he brought the bottles in.

Before noon Willie was home again, giddy with the morning's excitement, tired, and wondering if he should go over to McCaffreys' house that afternoon and tell Father Joe about his job. He decided to wait until the end of the week and went upstairs to sleep in the hot attic until the heat of the afternoon woke him up. Restless, unable to read when he tried, he walked down to the foundry to meet his grandfather on his way home and tell him all about the job. Ned was pleased, but warned him against trying to lift more than he was able, told him to be careful at all times with the horse so he wouldn't get himself kicked and crippled, and said he wasn't sure whether he liked the idea of him working at all; time enough for all that later.

There was something of a sneer, Willie thought, about the way Byron Searles looked at him when he told them at McCaffreys' house that he was working on the milk wagon. Father Joe said they had missed him afternoons and hoped that for the rest of the summer, and that was not long, either, Willie would be able to come over there more often. He would soon have to be going back to Washington, the priest said, and there were so many things he had wanted to talk with them about before he went he feared there wouldn't be time. They were beginning an important period of their lives when they started high school in the fall, he told them, and he wished that they were going to the Christian Brothers instead of to the public high school. He had hoped there might have been time during the summer to have read and talked more about Thomas Aquinas and his incomparable writings and thoughts, but he wanted them to know of the great men of the Church who came before him, great saints of the Church whose teachings blossomed again and again, like the spring in Cardinal Newman's sermon, in Aquinas' works.

Yes, they were both very, very young, but they must each find a way, they must determine to read and read and read this Angelic Doctor, for all the thinking of the Church before him led only to him and the thinking that followed returned to him as it would to a fountain. It was not "vain testimony," as the great Leo XIII said, Father Joe declared, that the heretical leaders for centuries had asserted that if the writing of Aquinas were taken away they could easily dispute all Catholic teachers and destroy the Church.

Let them think of their faith as of the gold and silver vessels and the precious robes of the Egyptians that the Hebrews, about to leave that country after their wanderings, were commanded to bring with them and dedicate to the glory of God. Let them think of Cyprian of Alexandria, whom Augustine called the mildest of doctors and most blessed of martyrs, going out of Egypt with those vessels and vestments of grace and fruitful doctrine.

He wished he could be with them longer, that he could talk with them frequently and share with them his own poor store of knowledge. And now, except when they were serving him at mass, they had not prayed together. So they prayed, each of them with his own heart and each with his own hope, silently under the late August sun which burned over the maple. Looking into the branches above him Willie saw one reddening leaf among the swaying fans of green.

No, there would be no one with him at the station when he was leaving, Father Joe said. Such honor was not for him and besides, if he went alone when it was time to go it would seem that he had just gone on a short visit and the winter would not be so long. When he returned in the spring he would find them both richer, he knew, far richer in spirit if they began to know the works of the great men he had told them about than if they had spent their hours listening to his own poor words.

Chapter Thirty-Eight

WHEN Willie looked at Miss Grace Latham, towering over the class like a thin, leafless winter, and heard her chop their days into periods of algebra, history, English and Latin, all with bells to start and stop them, he tumbled from the heights where he had been dreaming since the last time he had heard Father Joe talk. Miss Latham gave them books, among them a wretchedly small *Sir Roger de Coverley Papers*, with the same reluctance, he thought, that the women in the library parted with the treasures for which he was so hungry.

Before he really knew what was happening, Miss Latham had carved the class into two sections and, when the bell rang, herded one group into a small recitation room. Then she stood on the dais in front of them again and began to read the Latin poem about the little star. Her voice seemed to have the low, angry whistle that a hungry cat has when it gnaws the last shreds of meat from a dirty, discarded bone, or the flesh from the skeleton of a codfish. Willie could not recognize her words as having been born in the same language that Father Joe spoke, or Father Jim, or that Father Hanlon sang at high mass. Her voice killed all the meaning of the printed words in front of him and he turned the pages furtively to escape her.

Then crawling among the drawings of tombs, cracked columns, crumbling walls and round, eyeless heads on the pages, all colorless, cold and dead, he found himself alone in a desolate world, bewildered and afraid.

Weeks and weeks of it followed, and no matter how frantically he tried to hold to what they taught or how desperately he studied, his mind did not fasten to the facts, and he was miserable. His marks sagged with each report card and it was harder and harder to face his grandfather during the winter. The algebra tortured him and it was decided, after the midyear term when he was so far behind the rest of the class that there seemed to be no catching up, that he should go over to Joe Flynn's house three nights a week and let Joe help him. Catherine Daly said that she would be happy to do it, but that she had so many things to do and she was not very good at mathematics herself.

He spent many hours in Joe's kitchen, stifling from the heat of the coal stove while Nell's brother tried to help him. But he learned nothing. He would look at Joe's broad, pallid forehead, his greasy nose glasses, listen to his choking asthmatic voice, and watch him spit tobacco juice into an AUTOCRAT coffee can on the floor. Joe did the lessons, often arriving at the conclusions by methods Willie had no grasp of, and Willie would copy them out in his own figures when he reached home again. He was humiliated time after time in class when he would not be able to explain how he had done the work, and when examinations came he inevitably failed them.

If he had dared, he would have asked his grandfather to let him leave school at times when his failures would crush him. Yet clutching Father Joe's words to himself, he would determine to struggle on and somehow win. He knew it was the way he must go.

Chapter Thirty-Nine

STREAMING from Pete McNally's nearly lipless mouth and splashed with his brogue, the Latin sounded very strange to Willie when they first served mass together just after Pete had come back from Ireland where he had spent a while with his grandparents. Pete had been on the altar for a short time before he went to Ireland and when he came back he was even more arrogant than when he had left. Pipe-thin and lithe as a cat, he could run faster and fight or wrestle better than most of the altar boys, some of whom tried it with him the first time he came to a meeting in the sacristy.

His habit of coughing a little or snapping his fingers to remind Willie that it was time to change the missal from one side of the altar to the other, time to get the wine and water or ring the sanctus bell, was, Willie felt, Pete's way of telling him that he was the master. He took it on himself to inspect Willie's appearance, too, before they went out on the altar, telling him one morning before the half past seven mass that he ought at least to shine his shoes before coming to serve mass. Whatever Willie did, Pete had some comment to make about it, if only an approving nod of his head while they were out on the altar. "That's right, McDermott," it seemed to say. "Ring the bell, McDermott," or perhaps, "Up, McDermott, time for the wine and water—follow me." Waiting for the priest to come over to them with the chalice he would elbow Willie to be ready with his cruet. "Hold it up, up!" he might whisper, hardly moving his lips. Willie did everything he could to escape McNally; volunteered to serve earlier mass, asked directly at the meetings for masses he thought McNally wouldn't want, but there seemed to be no dodging him. He intruded himself when Willie left the meetings with Byron Searles or Leo Dion, and always found ways to remind them that his father, whom they met one night in Cahill's drugstore when they went in for a lemon-and-lime, had put on another salesman, his father was thinking of opening a branch in Pawtucket, or Woonsocket.

His father, a pious man who was reputedly very close with the pennies, owned an "art" business which was making him one of the richest men in the parish. In his office he kept close tabs on all the deaths in Catholic families and a week or so after the funerals, before the tears were dried or the insurance, if there were any, spent, one of his salesmen would appear at the home of the family and somehow wheedle a picture of the deceased from them. Then one of the "artists" would make a copy, enlarged and in color, of the photo, which the salesman would sell very cheaply to the bereaved family, the widow, the mother, the father, son or the daughter. Who didn't want such a beautiful portrait? Yes, but the eyes, the eyes were bluer and the hair was darker. Why, madam, McNally would fix that, nothing at all, no charge. The suit was lighter, as you remember it, madam, the dress was pink, you want the stickpin you gave him put in the necktie? McNally was happy to make any alterations. No charge at all, madam, no charge. Now, madam, you have the picture for less than it cost to make the snapshot. Entirely satisfied with it? Why, if you haven't a frame I can take it back to McNally and make a frame that will really suit the portrait. And, madam, if you don't buy the frame, for that's where McNally makes his profit, it will be a long, long time before you see the handsome portrait again. You're going to buy that frame, madam!

McNally didn't stop at deaths. There were weddings from which two or even three copies and three frames might be sold, and christenings and first Holy Communions and confirmations and there were graduations and Italians by the thousand; there were the French and the Poles, too. McNally had, besides his regular staff that were all either Irish or Irish-American, an Italian salesman and a French salesman. Pete naturally went to the Brothers academy instead of the public high school where most of the other altar boys went.

"Look, McNally," Willie said to Pete one morning after early mass, "you're not cardinal primate of Ireland here, you know. You're just an altar boy. Maybe they snap and grunt in Ireland when they're serving mass, but we don't. And don't poke me in the ribs any more and don't snap the fingers at me. I don't like it."

"McDermott!" the boy laughed. "I do believe we're getting our dander up! Why, McDermott!"

"You heard me, McNally, I don't like it. You'll do it once too often."

"Only to guide you, McDermott."

"When I want you to guide me, McNally, I'll ask you. Until I do, don't snap your fingers at me."

"Guidance is what you need, Willie darlin'," McNally said scornfully.

"Why should I argue with you? This is no place for it, anyway. Get wise to yourself. You'll last longer."

McNally quit snapping his fingers after that, but their relations were never friendly because Willie always had the feeling when McNally was near him that the other boy was just about to crack a whip over him, and he thought that if he ever got the chance, he would like to battle McNally and beat his brains out. It was the only solution he could think of; arguments with McNally never achieved anything because McNally, if he saw he was being cornered, would begin to throw taunts which only made Willie want to fight him. He wasn't even sure he could whip McNally, but he thought he could. It was wretched to think, though, that McNally was so clever and so sure of himself a fist fight was the only way to stop him. When it was possible Willie avoided him, because if they fought Father McCaffrey was sure to hear about it; he had a genius for knowing what was going on among the altar boys.

A battle royal started on the lawn of the church one night after a meeting when someone pulled another boy's cap down over his ears, and in the middle of the brawl Willie found himself slugging it out and wrestling with McNally. For the rest of them, except Byron Searles who usually managed to stay out of such scrimmages, it was not unfriendly. They clipped each other, dumped the next, if they could, or were dumped. McNally lashed out with his fist, however, and stung Willie on the nose, making it bleed. Willie called him a son of a bitch and drove back at him. McNally was taller, but Willie was a little heavier. In a minute it was clear that they were in earnest and the rest of the boys stopped to watch them. They didn't kick, but they did everything else they could to smash each other up and Willie, sensing that McNally would wear him down if he stood up and traded punches with him, closed in on the taller boy and threw him.

They were rolling around the lawn, each of them slipping in a punch when he could, when Father McCaffrey came out of the church. If it had been in friendly spirit they were battling he would have let them pummel each other all night if they wanted to, but he was irate that, as he could tell from what the boys watching were saying, McDermott and McNally were having a serious fight. He hopped over the lawn and hauled them to their feet, knocking their heads together with a sickening crack when he got them up. When the others began to drift off, carelessly, as though they had not been interested in the first place, he called them all back to him. The priest let go a tirade against the whole group, the two fighting first of all, and the rest of them for standing there watching. On second thought, he said, they might as well all go back into the sacristy because he had a few words to say to them that he didn't want people on the street to hear. He paced angrily up and down in front of the long dresser where the vestments were set out while they unfolded their seats and sat.

He'd try, he said, to go into the whole thing for them as he saw it and he hoped they would. It was more serious than they thought. Not that there couldn't be arguments and yes, even a fight among them now and then even if they were altar boys; he didn't expect any angels to appear suddenly in St. Malachi's. But let them get together like gentlemen, if they had any conception of what the word meant, and thrash things out in private, just the two that were involved. But why did they have to fight among themselves, among their own kind? If there were fighting to be done, he should think they could find someone else to fight with.

"Well, I'm proud of you all. You certainly honor yourselves and your people and your Church. It does take the genius of the Irish to transform a meeting of altar boys into a street brawl, doesn't it? Only a step from the sacristy to the gutter for you, isn't it? You know, I am beginning to believe myself all the rotten slanders were ever made against the Irish. I can't do anything else when I'm faced with a crowd of ruffians like you. Frankly.

"It fills my heart with pride, as you can easily understand, to know that I'm your—well, we have to find a place for me in this gang, don't we? Am I the leader of the mob? Is that what you'd call me? Am I your Fagin, perhaps? Let me assure you I'm not, gentlemen. Let me just remind you, in case it might have slipped your minds, that I was ordained in the Catholic priesthood. Perhaps some time we might go into the meaning and the significance of the sacrament of Holy Orders—some time when you are in a less frenzied state of savagery, I suggest.

"My relation to you, gentlemen, is that of a spiritual leader, if you can grasp that. It is not precisely a tribute to myself to have you rush out of my sight and hearing to engage in a low brawl on the very lawn of the church. Do you really think I will tolerate such conduct in you? You're quite mistaken if you do.

"While we're on the subject of fighting and street brawling, by the way, I want to tell of an incident that was reported to me the other day by Mr. Shapiro, the tailor over there on Melrose Avenue, a very revolting incident. It happens that I am one of Mr. Shapiro's customers—I believe all the priests in the parish are. I find it necessary from time to time to drop in at his shop. Mr. Shapiro, I would like to inform the unenlightened, is a very hard-working man with a very large family and he finds it necessary to spend long hours in the shop to earn a living for them. When he stays late at the shop his boys bring him his supper. One night recently, so he tells me, the boy arrived very late and had no supper for Mr. Shapiro. The boy was pretty well beaten up in the bargain. He was stopped in the street—right near the shop—I mean right in this very neighborhood, by a pack of young wolves that knocked the dishes from his hands and then proceeded to beat him up, just by way of welcome into the neighborhood, I suppose. Yes, the boy was alone and there were five or six of them in the gang that attacked him.

"Don't worry, gentlemen, and don't let your knees knock together so loudly. Mr. Shapiro did not know the names of the young scoundrels who attacked his boy. At least, if he did, and I have a suspicion that he did know them, he spared me the embarrassment of telling me. After witnessing tonight's performance I am certain it was the latter. I think it might be very embarrassing at this moment if I asked for a show of hands as to who among you was there and who was not there, wouldn't it, gentlemen? Well, I'm not going to, so you can put your minds at rest. What disturbs me most is not whether any special one of you were there or not but that, after seeing your behavior tonight I have the feeling that any one of you *might* have been there.

"Would you barbarians permit me to remind you of a few words of St. Paul, assuming you might listen to him even if you are tired of listening to me, Ganley. Yes, thank you for your attention. 'Be without offense,' he said, Ganley. 'Be without offense to the Jews and the Gentiles and to the Church of God.' That might be of some significance to you, Ganley, if you think you can get away with injuring one without injuring all. I didn't say you were there did I, Ganley? No, you're right, I didn't. But you were there on the lawn tonight, Ganley, you were all there on the lawn tonight while the two—the two knights of the Holy Sepulchre were defending their honor! And if you think *that* doesn't give offense to the Holy Mother Church, I'd like to know what you think does!"

If they were such militant young Catholics, there was fighting to be done in the world that wasn't done with fists. Let them strengthen their minds and serve God with as much zeal as they strengthened their bodies and served themselves; fortify themselves in faith and morals and at least, once again, among themselves try to behave with forbearance and friendship. He called Willie and McNally from their seats and stood between them smiling to indicate that while he didn't condone what they had been doing, he forgave them. Shake hands, he said.

McNally, grinning, hanging his head, put his hand out across the priest's cassock toward Willie who tentatively began to raise his own—and drew it suddenly back again.

"I don't want to shake hands with him, Father," he said.

"Shake hands, I said," Father McCaffrey ordered, astounded.

"Father, I don't want to and I won't!"

"Why won't you?" the priest asked sharply.

"Because I don't forgive—I don't want to be friends with him." Willie was shocked at his courage and wished he could find it in himself to shake hands with McNally whether he meant it or not, as he suspected McNally was doing, but he couldn't. McNally had goaded him too long and too bitterly; he hadn't realized how bitterly until they began fighting.

"Well, Father Joe's long talks to you have certainly inculcated Christian doctrine in you, haven't they?" said Father McCaffrey. "I'm sure he'd be delighted to know how deeply you have been affected by them, McDermott. Yes, it would be extremely gratifying to him, I'm sure, to know. I think you'd better go home, McDermott, and not come around again until you have given this matter some very serious thought. I might add, before you leave, that I don't think I have ever encountered such an outrageously vicious attitude in a Catholic boy. You'd better do some very serious thinking, about this thing. Frankly, I shouldn't like to have to sleep with your conscience tonight. You can go home now."

"Yes, Will, the priest is right," Ned said when, after troubled days and nights, the boy at last brought his wretchedness to him. "You must go to what's-his-name and shake hands with him and get it over with. The sooner you do it the better. Why should you be fighting and quarreling amongst yourselves anyhow? The priest is right. Go to what's-his-name and shake hands with him. Tell me—did he lick you?"

"No," Willie said. "He didn't, but he probably would have if we weren't separated—"

"Well, go to him anyhow and shake hands and make friends with him and you'll feel better all around."

"I still don't want to," Willie said unhappily. "He's no friend of mine and I don't want to be friends with him. He's always bragging—he thinks he's better than anyone else. Everyone has to do what he wants to do—"

"Now, now," his grandfather cautioned. "What's that to do with it? What's that to do with you not storing up anger and hatred in your heart against him? It's you I'm thinking of and not Mc-what's-his-name."

"He's always causing me trouble," the boy said. "He snaps his fingers at you when you're serving mass and he's always telling you what you should do next. He thinks he knows more than anyone else. One morning he even told me to shine my shoes before I came to serve mass. Why should I have to shake hands and be friendly with someone like that?"

"Well, maybe the shoes did need a blacking," Ned declared. "You must be careful about things like that. It's what they always say, d'you see, that the Irish is forever fighting among themselves and with everybody else. You must be careful not to give them the chance to say that, you know. Not about you. They say the Irish can never get along with anyone."

"It was his idea to all gang up on Shapiro one night he brought his father's supper to the tailor shop," Willie blurted out almost without realizing what he was saying.

"You wasn't mixed up in that, I hope?" his grandfather asked.

"No, I came home when they did."

"Was young Pat and John?"

"No," Willie answered. "They weren't there."

"Good. I'm damn glad of that, anyhow."

Watching the boy as he spoke, Ned saw how troubled he was.

He wanted to end the talk as quickly as he could and, as always, hoped he could say what he meant without leaving a sting that would smart after he had finished.

"Come," he said, "tell me you'll find this Johnny-come-lately, whatever his name is, and shake hands with him. No harboring a grudge against him whatever he's done. You have a right to do that and if later on you don't want to be friends with him you have a right to do that, too, but not to be having hard feelings against him, anyhow. Come, tell me you'll do that."

"All right," Willie said reluctantly. "I'll do it—"

"That's the ticket," Ned said happily. "That's the way to talk. Go to him now and tell him you thought it all over by yourself and you thought the thing to do was, after all, to do what the priest told you to do the other night. It's only right and it's what I'd do myself if I had to do it. I'd go to the man I quarreled with and say I thought it all over and decided it was time to end the fighting and shake hands and get it over with once and for all. I'd say that to him and then—well, then if he hadn't the good sense to see the point of what I was trying to tell, d'you see, or if he tried any of the old tricks on me, if he snapped his fingers at me again or anything like that, why then I'd—I'd give him the licking of his dear life—I would so. If he tried any of the old tricks on me, I'd beat the daylights out of him so he'd never forget it. Then I'd put out my hand and shake hands with him whether he liked it or not and I'd feel better about the whole damn thing, anyhow. And the sooner you go and tell him that, the better for yourself and all concerned, especially Mc-what's-his-name."

Chapter Forty

NED was shining his shoes, as he did every Sunday morning, when Johnnie McDermott, too breathless to speak, ran into the house. The old man looked up at the boy and went on with his polishing, spitting on the toes of the shoes and skimming the brush over them. He told the boy to sit down and asked him if he were up before breakfast that morning and in such a rush.

"Pa's hurt," Johnnie said. "Ma wants you to come over to the house. He's spitting blood. He spit blood all night she says, and he's hurt."

"What in the name of God is this?" Ned cried. "What happened? What happened to him?"

Ned grabbed a shawl and scurried out while he was putting on his shoes. Johnnie sat down. Without bothering to lace his shoes Ned pulled his cap on and bolted out the door, the boy trailing after him. He raced up the little alley and into the kitchen where Mollie was sitting at the kitchen table, crying.

"Where is he?" Ned shouted. "Where's Pat?"

Mollie pointed to the bedroom. Ned clumped into the room and saw his son in the bed, pillows propped up behind him. Pat's face was blue and swollen, his lips were puffed out and one eye nearly closed. He smiled when his father came in and patted his mother's hand as she sat in front of him on the edge of the bed. His mother was crying.

"What?" Ned began.

"Now, take your time. Nothing serious," Pat said in a voice that sounded as though someone in another room were doing the talking.

"What the hell happened?" Ned yelled.

"Nothing serious," Pat said again. "Nothing serious."

"Oh, dear, I can't get a word out of him," Nell groaned.

"He wouldn't tell me anything, either," said Mollie, coming into the room.

"Has he had the doctor?" Ned asked.

"No," said Mollie. "He won't let me call the doctor."

251

"Go fetch the doctor," Ned ordered her. "Here, Patrick, go fetch the doctor. Now," he turned to his son as his grandson ran out of the house, "what the hell happened?"

Patrick came running back into the house and asked them if they wanted him to get Dr. O'Neill and did they want him to telephone. If they did, he said, someone better give him a nickel. Ned thrust a coin into the boy's hand and told him to go as quick as God would let him.

"Who hit you?" Ned demanded. "What son of a bitch hit you?"

"Take your time," Pat answered. "I'm tired. Take your time. I'll tell you all about it in a minute."

"If any son of a bitch," Ned muttered, "if I had the one that . . . who was it?"

"Leave the boy alone, Ned," Nell said. "Don't try to talk, Pat dear, rest yourself, now. Don't try to talk."

"Do you want some more water, Pat?" Mollie asked. "Can I get you some water?"

"Ummhmm," Pat mumbled.

She brought him a glass of fresh water and he took a mouthful to slush around his teeth and spit again into a hand basin which she held up under his chin while he was drinking. He smiled and pushed the glass toward her again.

"No more," he said.

"I'd like to know who did it," Ned grunted. "Where in the hell is that boy with the doctor?"

The doctor herded them out of the room when he arrived.

"Hmmm," he said, stripping the bedclothes down to examine Pat. "Hit by a streetcar?"

"You're a scream," Pat said. "My side hurts."

"Your face is a mess," the doctor said, pressing his fingers around the man's ribs. "Does that hurt you? It ought to, I think two of them are broken. How did it happen? I'll have to report this, you know."

"I fell," Pat said.

"Spit much blood?"

"All night," Pat said.

"I'm afraid of this," the doctor said. "We'd better get you to St. Joseph's."

"Like hell," Pat said.

"Were you kicked? What happened?"

"I fell," Pat repeated.

"Well, two ribs are gone," the doctor continued pressing Tom's sides and his back. "And I don't know what's wrong inside. You'll have to go to St. Joseph's."

"Not me," Pat asserted. "Tie up the ribs."

The doctor opened the door and they filed into the room—Ned, Mollie, Nell and Chris McDermott who had arrived in the meantime.

"This man will have to go to the hospital," the doctor said to Ned. "He has two broken ribs and I'm worried about that blood he's spitting."

"Yes," Ned said, looking at Pat.

"No hospital," Pat declared.

"You'll have to go if the doctor says so, Pat," Chris cut in.

But Pat wouldn't go and Ned at last had to order them to stop badgering the man. The doctor said he would do what he could and if the bleeding cleared up a little he might be all right; you couldn't tell. He said he'd feel a lot safer, though, if he could get him to a hospital and be sure he'd get the proper care. Mollie said she could take care of him as well as any nurse and Nell assured the doctor that she would be there, too, to do what she could for her boy. Chris McDermott said it was the damndest family he ever saw and that he'd come back after mass to see how Pat was feeling.

"Now," said Ned when the others had gone out of the room, "tell me."

"Nothing, nothing."

"I want to know, Pat," his father said. "And I will."

"A fight, then," Pat's voice was barely audible to the old man.

"With who? Where?"

"Whole crowd," Pat murmured.

"Drunk?"

"Christ, no. Meeting. I was at a meeting. Fight started. Everybody was fighting. I was in the middle, I guess."

Larry McDermott's warning rose in Ned's mind. Pat coughed and spat into a cloth Mollie had left for him.

"Was you with Trenn and them Socialists, Pat?" Ned asked.

"Yes," said Pat. "With Trenn and them Socialists. Trenn was speaking when the fight started. Don't bother me any more, I'm tired."

"Who started the fight?" Ned could not restrain himself.

"We don't know. Don't know."

"Did you?"

"Christ, no. I told you, Trenn was speaking. We were listening to him."

Nell came in with a glass of water and told Ned to stop talking to Pat and making him answer questions when he was so tired and hardly able to speak at all. Ned whisked her out of the room when Pat had rinsed his mouth with the water. Pat tried to turn on his side and groaned with pain.

"Ah, it hurts you," Ned stood up. "Who was it started the fight, Pat?"

"Don't know—some son of a bitch in the crowd."

"Why did he? Was there talk against the Church or what?"

"No, no. We did all right until the cops came . . ."

"The cops was there too?"

"Ummhmm."

"Many of them?"

"Ummm."

"Was Larry McDermott there?"

"Ummm."

"Was it Larry? Was it Larry hit you, Pat? Pat, was it Larry hit you?"

Pat had dropped away to sleep, breathing fretfully with his bruised mouth open and the saliva running pink down from the corners of his lips. Ned wiped it away with his handkerchief. He put his hand on Pat's burning forehead and Pat seemed to be trying to open his eyes again. Ned tiptoed out of the room and told Nell to sit in there with Pat for a while. He said he was going to mass and would come there as soon as it was over.

Pat was still sleeping when Ned came in again from mass. He wouldn't eat, but drank a cup of tea and went out into the yard to tramp around, smoking his pipe and tormented with the thought that Larry had been right about Pat hanging out with the Socialist Trenn in Olneyville. He had told them to call him as soon as Pat woke up again, and he hoped it would be soon because he wanted to ask him again how much Larry had to do with the fight the night before. He knew Larry was a vicious fighter, but breaking the ribs, that must have been done when Pat was on the ground; no, he couldn't believe Larry would kick a man when he was down.

254

Not Pat, anyway. However it was, Pat was his son and by God, whoever did, let him watch out.

It was late in the afternoon when Pat woke up at last. The discoloration had spread around his eyes and the slits that showed when he tried to open them were little ditches of blood. Mollie gave him water again to rinse his mouth and asked him if he could eat something, but he shook his head. She felt his forehead and bathed it with cold water. Pat smiled and nodded his thanks. Mollie started to comb his hair for him but he shook his head.

"Hurts me," he said.

To Ned his son looked terribly beaten and still no worse than he had seen Pete or Mick on many a morning after they would have been in a fight with someone; Pete had often looked worse, with even his head bandaged up. They would lie in bed for a day and be up and off the next, ready for a fight again and perhaps even looking for the man who gave them the licking the night before. Pat was as big and strong as either of them, surely. Just let him rest for a day and he'd be on his feet again. Ned would ask him more about Trenn and the Socialists and all about the fight when he was up out of bed.

Larry had been there, all right. Perhaps he would come over to the house and tell him about what had happened, though Ned wished that Pat himself would tell him all there was to know about it before Larry got there with his tale of woe. If Pat showed signs of feeling better later on he would ask him more about it. He noticed for the first time, as Mollie bent over Pat to clean off the trickle of blood that ran darker now on his son's chin, that her body, pinched as a hungry child's at the shoulders, seemed to sag heavily out over the bed. He hadn't known there was going to be another baby in Pat's family and, looking at Mollie critically, her reeds of arms, bony nervous hands and her eyes, bright but sunken, he wondered if she would ever be able to stand it.

He was going out in the yard again when Pat burst into a tempest of coughing, and he ran into the room to see Mollie trying to hold his son up and wipe the blood from his mouth at the same time. Pat's nose was bleeding now, too. Ned, helping Mollie, told her he thought they should have the doctor there again and Mollie said she would send one of the boys for him right away. Pat's cough subsided and he sank exhausted back on

255

the pillow again, his eyes closed. Nell came into the room and bathed her son's face again. Ned sat beside the bed for a while and then went into the kitchen where he asked Mollie what she knew about what had happened to her husband. Nothing, she told him; she didn't know a thing except that he came home late Saturday night all covered with blood and his clothing all dirty and torn. She said she thought she had heard Pat say good night to someone before he came in the house, but she wasn't sure about it because she had fallen asleep waiting for him. She said she always waited up for Pat when he was out at night and she often fell asleep in the chair before he got home.

It was very late when the doctor came the second time, and twice before he arrived Pat broke into horrible fits of coughing and spitting. There was nothing they could do for him and he did not speak or even appear to know any of them when his eyes opened. Dr. O'Neill said if they wanted a priest they had better send for one because there wasn't much more that he could do for him except to make him as comfortable as he could. Father Jim McCaffrey came back with Johnnie McDermott, but they could not rouse Pat for the priest to hear his confession. Father Jim anointed the injured man and sat with Ned in the kitchen afterwards, trying to reassure him that his son might pull through after all. Ned sadly told the priest that he was afraid his son had been beaten so badly he would never get up out of the bed again.

Father Jim stayed nearly the whole night with them, but Pat did not rally again and before the roosters in old man Reed's yard crowed Pat was dead.

Nora and Nell washed the body themselves. Ned, shaken by the suddenness with which it had all happened, dared not even think of what the blow would do to his schemes. The little hoard he was accumulating for Willie so painfully would have to go at one gasp, he knew that, but then what? Here were three mouths to feed and another would be along soon. He couldn't ask his son Chris just ready to marry, to take on the burden of Pat's family and he'd be damned if he'd let the boys go to work yet. They were too young for it, and much as he determined to do for Willie he couldn't do it and see the other boys starve now that they had no father to take care of them. Well, with God's help it would have to be done somehow, but how?

Nothing for it but to take the money that was being put away all these years for Willie's schooling. He couldn't even guess how much there might be, but enough, anyhow, to take care of the doctor and the funeral. He told Nell, while they were having a cup of tea, to fetch over whatever she had. She knew what he meant and she thought how very few dollars were tucked away under Anthony's robes now. In her panic she nearly told him what she had done with the savings, but caught herself in time. She dreaded what Ned might do if he learned what had happened, for Kate Reagan had never repaid her the loan she made to buy the material for the Murtaughs' dresses. One thing or another had always happened—sickness, troubles Kate had collecting her bills, even the bill from the Murtaughs, she said—so that not a penny of the loan was ever paid back and Nell had given up hope of ever getting her money. It wouldn't do to tell Ned, whatever else she had to do. He probably would never ask Mollie about it and he wouldn't see the bills when they came. Even if she could lie to Ned about it, and that she had never done as long as she knew him, there was still Mollie and the two boys and the baby coming along. Kate would have to—but it was a hopeless thought. Kate didn't have it and couldn't get it, Nell knew. What a fool she had been to let Kate con her along and get the money in the first place and what a fool Kate was, too, letting the Murtaughs do her out of the money they owed her. Nell could see the Murtaughs riding in their cars with her own dollar bills, three hundred of them, too, dripping from their dresses. She slipped across the lane home to wait until Willie had gone upstairs to bed and Chris had come home from Catherine Daly's house.

She put the bills before her on the table and counted them over. Hardly enough to buy Mollie her widow's weeds and the boys new clothes for the funeral of their own father. She brought that much over to Mollie, however, and made sure Ned saw her when she was giving it to her. She hurried back to the house again before Chris would be in his bed. But he stopped in at Pat's house after leaving Catherine Daly, and it was after three when he came into the kitchen. She told him, choking with sobs, what had happened to the money.

Chris McDermott was sodden with sorrow. Pat was so much older than he was that he had never known his brother really well. Pat had been married about the time their brother Will died of his burns. He, Chris, was a boy in the Brothers' school at the time, a sickly, lonesome boy who had four eyes, skinny and not very tall. The others, Will and Pat, neither of them giants, were solid, muscled men when they were seventeen, working hard and earning their ways. It had taken him so long, looking at the world from behind the thick glasses he wore, to reach where he was, ready to marry Catherine Daly and settle down with her for the rest of his days. Will had never helped him and neither had Pat. Will's son was brought into the house and robbed him of what love and help Ned might have given him along the way. He lacked the strength to say what he wanted to say—they could all, all of them, go to hell—his mother, his father, Pat, Pat's family, Willie. They could all go to hell and he would take what he had, and that was not too much, and marry Catherine Daly.

But there was more to think of than just that. He told his mother she would have the money—How much was it, three hundred?—at noon the next day. That was settled. And now, he asked her, what about Kate Reagan? She must pay them what she owed them. Had his mother a note or something like that? She hadn't. Bad. However, he'd see Kate himself and find out what could be done to get the three hundred back from her.

"Chris darling," Nell said, "Kate has no money and we'll never get it from her."

"But, Mother," he said, "we'll have to. What I give you tomorrow I'll be taking from what I've saved up to get married with. What would Catherine say if I told her now we would have to wait a while longer before we got married. I'll *have* to get it from Kate!"

"Yes, pet, you will," his mother said. "Kate will have to pay up now."

But she knew Kate couldn't, or wouldn't.

Chapter Forty-One

MOLLIE, in hissing black taffeta, stood alone in the carpeted hallway under the jonquil of gaslight, slowly moving her blistered eyes to look into the parlor at Pat lying so still on the satin froth of the pillow in the coffin, still not quite able to believe it was really Pat there, but only some violent dream of her own, perhaps, where the beautiful flowers banking the casket only blurred her terror and hopelessness, the unspeakable loneliness freezing her heart. How awful short the years had been, now that the joy in them was gone. Yes, she had her two boys and she loved them both dearly, but you can't cling to them in the night and you can't look across the pillow at them when the cold morning light crowds into the room with you and you will get up, leaving him still sleeping while you go into the dreary little kitchen to light the fire, wondering, and fearing, too, what troubles the day may bring. No, you can't rest at night, sitting on the floor before the warm fire with your head on his lap while Pat sits in the rocker reading and reading things you never understand, and you don't even face him but stare at the ceiling with its thin plaster peeling off in little coins. As he rocks slowly, a hand will reach from the little book he is reading and dance into your hair that has drifted down between his legs. The hand will swim easily there for a while and then he will bend down to kiss you and you will feel the warmth of his lips where the part is in your hair. Soon you will feel him move and hear the book drop on the table when he throws it there. He will help you get up and you will stand in his arms and kiss while the last glow of the stove spreads over you before you go to bed. No, there'll be no more of that, never again. It's gone with him.

Will the sight of him vanish, to, like those things, the sight of him coming home Saturday night, stumbling against the side of the house as he came up the alley, his face dirty and bruised, swollen and cut at his burning eyes, and one of the white teeth in front of his mouth twisted, smeared with red and sagging from the gum? When will that sight vanish, or the pained smile that died on his puffed lips when he covered them with a nervous, shaking hand? Oh, Pat, will she ever know who did that to you, that she can hate them and damn them with all that is left of her heart for as long as she lives, and will she ever know what made you go where you did and think the things you did, that made your eyes bright with passion she never shared. A sob strangled a laugh that burst timidly from within her when she thought of the things he had said to her that first winter they were married, before the baby was born and she was so afraid of what might happen to her. He was afraid, too, and she knew it, but he said: Why, Moll, when you die I'll wear a big black and white check suit to your funeral and a green silk ascot tie as big as a cabbage with silver—studded all over with silver horseshoes. I'll wear a batwing collar, Mollie, and lemon-yellow gloves and a gabardine reefer with white pearl buttons, a double-breasted one with pearl buttons as big as silver dollars. I'll walk along the Bois du Boulogne with an independent air that day, all right. Wouldn't you like to see me then with fawn spats and a cane? That's what I'll wear to the funeral and that's the day I'll break the bank at Monte Carlo. You can hear the people all declare, Oh, he must be a millionaire (he was singing to her) *for he's the man that broke the bank at Monte Carlo.*

Oh, Jesus, Mollie, nothing will happen, nothing in the world will happen to you, because if it did what would I do? Why what would I do if it did? No, something tells me I'll never get the chance to wear the check suit with the ascot tie and silver horsc-shoes or my lemon gloves or the gabardine reefer—there ought to be a light brown derby hat to go with all those things, don't you think so, Mollie—besides, wouldn't I look like a goddam fool? You don't want me waltzing around the streets of Providence looking like a damned fool, do you, Mollie? Oh, Jesus, sit in the rocker here with me—put your feet up on the hearth there and I'll sing a song about *two little girls in blue,* dear for you, or *wait till the clouds roll by, Nellie.* Do you like that one? There's lots of songs you don't know and you'll have to learn them pretty soon, because I can't do all the singing for this family.

He sang until she fell asleep and when she woke up he was asleep, too, and the fire had gone out. His hands had fallen down into her lap, his head had dropped on her shoulder.

With Pat you didn't worry, he would not let you, and if you had been worrying while he was away at work, he knew it the minute he stepped into the house. What could have been worse than that first winter? There wasn't any work and there wasn't any coal, but he would go out at night and come back with a sack of it on his back, never tell you where it came from or how he got it, but there it was to keep the house warm and he would put it in back of the stove for you without a word. If you were in bed he would do it without making the least noise; he never once woke your father up, but you would hear the coal crunch in the sack when he put it on the floor and you would hear him stepping softly into the next room to see how the old man was, if he were sleeping, if he needed anything and then you would hear him drawing a fresh glass of water to put beside your father's bed on the little table. He would never let you carry the rags or the cloths from your father's room to burn them in the stove. He would stand beside you talking to him while you combed out the curls that gathered in your father's beard and you watched the roses of death blooming scarlet above the chestnut hair of the beard.

Fear romped the house and trod on your heart when you were alone in it with the old man, but when Pat came home it fled. The days that were filled with fear and nights that were filled with hope. The old man was dying, as so many many of them died, with their lungs rotting away inside them, their eyes luminous with wonder, and bewildered that it was really happening to them, coughing, coughing, coughing and spitting until they were gone. There was hope with Pat, in spite of all the fears, because the baby was coming, but it was painful, too; because the old man wanted so much to live until it came. It seemed, when he did die, only a few days before the baby was born, that no one would ever die again, that dying had ended and babies would be born. Pat could make you think that. With the baby growing and Pat so tender, nothing else could be real, nothing else could be true.

It was the first Sunday he didn't go to mass; when he said he'd stay home and take care of the baby while you went to early mass and then, when you came home, he had the breakfast waiting for you on the table; he sat down to eat with you and when you told him he'd better hurry if he wanted to be on time, he said not to worry about it. He didn't leave the house that day at all, and when Ned came in later to say he was worried that he hadn't seen Pat at mass, Pat just laughed. You saw Ned's eyes drop; he looked as though he had been whipped and had fallen. All he said to his son, though, was that he would see him at mass the next Sunday. Then he sprawled down on the floor and began to play with the baby. At least, he said, when he was leaving the house, he could tell Pat's mother when she asked him if he had seen Pat, as she always did, that he *had* seen him and just stopped in for a while to see the baby before he went home to his dinner. He came every Sunday after that while they were living in the house on Christian Hill and it was always the same. The only time Pat ever went to church from then on was to his brother Will's funeral mass, the only time until tomorrow morning when they would carry him into St. Malachi's for his own.

Whatever happened to Pat then? Who were the men who came to the house to see him and sat long hours after you had gone to bed, talking and talking in the kitchen? The books and papers they gave him to read that you could never understand, the long nights he would spend away from you and the nights he wouldn't even come home to his supper, nights you would lie wondering and thinking and thinking until at last he *would* come home to you. Nights that were bleaker and longer than a whole winter. No, it wasn't worry, it was only you were hungry for that part of him the devils hiding in the pages of those damned books had stolen from you, and it was a fear in you that trembled to think where they would take him. The devils you did know, that Maggie Monaghan and that Bessie McGinn, they were never the devils that troubled her, it was those devils that slunk behind the covers of the books, devils she didn't know. Yet, when he was with her she didn't fear them either, there was so much of him, he was so full and he made her know she didn't share him with anyone or anything, that he was happier there with her than anyone ever was anywhere in the wide world.

Those devils were strong, though. Strong enough to pull him out of the arms of the Church and nearly out of her own arms too. What had they ever whispered to him? Tessie Butler pleaded with him the year he lost so many jobs, the year when if they ate a full meal they ate it at Ned McDermott's, when Ned would drop a five or at least a two into her bag when they were going home. Tessie pleaded with him to forget the false friends that took him out of his home and away from the Church and at least go this year and make his Easter duty. Pat, darlin', do it this once, only this once for Mollie and the dear boys. When Tessie went up to her room they sat by the stove in the kitchen and she put her head on his leg as she had done so often. While he stroked her cheek with his hand she asked him what it was, didn't he care for them anymore? Don't you care what happens to us, Pat, dear, don't you want us to be happy? What is it that takes you away from us? You're always with strangers, Pat. When they don't come to you, you're away with them somewhere. The books are as bad as the strangers, Pat. Strangers I never could like. I hate them, Pat, I hate them.

His fingers were pressing gently on her face and he bent over until his mouth was beside her ear. It's not that I don't care, Mollie, it's that I do care. It's never strangers, Mollie. Never strangers. I do want you to be happy. I wouldn't hurt you for all the world. Don't you know that? I wouldn't have anybody un-happy—there don't have to be. If there's trouble and misery and everything is rotten everywhere around us, I didn't put them there. If they don't like the things I say and they won't hire me, or if they hire me one day and fire me the next—oh, Jesus Christ! He sprang up, leaving her there sitting on the floor puzzled and hurt, the first time he had ever left her so. He was always so gentle, so patient. What the hell is the sense in my trying to tell you, Mollie, you'd never understand a goddam word of it anyway. You'd run crying to St. Malachi's—you'd run to my mother's . . .

Did I ever run to them crying, Pat? Did I ever run to your mother's or did I ever run to St. Malachi's crying? Oh, Pat (she sat where she was on the floor and she was crying, the tears dropping on her hands), why did you ever say that? I have no one to run to, Pat. What would I say to them if I ran to them crying? I'd never do that, Pat, no matter what it was, no matter what you said or what you did. This is where I want to be. It's to you I'd run crying. This is where I'll always be, as long as you want me, as long as I live.

When she looked up at him the anger had passed from his face and he was bending down to help her up. He kissed her as he had never kissed her before and they never spoke about things like that again. She never let Tessie speak to him again about going to mass and she even told his mother and his Aunt Nora never to ask him. Only when Father McCaffrey came to the house to ask her if the boys couldn't go on the altar, did she ever mention such things to him. Then he said if she wanted them to go on the altar and they wanted to, it was the same to him. They were her boys as much as they were his, he said, and if it would make her happy to have them on the altar, let them join.

When the third baby died, almost before it began to breathe, she thought she would never get well again herself. Before the year was done her teeth, that Pat always said he loved so much, began to bother her. She had never noticed it, but soon there were only broken shells of them in the front. Her hair began to gray and one morning, choking from the ashes when she was cleaning out the kitchen stove, she began to cough. She was terrified when she saw she had spit blood into the powdery white ashes in the hearth. But then she didn't care, for Pat was never nearer to her, never leaving the house at night, never leaving her side only to go to work. Weak, tired, hardly able to walk across the room, she was happier than she had been for so long. Then, she knew, there were no strangers with him, he was all hers once more. She reminded him about the lemon-colored gloves, the green ascot tie as big as a cabbage, and he laughed.

Now he was gone. When he came home Saturday night, bruised, cut, he let her put him to bed like a little baby, only groaning a little when he said the side of his head hurt him. There was a fight, he said. Yes, she knew there had been a fight, but Pat wasn't the kind of a man that went around fighting. There was a meeting, he said, and the cops broke it up; there was a fight. That was all she could get out of him. But she hated them, she wanted to know who they were.

She realized that while she had been standing there under the gaslight people had been going out and saying good night to her. That was why she had been standing there. The spring wind pushed the door open and she closed it. In the parlor there was only Pat's Aunt Nora, sitting near the coffin, nodding, with her rosary in her hand. Mollie brushed Pat's black hair with her hand and saw Nora look up at her as she went to the kitchen. His father sat in Pat's rocker by the stove, smoking his pipe. Mollie started into the bedroom, but the sight of the vast empty bed drove her out and she asked the old man if he would drink a cup of tea with her. Ned said he was parched for one. While she was pouring the tea she asked Ned if Pat, when he was younger, before they were married, she meant, if he ever wore a reefer with pearl buttons as big as silver dollars.

"Did he what?"

"Did he ever wear a green ascot tie," she asked, "or lemon-yellow gloves when he was young? Did he ever wear a black and white check suit before we were married?"

"Christ, no, Mollie, Pat never cared a damn for them things."

"Oh, what am I saying?" Mollie said, staring at the tea. "Of course he didn't. Pat would look like a damned fool in things like that, wouldn't he?"

Chapter Forty-Two

SOLEMNLY Pete Carron assured the widow of his deepest sympathy for her in her trouble and declared that if there were anything he could do for her or the boys she had only to call on him, anything in the world he could do for her. The distraught little widow thanked him, saying she didn't know what she was going to do with the two boys to take care of and another baby coming. She said as soon as she could she would go out and find work but no one would hire her the way she was. She said she thought as soon as the baby was born and she was able she would go back to the mill to see if she couldn't get work. Pete sympathized with her and again assured her that anything he could do for her and the boys he would be only too happy to do it. Ned, overhearing him, said it wouldn't be necessary for him to do anything for the widow or the boys; the only thing he could do for them was to remember them in his prayers, Ned said.

It was a great temptation, though, for Ned to tell Pete there was something he could do for them. It would have relieved him of a great care. But it was one of the gestures Pete Carron always made at wakes in the family and Ned knew that he had no intention of ever doing anything more than talk about it. How damn nice it *would* be, the old man thought, if he had a house or something that could be mortgaged and he could get some money from Pete Carron that way. But, be damned, he decided; if you had a house or what to mortgage there wouldn't be any need of mortgaging it to Pete Carron, then you wouldn't need Pete Carron.

"We never know, Ned," Pete declared, "when we'll need the helping hand. What little I have I'm only too happy to share with those in need, especially one of my own people, my own family. Who knows but one day I might even be coming to you, Ned."

"Ah, there's damn little chance of that," Ned said, regarding Pete carefully and thinking that it was the son of a bitch's way of reminding him of the difference between them.

"Who owns the house here, Ned?" Pete asked.

"God only knows," Ned answered. "When Tessie Butler died

here it was hers and I suppose she'd leave it to Mollie. But the whole thing's in the damnedest tangle you ever seen. Tessie left no will, you see, and if Mollie, there, was to claim the house as the next of kin the city would be on her neck for the taxes. . . ."

"But I mean who do they pay the rent to?" Pete asked.

"Be damned if I know," Ned said truthfully. "It might be since Tessie's death they paid none at all. Who the hell would they pay it to then?"

"I was asking you, Ned," said Pete.

"Well, they couldn't pay it to Tessie that owned the house and she dead, could they? And they couldn't pay it to anyone else either, could they? It seems to me they mustn't have paid any rent."

"It's a nice little piece of property, Ned," Pete said. "Too bad, now, Mollie couldn't have it for herself."

"Yes, it is. It is too bad, but that's the way things goes. Her that needs it for a home can't have it, and her that's dead don't need it and some son of a bitch that don't need it either will come along and snap it up for next to nothing."

"I should think you'd want to buy it up yourself, Ned," Pete was angling now for a little business.

"I thought of that, too, Pete," he said. "But where the hell would I get the money for it?"

"It couldn't be too much, Ned."

"That much," Ned said. "Even that is more than I have."

"It's a nice little piece of property," Pete said.

After his talk with Pete Carron Ned stayed at his own house for the rest of the time the wake was going on across the lane. He could not bear to look longer on the corpse of his son and couldn't listen any longer to the talk about what poor Mollie and her boys were going to do now that Pat was dead. The past few years, married and away from home, Pat and his troubles had not entered more than casually into Ned's life. His hopes and thoughts had been almost wholly for Willie, and Pat's boys had had very little from him. Years flew now on quicker wings than ever they had. Ned's conscience seared him for having neglected his son and young Pat and John. He had simply never thought, beyond the loan of a few dollars now and then which he never expected to be repaid, of having to provide anything for Pat's family. Now near the end of the race, and he knew he hadn't much farther to run, he would have to make up for it. Well, he had only his two

267

hands and they not what they were once. He must do what was right for Mollie, who had no one of her own family to help her. But he must not let go his schemes for Willie, never.

"Will," he asked "does it cost a great pile of money for the colleges and all now?"

"I don't know." Willie had never thought of what it might cost to achieve the things his grandfather had taught him must be accomplished.

"I mean, say," Ned speculated, "would you have some help, do you think, from the priest there that was so interested in you? Would he find a place where you could study that wouldn't cost you a pile of money? Do they—well, can you—ah—is there some way d'you suppose that you could study without it costing a pile of money? For there's very damn little of it, d'you see? Very damn little and damned if I know where there'll be much more of it.

"D'you see, if I was to borrow money now and anything should happen to me, why, then, you'd have it to pay back—every cent— or Chris would. That's if I borrowed of Pete Carron, though I'd never do that. But say I did, now, if I was to borrow from Pete Carron and anything'd happen to me, why there'd be the whole thing for you or Chris to pay him back and it'd be years before ever you could, see?

"I thought, maybe, the priest there might know of some way you could study, for that you must, I'm determined. Casey or any of them fellas I might get a few dollars from would have to be paid back the same as Pete Carron, and if anything was to happen to me, though I don't think it will—but look at poor Pat there, Lord have mercy on him—and who in the hell would ever think anything would happen to him, a young man like that?

"Tim Lee has little or nothing himself, only the rent from that rookery he owns down there on the waterfront and that's barely enough to keep him and Annie alive, he tells me, what with taxes and mortgages and that kind of thing. So I can't borrow from him, d'you see, though God knows if he had it he'd be the first to let me have it, that I'm sure of.

"Ah, we'll find a way somehow, I'm sure, but for the life of me I can't think of the way now that we'll do it. So, when you write them letters to the priest you might ask him, in that kind of a way that he wouldn't think you was a pauper begging from him or anything, if he knows some way we can do it."

Willie said that the next time he wrote Father Joe he would ask him what his grandfather wanted him to.

"Fine. Fine," said Ned. "The influence of a priest is a great thing you know to have on your side when you're in trouble—and God knows, Willie, we're in trouble enough now."

The death of his uncle had not touched Willie McDermott greatly until he saw how deeply affected by it his grandfather was. Pat was like many of the other people who came to his grandfather's house, neither great nor dear to him. Pat's dying, he knew, struck pain into his grandfather's heart, but the boy did not realize the many and sharp blows that were assailing the old man. He did not know what he would write to Father Joe, but he would do it.

Chapter Forty-Three

SINCE Pat's death, Ned's step on the stairs when he came home from the foundry had grown slower and slower, but when he came home in the middle of the afternoon a week before Easter Nell looked at Nora, wondering, when they heard him. Whoever it was would take a step and stop, take another and stop. Willie went out in the hallway, to see who it was and found his grandfather leaning against the wall, his breath sounding like bubbles breaking in a pot of soup boiling under a cover. He was standing near the top stair and the boy went down to help him the rest of the way, taking the dinner pail from his grandfather's hand. Ned was shaking his head as though he were in pain, but smiling weakly. In the kitchen he leaned with both hands on the edge of the table, heaving like a winded horse. Nell asked him what was wrong at the shop he was home so early in the day, hours before he usually came. The old man raised a hand to silence her.

"Sloan's," he asked. "Is there any Sloan's in the house? I couldn't stick it another minute—Skinny Byer's pouring the floor —is there any whisky?"

"There is," Nell said bumping Nora out of her way as she hustled into the bathroom for the bottle of liniment.

Nora glared at her and hurried into the pantry for the whisky bottle.

"What the hell is that smell?" Ned groaned, his eyes closing as he wrinkled up his mouth. "Smells like a wake—hasn't there been wake enough in this family for you?"

"A pot of flowers I bought of the peddler for Easter," Nell said handing him the bottle of liniment. "Get into your bed."

"Throw them out—I don't like the smell of a wake in the house."

He pushed Willie's hand away from his arm as he started to go to the bedroom. Nora had the kettle already jumping and hissing on the stove and she was pouring a measure of whisky into a water tumbler. Nell ladled sugar into the tumbler and filled the glass with the boiling water. She told Willie to help his grandfather off with his shoes. Ned drank the whisky with shivering hands while the boy unlaced the heavy shoes.

"Ah," he said when he had emptied the glass and was lying back in the bed in his long underdrawers. "Good—good—hand me the Sloan's."

They went out into the kitchen again, but they could hear him coughing and grunting to himself. Nell fussed with the stove and said she wished Chris were there so she'd know what to do for him.

"The doctor," Nora suggested. "He's the one will know what to do."

"He's taken cold, that's all it is," Nell tried to reassure herself.

Suddenly Ned, reeking of the liniment, the throat of his shirt open where he had been rubbing it on his chest, wheezed by them and went into the bathroom, slamming the door after himself. They stood looking at the closed door as though it would speak to them in a moment. Then they heard him scream out in agony and the door flew open. He staggered out, still screaming and doubled over, his hands cupped over his groin.

"Water!" he gasped.

"Oh, God!" Nell cried. "The Sloan's! He has the Sloan's on his parts!"

Nora ran a little pot of water full at the sink and flung it on him. He gasped. Nell ran into the bathroom and ran the water in the tub.

"Into the tub, Ned!" she cried. "Get into the tub!"

"Squat, Ned," Nora urged running after him with another pot of water that she threw on his backside as he was climbing into the tub with one hand still holding himself.

He sat shivering in the tub while the cold water poured over him and the tub filled. He waved them out of the bathroom, muttering that they were his own private parts and he could take care of them himself and for the love of God to leave a man alone, stop plaguing him when his parts is blazing and burning off of him! He splashed and pounded with his fists against the tin sides of the tub and when they could hear him getting out of it again Nell ran to get him clean dry underwear. His teeth were chattering with cold when he went to the bedroom again and moaning crawled into the bed.

Now, Nell decided, it had gone far enough, and she sent Willie to the store with a nickel to telephone to Dr. O'Neill to rush right over for his grandfather was taken sick, and tell him, she added, to rush over right away for the man was in great pain.

"It's Ned," Nora said when she went down to let the doctor in. "It's Ned has Sloan's on his parts, Doctor! He's suffering torments. This way, Doctor. Oh, he's burned to a cinder, Doctor, burned to a cinder!"

"We'll see," the doctor said cheerfully. "We'll see what we can do for him."

While he was in the room with his patient the dining room filled with people. Mollie came over with her two boys. She stood flushing her apron out in front of her over another McDermott she carried there, or maybe two, Nora said, maybe two, she was that big. Old man Read was there, cap in hand, looking very bewildered. Catherine Daly sat at the table, for the news had sped down the lane from house to house very quickly, and Mrs. Deignan, with a shawl on her shoulders, had come over, too. There was a rush for the kitchen when the doctor called from the bedroom for a glass of water and a teaspoon.

"The man has pneumonia," said Dr. O'Neill when he came out of the room and sat at the table to write his prescriptions. "He's a very sick man. That window in there is shut fast. Open it up and keep it open."

"Oh, God," Nell wept, "pneumonia!"

"—And drownding in flames of Sloan's," Nora added. "Oh, dear, oh dear!"

Well, there was nothing anyone could do, Nell said. When the doctor had gone the coughing stopped for a while, and the people started to go. She went into the bedroom where Ned was slowly opening his eyes to stare at the ceiling and closing them slowly again as he fell away into a doze.

All during Holy Week he lay burning with fever, sometimes reaching through a fog of weariness with fierce determination only to sink back again exhausted, with bitter tears of defeat rolling down his face. His voice was throttled down to a whisper and his words were like cinders falling away from a wreck, which hissed for a fragment of a moment before they sank forever beneath the waves. There was very little hope now, the doctor said, that he would rally again because he was too old and too far gone. If they wanted the priest, he said they had better be prepared and send for one before it was too late. He said eggnog would be about the best thing the patient could drink and Ned insisted Willie make them for him with a stick of whisky to strengthen them.

Tim Lee, who heard from the moulders that Ned had gone home sick, called to see him Holy Thursday. He sat with his derby on and collar of his coat up around his neck until Ned motioned to him to shut the window down. He sank his wasting hand into the lapels of Tim's coat and drew his friend closer to him.

"I'll pound no more sand, Tim," he whispered slowly, the hand still clutching Tim's coat. "The last flask is poured for me, Tim, and too soon. Too soon for what I have to do—"

"Ah, sshh," Tim stuttered, "you'll be up and out of this in no time. Sure I seen us both worse off many a time than you are now. You'll be up in no time, Ned."

"Don't con me, Tim, I know. It's the last end, Tim, and it's here too soon for what I wanted to do and there's no one will do it for me. The boy is only after starting along the road to where he'll go and I wanted to be along with him. I did so. There was so many things I could have told him over the years and I too ignorant to tell him the half of what I wanted to. I don't want to leave him now. Ah, it's too soon, Tim, I tell you, for all I have their promises they'll help him. Promises—promises is piss in the pot. I won't be here to see they're kept, will I? No. They'll promise me anything now to shut me up. When I'm gone—"

"Hush, man dear, don't talk like that!"

"No matter, Tim," the words sifting slower across his cracked, parched lips. "We got the best of them after all for we made a scholar of him in spite of them. Yes, we did that. A scholar. There's no one now can rob him of what he knows; there's no one can steal it from him now, by God! And hungry and thirsty for more of it, too. It was me and him did it. Him a chit of a boy and me an ignorant old man. With God's help we did it alone by ourselves. Made a scholar of him that can match wits with the best of them and never will have to pound sand for some Yankee son of a bitch nor cast his goddam iron. No, Tim, you'll never see that lad sitting his arse on a stool somewhere writing figures down in a book for a thief like Deignan. No, you'll never see him with a pick nor a shovel in his hand. No! Not him."

He let Tim's coat go and settled back against the pillow with his chin resting on his heaving chest. His eyes opened wide and he swung his arm toward his friend.

273

"No! Was it the priest made a scholar of him with a talk here and talk there? Flying away on the poor boy like the geese in the fall? Leaving him alone for the whole winter through? No, it was not the priest did it! It was not the priest, God forgive me, sat night after night with him and him reading and reading from whatever we could lay our hands on. It's that did it, Tim, and it was me did that. Me, Tim and not the priest, nor the teachers, Chris, nor Catherine, nor a goddam one but me. 'Twas me when the teachers robbed him of the medal made him keep at it, and he did. It was not the nuns that first taught him his letters and it was never out of my mind a minute. And how did I teach him to read not knowing a word of it myself, Tim? How did I teach him to read what Emmett wrote then, and never know myself? But I did that and how I'll not tell you. No, I'll not tell you how, but I did it. I swore I'd do it and I did."

He lurched up from the pillow, knifing his glittering eyes into Tim's and seizing his coat again.

"Rest yourself, Ned," Tim said. "Ah, rest, Ned."

"Soon enough and a long time, Tim. God help me the job is only half done, only started. It's only the pattern is put into the flask and the sand pounded around it, the iron's not poured into it. The wind's on the cupola and the first heat's ready. I can hear it roaring in my ears. I can see that iron streaming out. Ah, Tim, it'll run clear as a fountain sometimes but when you pour the mold there'll be a tit of slag was in it and when the casting comes out there's a rattail to mar it. If I was here I'd see the slag if it tried to creep in, d'you see, and I'd have it out before the harm was done, so there wouldn't be a mark or a blemish on it. I'd have it as bright as the blood in the veins of a saint. I'd have a casting the like of it you never seen!

"Time's all's needed now. Oh, if it was the will of God to spare me a pinch more of it! Wouldn't you think, Tim, with all He has of it, with all eternity and a day after that if He wants it, wouldn't you think there'd be a pinch more of it to spare for me? When I need it? Ah, He said, you have your time and you have your days and you know best what you'll do with them. Only He didn't warn me, Tim, how fast they fly away."

"You done what you could, Ned. No man can do more than that. No man."

"I'm—I'm standing, Tim, with the empty ladle in my hands, the job only half done."

274

His hand dropped to the covers as he let himself fall away to the pillow. Tim covered the hand with his own.

"Half done," he repeated tiredly. "Still and all I know he will do the rest of it, hard as it will be to do it alone. Oh, it'll be hard for him now, Tim, for there's stacks and stacks of more books to read and a whole lashing of things must be done. How I know he'll do them is beyond me, but he will. He's bound and determined, to. Once I thought, well, I have this one and that to count on if anything should happen I wouldn't be able to do the whole thing. I thought of Pete Carron and Torpedo and I thought of others. But now the time is come for it and I don't want them if I could have them to lend a hand. I want no one to share it but me and him, no one at all. If I won't be here myself to do it with him, I don't want them to have a hand in it. The ways of God is strange and the more ignorant a man is the more strange they are to him. You'd think he might have dropped a lad like that into me lap sooner. But you have your time, He said, and he has his, so and so many for this one and so many for the other one, and you'll have to do the best you can with them.

"God's will be done. But still, a pinch more time would never be missed by Him, Tim, with all He has on His hands and a few minutes more or less out of eternity would, only a few minutes more of it here below is all I'd ask, would—"

"Don't wear yourself out, Ned. Lie back there and rest yourself. Lie quiet and save your strength for you need it."

"Is it growing dark in here, Tim? Will, Will," he called hoarsely. "Will, fetch us in a light."

Willie lit the gas jet above Tim's head and Nell, standing at the doorway in its brassy glare, asked Ned if he would have anything to eat. She said he seemed better that afternoon than he had since he was took sick and that the priest was coming to see him in the morning.

Friday he was weaker, sleeping a little, waking up to mumble a few words no one could understand, and collapsing again in sleep. Dr. O'Neill was in the room with him when Father O'Farrell arrived and was saying his prayers in the kitchen, and the doctor was amazed that Ned rallied to ask who the hell it was mumbling in the kitchen. When they told him it was the priest, he asked why the hell they had sent a foreigner to a man dying and hadn't he been long enough in the cathedral parish to have an Irish priest sent to him when he was not able to go himself?

"Pay no attention to what he says, Father," said Nora. "His mind's wandering the whole night long and he don't know what he's saying."

Ned rolled incoherently on when the priest came into the room, recognizing no one. His voice gasped like a sandy bellows with a rip in it, sucking wind it couldn't hold, and his hungry hands clawed ceaselessly at the covers of the bed, pulling little pinches of the cloth and letting it go again as gently as he used to pluck and stroke the leaves of Peg's ears, Willie thought, straining to catch a word of what he might be saying. He might have been in the foundry, he might have been at a cockfight or sailing down the river on the wrong boat, he might have been anywhere except where he was, an old man dying in his bed.

Father O'Farrell gave him the last rites of Extreme Unction. The long day grew dark and during the night they sat, one after the other, watching at his bedside. Only Nora, after stacking a plateful of hot-cross buns and putting them on the table, went to bed. Nell sat most of the night with him, leaving a couple times to snatch a few minutes' rest on the couch when Chris insisted on it. While she was in there with him Willie and Chris sat at the table in the kitchen, not speaking to each other because there was nothing to be said, and if there had been neither one of them could have said it to the other. Willie could hear his grandfather's labored breathing, the steady little whining of his grandmother's rocker and now and then a troubled little snore from Nora's room.

A sunless silver day spread itself over the windows, and his uncle asked him if he would sit a while with his grandfather while his grandmother rested again. Willie saw the pale light grow stronger as he sat and when the sun at last had risen he saw his grandfather's eyes open and turn to him. He asked, stifling his tears, if his grandfather would have his eggnog now and the old man, after vainly trying to find a voice to answer, winked his eye to him, yes, he would.

Willie went downstairs into the sweet spring morning for the fresh milk and mixed the drink in the kitchen. Chris said he didn't know how wise it would be to give his father a drink; he was pretty far gone, he said. Willie looked scornfully and defiantly at him.

"He wants it," he said, grinding the egg beater.

His grandfather's eyes were still opened when he brought the drink into the bedroom and Willie, pointing to the whisky bottle standing among the medicines on the commode, asked him if he wanted a stick in it. The eye winked again, yes, he would. Ned was too weak to raise himself from the pillow or even lift his hand to take the glass and Willie put his free arm under his grandfather's shoulders to lift him, holding the glass to his lips. Ned barely sipped at it and let his head fall back on the boy's arm. Willie put the glass on the commode and lowered his grandfather gently down onto the pillow, wiping a little froth from the fragrant drink away from his mustache. Ned's eyes closed.

Nora was stirring in the kitchen, prodding the fire, making tea and cooking a pot of oatmeal. Nell would have only a cup of tea, but scalding hot, she said. Chris McDermott ate sparingly at the oatmeal and said he thought he would shave to freshen himself up a little because he was worn out. He went into the bathroom and Willie sat at the table.

It seemed hours later, or it might have been a moment, that he heard the words of a litany from his grandfather's room and went in again. His uncle stood with his head bowed at the foot of the bed. Nora sat in the rocker and his grandmother on the bed facing his grandfather.

"Lord have mercy on us," Nell prayed.

"Christ have mercy on us," Nora intoned. ("He's having a hard time of it, ain't he?")

"Christ hear us," said Nell.

"Christ graciously hear us," Nora said.

"God, the Father of heaven have mercy on us."

"God, the Son, Redeemer of the world, have mercy on us."

Ned was pouring the biggest mould he ever cast, a windlass, it seemed, towering above him, its cope like the cover of the biggest book in the world, so heavy he could hardly close it over the flask. The ship wasn't built that would carry a windlass that size. He was ready to take the first iron in a ladle no one but him could lift. O, merciful Jesus, he wouldn't have time to lift it! He was calling Willie, Willie, his own Will, Nell, Chris, he was calling Skinny Byer, Tim Lee, Pat, Joe, John, Pete, all of you, Torpedo John, Owen Tegue, Larry, Patrick, where are you all? He was calling them to help him as the bright stream of fire gushed from the cupola, burning and blinding.

"From sudden and unprovided death."

"Lamb of God who takes away the sins of the world."

"Spare us, Oh Lord."

"He's gone! Oh, he's gone!" Nell cried, falling over him.

"Yes, he's gone. Lord have mercy on him," said Nora. She rose from the rocker as Chris McDermott lifted his mother from the bed and Willie ran out of the room. She saw the eggnog on the commode where Willie had put it and carried it with her to the kitchen. She was about to pour it down the pantry sink when her hand stopped.

"Why waste it?" she muttered, drinking it.

Chapter Forty-Four

NED'S brother Joe, who had the farthest to come for the funeral, arrived from Brooklyn early Easter Sunday night. He dropped his tears and an "Our Father" kneeling at the coffin, blessed himself and started for the kitchen where he knew he would find the other brothers whom he had not seen in many years. Willie recognized him among the many men he had never seen before by the hurried step of the legs, not bowed, but bent out a little like his grandfather's as though he were always carrying something heavy, the same cairn rising on his back and his proud face when Joe turned to him to ask which door went to the kitchen.

Mick, up from the soldiers' home in Bristol for the first time in a long while, sat in Ned's rocker at the kitchen window with his pipe in his mouth, a heavy blackthorn, his best leg, held between his knees and a little mustard jar half filled with whisky on the table in front of him. Ned's brothers—Pat, Pete and Joe, and Mick with their friends and Ned's, Tim Lee, Owen Tegue, Torpedo Casey sat on the big kitchen chairs. Nell's family, whom none of the McDermotts ever liked very much, squatted on the uncomfortable campstools the undertaker had brought or, snatching a hasty drink from the bottle on the table, hurried into the other room again to sit for a while with their wives and daughters. When one of them would come in Pete would wink at Pat or Mick would wink at Pete and they would all grunt a contemptuous, half-tolerant grunt and go on talking about their own family. Lonely Mick, whose Dolly Varden of a wife skipped away on him years before while he was away as a teamster with the circus, listened to them telling that this one was getting married soon, or that one had a baby, a christening, and he wished now that in his old age he had a son or a daughter to turn to instead of dreaming away his days in Bristol. All he could say to them then was that he had stopped drinking entirely, except on such occasions as this, and he thought to himself when he was saying it that he had surely put away a penny or two these last few years and thank

God none of them knew he had, and it right there in the little chamois bag that hung with scapulars on his chest.

Joe dragged one of the stools over near Mick. Looking from one brother to another, it seemed to him that they were no closer to him now than some stranger he might have passed on the road when he was a young man. He said it must have been very sudden, Ned passing away like that. They hadn't even known in Brooklyn that he was sick until they got the telegram saying he was dead, and that the funeral was to be Monday. What was wrong with him, he asked.

"Worked himself to death," Mick said scornfully.

"You'll never die of that, will you, Mick?" said Pat bitterly.

"He's too mean to die the way a good Catholic should," Pete declared. "They'll have to take an ax to him at last, or shoot him when he gets so he can't walk no more."

"How are you feeling yourself, Mick?" Joe had always liked Mick and his wild ways better than any of the others except Ned.

"Younger and heartier than any one of you," Mick answered, belligerently downing the drink.

"Ned was long past seventy," Tim Lee said.

Torpedo, shaking his head and stroking the anchor on his cap, recalled the last time he had seen Ned in the old house, how they had talked in the kitchen, Ned so damn set on making a scholar of the grandson. This was the first time he had ever been to this house to see Ned, and the last, he said sadly.

"Do you remember the little house they lived in when they were first married up on Federal Hill there?" Joe asked. "I was serving my time in the foundry and boarding with them. None of the children was born then. Do you remember the time of the riot? When the Guineas were going to drive the Irish off the hill, or the Irish drive the Guineas. Which was it, Pete? That was a hell of a fight. With sticks, stones, anything they could lay their hands to. . . ."

"I remember it well," Mick said. "I was in Ned's house that day and he come running in and grabbed the big kitchen knife and my sister Mary, Lord have mercy on her, tried to take it from him and. . . ."

"It was Pete grabbed the knife," Joe interrupted.

"I never cut a man with a knife in my life," Pete declared.

"Ned had the knife," Mick continued. . . .

"Joe is right," Pat said.

"Whoever it was," said Joe, "Ned or Pete, pulled the knife and Mary hung on to it and it damn near sliced the hand off her."

"That's right," Pat said, "but it was Pete, not Ned. I remember that day well, for I had a burn where the iron splashed on me in the shop and I was on crutches. Ned and me was backed up against a tree on the hill there where the park is now and me lashing out with the crutch every time a Guinea run past. Ned had no knife, I know; he had my other crutch. It broke his heart, though, when old Bid Mulalley, she was half blind anyhow, shoved her fist up under Ned's nose and says, 'God damn yez, we'll drive every last one of you dirty Guineas off this hill yet.' "

"Ah, yes it would," Tim Lee sighed. "He was a proud man always and it would break his heart to be called a dirty anything by old Bid."

"Yes, he was. Proud and fearless," Pat continued. "When we were younger we had the floors next to each other in the foundry and one day, to stir him up, I says it was going all around the shop that he was afraid of Neil Thomas, that was the foreman. 'Am I,' he says, 'wait'll you see.' Neil was walking down the gangway minding his own business and Ned, working way in the back of the sand heap, calls him over to the floor. Neil come up on the floor, walking the length of the sand heap, and stood beside him. 'Now,' Ned says holding the rammer in his hand, 'get off this floor, you son of a bitch, and never set foot on it again until you're asked to.' In them days a moulder's floor was his own, of course, and the foreman had no right on it. Neil was dumbfounded, but there was Ned with the brass rammer in his hand standing there, so off the floor he got without saying a word. Or the time we were coming from the foundry one night and standing at the trolley switch there by the big elm tree just up from Finley's. It was the time right after the car strike in Pawtucket, and I told him the motorman coming into the switch on the Melrose Avenue car was one of the scabs from the Pawtucket strike. Ned let fly with the dinner pail, thank God it was empty, and it crashed through the front window of the car and the glass spread all over. The motorman kicked the pail out and come running up to Ned, but there was quite a crowd of moulders there and he said nothing. Sure the man never seen Pawtucket in his life."

"It's a great wonder you lived as long as you have, making as much trouble for others as you have all your life, Pat, with your dirty tongue," Mick said.

Pete Carron, waving his derby to this one and that one, came into the kitchen and went directly to the table where he carefully examined a glass and poured himself a generous drink. Not a single one of them would honor him enough to call him Mr. Carron and none of them felt enough at ease with him to call him Pete. He recognized Joe, whom he had not seen in many years.

"Well, it's Joe, isn't it?" he said. "Well, how'dyou do, Joe, and how is the family, God bless them. And how are things in Boston these days? Well, well, it's a long time since I've seen you!"

"Fine," Joe answered in a surly voice. "We live in Brooklyn."

"Ah, yes, Brooklyn. Why, bless me, yes, Nell was telling me that only a while ago. And the family is well? Ah, my good friend Bishop Mundeen is in the Brooklyn diocese. Yes, I'm well acquainted in Brooklyn. The Haggertys there, I suppose you've heard of them? John A. and the others, Waterford people. Left-handers, I'm afraid, but great Irishmen, great Irishmen. You've heard of the bishop, of course?"

"I never seen the man in my life," Joe answered, just as surly as before. "We live in St. Augustine's parish."

"Oh, yes, St. Augustine's," Pete murmured going into the other room to pay his respects to the widow.

"Is that Pete Carron?" asked Joe when he had gone.

"Yes," said Pat, "that's Pete Carron, the son of a bitch."

"We're the well-connected family, ain't we?" Pete sneered, "bankers and policemen, nuns by the score. . . ."

"What's this about the police?" Larry asked pleasantly as he came into the kitchen, followed by Willie McDermott.

"Is that the grandson?" Casey asked Tim Lee, as he bowed to Larry.

"Yes," Pete said, "Ned had great schemes for that boy."

"I know he did," Casey nodded. "He's Will's son, ain't he? Who did he marry?"

"Who, him?"

"No, no," said Casey impatiently. "His father—who was his mother, I mean?"

"Oh, she was Kitty McDonough," Tim said. "John McDonough's youngest daughter. Did you ever know John?"

"No, who was he?"

"Great singer, John was," Tim recalled. "He was a machinist, you know. Oh, John could read a blueprint or anything about a machine or the like of that and make it with his own hands. Damn few in his day could do it, Casey."

"Damn few can today," Torpedo said laughing.

"That's what I'm telling you," Tim said. "John was in the war, too, when he first come out here. He was a fine-looking man, as big as Pete here, but not so thick, a quiet, sober man. Wore a beard all his life and you'd hardly hear him raise his voice behind it, except when he was singing in St. John's parish on the hill. They would come there to last mass from all over the city to hear him sing. Many a time he was asked to go and sing at the cathedral. There was no one could sing the Tenebrae like he could, but he never would go. Only in his own parish there would he sing."

"What do you think of that?" Casey was impressed. "He was in the war, too? Mick would know him, then. Mick won the goddamn war.—Did you know John MacDonough, Mick? I say did you ever know John McDonough?"

"No," Mick growled. "Who in hell is he?"

The music of that Tenebrae and the voice of John McDonough singing it had vanished from him like his own father and mother before he had ever heard them, Willie thought. If he had known them, perhaps, the loss of his grandfather would not be so hard to bear, or, he didn't know, it might have been.

"Hello, Will," Tim said. "Too late now for any of Ned's schemes," he said turning to Casey again.

"Big enough, ain't he?" said Casey.

"Yes."

"Be a damn good time for him to get into the Navy."

"Ned was bound to make a scholar of him," Tim objected.

"What the hell use is a scholar these days?"

"That's what Ned wanted."

"Strapping lad. Will you have a nice drink, Tim?"

"I will." Tim knew if he waited for the McDermotts to pour it for him he would be thirsty all night long.

"Why didn't Ned bring the lad into the foundry with him?"

"Often said he didn't want him pounding sand all his days as he had done." Tim drank. "Said the boy was as smart and bright as any Yankee ever come down the pike, didn't want him in the foundry."

"Ned leave anything so's the lad can go to school?"

283

"Not's I know of," Tim said. "If there's enough to bury him, it's a lot. He hadn't a penny, you know, giving every cent he could spare to his Pat's widow and all."

"Hadn't he anyone he could turn to then to help him out?"

"God, Torpedo, if I had anything myself, I'd be only too glad to help the boy. But what the hell have I? Sure I haven't done a tap of work in years. All I have is the house the Bravas live in and there's damn little left out of what I get from the rents of that when the mortgage and the taxes and water bills and the like is paid. Besides there's a doctor bill for Annie staring me in the face every month. She has cancer, you know."

"Ah, too bad," Casey said. "Too bad there's not some way the boy could get what his grandfather wanted for him."

Tim said it was, indeed.

Larry sat beside Joe and asked him how things were in Brooklyn and if they had picked up any since the war started. Joe said they had more than enough work now, though wages were no better than they had ever been. Larry asked him if he ever run into that young anarchist of a moulder in his travels around the country, the one that blew up the parade in San Francisco. They ought to hang him, he said.

"I run into him, Larry," Paddy Murray, a moulder from the Clydeside, said. "Right here in Providence and a damn good man he was, too. I don't believe he done it."

"In Providence?" Larry didn't believe it.

"Aye, in Providence," Paddy said definitely. "Spoke to the union meeting when there was a strike in Whitinsville, or Taunton, I don't remember which now."

"There was strikes in both them towns a few years back," Pat told them.

Larry said the quicker the union cut loose from a thug of that kind the better off it would be. Paddy insisted the man was innocent.

"Ned was a great man for the union," Pat said. "I remember going with him to Boston one time the moulders' convention was on there."

"There was a fight on the floor of the convention about the moulding machines that was just coming in at the time. It was nothing to Ned, d'you see, for the machines was only used by the bench moulders anyhow, or meant to be used by them. It was the bench moulders started the fight. They would have nothing to do with the new moulding machines, though they could turn out double the work if they used them, it seems; they was afraid if they did the company would cut down the rate for the piece work. The companies was bound and determined the machines was going in.

"In them days, you know, there wasn't‚ a Guinea in the foundry. I beg your pardon, Johnnie," he said turning to Johnnie Nitti who had been sitting unnoticed in a corner.

" 'At's all right, Pat," Johnnie said pleasantly, "I call you Micks, too, just the same."

"Well, they was Eyetalians in the shop, of course," Pat said, "but not moulders. They were laborers cutting over the sand heaps and working in the yard and on the cupola, and the like of that, but not moulders, you see."

"You see?" Mick echoed, glaring at Johnnie Nitti.

"So what does the company do but take the Gui—the Eyetalians off the cupola and out of the yard and put them to work on the moulding machines on the bench work. Well, once they was moulding, and mind you they was still getting the laborer's pay, they up and try to join the union. I guess Johnnie there might have been one of them for all I know.

"Paddy Coughlin was the head of the local then and Paddy says no. Now he never liked the bench moulders themselves a hell of a lot, anyhow—the baker boys or the mud-pie boys was what Paddy always called the bench moulders. Nor he didn't like the Guineas —I beg your pardon, Johnnie. Nor he didn't like the machines coming into the shop. The local, Paddy says at the next meeting, will hold the whole matter in obedience until the proper time. . . ."

"Abeyance," Larry corrected him.

"Obedience was what Paddy said," Pat insisted, "And obedience was what he got on all sides for that matter. Well, that was the whole thing, d'you see, and now here was the bench moulders making a hell of a fight against the Guineas and against the machines coming into the union and the foundry and there was the Guineas outside the door clamoring to be let in."

"What in hell, has all this to do with Ned," Mick asked.

"Pour a drink into that one, will you, Joe?" Pat asked. "In Boston there the fight was on and getting nowhere, with all sides bedeviling all other sides, except the Guineas outside the door and no one to raise a voice for them at all. The more they argued the worse it got. Finally, Ned got the floor. I was surprised myself he wanted to talk for he was always one to mind his own business and not go poking his nose into other people's, but up he got, anyhow.

"Now, he says, we're licked before we start at all if we think we can keep the machines out of the foundry. We might raise hell enough to keep them out this year and the next, but sooner or later they'll be in. When the company makes up its mind to that, it'll bring them in. And why in the hell shouldn't they come in if they will make a day's work easier? I only wish to God they had come in forty years ago and my back might be straighter than it is today.

"Where I live, he said, there's a hell of a big hill—it's so damn high and steep a man has to get down on his hands and knees and crawl to walk up it. On the top of it is the college and sometimes I think it was put there for no other reason than to keep too many from walking up to it. Anyhow, they have trolleys running up the hill. Well, they go up the hill and don't run at all for they're dragged up it by horses. The trolleys run with the electric every-where else in the town but up the hill they're pulled by the horses. Once upon a time they was all pulled by the horses and someday they'll be pulled over that hill by the electric just as they are everywhere else. Now when that day comes, and you can be damn sure it'll come, I don't think them horses is going to get together and say—Look here, now, that's our work and you shan't take it from us. We want to break our backs and bust the eyes out of our heads pulling them cars over the hill and you must keep the electric the hell out of it. No, they won't! And what goddam fools they'd be if they did! There's too damn much good sense in a horse for that. Well and good, them horses will say, pull the damn things over the hill with the electric if you can, we'll be damn glad to let you.

"Indeed,' says Ned, 'I think if there's some slick Yankee was smart enough to sit down and scheme out a way for you to spare your backs and let a machine do the heft of the work for you, it's not you should be up on your hind legs roaring to keep it out of the foundry. Some will say if the machines comes in the prices of the piece work will be cut and no doubt they'll try that, too. And I say let them try it for that's why we're joined and banded together here in a union for—to stop such things as that, but not to stop the coming in of anything that'll make our work easier and our days longer.

"And what is this about keeping the Eyetalians out of the union? What's that for, I'd like to know. If you're as thick as you sound, go ahead and keep them out. Try to keep them out of the union and the machines out of the foundry and the first thing you know they'll both be in and you'll be outside there knocking on the door and no one to listen to you. That's what it will come to and no worse nor better than you deserve for your thick-headedness.

"What the hell, he says, is the Iron Moulders Union? What the hell right has it or you to bar any man out of it that works in the shop? Is it because he's an Eyetalian you won't let him in? Well, now! You won't let them in the union! Well, I never heard of one of them barred out of the Church yet, did you, because he was an Eyetalian? No, I didn't! For it's an Eyetalian Pope runs the whole show! And where in the hell would you be, then, if the Eyetalian Pope, God bless him, took it into his head one fine day to bar you out of *his* union? Well!

"Well, then, Ned went on whilst you could hear a pin drop, you better think it over again, then, before you bar them out. You better think it over before you do. You better think twice about it and whilst you're at it you better open them goddam doors in the back of the hall there and let them in.

"Well, Lord have mercy on him, they cheered and cheered him! They threatened to pull the roof down," Pat was crying a little now as he spoke. "He sat down and leaned over to me and says, Pat, he says, why the hell didn't you stop me? I never talked so damn much in my life. Then they voted, of course, and they voted the machines in and the Eyetalians in and that was all there was to that. But Ned says to me while they're wrangling over the next thing that come up whatever it was, Why the hell didn't you stop me, Pat, before I talked so damn much? But, he says, I licked them sons of bitches, didn't I? I carried the point that time all right and the hell with them!"

Willie wished he might have been with his grandfather that time and so many other times these old men knew about that they had spent with Ned. He did remember Boston, remembered the car of the train and the whisky bottle cutting through the smoke, all the moulders, the greatest men in the world, and his grandfather happy and laughing all the way there, his grandfather guiding him across the great cobbled plain in front of the station that seemed wider than the world had ever been before and his grandfather saying it was Irish, all Irish from Mansfield, Norwood right in to Boston and out again to Cambridge, every stick and stone of it. The moulders were all wearing silver badges on their coats with green silk ribbons under them and his grandfather got one for him. They rode far out on a train one afternoon and when he looked below him as the car sped along there was a delirium of cities and people, of carts and noise and rivers roaring. He sat for a long time with a wrinkled old woman drinking tea that had condensed milk in it to sweeten it and eating floury currant bread that pasted itself to his mouth and made him thirstier. Later they saw jugglers, dancers, singers, acrobats and a moving picture afterwards where kilted Highlanders marched behind the pipers while the orchestra played "The Campbells are Coming" and the British tied the Sepoys to the mouths of the cannon to punish them for revolting.

Mick had taken a whisky every time anyone else took one.

"Ah," he said, "you make me sick. You make me sick with your stories and your blubbering and your goddam tears. And what will you do now? You'll wipe the tears away, you sons of bitches, with a Hail Mary or two, and you'll go home to your wife or your young ones and you'll slobber over them, you will, or you'll give them a cuff on the side of the head and they'll tuck you into your beds as nice as you damn please. That's what you'll do! But what in the hell will Torpedo there, what'll he do after tossing around and slatted from hell to breakfast on some goddam ship? What'll he do with a furlough now and no Ned to come and see and talk to? Why, the poor son of a bitch he'll be as lonely as the end of a bit of a rope that's worn out and cut off a line. You know that, Owen Tegue! You might think of that when you're tucked in your nice warm beds there. And what the hell will I do now? Yes. What the hell will I do? Sit the rest of my days among them dried-up relics there in Bristol while they load me up with lies about what they done in the war and I load them up with lies about what I done? What am I to do when I have a day off now and no Ned to come and see? Ha! Will I hobble on my sticks over to Pete's, do you think, that ain't half the man Ned was, as big as he is? And will I sit and listen to him lie about this one he licked and that one he pulverized? Will I?

With the young ones walking around in back of him laughing at us both? Or will I go to Pat's then, and stare at that scarecrow of a wife of his whilst he'll be weeping and wailing about the dear days that's gone? Yes, you'll miss Ned! *I'll* miss Ned! *I'll* miss him, you sons of bitches!"

Chris McDermott had come into the kitchen and heard the last of what Mick said.

"Uncle Mick," he said, a sharp sigh cutting into his words, "you know you always will be welcomed here."

"Ah, *shit!*" Mick said. Who'll I talk to *now—*you?"

"I'll never forget," Pat would have spurred them on any other night, "going to Gyp Burns's funeral with Ned years ago. It was a Monday, cold and freezing, and the burial way the hell out in St. Anne's halfway to Canada. It seems Ned was at a cockfight the day before, probably with Tim Lee for all I know, and he lost his coat.

"Chris there borrowed a coat for him from one of his swell friends with a black velvet collar and all, just the thing for a funeral, and the three of us went in the hack. I was sitting in the middle with Chris on the one side and Ned, Lord have mercy on him, on the other. Cold as it was Ned had the window of the hack open for he was chewing tobacco, so that he could spit out.

"In the middle there between them I noticed it, I suppose, more than I would, but every time Ned would spit, up would come Chris's hand right across me and hold it over the black velvet in the front of the coat. Ned would give him a look when he did it, but he said nothing all the way to the cemetery. Every damn time Ned spit Chris stuck out the hand in front of him. Well there we are standing at the grave side and the priest, I think it was Father O'Reilly, reading the prayers when I see Ned, with the head bent, take a quick look at Chris that's standing right beside him now and me on the other side of him. He opens his lips to let go a quiet spit with no one the wiser when out comes the hand again and down it claps on the front of the coat.

"Well, if I ever seen a man mad, it was Ned. Not a word out of him though, but he offs with the coat and drops it in the snow and he away again to the hack. You could hear him spit as he went."

The roars of their laughter rose above the sounds of the prayers being said in the other rooms.

"Ned was always a proud man," Tim Lee said without the trace of a smile.

Chapter Forty-Five

CATHERINE DALY was a fresh wind blowing over the scorched meadows of their sorrow. Nell said she had been an angel, no less, doing a thousand things that needed doing around the house on Saturday and Sunday, the thousand things Nell and Nora would forget and Chris McDermott wouldn't even know had to be done. She was drooping with weariness Sunday night, and after people began going home she went into Chris's room to rest, lying on his bed with the window open, her head and shoulders high on the pillow. Chris McDermott, smarting from Mick's cut, looked for her through the other rooms and found her at last on his bed. He had never seen her slender beauty at rest in a bed before and, quietly standing in the dark looking at her, he knew his hungry eyes might never feast this way again. There were plains of years, timelessly stretching themselves without horizons, separating them. He was neither bitter nor angry, but sad about it, very sad and stunned to realize it. He would have to live a lifetime, he thought, standing there a few moments while she slept. Catherine opened her eyes at last and seeing him there, held her hand out to him.

"Poor Chris," she whispered. "You're so tired and unhappy. Oh, I wish I could do something, Chris, or say something to—to lighten your sorrow. But what can I say?"

"Nothing, Catherine," he answered. "Nothing anyone could say now would do that."

"I know it, Chris."

He took her hand and touched his lips to her cheek, barely touched and as cooly and hastily as her father might, she thought, almost reluctantly touched her. She felt his cold fingers relax and he let her hand go again, thrusting his own into his pockets as though he were shivering in a drafty alleyway. She knew how deeply troubled he was and wished she knew a way to reach him. He began talking slowly and so low she could hardly hear him. He was saying something about money and she wished he wouldn't because it seemed sordid to speak of that now. If he needed money she could get what he wanted from her father for the asking. Chris mumbled on though, methodically, sparing of his words, in his own way. There had been a few hundred dollars, he was saying, his father had saved for Willie's education, he supposed, but that was loaned to one of the family, it made no difference to whom, and never paid back. Probably never could be returned, and when Pat died and money was needed quickly, it had to be replaced because his father was not told it had been loaned out. His mother made the loan and never said anything about it until his father told her —it must have broken his heart to do it—to give what there was to Mollie. Well, he had to take his own money, money he had been saving for a long time, money he thought they would use to set up housekeeping with when they were—when they were married. He thought, yes, and he tried since then more than once to get the money from the one it was loaned to, but she never was able to repay it, and he had not been able to save up what he had given his mother. In a way he was glad he had been able to spare his father the pain of knowing the money was gone in the first place and his mother the humiliation of having to tell his father what she had done.

"Don't think about it now, Chris," Catherine urged him softly, touched, though, that even in his deep sorrow she was still in his thoughts. "Don't even think about those things now. It will only upset you more. . . ."

But he had to think about it now, because it made all the difference in the world. Oh, that was only part of it, only a part of what he had to tell her, what he had to tell her now, because if he waited he would be afraid to tell her. In the morning he would be burying his father and he might as well. . . .

"What?" Oh, Chris! What?"

There was no one now, he told her, to take care of his mother and Nora. They were getting old; he had never noticed how his mother had aged until he looked at her standing beside his father's coffin. Nora, well, it was different with Nora, but, still, there she was, growing old and helpless with no one, no one to look after her and she was his mother's sister. His father had taken care of her when he was alive and now that he was gone someone else had to do it. There wasn't anyone but himself and he would have to take up the burden where his father let it down. He couldn't leave his mother, he couldn't marry and go away, not while she was living. . . .

"Then we can't—oh. . . ." Catherine began to cry.

Willie, alone in the dining room since his cousins Patrick and

John had gone home and Mick was stretched out on the couch, babbling, heard her. There had been so much weeping in the house it did not disturb him at first, but when he heard his uncle's voice, so dull, so careful and deadly, he listened to what they were saying more closely. Soon, however, the overpowering monotony of his uncle's voice lulled him into half a sleep from which he stirred only when a sharp cry from Catherine came out of the darkness of the room.

There was no way out of it, not now, at least, Chris McDermott was saying; he couldn't leave his mother. . . .

"But, Chris," Catherine moaned, "you can't leave me. . . ."

He couldn't leave his mother, he went on, and Catherine would never be happy if they were to get married and he had to bring her there to live in this house with his mother and Nora and Willie. She wouldn't be happy and his mother wouldn't be happy and besides he wanted to bring Catherine into a home of her own when they were married. It was strange, he said, that while his father was alive he had never thought of these things. He knew the old people couldn't live forever, but he never had thought things would turn out this way for him. He hoped she knew how it hurt him to have to say these things to her; he never thought he would ever have to, never in the world.

"There must be *something*, Chris," Catherine said, sitting up in the bed and shaking her head like a child who has just fled the terrors of a wicked dream. "Isn't there something? Surely your mother doesn't expect you to give up your whole life for her! How—how can she?"

"What?" he asked her, his tone changing ever so little. "Why shouldn't—no, Catherine, dear, she doesn't expect me to. But if she—what *else* can I do?"

If you wanted me the way I want you to, the way I thought you did, Catherine was saying bitterly to herself, you would know what else there is you could do now, or nothing would stop you until you did find out what else there is you can do. Not your mother, or Nora, or anything in the world would stop you. You would not stand there like a beggar waiting for someone to drop a nickel's worth of hope, or ten cents' worth of courage into your hand. All her tenderness dissolved in the boiling broth of her anger. She hated his mother and then she hated herself for hating her. It couldn't be true; he was completely upset; she would wait.

"Father would want me to stay with her," Chris said. "I know he would want me to take care of her. There won't be much insurance or anything, you know, probably only enough to bury him. There won't be anything left after that. Who would take care of my mother? Willie isn't old enough to do it. He'll have to have a home, too, of course. And he will as long as he needs one. Father would want me to do that too. He would want me to provide a home for him, but, of course, he'll have to leave school now and find a job for himself, because I can't take the burden of his support entirely on my shoulders. . . ."

"Oh, Chris, he won't have to leave school, will he? Your father . . ."

"I wish I could see my way clear to keep him in school, Catherine, but I don't see how it can be done."

"But he's only started," she said pleading.

"I know it seems hard. It will be hard on him. I know it will. But it will be all I can do to provide a home for him. Everyone will have to make sacrifices. . . ."

Leave school? The meaning of what his uncle was saying slipped by Willie at first. Why, his grandfather—but he had forgotten for a moment that his grandfather could not speak for him now. He was acutely aware that of all the things his grandfather had said and wished for him, the only ones which counted now were those he had said to Willie himself directly; nothing ever said to anyone else would be remembered or done. Yesterday was his grandfather's and his own; tomorrow would be his to fight for, to fight for against his uncle first and then whoever else there might be.

Catherine said she was going home and she would come back the first thing in the morning; probably might be home only a few minutes. Chris told her he would walk her home.

"No, Chris," she said, her anger rising before she could restrain it. "Stay here with your mother. Willie will walk me home."

Stunned and hurt, too unhappy to dispute her, he told the boy to get his things on and go with Catherine.

Catherine wished she could tell Willie how sorry she felt that his uncle had decided he would have to leave school, but it seemed so cruel even to speak of and yet so slight compared to the blow Chris had struck her. Willie was so young, there was so much to say, that she thought she had better not begin.

293

Walking alone with her was enchantment for Willie. In the still, sheltering night his troubles dissolved, the sounds of their footsteps were smothered as they dropped in the soft sand of the lane. When he looked into the sky he saw a star speed across it in a swift breathless arc. Another soul, free at last, reaching for heaven, he thought, remembering that Rose Riordan had said that one night when they saw it happen while they were sitting on the back steps of the old house waiting for his grandfather and Peg to come home from Deignan's. They walked through the fragrance that poured out of the greenhouse and then under the hush of the big elms near Daly's back fence where it seemed to be even darker.

"Help me up, Willie," Catherine said, putting a hand on his shoulder.

Slightly crouching, he leaned his shoulder against the fence and clasped his hands with the fingers laced tightly together and hung them between his knees. Catherine put her foot into the stirrup the fingers made and her hands on the top of the fence; then she lightly sprang up on it, twisting her body as she did, and sitting there with her legs dangling down in front of him.

"Could you hear what your uncle was saying to me tonight?" she asked him.

"Some of it," he answered defensively.

"Don't worry about it," she said, swinging her legs up over the fence and dropping down into the darkness. "Good night, Willie."

Chapter Forty-Six

BESET by the flowers, the lovely chaos of their color flaming from the roses within the arms of the cross, in scarlet and bleeding clusters at the foot of the coffin in back of which sang the fringed sweetness of the carnations, the desolate boy sat nodding drunkenly in the arms of the horsehair chair, alone in the parlor with the corpse while the dirge of the rosary from the drawn and ebbing lips of the old women in the next room washed over him in frosty waves. The column of the candle had burned down and the flame, steady in the still room, shone saffron on the drawn skin of the forehead. The boy lifted his eyes to the pocketed petal of the gaslight, wishing it might burn on forever, that the sun he knew by now must be bursting its brilliance into the kitchen might not shine that day. I wouldn't miss you, he thought, and remembered him in the satin bed of the coffin, so many times in the early morning light with his white head beside him on a pillow, so many times under the gaslight lying on the couch with the pipe upside down in his mouth and Peg curled up at his feet; saw him in joy and sorrow, the still hands now laced with the black rosary stretching out to Robert Emmet, or, taking his own hand, reminding him of blue and cloudless skies. The storms of his wrath thundered again and the tear buds of his grief dropped from brown eyes that were closed forever.

When the surging of the prayer died away, and the boy could hear them rising from their knees, he went out of the parlor to see Catherine Daly pulling at the tassels of the curtains to let the morning in. She turned her head to him over her arm as though she hadn't expected to see him come out of the parlor. The light of the day was pale on the black dresses of the old women and on the golden oval frame of the picture of his grandfather and grandmother on their wedding day. A hurried rain was showering and when Catherine Daly opened the window a few inches at the bottom, it leaped into the room. She followed the boy into the kitchen where Nora was making tea for Mick and Pete. The stairs creaked under old man Reed going down to feed his hens and let them out in the yard for the day. Nell, said Nora, had fallen off into a doze on the bed and let her rest, poor soul, until it was time for the hacks to start arriving. Chris, too, she said, was lying on his bed with all his clothes on, worn out. The boy went down into the yard and watched the clucking hens waddle· out of their house, the handsome bold white rooster preen himself, wings spread out as if to catch the lightly falling rain. Across the lane his cousins were moving around their house.

Tea and tears flooded the kitchen when he got upstairs again. People were beginning to arrive for the funeral. The mourners crowded every room waiting for Austin McDonough, the undertaker, to call them to their cars in the order of their closeness to the family. It took a long time, because the shop had shut down for the day in respect to Ned's memory and nearly all the moulders were present. At last the cars began to move away from the house, the hearse was drawn up and the family—Nell, Chris, Nora and Willie went slowly down to the car.

The rolling Miserere, Father McCaffrey in the black chasuble with its snowy cross and border, the deep-throated organ's keen and the sad "Agnus Dèi" hardly penetrated the boy's stunned consciousness until, the mass finished, Father McCaffrey, with the long cape over him, came to the casket outside the altar rail, the altar boys carrying the holy water and the censer, and began to read the final prayers of the ceremony.

"Eternal rest grant unto him, O, Lord, and let perpetual light shine upon him," the priest said.

The remainder of the prayer was lost for the boy. He stood, knelt and stood again mechanically as the rest of the congregation did, Nora nudging him with her elbow when it was time to do it. He murmured the "Our Father" at the priest's direction when the others did, hardly knowing what he said. He looked at the casket, its silver handles, silver name plate with the date of his grandfather's death on the top, dimly aware of it. One thought coursed through his mind, so acute, so terrifying to him it extinguished everything else—he was dead, dead.

Chapter Forty-Seven

EMPTY and tired, they returned from the cemetery to the silent house that was still oppressively fragrant with the flowers. The fire burned in the kitchen stove and Willie stood beside it to warm himself while Nora, making a pot of tea, nervously clattered the cups and saucers. The kettle slopped over when she poured the water from it and what dropped on the stove hissed loud and briefly. His grandmother called him to come into the dining room for a cup of tea and he went in to see her absently stirring the sugar in her cup, and his uncle sitting in the chair with the arms on it at the head of the table where his grandfather always sat. It was not unusual, when his grandfather was not at home, for one of them to sit in the chair, but his uncle sat there now with an unaccustomed air of authority and, it seemed to Willie, belligerency. He felt that when his uncle looked up at him when he came in, it was to make sure that he had seen him sitting in the chair at the head of the table. Willie hesitated to sit in the chair at the right of his uncle where he always sat; he was reluctant to be that close to the man. No one spoke because there was nothing they could say to each other that hadn't been said in sorrow a thousand times since Saturday. His grandmother continued stirring the sugar in the tea and the spoon rang loudly against the sides of the cup in the quiet room. Chris told her she ought to lie down for a while, but she did not answer him. Then, at last, she told Nora to come with her and she went into the bedroom. Soon they could hear her sobbing and the sound of Nora's voice trying to comfort her. Nora closed the door on them and the sounds of the sobbing grew softer, then stopped.

Even in the other house, sleeping so long in beds that close either of them might have reached out with his arm and have touched the other, so near that the frenzied gnashing and grinding of his uncle's teeth in the night had often split his dreams, Willie had never had the feeling of being alone with him before now. They had never been nearer each other in their thoughts than strangers riding the same streetcar to separate destinations. To see the man now sitting in the chair from which his grandfather had so often spoken words of encouragement and hope stirred an indefinable anger in Willie. He wished, if someone had to die, it had been his uncle; then, for a while his grandfather would have been sad and unhappy, talked hardly at all to anyone when he came home from the foundry, but their lives would soon have resumed their steady beat again, despite it.

"Willie," his uncle said slowly, "we'll have to have a talk soon about what we're going to do."

"Do?" Willie asked him. "What can we do now?"

"I mean about how we're going to get along now that Father's gone."

Willie hadn't been thinking about it; there had been no room in his mind for any thoughts beyond his own grief. His uncle's words, however, brought back to him the snatches of talk he had heard last night, or was it the night before—he couldn't remember—between his uncle and Catherine Daly.

"You mean," Willie said, "I have to leave school, don't you?"

"We don't have to talk about it now, Willie," his uncle assured him with a kindness Willie resented, "there's plenty of time to talk it over—when you're feeling better."

"I heard you telling Catherine Daly," Willie said.

"Why, Willie," his uncle said, "I didn't think you were spying on me when I was talking with Catherine the other night. I had many things to say to her that hurt me very much to say. Did you hear everything I said to her?"

"I wasn't spying on you," Willie defended himself quickly. "I couldn't help hearing what you said."

"Spying on people when they are talking is one of the most despicable things you could do, Willie," his uncle said sternly and righteously. "One of the worst things you could have done."

"I wasn't spying, I told you," the boy said. "I couldn't help hearing you. You never cared whether I went to school or not, anyway, did you? Only my grandfather wanted me to go to school and—"

"You're upset," his uncle said with the same adulterated kindness. He told him that now that his grandfather was no longer there to help him, many things would be different in all their lives. Perhaps, he said, sighing, if he would not have to help Pat's family out, Willie might still keep on with school until the end of the term at least. But his cousins were going to have to leave school now, too. Patrick certainly, and perhaps Johnnie could get a job when summer came and keep right on with it in the fall. In a way Willie should be glad he would have this chance to do something for his grandmother, who had been so good to him ever since he was a little baby.

"You don't have to tell me any more," Willie interrupted him. He sullenly got up from the table and started slowly for the kitchen, his uncle hurrying after him and putting his hand on the boy's shoulder.

"Take your hand off me," Willie said, pulling away from him.

His uncle tightened the grip on his shoulder and Willie spun around to knock the hand away, surprised a little at his own action and catching the same look of surprise in his uncle's eyes. His uncle reached out again, and Willie, thinking he was going to hit him, struck at his uncle's hand and pushed him away. It excited him, and there was a touch of fear, he thought, in his uncle's eyes now.

"Wait," his uncle began, reaching again.

"For what?" Willie said. "Keep your hands off me, God damn you!"

But he retreated, knocking against the stove.

His grandmother must have heard him swearing at his uncle and she rushed toward him, whacking him in the face with her hand, the heavy gold wedding ring catching him in the forehead before he could draw away from her.

His uncle said he was having a little trouble with the young whelp but that he would soon settle it; that she ought to go back to her room and rest.

"Rest is it? Rest!" his grandmother cried. "With this going on and Ned not cold in the grave." She turned on Willie again. "You wicked boy, do you want to drive me out of my senses entirely?"

"He's a selfish ungrateful boy," Chris declared bitterly. "But I'll take some of it out of him before long. Go and lie down and rest, Mother. I'll handle him."

"Get out!" his grandmother shrieked at Willie. "Get out and go to your room!"

"No, Mother," Chris said. "I want him to stay here. I have something to say to him. Go and rest yourself."

"Ah," she said resignedly, "I suppose. What can I do, anyhow? This is the thanks your father has, God rest his soul, for all he has done for him."

"I know," Chris said. "I know. I'll try to reason with him. Sit down there, Willie."

Ashamed, but still smoldering with anger, Willie sat in the rocker by the window where he could look out on the lane. While his uncle talked he watched the chickens in old man Reed's yard scratching over the damp earth and incessantly pecking at the mud. He could not look at his uncle, but he heard the voice running endlessly on reminding him that whatever plans had been made for the future, whatever plans, even his own marrying of Catherine Daly, would have to be put away now. Put away and probably forgotten, well, not forgotten perhaps, but never realized. Never. Willie listened, untouched by his uncle's words; the awful reality had happened and repeating it to him made it no worse. He wished only that the man would stop talking. Yes, his uncle said, he wanted a family of his own someday, though now he might never have it; it seemed that the will of God had decided otherwise for him and he must abide by it. Think how Catherine must feel, he begged, think of how she must feel about this.

Well, giving up his schooling, he said, was no harder for Willie to bear than it was for him to have to give up his hope of marrying Catherine Daly; think of it that way. When sacrifices have to be made it was the duty of a Catholic and Christian to make them without anger and without envying those who might have the very things he had to sacrifice. Did Willie think that now he had the right to ask him to let him keep on with school, that he should have to bear the whole burden of his grandfather's family all alone?

"No," Willie said. "No, I don't."

His uncle said it surprised him that a boy who had the advice and friendship of a priest as Willie had shouldn't know these things without having to be told about them and that he should want to strike his own uncle.

"I'm sorry I did it," Willie said earnestly.

Yes, his uncle was sure that when he thought about it he would be. He was sorry, too, that they had had to get angry with one another at such a time. It hurt him deeply not to be able to carry out his father's wishes to send Willie to school as long as he needed to go to school.

"Don't talk about it any more," Willie said. "I don't want to talk about it any more at all. Never."

He heard his uncle saying he ought to go into his grandmother's room and tell her he was sorry he had made such trouble in the house on the day his grandfather was buried. Willie went slowly into his grandmother's room and she put her hand on his arm as he stood beside the bed.

"Be a good boy, now, Willie," she said to him. "It's hard on all of us. Be a good boy now and do what your uncle says."

He looked down on her distressed face, on the anguished eyes slowly closing and opening, on the lips restlessly moving. She seemed to have shrunken and the hair he remembered so thick and black was gray and sparse. The arms so rounded and bold were wasted and were bony near the wrists, the flesh mottled and purplish, dry. He saw them splashing water over her chest in the old house, flipping it up like a bird thrashing itself wet in a puddle or, powdered with flour, plunging themselves into the mounds of dough to knead the week's bread. The golden band on her finger hung loose. It pained him to think he had caused her more wearying trouble on the very day of her deepest grief. The fingers grasping his arm began to relax their grip and were no more than a little weight on him. He stepped quietly from the room without waking her and, passing into the kitchen again, saw his uncle sitting in the rocker where he himself had been a few minutes before, looking down the lane toward the back fence of the house where Catherine Daly lived. Strangely enough, he thought, he didn't care what his uncle would have to sacrifice. He didn't believe his uncle. He hated him, he thought, and knew that his uncle hated him because his grandfather had loved him more than he had ever loved his uncle. It was a great joy to him.

"She's asleep now," he said as his uncle looked up when he had reached the kitchen door.

His uncle nodded his head, turning back again at once to stare out the window.

His own hypocrisy disturbed him when he reached his own room, and he stood watching the clouds tumble across the sky over the tops of the budding elms, thinking about it. When he stood beside his grandmother's bed with her hand on his arm had she been kind and gentle and forgiving to him, as he had been to her, only because she knew he was troubled and unhappy? He was certain his uncle's words, his whole attitude, had been only to spare his grandmother—not out of any consideration for himself. And why

301

shouldn't they have been; his uncle was doing what he determined to do, wasn't he? Willie wished he had walked out of the house never to go back into it. The thought stayed with him. Why shouldn't he? If he stayed here now, knuckling under the rule of his uncle, and he knew Chris would be hard and merciless with him, thwarted as he was in his plan to marry Catherine Daly, there was little to hope for, certainly nothing that he had spent all his days hoping for and dreaming of with his grandfather. Well, if he went to work where would it be? He thought first of the foundry and it was not unpleasant, its heaps of damp sand neatly piled on the floors, the precise modeling of the sand in the flasks and the roaring, singing white iron to carry, to pour into the moulds as his own father had done and his grandfather had. He quickly banished the idea of going with his uncle into Ryan's ship chandlery and speculated on the chances of his uncle Owen Tegue's getting him a berth on a tanker or a collier or any of the other ships that made the port. But why, he thought, couldn't he go into the Navy or the Army? Probably the Navy would be better; that's where Joe Riordan had gone by now, undoubtedly, as so many of the others had. The first thing to do was to get out of the house, out of the city, to get somewhere no one knew him.

Exhausted, Willie dropped himself across the width of his bed. Desolate and sick, he stumbled through the darkness of his loneliness for the comforting light of his prayers and found himself sending up his sighs, mourning and weeping in a vale of tears bitter and deeper than he could sound his thoughts. Oh, Mother of the Eternal Word, he cried again and again until the aching silence of his spirit echoed with its sound, adopt me as thy child, adopt me as thy child. . . .

He did not know how long he had been there asleep, but when he woke up again it was dark in the room, and he jumped to his feet. He looked out of the window and could see the lights burning in the houses around them and on the lampposts in the street below. Running downstairs, he thought it was too late to start anywhere now, but he could do it the first thing in the morning, before his grandmother or anyone else in the house was awake.

Ned's hat, battered and sandy from its many trips to the foundry, hung on the nail on the kitchen door where he had hung it himself the last time he came home. Looking at it, Willie wondered who would take it down, if they were going to take it down, and when they would do it. What would they say when they did? He knew Nora would never touch it if it hung there forever and a day. His grandmother, stifling a sodden tear, perhaps, might take it down sometime when she was cleaning the house, but then his grandmother was never one of those women who go sweeping fanatically through a house with a scrubbing brush in their hands. She might never touch it. If anyone else was in the room his uncle would never take the hat down, because he would not know what to say while he was doing it. Might he slip into the kitchen some morning, perhaps, when he was all alone, and take it down? What could he do with it if he did? He would never dare burn it and he would not dare throw it into the trash; surely he couldn't take it from where it was and hang it outside the door on one of the wall nails there. No, he wouldn't dare lift it out of the house, not in the morning. Could he slip out the back way with it some day? No, he couldn't do that, either, because he would have to say, then, that he had taken it away. Then it would have to be at night when everyone else in the house was asleep. That was the only time his uncle would ever find to remove it. But what could he say to them in the morning? Either Nora or his grandmother was sure to notice its disappearance and if they didn't, Willie decided, he would.

The hat might be there a long long time, as long as his grandmother and Nora were there. But that itself might not be so long, either. Soon, Willie thought, all these old people would be lying out there under the willows at St. Ann's where his grandfather lay —his grandmother, Nora, dear Tim Lee, Torpedo Casey, old Mr. Devine, Gyp McGlinn, Mick, Pat, Pete, all of them. They would be out there where his grandfather was or, perhaps, in the Holy Name on the other side of the city where Tessie Butler was, leaving behind them what? A little shell of a house someone would snatch from those dear to them, probably, an old hat, a pair of silver rosary beads and the memory of a few bright words in the hearts of those they left behind. When they were all gone, the world Willie would live in would be peopled by his uncle, Larry McDermott, McNally, Byron Searles, brutal little men with red jackets at the circus, sly men like Martin, a world without great joy, or great sorrow or great anything, a world, as Billy Cudahy said, of bush leagues, where Catherine Dalys and Rose Riordans did not live, where Father Joes did not speak.

303

Frantically, Willie dredged the waters of his memory for the indestructible words his grandfather and Father Joe had spoken to him, but he could not bring them up. Yet he knew they were there. He knew he could never run away from these people or from the house. He surrendered, knowing that the trellis of dreams, more than dreams, of faith and hope his grandfather had built for him was there for him to cling to and climb, even with the wicked little flames of hatreds and defeats and despair licking at his heels. Perhaps he might not realize in himself the great stranger his grandfather would have made of him, but, clinging and climbing, he would never have to know the bitterness, either, of having to say good-by to him.

THE IRISH-AMERICANS

An Arno Press Collection

Athearn, Robert G. **THOMAS FRANCIS MEAGHER:** An Irish Revolutionary in America. 1949

Biever, Bruce Francis. **RELIGION, CULTURE AND VALUES:** A Cross-Cultural Analysis of Motivational Factors in Native Irish and American Irish Catholicism. 1976

Bolger, Stephen Garrett. **THE IRISH CHARACTER IN AMERICAN FICTION, 1830-1860.** 1976

Browne, Henry J. **THE CATHOLIC CHURCH AND THE KNIGHTS OF LABOR.** 1949

Buckley, John Patrick. **THE NEW YORK IRISH:** Their View of American Foreign Policy, 1914-1921. 1976

Cochran, Alice Lida. **THE SAGA OF AN IRISH IMMIGRANT FAMILY:** The Descendants of John Mullanphy. 1976

Corbett, James J. **THE ROAR OF THE CROWD.** 1925

Cronin, Harry C. **EUGENE O'NEILL:** Irish and American; A Study in Cultural Context. 1976

Cuddy, Joseph Edward. **IRISH-AMERICAN AND NATIONAL ISOLATIONISM, 1914-1920.** 1976

Curley, James Michael. **I'D DO IT AGAIN:** A Record of All My Uproarious Years. 1957

Deasy, Mary. **THE HOUR OF SPRING.** 1948

Dinneen, Joseph. **WARD EIGHT.** 1936

Doyle, David Noel. **IRISH-AMERICANS, NATIVE RIGHTS AND NATIONAL EMPIRES:** The Structure, Divisions and Attitudes of the Catholic Minority in the Decade of Expansion, 1890-1901. 1976

Dunphy, Jack. **JOHN FURY.** 1946

Fanning, Charles, ed. **MR. DOOLEY AND THE CHICAGO IRISH:** An Anthology. 1976

Farrell, James T. **FATHER AND SON.** 1940

Fleming, Thomas J. **ALL GOOD MEN.** 1961

Funchion, Michael F. **CHICAGO'S IRISH NATIONALISTS, 1881-1890.** 1976

Gudelunas, William A., Jr. and William G. Shade. **BEFORE THE MOLLY MAGUIRES:** The Emergence of the Ethno-Religious Factor in the Politics of the Lower Anthracite Region, 1844-1872. 1976

Henderson, Thomas McLean. **TAMMANY HALL AND THE NEW IMMIGRANTS:** The Progressive Years. 1976

Hueston, Robert Francis. **THE CATHOLIC PRESS AND NATIVISM, 1840-1860.** 1976

Joyce, William Leonard. **EDITORS AND ETHNICITY:**
A History of the Irish-American Press, 1848-1883. 1976

Larkin, Emmet. **THE HISTORICAL DIMENSIONS OF IRISH CATHOLICISM.** 1976

Lockhart, Audrey. **SOME ASPECTS OF EMIGRATION FROM IRELAND TO THE NORTH AMERICAN COLONIES BETWEEN 1660-1775.** 1976

Maguire, Edward J., ed. **REVEREND JOHN O'HANLON'S *THE IRISH EMIGRANT'S GUIDE FOR THE UNITED STATES:* A** Critical Edition with Introduction and Commentary. 1976

McCaffrey, Lawrence J., ed. **IRISH NATIONALISM AND THE AMERICAN CONTRIBUTION.** 1976

McDonald, Grace. **HISTORY OF THE IRISH IN WISCONSIN IN THE NINETEENTH CENTURY.** 1954

McManamin, Francis G. **THE AMERICAN YEARS OF JOHN BOYLE O'REILLY, 1870-1890.** 1976

McSorley, Edward. **OUR OWN KIND.** 1946

Moynihan, James H. **THE LIFE OF ARCHBISHOP JOHN IRELAND.** 1953

Niehaus, Earl F. **THE IRISH IN NEW ORLEANS, 1800-1860.** 1965

O'Grady, Joseph Patrick. **IRISH-AMERICANS AND ANGLO-AMERICAN RELATIONS, 1880-1888.** 1976

Rodechko, James Paul. **PATRICK FORD AND HIS SEARCH FOR AMERICA:** A Case Study of Irish-American Journalism, 1870-1913. 1976

Roney, Frank. **IRISH REBEL AND CALIFORNIA LABOR LEADER:** An Autobiography. Edited by Ira B. Cross. 1931

Roohan, James Edmund. **AMERICAN CATHOLICS AND THE SOCIAL QUESTION, 1865-1900.** 1976

Shannon, James. **CATHOLIC COLONIZATION ON THE WESTERN FRONTIER.** 1957

Shaw, Douglas V. **THE MAKING OF AN IMMIGRANT CITY:** Ethnic and Cultural Conflict in Jersey City, New Jersey, 1850-1877. 1976

Sylvester, Harry. **MOON GAFFNEY.** 1947

Tarpey, Marie Veronica. **THE ROLE OF JOSEPH McGARRITY IN THE STRUGGLE FOR IRISH INDEPENDENCE.** 1976

Vinyard, JoEllen McNergney. **THE IRISH ON THE URBAN FRONTIER:** Nineteenth Century Detroit. 1976

Walsh, James P., ed. **THE IRISH: AMERICA'S POLITICAL CLASS.** 1976

Weisz, Howard Ralph. **IRISH-AMERICAN AND ITALIAN-AMERICAN EDUCATIONAL VIEWS AND ACTIVITIES, 1870-1900:** A Comparison. 1976